She wasn't jealous—absolutely not—but there was something deeply unsettling about the way he looked at *that woman*...

Emmeline looked up and saw Veronica Cabot, her "nephew," and another couple getting up from a table across the room. "Speaking of cruel women," she murmured.

"What? Who is it?"

"It's Sir Frederick Cabot's *much* younger wife. She's here with her husband's nephew. Rosemary and I saw them when they arrived this afternoon. They don't even try to hide it." Emmeline sat back in her chair and crossed her arms over her chest. "It's disgusting."

Gregory craned his neck around. He only caught glimpse of the back of Lady Cabot's head, but he saw Trevor Mayhew as he ushered her out of the bar and held the door open for their companions to pass.

Gregory turned back and swallowed hard. "It couldn't be. It *can't* be. *It can't*," he muttered under his breath. He downed what remained of his whiskey in one gulp. It burned as it slid down his throat. He was unnerved to see that the hand that held the tumbler trembled slightly.

The light-hearted flirting of only moments ago had disappeared. Emmeline touched his sleeve. "What is it? Are you all right?"

His head shot up, as if suddenly remembering where he was. The color had drained from his cheeks. There was a wild, hunted expression in his cinnamon eyes.

"Gregory, are you all right?" Emmeline asked again. Her voice was tinged with urgency as her gaze scanned the room to determine what had disturbed him. "You look as if you've seen a ghost."

Buried secrets can kill...

The seaside resort of Torquay, along the English Riviera in Devon, is the perfect place for a restful holiday. That's what journalist Emmeline Kirby desperately needs after her harrowing escapes from spies and others with nefarious intentions back in London. She also needs distance to sort out her conflicted feelings for jewel thief Gregory Longdon, who once stole her heart. But who should turn up out of the blue? The ever-charming, devastatingly handsome Gregory. That's when secrets from his past—and murder—shatter the serenity of this picturesque haven.

Lead Me into Danger

"Adventure from Venice to London with an engaging cast of characters in this fresh, fast-paced mystery filled with jewel thefts, international intrigue, unexpected twists, and a lovely touch of romance." ~ Tracy Grant, bestselling author of *The Mayfair Affair*

Deadly Legacy

"Stolen diamonds, revenge and murder are served up at a cracking pace as Emmeline unites with Gregory once again in this intriguing second installment of Daniella Bernett's mystery series." ~ Tessa Arlen, author of the Lady Montfort series and Agatha Award finalist

"Emmeline and Gregory's new adventure is a delightful blend of mystery and romance, filled with dazzling twists and turns, unexpected dangers, and old and new tensions in their relationship." ~ Tracy Grant, author of *London Gambit*

From Beyond the Grave

"Escape to Torquay with Emmeline and Gregory for a seaside whirlwind of mystery, romance, and unexpected secrets that will leave you eagerly anticipating the next book in the series!" ~ Tracy Grant, author of *Gilded Deceit*

"Dark secrets, deceit and murder threaten Emmeline and Gregory's future along the scenic Devon coast...A story sure to please fans of romantic suspense." ~ D.E. Ireland, authors of the Agatha-nominated Eliza Doolittle and Henry Higgins Mysteries

ACKNOWLEDGMENTS

I would like to thank Acquisitions Editor Lauri Wellington, who continues to have confidence in my work; editor Faith C., who gives my books the extra polish they need; and Jack Jackson, a master designer who creates the beautiful covers for my books.

My continued gratitude to the Mystery Writers of America New York Chapter for its support—particularly Sheila and Gerald Levine, and Richie Narvaez.

I would like to thank bestselling author Tracy Grant, who has been on this journey with me from the beginning. I would be remiss if I didn't thank authors Emma Jameson, Tessa Arlen, Alyssa Maxwell, Meg Mims, and Sharon Piscareta, with whom I became friends via Facebook and exchange lively ideas about writing and life.

Other Books in the Emmeline Kirby/Gregory Longdon Mystery Series

Lead Me Into Danger
Deadly Legacy

FROM

BEYOND THE

GRAVE

An Emmeline Kirby/
Gregory Longdon Mystery

Daniella Bernett

A Black Opal Books Publication

GENRE: PSYCHOLOGICAL SUSPENSE/MYSTERY/THRILLER

FROM BEYOND THE GRAVE
Copyright © 2014 by Daniella Bernett
Cover Design by Jackson Cover Designs
All cover art copyright © 2017
All Rights Reserved
Print ISBN: 978-1-626947-01-6

First Publication: SEPTEMBER 2017

Published by Black Opal Books http://www.blackopalbooks.com

*To my parents and my sister Vivian, with love.
You are the ones who are always there for me.*

PROLOGUE

Toronto, Canada 1998:

The young man, the accused as he was referred to, gripped his knees hard to stop his legs from trembling. His palms were damp. A single droplet of sweat wended its slow, torturous way from the nape of his neck all the way down to the small of his back. He nervously fingered the collar of what had been a crisp, white shirt, but which had now gone limp. Was it only him or was it inordinately warm? Stifling, in fact.

His blue gaze flickered around the wood-paneled courtroom. It fell first on the Crown prosecutor. From his vantage point in the box behind the two lawyers, he could only see her back and a bit of her profile when she shifted slightly in her chair. Her chestnut hair was pulled back and piled neatly atop her head. She sat ramrod straight as she listened to the judge. Over the course of the three-week trial, she had shown herself to be hard as nails. There was not an ounce of forgiveness or empathy in her soul. To her "the accused" was always guilty. Next, he caught the eye of his defense counsel, who glanced over his shoulder to give him a watery smile. It was half in apology and half in resignation. To be fair, he had done his best but the cards had been stacked against him from the start. Finally, the young man's gaze came to rest on the jury in its box to the right of the prosecutor, the seven women and five men in whose hands his life rested. He studied each juror's face, trying to discern what their collective decision had been. No one looked at him. Not a good sign. No, not good at all.

"Foreman, has the jury reached a verdict?" the superior court judge asked sententiously.

"We have, your honor. We find the accused—" The young man held his breath. "—guilty."

He heard what the foreman had said, but his mind still couldn't quite comprehend it. *Guilty*. The word thundered in his ears. *Guilty*. A low murmuring suddenly erupted amongst the benches in the public seating area.

"Quiet in the court," the judge ordered. "Quiet."

He sat there waiting, peering down from his perch. Only his hands, white and blue-veined, peeped out from the voluminous folds of his black robe. When silence reigned once more, the judge cleared his throat. Beneath his tuft of receding steel-gray hair, deep lines furrowed his brow and fanned out from the corners of his cold brown eyes. The young man swallowed hard. He would never forget the judge's eyes boring into every fiber of his being.

"Will the accused please rise."

The young man shuffled to his feet. He didn't think that his legs would be able to sustain his weight. His knuckles were white and distended from holding the edge of the box so tightly.

"Edward William Prichard," the judge intoned with all the gravitas of his office, "a jury of your peers has found you guilty of murder in the death of Henry Cummings. By your own account, Mr. Cummings took you into his home and treated you as another son when you found yourself in need. And how did you repay this kindness and generosity? By stealing from him and ultimately taking his life. Under the Criminal Code of Canada, I sentence you to twenty years in prison for your crimes."

Edward slammed his hand down and shouted, "But I

didn't do it. I'm innocent. I didn't do it." His voice cracked. "You must believe me," he implored the jury. "I didn't do it. It wasn't me."

At that moment, out of the corner of his eye, he caught some movement in the public seating area behind him. Edward looked over his shoulder in time to see a woman quietly slipping out of the courtroom. The woman he loved. The woman who had set him up.

The judge was muttering on about his right to appeal, but Edward wasn't listening. What did it matter? Without her, his life was meaningless.

And so that night in his jail cell, Edward turned his back on the world and killed himself.

CHAPTER 1

England, April 2010:

Dazzling sunlight greeted Emmeline as she emerged from the Torquay railway station. She had caught the ten-o-six train from Paddington in London and now, nearly three hours later, she was in lovely Torquay, one of the resort towns on Devon's south coast that together make up the English Riviera. Torquay, with its near Mediterranean climate, was nestled on seven hills and afforded stunning views across Torbay. The town became a fashionable seaside resort during the Napoleonic Wars. Torquay also had been home to writer Agatha Christie, whose mystery novels Emmeline had devoured as a child when she and her grandmother settled by a crackling fire on cold winter afternoons in Kent.

Torquay was the perfect place for Emmeline to escape from everything that had happened over the last few weeks. It was a world away from the Sedgwicks and their dirty secrets, and a world away from poor Ambrose Trent—the cousin she never knew existed and now would never get to know. Her thoughts clouded over as she remembered Ambrose. She still felt guilty, although logically she knew it wasn't her fault. It was all such a terrible tragedy. A lie that had its birth in World War II and condemned three generations of a family—her family—to seek vengeance because there had been no justice.

Emmeline sighed. Right, she had had enough mysteries to last her a lifetime. "Sorry, Agatha, it's time to move on," she said resolutely.

Her dark curls bounced with determination as she gathered up her bags. Gran had been right. She needed to get away for a bit. Now that she had recovered from the concussion and the stab wound was on the mend, Emmeline needed time to forget and to figure out what would be the next step in her career. Once word had gotten around that she had been sacked from *The Times*, her phone hadn't stopped ringing with offers from rival papers, as well as the BBC and Sky News. Emmeline had been flattered to see that her work engendered such respect, but she hadn't made any decisions yet. Perhaps she would freelance for a while. One thing was certain, she would never, *never* return to *The Times*. James Sloane, her former editor and former friend, had come crawling on bended knee and cravenly begged her to come back to the paper. Well, it was too bloody late. Her stomach still twisted in knots when she recalled how he had refused to stand up for her. James and the paper would just have to muddle along without her.

She hailed a taxi to take her to her hotel, which was only a mile from the station. As she slipped into the back seat, Emmeline had to admit to herself that this little holiday would also give her time to think about the vexing problem of Gregory. There was rarely a moment lately when he wasn't in her thoughts. Perhaps, the problem wasn't him but *her*. If she were truly honest, in her heart of hearts, Emmeline knew that she wanted him back in her life. It was no use denying it anymore, especially to herself. However, it wasn't the loss of the baby or the fact that he was a jewel thief that held her back, but fear. Fear of giving herself completely again, fear of being hurt, and, most of all, fear that he would disappear for good this time. She had been shattered when he left the first time. What if it happened again? Was she strong enough to survive? Maybe by the time she left Torquay, she would have the answers to these unsettling questions.

"Here you are, miss," the cab driver said cheerfully as he turned off Park Hill Road and pulled up in front of the Royal Devon Hotel, which loomed over the bay from its sheltered clifftop perch. He was a smallish man with rosy cheeks and friendly hazel eyes. Although he tended toward the tubby side, he quickly bustled round the car to open the door for her.

"Thank you very much. How much will that be?"

He told her and she settled the fare.

"Shall I nip your bags inside for you?" he asked helpfully.

Emmeline smiled. "That's very kind of you, but I can manage."

The driver touched his finger to his forehead in a little salute. "Then I'll be off, miss. Enjoy your stay in Torquay."

"I intend to. How could you not in such a beautiful setting? Thanks again."

Emmeline felt her body starting to relax as she headed up the steps and into the pristine lobby with its cream-colored walls and ornate moldings and columns. In her jeans and lemon knit blouse, she wondered whether she might be a trifle underdressed for the elegant four-star hotel. But after all, Torquay was a resort where people came to unwind and enjoy a host of leisure activities, from sailing and swimming to cycling and walking. It was silly to worry about how she was dressed. She had never been one of those women who was obsessed with her appearance. In fact, the only makeup Emmeline wore was a touch of lipstick. Just something to give her face a bit of color. She couldn't be bothered with the rest of it.

Her leather pumps barely made a sound on the green and white marble floor as she crossed the lobby to reception.

"Good afternoon, madam," said the woman behind the desk with a pleasant smile. "How may I help you?" She had a long, oval face with high cheekbones and bright blue eyes. Her golden hair fell to her shoulders in neat waves. Emmeline guessed that she was probably only a few years older than she was.

"Good afternoon, my name's Emmeline Kirby. I have a reservation for a fortnight."

"Just give me one moment to verify that, madam." Her fingers rapidly punched at the keyboard in front of her. "Ah, yes. Here it is. However, Miss Kirby, I'm afraid your room isn't ready yet. Check-in time is two o'clock."

Emmeline glanced at her watch. It was a little after one.

"You're welcome to wait in the bar or the conservatory. Light snacks are available there."

After three hours on the train, Emmeline was itching to get out and see the town. "Would it be all right if I left my bags while I go into town and then I could collect my key later?"

The woman smiled. "Of course. I'll just make a note for my colleague, in case I'm away from the desk when you return. Leave your bags there. I'll have the porter take them to your room when it's ready."

"Super. Thank you. Any suggestions where I can grab a bite to eat?"

"You'll find a number of cafés and pubs along the promenade. There are also some gardens along the seafront where you might like to stroll after lunch. It's a short walk from the hotel. Just go back out the front door and make a right at the end of the drive. Here let me show you." She slipped a hand under the desk to pull out a map.

"No, that's fine." Emmeline waved a hand dismissively. "I'm sure I can't get lost. Even if I do, I'm not on a timetable now. I'm on holiday. I always find it jolly fun to discover new places."

The young woman smiled at her conspiratorially. "I'm the same way. Well, I hope you enjoy your stay with us, Miss Kirby. My name's Connie, in case you need anything."

Emmeline returned her smile. "I'll keep that in mind. Now, I'm off to explore. Thanks again."

With a sense of renewed purpose, she pushed the glass door open and once again felt the golden strands of sunlight caressing her face. She started humming a little tune of her own creation as she let her feet lead the way down to the harbor. Twenty minutes later, she was comfortably ensconced at a window table in a quaint café across the road from the promenade. After perusing the menu, Emmeline settled on a warm tarragon chicken salad and a glass of sauvignon blanc. Within minutes of ordering, the waitress was placing the glass of wine in front of her and a basket of fresh homemade brown bread on the table. Emmeline took a sip of the chilled wine and allowed it to roll around her tongue for a moment before swallowing it. Ah, crisp, light, and refreshing.

Her mind wandered as she munched on a piece of the delicious bread and watched as people ambled back and forth along the pavement. They weren't in a great hurry and why should they be? Torquay was not London, where people were always rushing about. Torquay was meant to be savored slowly. A smile curled around her lips as she took another sip of wine and leaned back in her chair. Nothing was going to spoil her stay in Torquay. After all, what could possibly happen here?

Mother Nature was at the height of her seductive powers on this afternoon, and Emmeline was drawn to the harbor after lunch. Yachts and speedboats jostled alongside sailboats as they glissaded in and out of the marina. Wisps of gauzy clouds drifted aimlessly in the cerulean sky. The silken waters of the aquamarine bay undulated and winked knowingly as they captured the still smoldering embers of sunlight that tumbled from the heavens. Emmeline walked all the way to the end of Princess Pier, with its white railings and uninterrupted benches lining either side, to admire the inner harbor. She sat down to watch the teeming activity for a little while and was soon joined by a plump seagull who screeched and eyed her suspiciously at first. Once he was satisfied that she posed no threat, they settled into a companionable silence. Soon though, it was time for Emmeline to make her way back to the hotel.

She wandered through the neatly manicured gardens along the promenade. Her eyes were assailed by the blaze of color and textures. A golden sea of daffodils with orange faces bobbed and curtsied in the breeze, while scarlet, plum, and pink tulips preened and a host of tropical plants indolently nuzzled together nearby. Cabbage trees, or Torbay Palms as they were ubiquitously known, could be seen everywhere and gave the town a Mediterranean flavor. The trees had been introduced to the area from New Zealand in 1820 and had flourished.

Emmeline was looking out across the bay, when her attention was arrested by the sound of a woman weeping. It struck a strident chord when it mingled with the unending stream of merry chatter bubbling forth from the fountain in the center of the lawn. She turned and saw that, not too far away from her, there was an older woman leaning against one of the palm trees with her fists pressed tightly to her eyes. Her snowy white head shook from side to side as sobs wracked her frail body.

"Poor woman," Emmeline murmured under her breath. Perhaps she should go over there and see if there was anything she could do. She took half a step and then hesitated. On the other hand, the woman might not appreciate a stranger intruding into her private affairs. However, when Emmeline saw the woman stumble, the decision was taken out of her hands. She dashed across the lawn, grabbing the woman's elbow just in time to prevent her from falling. "Are you all right?"

"What?" The woman blinked a few times. She slowly turned her head and fixed her bewildered slate-blue stare on Emmeline, as if suddenly becoming aware of her presence. Things were starting to come back into focus.

"I said, are you all right?" Emmeline repeated. "Shall I fetch a doctor?"

"No, no. No need for that." She patted Emmeline's arm with a blue-veined hand. "I'm perfectly all right now. I'm sorry I gave you a fright, my dear. It was simply an old woman being overwhelmed by her memories."

Color was starting to return to the woman's cheeks, but Emmeline was unconvinced. "Perhaps it might be a good idea if you sat down. There's a bench over there. I could sit with you for a bit, if you like."

The woman smiled and patted her arm again. "Don't be silly. I wouldn't dream of it. It would be very selfish of me. I'm sure you have better things to do than to fritter away your afternoon on an old woman."

Emmeline wagged a finger at her, but her smile and gentle tone softened the scolding. "That's the second time you've said old woman in as many minutes. You're not old. As my gran would say, you're mature."

The woman laughed at this, a genuine laugh that lit up her entire face and gave Emmeline a glimpse of the beauty she must have been. "Your grandmother sounds like a very wise woman."

"Oh, she is." Emmeline nodded emphatically. "Very wise and very wily. Nothing gets past her. I learned that the hard way on several occasions when I was a child. At any rate, age is just a number. It's how you feel that counts. Now, shall we sit down? That bench looks awfully inviting. Here lean on me. I'm stronger than I look."

In the end, the woman allowed herself to be led by the elbow toward the bench. Little did she know that Emmeline had no intention of taking no for an answer.

"There, isn't that better," Emmeline said. "And just look at that view across Torbay."

The tide was starting to come in, and they could see frothy crests rise and fall as the waves gently lapped against the shore.

They were quiet for a few moments. Emmeline had always been drawn to the sea. She could sit for hours just watching the hypnotic, almost balletic, grace of the rollers as they crashed upon jagged rocks or the velvet sands of a beach.

"Thank you again, my dear. Not everyone would have taken the trouble to stop."

Emmeline waved a hand dismissively in the air. "You give me far too much credit, madam. I assure you that I have done nothing."

"You took pity on an old—"

"Ah. Ah." Emmeline raised a finger in the air. "I thought we settled that point already. You are *not* to use that word. You must eradicate it from your vocabulary. The word is *mature*."

The tiny folds around the woman's eyes crinkled when she chuckled. "Really, you are a most extraordinary young woman. You remind me a little of my daughter. Not in looks, for she's fair, but in your manner. You both have an uncanny ability to see the bright side of things in any situation." She sighed and her eyes clouded as she turned her gaze toward the bay. "Unfortunately, I've lived too long and seen too many awful things in this life to ever be so cheerful again."

"Nonsense. Don't talk such rubbish. You're just a bit down this afternoon. That's all. It happens to all of us. Now, tell me more about your daughter. She sounds like an interesting person."

"Rosie? Oh, yes, she's definitely interesting. She's strong and independent. Very much her own person. We named her Rosemary after me. I suppose you might think that a bit of vanity—" She blushed self-consciously at this. "—but my Denis insisted. At home, we called her Rosie, but outside the family she insisted on going by her middle name. As I said, she wanted to stamp her own identity on the world. But she's extremely loyal to those she loves, and she always put family above all else. By the way, we've been sitting here all this time, and we haven't been properly introduced. My name's Rosemary Dunham."

Emmeline extended a hand. "Very pleased to make your acquaintance, Rosemary Dunham. I'm Emmeline Kirby."

"What a lovely name. It has a musical lilt to it."

"Alas, I cannot take credit for it. I have my parents to thank for bestowing such a pretty name upon me."

"They must be very proud of you."

A tear stung Emmeline's eyelid, as she thought about her parents. "I would like to think so. They were journalists, like me, and they died on an assignment in the Middle East when I was five years old. My gran, my mother's mother, is the one who raised me. The woman you see before you today is the product of her devoted love and care. Gran is my best friend. My rock. She has been there for me through thick and thin, through skinned knees and hurt feelings, through everything."

"You're very lucky. Do you have any siblings?"

"No, it's just me."

"When you were growing up, did you miss not having a brother or a sister?"

"No, because I had Gran. She was mother, father, brother, sister all rolled into one. What about you? Do you have any other children besides Rosie?"

"Yes, two sons. Teddy, the oldest, and Kit, the baby. Rosie is the middle child."

"Did they all get along as children?"

"Well, Rosie and Kit are only three years apart, so they were fairly close. Teddy was eight years older. You see, I was married twice. Teddy was from my first marriage to Arthur. He was only a year old when Arthur died."

Emmeline squeezed Rosemary's hand sympathetically. "Oh, how awful."

"Thank you, my dear. I don't mind telling you that we struggled in those years after Arthur's death. I took two jobs to make sure Teddy went to bed with a full belly. Then when I had resigned myself to my lot in life, I met Denis.

Warm, funny, loving Denis. Suddenly, the loneliness and misery lifted and I was laughing again. Actually laughing. And he was wonderful with Teddy. In no time at all, he had my five-year-old son eating out of the palm of his hand. You never saw anything like it. Denis was a natural-born father if there ever was one. We were married five months later."

"How marvelous that you were able to find love twice in a lifetime. Not everyone is lucky enough to find it once."

"Yes," Rosemary murmured distractedly. "Yes, lucky." She frowned at the bay.

"Have I said the wrong thing?" Emmeline asked, confused.

Rosemary patted her hand. "No, not at all, my dear. It's just that today is exactly six months since Denis died."

"Oh, I'm terribly sorry."

"There's no need to be. You couldn't have known. Besides, it was a relief for him and for me. He had been very ill, and it was difficult to watch him wasting away little by little each day."

"Is that why you were so upset just now? Because you were thinking of Denis."

"Yes, that and other things. Today is also the anniversary of Teddy's death. He died years ago. But, I never had the chance to say goodbye. Both my boys were bitten by wanderlust at a very young age and, at the first opportunity, they set off to see the world. Only Rosie was content to remain at home here in England. I suppose girls always do stay close to the nest."

"How tragic about Teddy. You must have been devastated."

A stray tear trickled down Rosemary's cheek. She impatiently wiped it away with the back her hand. "Yes. He was twenty-seven and in the prime of life. I know it's wrong and you should never have a favorite, but Teddy was my first born and he held a special place in my heart." She choked back a sob. "A parent should never have to bury a child.

Never. It is the worst thing imaginable. No matter what his age."

"Yes," Emmeline replied, as she was assailed by thoughts of the baby she had lost.

Something in the tone of Emmeline's voice made Rosemary turn. "Do you have any children?"

Emmeline shook her head and swallowed the lump that formed in her throat. "No." This came out as a hoarse croak. She struggled hard against the still-fresh pain. "No, but I would like to have children. Very much."

They fell silent as Emmeline tried to collect herself. Once she seemed to calm down a bit, Rosemary ventured quietly, "I'm sure you will make a wonderful mother one day."

"Do you think so?" Emmeline asked, needing reassurance.

"Yes. You just have to find a nice young man. Is there a special someone in your life?"

Emmeline dropped her head between her hands and groaned. "It's very complicated. That's part of the reason I came to Torquay." She lifted her head again. "I needed time to think."

Rosemary smiled. "Nothing is complicated if you love each other. Do you love him?"

Emmeline's eyes searched Rosemary's face as if answers were written there. Of course, that was silly. She was the only one who *could* have the answers. Maybe she already knew the answers and was simply afraid to listen. "I—I—"

"Forgive me," Rosemary apologized. "I shouldn't have asked that. None of my business. I didn't mean to pry."

"I didn't think you were. I just can't answer the question. Not quite yet."

"Well, you couldn't have picked a more beautiful setting to chase away the cobwebs in your mind. Torquay will do wonders for you. I should know. My parents sent me here from London when I was a child during the war. Torquay was considered safer than the towns in the southeast. However, it did sustain some bomb damage, largely from planes dumping excess loads after participating in the Plymouth Blitz."

"Really? I wasn't aware of that. You must know the town extremely well then."

"Yes, I do. I stayed with my aunt, my father's sister. She and my uncle welcomed me with open arms. I was treated like another daughter. They had two girls, who were around my age, and a boy. He was seven years younger. The baby of the family and the apple of everyone's eye. We all got on famously from the start. I keep in touch with my cousins to this day. They still live down here. When my children were small, Denis and I brought them down here every summer, and we all had the most marvelous time together. Cousins mingled with cousins. One big happy family." A smile touched her lips at the memories. "I wish the children could have remained small forever. I could protect them back then." She sighed and turned back to Emmeline. "Ah, well. It was all a long time ago. This is the first time I've been back to Torquay in years. Rosie recently got a job down here and I came for a short visit."

"How nice. I must say I was awfully lucky to have run into you this afternoon, Rosemary. Would you care to continue our conversation over tea or is your daughter expecting you?"

"You've spent too much time already listening to the maudlin ramblings of an ol—" Emmeline lifted an eyebrow and cocked her head to one side. "—mature woman," Rosemary continued. "You're young. Go out and explore Torquay. Enjoy your holiday."

"But I am enjoying myself tremendously. I'm just sorry Gran isn't here. You'd like her very much. I'm guessing you're about the same age. I'm sure that the two of you would have a lot in common."

"We already do. We like you. In just half an hour, you've bucked me up no end."

"Oh." Emmeline blushed. "That's nice of you to say.

Sometimes it's simply easier to talk to a stranger."

"But we're not strangers anymore, my dear."

Emmeline smiled. "No, we're not. So can I tempt you with a cup of tea, friend?"

Rosemary tucked her arm in the crook of Emmeline's elbow. "I can't think of anything else I'd rather do. However, I insist that it be my treat."

"But—"

"No, my dear, I will brook no arguments."

Emmeline shrugged her shoulders in resignation. "All right. I saw several little cafés along the Strand. Shall we go there?"

"Would you mind terribly if we went back to my hotel? I'm feeling a bit tired and they do a lovely tea in the conservatory?"

"Of course, not. Where are you staying?"

"The Royal Devon."

"The Royal Devon? What a funny coincidence. That's where I'm staying too."

"Then we'll be seeing a lot of one another over the next few days."

"Yes. We can plan an outing together and perhaps I can even meet Rosie. I'm surprised you're not staying with your daughter."

"I didn't want to impose. She doesn't need her mother hovering about the house. Besides, all those years ago when I was a girl, I dreamed of one day having enough money to stay at the Royal Devon. So you see it's a treat for me."

"And for me too. Let's go."

✺✺✺

Emmeline and Rosemary found themselves swallowed into a beehive of activity the minute they entered through the double doors of the hotel lobby. Maids were rushing about polishing table surfaces and the chandelier, as well as buffing the already gleaming marble floor. "I wonder what's going on?" Rosemary asked as she was nearly knocked down by a porter, who apologized profusely.

"I have no idea," Emmeline said. She caught a glimpse of Connie at the reception desk as she pulled Rosemary out of the fray. "Here, why don't we go over to reception. I have to collect the key to my room and we can find out what the fuss is about from that nice young woman I spoke to earlier."

Rosemary mumbled something that Emmeline didn't quite catch, but assumed it was agreement. She gently guided her new friend across the lobby. "Hello again, Connie."

The young woman had returned the receiver to its cradle and was just punching something into the computer. "Oh, Miss Kirby," she said, startled. Her blue gaze swept over Emmeline and Rosemary. "And Mrs. Dunham. Good afternoon. Miss Kirby, your bags have been taken up to your room. Here is your key. You're in room three-o-three. It has a magnificent view of the sea." She handed over the key to Emmeline.

"Thanks very much. I can't wait to see it."

"Is there anything else I can do for you, Miss Kirby, or you, Mrs. Dunham?"

"Actually, Connie, we were wondering what's going on here?" Emmeline waved her hand at the bustle behind her.

A pink flush colored Connie's creamy cheeks. "On the Royal Devon's behalf, I must offer you ladies our sincerest apologies. Ever since we received the call about an hour ago that a VIP and his wife were coming to stay with us for two weeks, the staff has been at sixes and sevens, trying to ensure that everything is perfect."

"Surely, you've had other VIPs as guests before. What makes this couple so special?" Rosemary asked quietly.

Connie looked intently at the older woman for a second before responding. "I shouldn't be telling you this." She lowered her voice. "And you must promise to keep it to yourselves." Emmeline and Rosemary nodded and leaned in closer. "It's Sir Frederick Cabot and his wife."

"Frederick Cabot? The billionaire who has his finger in everything from oil and shipping to multimedia companies, and who was knighted by the Queen two years ago for his philanthropic works," Emmeline whispered.

Connie darted a glance to her right and left to make certain no one had overheard them. "That's him."

"He lives abroad, doesn't he? Somewhere in France, if I'm not mistaken."

Connie nodded. "That's right. However, he was born in Devon, near Exeter. He has a house here in Torquay and comes back every April. He usually stays about a month and then flees before the summer tourist season gets into full swing. This year, though, he's having some work done on the house. He's only coming down for a short visit. He wants to show his wife the villa and a bit of the area, before they're off to more exotic climes. I believe they only got married in October."

"Practically newlyweds," Rosemary murmured. Her slate-blue eyes never left Connie's face.

The younger woman inclined her head imperceptibly and went on. "From what I understand, Lady Cabot is *much* younger than her husband."

"Ah, that's the lay of the land, is it?" Emmeline said knowingly.

"Yes. Supposedly she's extremely beautiful, but she shuns the press like the plague. There's no photograph of her anywhere."

"That's rather curious, in view of the fact that her husband owns a string of newspapers and cable companies across two continents. You'd think a man like that would enjoy showing off his trophy wife."

"And another thing—"

"Constance, what's going on here?" A stern gentleman with a receding hairline and dressed in a charcoal suit suddenly materialized. He peered down imperiously at her through half-moon glasses.

"Oh, Mr. Harcourt, I didn't see you. I was just assisting Mrs. Dunham and Miss Kirby. They're new guests."

Emmeline sensed that Mr. Harcourt must be Connie's boss. "Yes, thank you, Connie. You've been most helpful. I think Rosemary and I will take your advice and visit Kent Caverns tomorrow. Perhaps, we'll do an outing to Cockington on Wednesday. You made the little thatched village sound so enchanting."

"It is. You'll love it, Miss Kirby," Connie replied aloud, while she mouthed a relieved thank you.

"And you said that we can take tea now in the conservatory?"

"Yes, that's right. It's just around the corner to your left."

"Thanks again. Mr. Harcourt, I must say that I've never been in a hotel where the staff is so kind and attentive," Emmeline said with a smile that was intended to melt even the stoniest of hearts.

"Yes, well, I must get on," he blustered to cover his embarrassment and quickly disappeared into the office.

Connie exhaled. "Thank you, Miss Kirby. I'm ever so grateful. He's not a bad sort, just a bit of a stickler." She jerked her head in the direction of the office door. "For a minute there, I thought he was going to sack me. I only started two weeks ago, but I really like it here."

"Don't worry, my dear," Rosemary said as she patted Connie's arm lightly. "We won't breathe a word of what you told us to anyone."

Connie put her strong young hand over the older woman's blue-veined one and gave it a quick squeeze. "Thanks. Now, I must go before Mr. Harcourt reappears."

❦

Emmeline and Rosemary had just ordered tea and were chatting amiably about novels they had recently read, when

Connie came hurrying across the conservatory toward their table. "Miss Kirby, I'm terribly sorry. What with all the fuss over the Cabots and Mr. Harcourt popping up like that, I forgot to give you this. It came while you were out." She handed Emmeline a small brown-paper parcel. It was stamped with the name of rare bookshop in London and had her name and the hotel's address printed across the front in bold capital letters.

"I don't understand. I didn't order any books. And certainly not to be delivered here. There was no note or anything with it?" Emmeline asked Connie in confusion.

"No, the gentleman just left it at the desk. I'm afraid I have to get back. I'll leave you to unravel the mystery."

"Yes, of course. Thanks, Connie."

Emmeline frowned as she turned over the package several times.

"Aren't you going to open it? You won't know what it is otherwise," Rosemary prompted.

Emmeline laughed at her friend's curiosity. "I already know that it's a book. But you're right. Perhaps there's a note inside." She proceeded to tear the paper. What emerged was an elegantly bound first edition of Elizabeth Barrett Browning's *Sonnets of the Portuguese*. She caressed the claret leather cover and carefully leafed through the volume, pausing from time to time to pour over familiar stanzas. But there was no trace of a note to be found anywhere.

"A volume of the most romantic love poetry. What a handsome gift. You must have a secret admirer. How exciting." Rosemary gleefully clapped her hands together as a child might do.

The kernel of a thought was forming in the back of Emmeline's mind. "A secret admirer. I don't think so," she mumbled. There was only one person who could have sent this book.

CHAPTER 2

"No, Rosemary. This is not from a secret admirer," Emmeline repeated as she carefully closed the poetry volume and put it down on the table.

"Then you know who it is?"

Emmeline folded her hands on the table. "I have a fairly good idea."

"Does this have to do with the complication we were discussing earlier? The man you were running away from?"

Emmeline's head snapped up. "Who said anything about running away?" she asked defensively. "I'm not running away from anyone. I told you I came to Torquay for a holiday."

"Yes, I remember you did say that. But you forget that I'm *mature* and I'm also a mother, so I can read between the lines. So what is this mystery man like? Obviously, he has good taste and is not short of a bob or two if he can send you gifts like that. Is he good looking? Is he amusing? Charming? What?"

Emmeline was momentarily at a loss for words. How did one describe the enigma that was Gregory? Her former lover, former fiancé, *and* a jewel thief. She sighed and shrugged her shoulders in resignation. "Well, he's...He's— Oh, my God, I can't believe it." Her eyes widened when she saw the object of her mental turmoil casually making his way toward their table. "This is not happening," she told herself. "It can't be. I must be imagining it."

When she looked up again, she saw that it was indeed Gregory, dressed casually in an open-necked peach shirt and beige trousers. He was fast closing the distance between the door and their table. And he had a bemused look on his face. Damn.

"I say," Rosemary whispered none too softly. "He's criminally attractive, isn't he?"

Emmeline was tempted to kick her shin under the table. Instead, she muttered *sotto voce*, "He's criminal all right." There was no time for more.

"Ah, Emmy, darling, I see that you received my little gift. I know how much you love poetry and the minute I laid eyes on it, I knew it would make the perfect birthday present." He stood there, all six feet of him, and beamed down at her.

"My birthday is not for another month," she responded churlishly, trying to figure out what he was up to.

"I simply couldn't resist." Gregory shrugged ever so endearingly, as he smiled conspiratorially at Rosemary. "You know how it is."

"Oh, I do indeed," she concurred earnestly. "Sometimes it is positively impossible to resist something when it catches your fancy." Her slate-blue eyes stared up adoringly at Gregory.

Emmeline shook her head and glared at him. In mere seconds, another unsuspecting female had succumbed to his silken charms. How did the man manage to do it? If Rosemary wasn't careful, she might be leaving the Royal Devon sans her jewels. Then again, she might be safe. Emmeline cocked her head to one side and studied her new friend. Although Rosemary's cream-colored blouse and mauve skirt were well-cut and made of good material, she didn't look the sort who had oodles of money stashed away.

"Forgive me," Gregory was saying as he extended a hand to Rosemary. "We haven't been introduced and, as

Emmeline appears tongue-tied, I see that I shall have to do the honors. I'm Gregory Longdon."

"And I'm Rosemary Dunham."

"Delighted to meet you, Mrs. Dunham."

"Rosemary, please."

Gregory flashed one of his most engaging smiles. "Rosemary. What an utterly charming name." He bent down to brush her knuckles with a kiss before relinquishing her hand.

"Oh. Oh, my." Rosemary blushed and tittered. "It's been a long time since a gentleman has kissed my hand."

"Has it, Rosemary? Then the men you know are complete fools. You should be showered with compliments every day."

She giggled again, while Emmeline rolled her eyes.

"Well, ladies, I didn't mean to interrupt your tea. I'll be staying here for a few days, so I'm certain that our paths will be crossing again."

"Not if I can help it," Emmeline mumbled.

"What was that, Emmy?" Gregory asked innocently.

"Nothing. Nothing at all. Don't mind me. Just pretend I'm not here."

"That's quite impossible," Rosemary piped in as she tapped Emmeline on the shoulder. "She's such a lovely girl, Gregory. But then, you obviously know that already."

"Yes, isn't she?" Gregory agreed as both he and Rosemary bestowed a fond smile upon Emmeline, who felt a flush rise to her cheeks.

"I have an idea. Why don't you join us for tea?" Rosemary said.

Emmeline shook her head at Gregory, but simply smiled when Rosemary turned toward her. "Wouldn't that be nice, Emmeline?"

Before she could answer, Gregory replied ingenuously, "I wouldn't want to impose. You ladies looked as if you were in a deep *tête-à-tête* when I arrived."

"Nonsense. You wouldn't be imposing. We were simply chatting. It would be jolly nice if you'd stay."

"Emmy, what do you say?"

"Why ask me? It seems as if things are settled."

"Well, if you're sure. I can't think of a better way to spend the afternoon."

Emmeline shot him a withering look, as he took the chair next to Rosemary.

The waitress soon returned with a tray laden with cups and saucers decorated with a delicate spray of tiny pink rosebuds, a teapot and assorted sandwiches and pastries. "Miss, could you bring another cup and saucer? These ladies have kindly asked me to join them."

"Right away, sir."

"Never mind about that, dear. The gentleman can have my cup. I'm suddenly feeling very tired. I think I'll go upstairs and lie down for a bit."

"Rosemary, don't let Gregory chase you away," Emmeline protested.

"Oh, I'm not. I'm just tired. Too much excitement for a *mature* woman in one afternoon," she replied as she pushed her chair back and stood up. Gregory rose as well. "No, please sit. Enjoy tea with Emmeline. I'm sure the two of you have a lot to talk about." She gave Emmeline a pointed look and then turned to Gregory. "I hope I'll be seeing more of you in the next few days."

"The pleasure will be all mine. I will count the minutes."

The older woman giggled as she slipped away quietly.

Emmeline crossed her arms over her chest and remained silent.

"Shall I be mother?" Gregory asked as he picked up the teapot. Receiving no response, he proceeded to pour out two cups of Earl Grey. Curls of steam floated upward and tickled Emmeline's nose, as he handed her a cup.

She waited until this little ritual had been completed and he was leaning back in his chair sipping tea and munching

on a dainty tomato sandwich. "Comfy?" she inquired solici-
tously.

"Darling, you should really try one of these sandwiches.
They're delicious." He wiped some crumbs from his mustache and took another sip of the amber liquid.

"Should I really?"

"Mmm."

"All right, Gregory. Let's drop the pretense. You and
Gran plotted this little sojourn between you, didn't you?
Gran was the only person who knew that I was coming out
to Torquay. In fact, she insisted that Torquay would be 'the
perfect place' to clear my head after everything that happened with Ambrose and Claire."

His eyes, which she had always thought of as two pools
of liquid cinnamon warmed by the summer sun, widened in
mock innocence, as he crossed two fingers over his heart.
"Emmy, I swear that I have absolutely no idea what you're
talking about. And I must say, it's rather mean-spirited of
you to even suggest that dear, sweet Helen and I would *plot*,
as you so unpleasantly put it, against you. We have nothing
but your best interests at heart, love."

Emmeline snorted. "Really?"

"Yes, really. Now, you must admit that you're just the
teeniest bit happy to see me. Aren't you?" He reached
across the table and traced his finger along the curve of her
cheek. "Aren't you?" he said more softly, sending a tingle
all the way down her spine.

Damn. Emmeline could feel herself weakening. She *was*
happy to see him. She couldn't deny it. Earlier when she
had been wandering down by the marina, at one point, she
had found herself wishing that he were in Torquay. And
now here he was. Perhaps it was Fate—in the form of
Gran—trying to tell her it was time to put the past behind
her and give Gregory another chance.

"Yes," she replied at last.

"Yes, what?"

"Yes, I'm happy that you're here. I—I missed you."

Emmeline cast a shy glance at him from beneath her lashes.

Gregory's right eyebrow arched upward in surprise. He realized how much courage it had taken her to finally admit it. He smiled and leaned across the table to press a tender kiss on her lips. "I missed you too, Emmy. You'll never know how much."

She put her hands to her face. Her cheeks were burning. It was suddenly very warm in the conservatory and it had nothing to do with the tea. "I—I—" Emmeline forced herself to look him directly in the eye. "I can't fight it anymore."

He took hold of one of her hands and rubbed his thumb along the side. "Can't fight what anymore?"

She took a deep breath and the words came tumbling out in a rush. "I would like us to start over. I would like us to be together again. My life was so gray and empty after you left. I was so lonely, especially after the baby. I kept hoping you would come back one day. It was just wounded pride that has prevented me from hurling myself into your arms these last couple months." She paused and swallowed hard. "There, I've said it."

She held her breath and waited for what seemed an eternity. A vein throbbed against her temple. Gregory simply stared at her. His face remained motionless. Had she got it wrong? Maybe he didn't feel the same way anymore? Just as she started to kick herself for putting her heart on her sleeve like that, he moved to the chair next to hers, took her face in his hands, and kissed her again—a deep, passionate kiss that erased all the doubts that had been racing through her mind.

Gregory pulled away first and smiled as he brushed a stray curl from her forehead. "I was rather hoping that that was the conclusion you would come to."

Emmeline smiled and rested her head against his shoulder, before becoming conscious of the fact that they were suddenly the center of attention. Everyone in the conservatory broke into applause, which Emmeline was sure made her turn a darker shade of crimson. She heard someone shout, "Lucky chap."

Gregory looked down at her. "He's right. I'm the luckiest chap in the world. And I'm never going to let you slip through my fingers again."

If only there weren't a niggling fear at the back of his mind that time was fast running out.

CHAPTER 3

S o where do we go from here?" Emmeline asked as they finished their tea and Gregory paid the bill.

He stood and proffered his arm. "Where do we go from here? How about a walk down to Meadfoot Beach before dinner, Miss Kirby? It's close by and the sea air is just the thing to work up an appetite. What do you say to that?"

Emmeline slipped her arm through the crook of his elbow and allowed him to lead her out of the conservatory. "A walk would be lovely. But that's not what I meant."

Gregory patted her hand. "I know what you meant, darling. However, I would prefer to discuss our future away from prying eyes and large ears." He indicated with his eyes all the people who were either smiling benevolently at them or casting surreptitious glances in their direction. It had suddenly gotten very quiet in the conservatory.

She nodded. "Point taken."

"That's my girl. I knew you would understand. After all, it's no one's business but ours."

"Ah, you're wrong about that," Emmeline said matter-of-factly as he gallantly held the door open for her.

His brow crinkled in confusion. "What do you mean?"

"Don't be naïve, Gregory. There are two people who have a vested interest in what happens between us."

They stopped in the middle of the lobby and he scratched his head. "Who might these interlopers be?"

"They go by the names of Gran and Maggie."

Gregory grinned at the mention of Emmeline's grandmother and her best friend. "What can I say, darling? With two such strong supporters on my side, you were bound to capitulate sooner or later. Although I must admit, it has taken rather longer than I had anticipated. It must be that stubborn streak in you."

"Arrogant beast," she replied in mock anger as she punched his arm.

He made a show of rubbing the spot. "I may be an arrogant beast, but you love me anyway."

She tilted her head back and looked up into his cinnamon eyes. "Yes," Emmeline whispered. "Yes, I love you anyway. Warts and all."

Gregory slipped his arm around her waist and pulled her toward him so that they were facing each other. He kissed the top of her head and held her close. She felt his warm breath against her ear as he murmured softly, "And I love you. More than life itself, my darling."

Emmeline smiled up at him and, for the first time in two years, she felt as if the other half of her soul had been restored to her. She never wanted to be parted from Gregory again. Ever.

"I say, Toby. It *is* you, isn't it?"

The man's voice came from behind her and interrupted their quiet moment. Emmeline felt Gregory's arms stiffen around her as they twisted around to see who the stranger was.

He dwarfed Emmeline, so he had to be about six foot one or two. As Gregory was forty-two and this fellow appeared to be slightly older, she guessed he was in his mid-forties. Slim, with a narrow waist above very long legs, there was an aura of rugged fitness about the stranger. His pale blue V-neck sweater molded itself to the contours of his trim muscular torso. He likely played tennis or rugby.

But what really drew one to him were his hazel eyes. They were full of intelligence and good humor. Emmeline found herself smiling back at him. There was something about him that immediately put one at ease. Perhaps it was the way his pleasant features meshed together—the oval face, the strong jawline and wide forehead.

The man clapped Gregory on the shoulder. "I say, Toby, it's good to see you after all these years. I couldn't believe my eyes when I came into the lobby and saw you standing there as large as life. I have so many questions. I hardly know where to begin, old chap."

Gregory looked down at the proffered hand and then directly into the stranger's eyes. For a second, a shadow seemed to pass over his face. It vanished in a flash, so Emmeline couldn't be certain whether she imagined it or not.

"I'm afraid you are under some misapprehension, sir," Gregory replied stiffly.

"Sir? Why so formal, Toby? Stop pulling my leg. It's me, Nigel."

"As I said, you are mistaken. My name is Gregory Longdon. Now, if you'll excuse us, we were just going out." Gregory put his hand on the small of Emmeline's back and made as if to go.

The man ran a hand distractedly through his chestnut hair. "I don't understand. You're Toby Crenshaw. I know it's been over twenty years, but I would have recognized you anywhere. You haven't changed a bit, except for the mustache of course."

Emmeline had kept silent during this exchange, but she spoke up now, "I assure you, Mr..."

"Sanborn. Nigel Sanborn."

"I assure you, Mr. Sanborn, that you are indeed mistaken."

He looked down at her and then back at Gregory in confusion. "I'm sorry to have troubled you, Mr. Longdon. I could have sworn that—"

Gregory cut him off. "It's quite all right. It happens. Shall we go, Emmy?" he asked briskly.

"Yes, well—I wouldn't want to keep you. I'm sorry again, Mr. Longdon. And you, Mrs. Longdon."

Emmeline felt her cheeks suffuse with heat. "I'm Emmeline Kirby. Not Mrs. Longdon."

"Not yet," Gregory interjected, "but I'm working on it. Now, if you'll excuse us, Mr. Sanborn."

He stepped aside to allow them to pass. "Yes. Yes, of course."

Emmeline cast a quick glance over her shoulder and saw that Sanborn was still standing in the middle of the lobby staring after them.

᙮᙮᙮

Crossing the hotel gardens, they cut through Lincombe Woods until they reached the steep cliff path. An old wooden staircase took them straight down onto Meadfoot Beach. Some of the boards were loose, so Emmeline cautiously tested each step with her toe before she put her full weight on it. Gregory was heedless to any danger. Soon they found themselves walking along a curving, sandy shingle drizzled with the warmth of the late afternoon sun. Meadfoot tended to be quieter because it was patronized largely by locals. Tourists tended to flock to the more popular beaches like Babbacombe and Oddicombe.

Gregory and Emmeline held hands like any other pair of lovers as they ambled in companionable silence. The velvet hiss of the incoming tide gliding over the sand and the occasional screech of a seagull overhead were the only sounds that reverberated around them.

There were only a handful of people scattered about the beach. After all, although Torquay's climate was mild, it was still only April.

"Emmy, why don't we go toward the eastern end of the beach? I think you'd like it. It's rocky in that section. We can find a spot to watch the tide come in and where we can be alone."

Emmeline laughed and stretched up on tiptoe to give him a peck on the cheek. "We're alone now. But let's go, it sounds lovely—well, everything is really lovely here. Or does it only seem that way because things have changed between us?"

Gregory smiled at her. "A bit of both, I think. Torquay and the surrounding towns are marvelous. Tomorrow, I'll take you exploring."

"I'll keep you to that promise. We can ask the hotel to pack us a picnic."

"Brilliant idea, darling. I knew there must be some reason why I loved you."

✐✐✐

It was common for people to fish from the rocks, but to-day sun, sky and sea conspired to ensure that Gregory and Emmeline had this section of the beach all to themselves. They perched side by side high up on a wide boulder. Gregory put his arm around her shoulders and Emmeline snuggled against him, breathing in the scent of his aftershave and feeling his heart beating in his chest.

They remained quiet for a long while, seduced by the undulating grace of the waves as they rolled in with greater frequency and crashed in a shower of froth against the jagged rocks below. They were simply content to be with one another.

Emmeline was the first to speak. She tilted her head back so that she could look into his eyes. "About what you said to that man in the lobby."

Annoyance flitted across Gregory's face. "Forget about him, Emmy. He's not important."

"No, it's not about him mistaking you for someone else. I meant what you said to him about us getting married."

"What about it? It's what we had been planning to do before—" Gregory broke off in mid-sentence.

"Yes, before you ran away, and I found out that you were a jewel thief."

"Darling, I told there were reasons—"

Emmeline put a finger to his lips to silence his protests. "Never mind all that. I've put it behind us. This is a new beginning, but I want us to take things slowly this time. I don't want us to repeat the same mistakes we made the first time."

"Are you saying that you *don't* want to get married?" he asked incredulously.

Emmeline smiled and placed a soft kiss on his cheek. "No. I want to be your wife more than anything in the world, but too much has happened in the last two years. I want us to have some time to get used to being around one another again before we jump into marriage. Surely you can see the sense in that."

"How much time, Emmy? Because I want you to know that my feelings for you have not changed."

"Just a little time, I promise you." She kissed him again.

Gregory pulled her toward him. "Fine," he said grudgingly. "Your wish is my command. But mind you, I hope you don't keep me dangling too long." He felt her giggling against his chest.

"I won't. You have my word on that. There's one more thing we need to settle right now." She pulled away and fixed her dark gaze on his face.

Gregory sighed and shook his head in resignation. "You have become very demanding in the last two years, my love. If you're not careful, I may change my mind about you."

Emmeline swatted his arm gently. "Listen, I'm being serious."

"I can see that. When those two little lines between your eyebrows knit together like that, I know that you're in deadly earnest. Now, what is it? You have my complete attention."

"You have to give up being a jewel thief. I will not marry a man who is a common criminal. You will have to find an honest form of employment to occupy your days."

The corners of Gregory's mouth twitched, but he suppressed the urge to laugh. "First of all, you are engaging in character assassination again. I can see you have been spending far too much time with our dear friend Oliver of late."

"We are not speaking of Chief Inspector Burnell at the moment. We are discussing *our* future. And I will not marry a thief."

Gregory winced in mock pain. "Must you hurl such vulgarities about, Emmy? I don't use such unflattering language when describing you."

Emmeline snorted. "That's because I'm not, nor have I ever been, on the wrong side of the law. I love you, but I will not tolerate it now that my eyes have been opened."

"Then why don't you close them again?" he suggested flippantly.

"Ah. So you admit it at last that you're a thief?"

Gregory pressed his lips against hers and, for a moment, Emmeline forgot what they had been discussing. "You know you're very alluring when you get all excited, but I admit nothing, my darling. Oliver and the rest of his police cronies are tilting at windmills. They have no proof that I've ever done anything illegal. It is mere speculation on their part. I'm a law-abiding citizen."

Emmeline groaned as she wagged a finger at him. "You, *my darling*, are incorrigible. However, you've been warned. Repent your wicked ways. The only thing that stands between us becoming man and wife is your chosen profession."

In a few days, these words would come back to haunt her.

CHAPTER 4

The tide chased them from their private nook as the sun dipped lower and lower in the sky, until it consummated its love affair with the sea. The amethyst haze of dusk pressed in around them as they retraced their steps across the beach to the staircase that led up to the cliff path. Somehow the stairs appeared even more rickety and steep when viewed from below.

"Gregory, isn't there some other way for us to get back to the hotel?" Emmeline asked hopefully.

"This is the most direct route. Why?"

"I can't explain it, but I don't fancy taking them. You can go ahead and laugh at me, if you like."

He smiled. "There's nothing to be afraid of. I assure you. Here take my hand." Emmeline hesitated. "Come on, love," he coaxed. "It's best if we start making our way up before it gets dark."

"You're right. I'm just being silly. Let's go."

Gregory led the way with Emmeline close on his heels. They had no choice but to go in single file. She held onto the handrail tightly and concentrated her attention on his back. One step after another. Halfway up, she was reproaching herself for her unreasonable attack of nerves, when her right foot slipped on a loose board. Her foot dangled upon the air and her arms flailed for a few seconds. But Gregory's reflexes were razor sharp, and he grabbed her wrist the minute she screamed. A split second longer and Emmeline would have plummeted to the rocks below.

He felt her body trembling and pressed her against the rock face. "Breathe, Emmy. You're all right. It was only a loose board. That's all."

Emmeline took great, big gulps of air. Her heart was pounding against her chest. She stared up into Gregory's eyes and forced herself to calm down. He had her arm in a vice-like grip. There was no way she could fall. "I'm all right now."

Concern was etched in every line of his face. "Sure?"

Emmeline smiled weakly and nodded. "Yes, I just want to get back to the hotel and take a nice hot shower."

Gregory squeezed her hand and brushed the top of her head with a quick kiss. "That's my girl. Then we'll have dinner and dance in the ballroom until the wee hours of morning."

"Sounds marvelous." Her legs still felt a little wobbly beneath her, but it was best to press on.

By the time they returned to the hotel again, Emmeline's good humor had been restored and the incident was forgotten. Gregory had teased her mercilessly the entire way. He always knew exactly which buttons to push, but she laughed anyway. Heads close together, linked arm in arm, they chatted and made plans for the rest of their holiday. It was as if they hadn't been apart for the last two years. How nice it was to be a couple again, Emmeline mused. Two halves of the same whole.

❧❧❧

Dinner had been superb. Emmeline couldn't remember when she had enjoyed a meal more. Her *sole meuniere* with asparagus and new potatoes were perfection itself. Meanwhile, Gregory had tucked into a juicy steak smothered in mushrooms and a red wine sauce, which had been accompanied by haricots vert. However, what really enhanced the excellent food was the understated ambience of the dining room, with its picture windows and breathtaking sea views.

Emmeline sat twirling the stem of her glass of pinot grigio between her fingers as she stared across the table at Gregory, a faint smile upon her lips. He looked so dashing in his navy, double-breasted suit, powder blue shirt and silver tie. There was no one else like him in the world. She felt like getting up in the middle of the dining room and telling all and sundry that he was all hers.

"What's so amusing, love? Have I got bits of food stuck between my teeth or something?" He dabbed at his mustache with his napkin.

"Nothing at all. Why do you ask?"

Gregory's right eyebrow arched upward. "You've got a very odd expression on your face."

She rested her chin on her hand. "Do I? I just like admiring you."

The corners of his mouth curled into a smile and he lowered his voice. "Then by all means admire away. I wouldn't want to interrupt. But I must say that you look absolutely ravishing in that silk confection that you're wearing. Coral is exactly the right hue to set off your dark looks, while the deep V-neckline in the front and the back sets off your lovely shoulders to perfection. It's enough to drive a man wild with desire."

Heat suffused her cheeks as he moved his chair closer and placed a hand on her knee. His cinnamon eyes danced with mischief. She was certain her blush must be deepening from pink to scarlet, as his warm lips left a tantalizing kiss on that soft spot where her neck and shoulder met.

She pushed him away gently. "I think we should order the coffee and dessert now." Her voice was low and hoarse.

"Do you, darling?" he asked innocently and leaned a fraction of inch closer. "Coffee was the furthest thing from my mind."

"I know. That's why I think we should order coffee, before things get dangerous."

"Dangerous? What could possibly be dangerous?" He took her hand in his larger one and flashed one of his devastatingly charming smiles. "We're simply two adults having dinner in a restaurant."

"Mmm. Things were tilting in a distinctly different direction a moment ago. Gregory, I told you. I don't want us to rush things this time."

He lifted her hand to his lips and brushed her knuckles with a kiss. "All right, Emmy. We'll do whatever you like. I won't press."

She touched his cheek lightly with her finger and whispered in his ear, "Thank you for understanding. I do love you."

"Yes, I know. I've always known. I was simply waiting for you to realize it." Their foreheads touched and they shared a smile. Then Gregory pulled his chair back. "Best to put some distance between us. I wouldn't want to be tempted and jeopardize my chances."

Emmeline giggled. "You're incorrigible, but never change."

"Now, where's that waiter? If we are to dance the night away, we need some coffee and dessert."

In the end, Emmeline had a pear and almond tart with banana ice cream while Gregory was content to have only an espresso. She was finishing her dessert and laughing at one of his jokes, when she noticed that seated a few tables away from them was the man they had run into that afternoon.

"Look, Gregory, there's that man again."

He had to swivel around in his chair. "What man?"

"Over there. That Nigel Sanborn. The one we met in the lobby. He keeps staring at us."

Sanborn lifted his wine glass in a silent toast and smiled at them. Emmeline and Gregory both inclined their heads in acknowledgement.

"It's funny that he was so certain that you were his friend," Emmeline said as she continued to look at Sanborn.

"Mmm. Funny." Gregory turned back and took a sip of his coffee.

Emmeline sensed a change in his mood. "Is something wrong?"

"Nothing's wrong, love. The man's simply confused. After all, he said himself that he hadn't seen his friend in over twenty years. People change after such a long time and the mind plays tricks on one."

"Yes, perhaps," she mumbled distractedly. "Toby Crenshaw."

"W—What?" Gregory spluttered.

"That was his friend's name. Toby Crenshaw."

"Rather a silly name, if you ask me. Now, are you ready to go? The dance floor awaits."

CHAPTER 5

Emmeline crawled into bed around midnight and fell into a deep, dreamless sleep the minute her head hit the pillow. They had danced until eleven-thirty and then Gregory had insisted on walking her to her room. Since his room was two floors up, he said that the least she could do was to give him a good night kiss to tide him over until he saw her again at breakfast. One kiss had turned into two, then three. She lost count after four. A little breathless and with her head spinning, it had taken all her willpower to pull back and send him on his way.

Now, as golden strands of sunlight slanted into the room and gently nudged her awake, Emmeline silently congratulated herself. She sat up in bed and pulled her knees under her chin. It had been the right decision not to invite Gregory to spend the night. She wanted things to be perfect this time. There was no reason to rush. They loved each other. That was the most important thing. That was the foundation of their relationship. It had to be. Without love—and trust in that love—they had nothing. But they weren't the same two people anymore, no matter how much Gregory protested to the contrary. A lot had happened in the last two years. She knew she had to get past it all, before she could embrace the future.

Emmeline threw off the bedclothes and got out of bed

with determination. "I'm going to do it," she said aloud as she padded across the room in her bare feet and pulled the glass sliding door open. She stepped out onto her balcony and took a deep lungful of clean, crisp air. "I'm going to get past it," she whispered, as she leaned her elbows on the railing to feast her eyes on the view of Torbay. "For us, Gregory. I promise."

☙☙☙

Showered and dressed in a red cotton sweater with a white collar and beige trousers, Emmeline made her way down to the restaurant half an hour later. Her gaze swept across the tables, but Gregory hadn't come down yet. She had the hostess seat her and ordered some coffee while she waited for him. Her mind wandered as she stared out the windows. She fingered the gold bracelet she always wore—the bracelet Gregory had given her—and smiled.

"Good morning. It's nice to see that someone's so cheerful at the crack of dawn."

Emmeline looked up to find Nigel Sanborn standing next to the table, a bemused expression in his hazel eyes. "Oh, good morning, Mr. Sanborn. I wouldn't call eight-thirty the crack of dawn. But, there's a lot to smile about. I'm alive. It's a beautiful day." She waved a hand toward the view outside the window. "And all's right with the world."

"Ah, there speaks a woman in love."

She felt a pink flush creeping up her cheeks. "Is it that obvious, Mr. Sanborn?"

"Please call me Nigel. Mr. Sanborn sounds so stuffy. Only my father is Mr. Sanborn. But to answer your question—yes, it is extremely obvious. Mr. Longdon is a very lucky man."

"If I am to call you Nigel, then I'm Emmeline. Well, Nigel, I would say that we were both lucky. It hasn't been easy, and we still have a few things to work out, but together we can get through anything. I see that now and that's the way it should always be."

"Quite right. Love conquers all. Best of luck to you both," he said sincerely and smiled down at her.

Emmeline returned his smile. She found that she liked Nigel Sanborn very much. He had a boyish enthusiasm and quiet charm that was irresistible. He was so open and friendly that before people realized it, they were telling him all sorts of things that they had never intended to when they first met him.

"I say, I hope I'm not stepping on your chap's toes by chatting with you like this."

"Oh, it's all right. Gregory's not down yet. He should be here any minute, though." Her gaze flicked toward the door.

"Good. I wouldn't want to upset him. I got the impression yesterday that I rather rubbed him the wrong way for some reason."

Emmeline looked down at her hands. She didn't know how to respond. She couldn't explain Gregory's reaction and his baffling antagonism to this man. It was not in his character to be so stand-offish upon first acquaintance. "I think you caught him off guard. That's all."

"Yes, of course. That must be it. But I could have sworn that he was Toby…" His voice trailed off and his hazel gaze drifted over her shoulder. He seemed lost somewhere in the past. After a moment, he apparently recollected his surroundings. "Have you known each other long?"

"We've known each other for three years, but certain circumstances have kept us apart the last two."

Sanborn nodded. "Hmm. I see," he said noncommittally. "At least you found your way back to one another. That's more than can be said for a lot of people. How did the two of you meet?"

"Emmy, what's going on here?"

Emmeline and Sanborn were both startled to see Gregory. They had been so engrossed in their conversation that they hadn't heard him approach the table.

Emmeline didn't know why, but she felt like a schoolgirl who had been caught doing something naughty. "Gregory, there you are at last." She smiled up at him. "Mr. San— Nigel and I were chatting while I waited for you."

"Good morning, Mr. Longdon. Please don't blame Emmeline. The fault is all mine. She was simply being polite," Sanborn explained, bowing his head gallantly toward Emmeline as he rose to his feet.

A tense silence suddenly filled space between the two men. Gregory's mouth was set in a tight line that Emmeline recognized only too well. Sanborn's eyes narrowed as he took a step toward Gregory, searching his features for some spark of recognition, of familiarity, in the hope of finding a man called Toby Crenshaw. Under the probing scrutiny, Gregory's face closed in on itself, becoming a mask of inscrutability, devoid of any emotion. Not a muscle moved. He didn't even blink. In the end, after what seemed to be an internal monologue, Sanborn shrugged his shoulders and turned back to Emmeline. "Well, I must be off. Nice chatting with you. Enjoy your day. Mr. Longdon." He inclined his head toward Gregory.

Gregory didn't budge. He watched as Sanborn walked toward a table at the other end of the dining room.

Emmeline tugged at Gregory's sleeve. "He must have very strong shoulders."

He looked down at her in confusion. "What?"

"I said that he must have very strong shoulders. Otherwise, a weaker man would have died already from all the daggers shooting out from your eyes."

"Don't be silly, Emmy. You're imagining things."

"*I'm* not the one who chose to start the day by being rude to a perfectly nice man."

"I wasn't being rude." Gregory jerked a thumb over his shoulder. "He's far too nosy for my liking. However, I see that he's already on a first name basis with you. Why was he asking you so many questions about us? Our personal affairs are none of his business."

Emmeline rolled her eyes. "Honestly. He was being friendly. It was merely idle chit chat. You make it sound as if I was being grilled by an MI5 agent."

"I don't like it," he replied tersely as he cast a quick glance across the room again.

"That is rather stating the obvious." She took his hand in hers and intertwined their fingers. "Forget about Nigel Sanborn. This is meant to be a holiday for the two of us."

He smiled as he caressed her curls. "Sorry." He bent down and nuzzled his cheek against hers. "You're absolutely right. Let's start all over again. Good morning, my love. Did you sleep well?"

Emmeline kissed his freshly shaven cheek. "Mmm. I slept like a baby."

He pressed a quick kiss to top of her head and lowered himself into the chair opposite her. "I'm glad that one of us could sleep," he said as he flicked open his napkin with a crack and draped it across his lap in one fluid motion.

"Oh, couldn't you sleep?"

"Not a wink all night long."

The corners of Emmeline's mouth turned downward in a sympathetic moue. "I'm surprised about that. The beds are extremely comfortable and the sound of the bay is so soothing."

"I think perhaps it had to do with the fact that I was all alone in my big empty room." He sighed melodramatically. "I'm rather afraid of the dark, you know." There was a playful glint in his eye.

Emmeline snorted derisively. "That's news to me. Since when are you afraid of the dark?"

He waved an elegant hand in the air. "Practically all my life. Didn't I tell you?"

"No, you never mentioned it."

"I suppose I was bit embarrassed. Probably my male ego. You know what psychiatrists say about the male ego. I'm sure I wouldn't be afraid if someone *shared* my room."

"Uh. Huh." Emmeline's right eyebrow arched upward

and she looked at him in askance. "And did you have anyone particular in mind for this therapy?"

Gregory reached across and took her hand. "Well, *we* seem to get along. I rather thought you might want to help me get over my fear."

"Did you now? I thought we agreed to take things slowly."

He cocked his head to one side and pretended to mull this over. "Yes." He nodded. "Yes, I do recall a conversation to that effect."

"Good. I'm happy to see that you're not losing your faculties. It would be a pity for a man in the prime of life."

"Thank for your concern, darling." He kissed her fingertips lightly. "But that still leaves my fear of the dark. I would like to abide by our agreement, naturally. I'm a man of my word, after all. So the only solution, if you won't come to my room, is for me to come to yours. I don't mind really. As long as I'm not alone."

The laughter bubbled up from her throat. "I bet you don't, you rogue. You win in either case."

"Do I, Emmy?" he asked with feigned innocence. "I hadn't thought about it, but I suppose you're right. Yes, I rather think you might have a point." He flashed her a cheeky grin.

She let go of his hand. "Oh, let's order already. It's much too lovely a day to waste it indoors."

Yes, Gregory thought. *Let's get away from the hotel and Nigel Sanborn.*

CHAPTER 6

Shortly after ten o'clock, armed with a picnic basket filled with tasty morsels, courtesy of the hotel, Gregory and Emmeline set out on the coastal path and followed the signs north to the town of Teignmouth. They dallied along the steep cliffs, drinking in the breathtaking views as a gentle wind ruffled the cobalt waters below in Lyme Bay. During their ramblings, they stumbled upon a secluded cove where seagulls stood sentinel on the rocky outcrop and frothy wavelets lapped against the tawny sand of the beach. Drizzled with the honey-gold light and warmth of the midday sun, it was the perfect spot for an *al fresco* lunch. The combination of the sea air and the walk made them suddenly ravenous, and they tucked into the contents of the basket with relish.

Once their hunger had been sated, they lingered on the beach chatting and laughing. Emmeline would have liked to take her shoes off and dip her feet in the bay but, although the air was mild, the water was still too cold. Regretfully, they said goodbye to their little cove and pushed on to Teignmouth. With one last look from the cliff, Emmeline made Gregory promise that they would come back before their holiday was over. He readily agreed.

The rest of the afternoon passed too quickly. At half past two, their feet led them into Teignmouth, an attractive seaside town on the River Teign just across from Shaldon. They walked out to the end of the Victorian pier, browsed in a few shops, and then made their way into the back streets, where they found a cozy café to have tea.

It had been a good day, Emmeline thought to herself as they entered the hotel again a few hours later. She stole a glance at Gregory's profile and smiled. He had enjoyed it too. It was written all over his handsome face. She touched his arm and reached up to kiss his cheek.

Gregory stopped and pulled her into his arms. "Not that I'm complaining, mind you, but what was that for, darling?"

"I love you and I just couldn't help myself."

"As I said, I'm not one to complain. It would be ungentlemanly to do so. But now that I find you in this receptive mood—" He bent down and kissed her neck. "—perhaps you will reconsider your unreasonable stance about helping me to overcome my fear of the dark by sharing my room."

He felt her warm breath against his ear as she laughed. "No," she said as she pulled away.

"But I'm in need of your tender ministrations."

Emmeline reached up on tiptoe and pressed a soft kiss on his nose. "The answer is still no. You will have to resolve your problem *alone*."

"You're a very hard woman, Emmeline Kirby," he replied in mock anger.

She laughed again. "And you—" But whatever she had been about to say was lost when Rosemary called to them from across the lobby.

"Emmeline, Gregory." The older woman waved and made her way toward them. "I was wondering whether I'd run into the two of you. Did you have a nice day?"

Emmeline felt a stab of guilt because she had been so caught up in her reconciliation with Gregory that she had completely forgotten about Rosemary. "Yes, we did. We took the coastal path and walked to Teignmouth. The hotel was kind enough to pack us a picnic lunch." She smiled as she swung the empty basket. "What about you?"

"Rosie had the day off, so I spent it with her and my grandsons."

"Oh, good." This assuaged Emmeline's conscience slightly. She turned to Gregory and explained, "Rosemary's daughter recently moved down here, so she's come for a short visit."

Gregory smiled as he slipped his arm around Emmeline's waist. "If your daughter's anything like you, then she must be a beauty."

Rosemary dismissed this with a wave of her hand. "What a lot of piffle you do talk. It's enough to make an old woman blush."

"Ah. Ah. I thought we settled this point already," Emmeline interjected. "*Old* is such a nasty word and it is so far from the truth."

"Emmy's right. With two such vibrant, attractive women around, I don't know where to turn first."

Rosemary laughed and placed a blue-veined hand on his strong arm. "Emmeline, I don't know where you found this flatterer, but I suggest you keep a tight leash on him. Otherwise, some designing female will try to steal him from you."

Emmeline looked up at Gregory. "Oh, don't worry. I don't intend to let him go. Not again. Not without a fight, at any rate."

He gave her waist a gentle squeeze and smiled.

"Well, I'm glad to see that the two of you have worked things out," Rosemary said with motherly affection. "If you hadn't taken this nice young man back, I was planning to have a serious talk with you."

"You hear what she said, Emmy? 'Nice young man.' I think you should listen to Rosemary. She's a very wise woman."

Emmeline groaned and shook her head. Here was another addition to his harem of admirers. Oh, well, she had no choice but to live with them. That was what happened when one was involved with the most handsome, most charming, most dashing man that walked this Earth. However, she sighed. She was only half joking when she told Rosemary just now that she would fight any rival for Gregory's affections. The only thing Emmeline worried about was whether she would come out the victor. *Let's face it, I'm not a leggy blonde supermodel who makes men drool.* Quite the contrary, she was short, petite, and dark. Although some said that she was pretty—namely Gran, who couldn't be characterized as unbiased judge—she would never be considered beautiful. Emmeline bit her bottom lip and frowned as she looked up at Gregory again. What did someone like him see in her? Could she ever be enough for him?

"All right, love?" Gregory asked, his puzzled gaze searching her face.

"Pardon? Sorry, my mind must have drifted for a moment." Her cheeks felt warm and she chided herself for her attack of self-doubt. After all, Gregory did come all the way to Torquay just to be with her.

"Am I boring you already? I suppose I will have to try harder to hold your attention."

"You could never bore me." She leaned into his embrace. "Now, what were you saying?"

"That's better. Anyway, Rosemary's told me of a lovely little restaurant in Torquay. I'm going to ask the desk to book a table for us tonight. Then, we can go to our rooms—our *separate* rooms—" He lifted his right eyebrow to emphasize his last point. "—to shower and change. I'll meet you here in the lobby around seven-thirty. All right?"

"Sounds perfect. I'll see you later."

"Good girl." He gave her a quick peck on the cheek and turned to Rosemary. "You don't know how it pains me to take my leave from you." He put a hand over his heart and gave a little bow. "However, I live in hope that I will be able to feast on your beauty again very soon."

Rosemary shook her head. "Oh, go on with you."

Gregory winked as he straightened up. He was whistling softly as he crossed the lobby with masculine grace. The two women watched as he spoke to the clerk on duty.

"Your young man's quite extraordinary, isn't he?" Rosemary said.

Emmeline nodded, her heart full of love. "There's no one like him." She blushed when she realized Rosemary's blue eyes were fixed on her. Emmeline cleared her throat. "Yes, well—I—"

Rosemary laughed and patted her arm. "No need to feel embarrassed, my dear. It's quite refreshing to see two people so in love in this age of quick divorces."

"Thank you," Emmeline replied quietly. "Sometimes when I look at Gregory, I can't believe that he chose me when he could easily have his pick of any number of beautiful women."

"What a lot of rot. Have you taken a look in the mirror lately? You are very pretty, Emmeline."

"But is that enough? I don't make heads turn when I enter a room."

"So what? That's not important," Rosemary scolded. "You've got a brain in your head. That's far more alluring. You've got a successful career. And above all, you have a man who loves you. Any fool with eyes in his head can see it. Some women would kill to have what you have. So we'll hear no more of this rubbish. You need to have more confidence in yourself."

Emmeline half-smiled. "You sound just like Gran."

"The more I hear about her, the more I like this woman."

Emmeline squeezed her hand and smiled. "Thanks."

"For what? I didn't do anything. I was only telling you what is as plain as day."

"Thanks, anyway. I've always been a little weak in the self-confidence department."

Rosemary's intelligent blue eyes widened in surprise. "But why?"

Emmeline sighed. "You don't really want to hear all my fears and foibles. You'd be bored to tears."

"Of course, I want to hear about them. I'd like to think

we were friends. You listened to my ramblings yesterday. Now, I'm here to listen to you. But I'm not as young as I used to be and my legs tend to get tired more easily these days. Do you think we could sit in those chairs over there?" She pointed to a quiet corner.

"Yes. Yes, of course," Emmeline replied and tucked Rosemary's hand through her elbow. "Lean on me. I'm sorry to have kept you standing, while I chuntered away like that. I should have realized."

Once they were settled in the overstuffed chintz armchairs covered in raspberry cabbage roses, Rosemary prompted, "Tell me, my dear. Perhaps I can help."

Emmeline smiled. Rosemary was right. They had become friends. It was amazing how quickly it had happened. She felt at ease talking with her. It was almost like talking to Gran. "That's very kind of you. But there's nothing you can do. No one can really. It's just my problem. I've always been plagued by self-doubt, ever since I was a little girl. It will sound silly to you."

"No, it will not. I assure you."

Emmeline twisted her hands in her lap. "When I was in school, I was always the one left out of everything. I don't know why. I've never had many friends. It takes me a long time to get to know people and to open up about myself. However, once I do make friends, I'm extremely loyal and would do anything for him or her."

Rosemary reached out to still Emmeline's restless hands. "I can see that. That's a very rare and admirable quality."

"I'm glad you think so. But because of that 'rare and admirable quality,' people tend to take advantage of my good nature, and I'm always the one who ends up hurt. After a while, I simply started turning inward to protect myself before I could get hurt. Thus coming full circle and winding up alone again."

"And you worry that Gregory will hurt you and you'll end up alone?" Rosemary asked, her round face full of sympathy.

Emmeline felt tears sting her eyes. "He's already hurt me. I won't bother to go into the details. It's too long a story. We're together again, but there's this voice that keeps swirling round and round my head. It keeps whispering that it's all a dream and I'm going to wake up one day soon and find him gone. Forever this time."

She choked back a sob. Rosemary rubbed her hand and remained silent while Emmeline collected herself. It didn't take her long. She wiped away a tear with the back of her hand and squared her shoulders.

She gave Rosemary a watery smile. "I'm a mess. You don't have to tell me."

"You're not a mess," Rosemary replied with motherly affection. "You're just a bit insecure. But there's absolutely no reason for it. It's all up here." She tapped Emmeline's temple with an arthritic finger. "Trust Gregory. He loves you."

Emmeline squeezed the older woman's hand. "I will." She nodded her head. "I will trust him," she replied in a stronger voice. "I have no choice. I love him."

"Just keep telling yourself that. Nothing else matters."

"Thanks for the moral support. I really needed it."

"You shouldn't need it, but I'm glad that I was here. Now, you had better go to your room and get ready for your dinner. You wouldn't want to keep Gregory waiting, would you?"

Emmeline laughed. "No. I would never hear the end of it." She scooped up her handbag and stood up. "Thank you again for listening. Perhaps we could go on an outing together one day."

Rosemary struggled to pull herself out of the soft armchair. Emmeline helped her up. "I don't think so, my dear. It would rather put a crimp in your young man's style. I would be a third wheel."

"You wouldn't. I assure you. Besides, Gregory could amuse himself for a few hours, while we went on an outing. Think about it. I would really enjoy it. Maybe we could go to Cockington Court or the Royal Terrace Gardens. It would be fun."

Rosemary was amused by Emmeline's enthusiasm. "I'll think about it."

A woman's loud laughter suddenly shattered the low buzz of conversation in the lobby. Emmeline and Rosemary turned around to see who was the cause of the commotion.

They weren't the only ones to stop and stare. For there in the middle of lobby, where she could be seen by everyone, was one of the most ravishing women that Emmeline had ever seen. Lush auburn tresses fell in thick waves down to her shoulders and her emerald silk wraparound dress clung to her svelte figure, emphasizing her full breasts, narrow waist, and round hips. The woman oozed sex appeal and she knew it. She laughed again at something the attractive chap with golden hair and blue eyes whispered in her ear. Emmeline judged that the woman must be around forty and the man looked to be at least ten years her junior. However, the closeness of their two bodies left no one in any doubt about their relationship. All the men in the lobby were envious, while their wives hated the woman on sight.

Emmeline and Rosemary shook their heads in disapproval. "Rather a tasteless display, if you ask me," Emmeline murmured as she stared at the couple.

"Revolting," Rosemary concurred. "She's no better than she should be." There was a hard edge to her voice and the look she cast in the woman's direction was full of loathing. She had to avert her eyes. "I must sit down again."

"Are you feeling ill?" Emmeline asked in concern and turned her back on the couple to concentrate on her friend.

"I'll be fine in a minute," Rosemary replied as she rooted around in her handbag for a handkerchief and wiped the beads of perspiration from her forehead.

"You look a little peaked. I'm going to have the desk call a doctor."

Emmeline had taken a half a step, when Rosemary touched her arm lightly. "No, don't. I'm fine. I just need to sit quietly for a few minutes and I'll be all right. Too much excitement for one day. That's all. Please stay with me." She patted the chair next to her. "Please," she implored.

Emmeline remained unconvinced but, against her better judgment, she acquiesced and lowered herself into the chair. Out of the corner of her eye, she could still see the tactile couple waiting for the porters to bring in their luggage. She could certainly hear them. You'd have to be deaf not to hear what they said.

"Really, Trevor." The woman wagged a finger at him as her husky voice drifted to Emmeline's ears. "You are *naughty*."

Whatever Trevor's reply was, it elicited another burst of silvery laughter from the woman, grating on Emmeline's nerves. She looked up just then and her gaze met the woman's cold green one.

Their eyes held for a long moment, before the woman turned away as Trevor tugged on her elbow and led her to reception.

With a look of disdain darkening his dour countenance, Mr. Harcourt was behind the desk to greet them. "Good afternoon, madam, sir," he said stiffly. "How may I assist you?"

"We'd like to check in," the young man replied.

"Of course. Your name please?"

"Cabot," the woman said.

Mr. Harcourt's dull gray eyes widened. "Cabot?"

"Yes, Cabot. We *do* have a reservation," was the woman's snippy rejoinder.

"Yes." Harcourt made a show of punching the information into the computer to cover his surprise. "Yes, here it is. Sir Frederick and Lady Veronica Cabot."

"There you see. That wasn't so hard, now was it?" the woman said, clearly irritated. "I'm Veronica Cabot."

"And this is Sir Frederick?" Harcourt asked incredulously, as his glance flicked toward the young man.

Emmeline had been listening to this little exchange, and

she turned to Rosemary. "That's not Sir Frederick Cabot," she whispered. "I interviewed him several years ago."

"I think everyone surmised that already," Rosemary mumbled. "Sir Frederick's photo has been in all the papers. I expect everyone knows who *he* is. Now, hush, my dear. We wouldn't want them to think we're spying." She sank back into the shadows surrounding their corner.

Emmeline chuckled. "There's no way we could be accused of that. They're not even *trying* to keep their voices down."

"No, obviously I'm not Sir Frederick," the man was saying, "but you're close. I'm his nephew, Trevor Mayhew. I have a reservation as well," he finished with a broad-toothed smile.

"You see, my husband was detained in London for a couple of days and my nephew here," Lady Cabot said as she looped her arm possessively through Trevor's, "was kind enough to escort me down to Torquay. To make certain that I got here all right. Such a sensitive young man. Always thinking of the welfare of others."

Harcourt blinked twice and cleared his throat. "Naturally, madam. Let me just see. Yes, here it is, Mr. Mayhew. You're in five-o-three and Sir Frederick and Lady Cabot are in five-ten."

"Same floor? I say what a splendid coincidence," Trevor remarked.

"Yes, isn't it?" Lady Cabot replied with a wink.

"Well, thank goodness they're not on my floor. I've had all that I can stand of this." Emmeline got to her feet. "I must go shower and change for dinner, but I don't want to leave you if you're still feeling unwell."

Rosemary smiled weakly. "You go on. I'm all right now, but I think I'll just sit down here for a few more minutes."

"You're sure?" Emmeline hesitated and stared at the older woman, looking for any outward signs of faintness or weakness.

"Yes. Stop fussing like a mother hen. That's my job.

You don't want to keep Gregory waiting. And remember what I said. Never doubt his love."

Emmeline bent down and kissed Rosemary's soft, dry cheek. "I won't. Perhaps we'll see you later?"

"Perhaps." Rosemary flapped a hand at her. "Now shoo."

"I'm going."

Emmeline crossed the lobby toward the bank of lifts. As she passed reception, Lady Cabot happened to turn her head. Her hard, green eyes raked Emmeline from head to toe with an expression of sardonic scorn. Emmeline shivered involuntarily. She was grateful when the lift doors opened and she was able to make her escape. There was something deeply unsettling about the beautiful Veronica Cabot.

CHAPTER 7

Dinner was heavenly. I'll have to thank Rosemary for her suggestion. And the company? Well, what can I say?" Gregory stopped and pulled Emmeline into his arms in the middle of the drive in front of the hotel. "The company was better than I could have hoped for," he murmured between kisses.

Emmeline giggled. "We'd better get out of the way, before a car comes and runs us over."

After a few more kisses, to which she enthusiastically responded, Gregory said, "They wouldn't dare, but better to be safe than sorry, Miss Kirby." He gave her a little bow and proffered an elbow as he guided them through the double doors. "Would you join me for a nightcap in the bar?"

Emmeline glanced at her watch. It was ten-thirty. "Well, just one."

"Excellent, Miss Kirby. Then I promise to escort you to your room."

"Gregory, that's unnecessary. I'm perfectly capable of finding my way to my own room."

"Ah, but the gentleman's code of conduct dictates that I escort to your door. It's Rule Twenty-Eight. You wouldn't want me to betray the code, would you?"

Emmeline halted on the threshold of the bar. "Gentleman's code of conduct? Rule Twenty-Eight? I've never heard of such a thing."

Gregory placed a hand over his heart. "Do not mock the code, Emmy. I live by the code," he said with solemnity.

She laughed again. "Rubbish. You're merely pulling my leg, as usual."

"No, my darling. I wouldn't dare. The code is held in high regard. Now, Rule Twenty-Nine says that once I escort you to your door, I must make a thorough check of the premises to ensure that no burglars had disturbed your room." There was a mischievous gleam in his eyes as he held the door open.

"Ah, I see. Rule Twenty-Nine. Well, you would certainly know about the criminal classes. But so that you don't labor under any illusions, my sweet." She reached up and kissed the tip of his nose. "You will be going back to your own room at the end of this evening." With that, she walked into the bar.

After they found a quiet table in a corner and had ordered a sweet vermouth with a twist of lemon for Emmeline and a whiskey and soda for Gregory, he picked up the thread of their conversation. "I must say that's not a very sporting attitude. You must try to be more broad-minded."

"Alas, we journalists are a cynical lot. I'm afraid we tend to start with the premise that there must be an ulterior motive somewhere in the equation." She raised an eyebrow. "Case in point."

"Me?" He put a hand to his chest in apparent disbelief. "What possible motive could I have? I'm an open book. I'm simply concerned about your welfare. It's my primal male instinct to protect."

Emmeline was enjoying this banter. She hadn't been so relaxed in ages. "I rather think it's another male instinct that's at work here."

"Darling, you quite shock me," he remarked as he touched her knee under the table. "If you go on like this, I'll start blushing."

"I'll bet. I'd like to see that. What a load of drivel," she replied without rancor. "Now, finish your drink."

"Yes, that's a good idea. The vermouth might make you see things more clearly."

"Plying me with liquor will *not* further your cause. If you remember, I only agreed to the one drink."

"How about a kiss? Will that 'further my cause,' as you put it? Perhaps we should test out the theory and see what happens."

Emmeline rested her chin on her hand and leaned closer to Gregory. "I don't know. Is it in the gentleman's code of conduct? I couldn't possibly allow you to kiss me, if it isn't in the code," she replied primly.

The corners of Gregory's mouth quivered. "You are in luck. It happens to be in Rule Twenty-Nine, subparagraph A, stroke One B."

"Stroke One B, really? How fortuitous. Somehow I had a feeling that it might be in the code."

"That's one of the qualities I admire about you, Emmy. Your perspicacity, it's second to none." She returned his grin and their lips met in the small space between them.

When they parted, Emmeline chuckled. "That, my love, will have to hold you until the morning."

"Cruel woman. You raised my hopes, only to dash them at the eleventh hour." He shook his head and repeated, "Cruel woman."

Laughter bubbled up in Emmeline's throat as she gave him a peck on the cheek. "I love you."

"I—" But before Gregory could finish what he had intended to say, the mingled sound of female laughter and plummy male voices drifted to their ears. Every muscle in his face froze.

Emmeline looked up and saw Veronica Cabot, her "nephew," and another couple getting up from a table across the room. "Speaking of cruel women," she murmured.

"What? Who is it?"

"It's Sir Frederick Cabot's *much* younger wife. She's

here with her husband's nephew. Rosemary and I saw them when they arrived this afternoon. They don't even try to hide it." Emmeline sat back in her chair and crossed her arms over her chest. "It's disgusting."

Gregory craned his neck around. He only caught glimpse of the back of Lady Cabot's head, but he saw Trevor Mayhew as he ushered her out of the bar and held the door open for their companions to pass.

Gregory turned back and swallowed hard. "It couldn't be. It *can't* be. *It can't*," he muttered under his breath. He downed what remained of his whiskey in one gulp. It burned as it slid down his throat. He was unnerved to see that the hand that held the tumbler trembled slightly.

The light-hearted flirting of only moments ago had disappeared. Emmeline touched his sleeve. "What is it? Are you all right?"

His head shot up, as if suddenly remembering where he was. The color had drained from his cheeks. There was a wild, hunted expression in his cinnamon eyes.

"Gregory, are you all right?" Emmeline asked again. Her voice was tinged with urgency as her gaze scanned the room to determine what had disturbed him. "You look as if you've seen a ghost."

"Ghost?" He gave a nervous laugh and patted her hand. "Yes, that's what it must have been. Of course. I must be tired and too much of this stuff—" He waggled the tumbler in the air. "—is playing tricks on my imagination. I was just caught off balance for a moment because the person I knew, the person I thought I saw, has been dead for years."

Has to be dead, for all our sakes, his brain screamed. *Has to be dead.*

ഐ

Dawn burst into life in a blaze of orange and gold the next morning, promising another glorious day for exploring.

When Gregory knocked on Emmeline's door to accompany her down to breakfast, there was no trace of last night's strange mood. He was his usual charming, witty self. She studied his profile surreptitiously from under her lashes as they rode down in the lift, but there was nothing to find. Emmeline exhaled deeply. She hadn't realized that she had been holding her breath. It was merely nerves, she told herself. Anyone would be thrown off-kilter if he thought he saw someone whom he knew was dead. She would think no more about it.

Emmeline reached up and twined her arms around his neck, since they were alone in the lift. "I didn't bid you a proper Good Morning when you came to my room, so I thought I'd give you a kiss now. That is, if you don't mind?"

Gregory's arms slipped around her waist and his lips curled into that smile she knew so well. "No, I don't mind at all, darling. You carry on."

But before they knew it, the doors were sliding open at the lobby. "We could go back up and come down again," Gregory suggested roguishly.

"At that rate, we'd never get out of the hotel today."

His finger was pressed on the Open button. "Would that be such a bad thing?"

Emmeline cocked her head to one side and laughed. "Incorrigible."

"I take that as a no." His mustache drooped downward in disappointment.

"Come on," she responded cheerfully. "Let's have breakfast. You promised to take me to Kent Caverns today."

"The things I do for love," Gregory mumbled as he allowed her to drag him toward the restaurant.

They ran into Rosemary by the reception desk. She was wearing a lemon-yellow cardigan over a cream-colored blouse and beige skirt. Her feet were shod in sensible brown suede shoes with crepe soles.

As usual, her snowy hair was swept high atop her head.

"Good morning, you two. Did you enjoy dinner last night?"

"You are a vision of loveliness, Rosemary," Gregory greeted her. "You set my heart aflutter."

"Piffle." She turned to Emmeline. "He never stops, does he?"

"No. He wakes up spouting flowery compliments to enchant unsuspecting females."

"I resent that, Emmy. You make me sound rather nefarious. You know I only have eyes for you, my darling. Mind you, if Rosemary was thirty years younger you'd have some stiff competition on your hands."

They all laughed at this. "Seriously, Rosemary, we must thank you for your suggestion," he said. "The restaurant was absolutely superb. We can't remember the last time we had such a wonderful meal."

"It's a good thing Gran is not here to hear you say that. I think you would become *persona non grata* down at Swaley."

Gregory sighed melodramatically. "Ah, my dear Helen. So many beautiful women, what is a chap to do?"

"Why don't we concentrate on cutting down on the number of women, shall we?" Emmeline suggested playfully.

"Emmy, you can't possibly be jealous of your grandmother and Rosemary."

"Oh, I'm not. So long as it remains only Gran and Rosemary."

"I am relieved. Thank you, darling."

Rosemary smiled with motherly fondness as she watched Emmeline and Gregory. Every word, every gesture, the tone of their voices when they teased one another, were evidence of how much they were in love. "What do you two have planned today?"

"Gregory has promised to take me to Kent Caverns and then I'd like to do a little shopping. Would you like to join us?"

Rosemary glanced up at Gregory. She could tell that he

would rather be alone with Emmeline. "I wouldn't dream of it, my dears. You young people don't need me hanging about."

"Oh, but we'd love for you to join us, wouldn't we, Gregory?"

He didn't hesitate for an instant. He flashed a dazzling smile at Rosemary and said, "Of course, we would. I'd be the envy of every man with a beautiful woman on each arm."

Rosemary laughed. "Ever the charmer, but the answer's still no."

"But what will you do all on your own?" Emmeline asked. "I remember you said that your daughter was working today."

"Yes, Rosie is working today. I'll see her later on this afternoon and have dinner with her and her family. As for the rest of the day, I thought I'd just wander about and see whether Torquay has changed over the years."

"At least, have breakfast with us, before you set off," Emmeline suggested. Gregory nodded his head in agreement.

"Sweet of you to ask, but I've already eaten. I don't sleep well and, therefore, I'm an early riser. I was just on my way to my room to gather my things before I wander down to Meadfoot Beach for a little while. The children used to love playing down there."

Emmeline's eyes widened in concern and she clutched Rosemary's arm. "You mustn't go to Meadfoot Beach alone."

"Why ever not? It's a wonderful place."

"The staircase leading down to the beach is extremely rickety. You'll slip and fall. I nearly did yesterday."

"Really?"

"Yes. If Gregory's reflexes hadn't been so quick, I would have been dashed on the rocks below. Promise me you won't go there alone." There was a plaintive note in Emmeline's voice.

Rosemary smiled and covered Emmeline's hand with her own. "Thank you for the warning, but I'm sure I'll be all right."

"Rosemary, someone could get killed."

"Nonsense, my dear, but to ease your mind, I'll go to the beach when Rosie's free. All right?"

Relief washed over Emmeline. "Yes. That's very wise."

"Good. I'm glad that's settled. Enjoy your day."

Gregory put an arm around Emmeline's shoulders. "We will. And you as well. Perhaps you'll join us for a drink in the bar tonight."

"It's very kind of you to invite me. I'll have to see. I can't promise anything. Now off you go. No more dawdling here in the lobby with me. Shoo. Kent Caverns await."

Emmeline leaned over and kissed Rosemary's feathery cheek. "I hope we'll see you later," she said as Gregory gave her a playful wink.

Rosemary watched as they made their way down the corridor. At one point, Emmeline tilted her head back to laugh at something Gregory whispered in her ear. "What a lovely couple they make," Rosemary murmured aloud. "But enough of that. I've busy day ahead of me. Very busy, indeed." She bustled toward the lift, every footstep full of purpose.

※※※

Veronica Cabot stretched with feline grace as she drowsily cocked one eye open and glanced at the clock on the bedside table. Eight o'clock. She groaned. Nearly the crack of dawn. She shut her eye again and burrowed deeper into the pillow. Beside her, Trevor's tousled blond head rested on her bare shoulder. The warm rise and fall of his rhythmic breathing tickled her neck. She nestled closer to him and allowed herself to be lulled into half-sleep.

Before long, Trevor began to stir. He turned over onto

his back and rubbed his eyes until the room came into focus. His blue gaze raked over the sheets, which molded perfectly to the slender curves of Veronica's slumbering body. A faint smile touched his lips.

"What do you think you're staring at?" Veronica asked, without opening her eyes.

The corners of Trevor's eyes crinkled together. "Sorry, darling. Didn't mean to wake you." He propped himself on one elbow and brushed her lips with a soft kiss. "Morning."

Veronica snaked her arms around his neck and pulled his head close to hers for a long, passionate kiss. "Now, that's a proper good morning." Her green eyes danced with mischief as she looked up into his face.

"I'll have to keep that in mind. Shall we get up or have a lie-in?"

"A lie-in," she purred. "Most definitely."

"Your wish is my command, my lady." He drew her body close to his and pressed a kiss against her temple.

They were content to remain curled in each other's arms for a little while. Trevor was the first to break the silence as he trailed a finger along the silky skin of her shoulder. "Ronnie, there's something I'd like to talk to you about."

Veronica grunted. "Oh, Lord. It's much too early in the day to tackle serious subjects. Can't this wait until later? Please."

"I'm afraid it can't wait. We must hash this out. Now."

"Very well, then." She sat up, pulling her knees under chin. Mild irritation was clearly etched on her face. "Go ahead. Talk."

"There's no need take on that tone, darling," he said soothingly.

"Trevor, just get on with whatever it is you have to say so that I can get back to sleep."

Now it was his turn to be annoyed. Sometimes she could be the most infuriating woman. "Very well. What are we going to do about Uncle Freddie?"

Her green eyes flashed with anger. "What do you mean *do*?"

"When are you going to ask him for a divorce?"

"Divorce? We can't rush these things. You'll have to be patient."

"Patient? *Patient*?" Trevor exploded. "We've been together for months. Virtually since you returned from your honeymoon. I've *been* bloody patient."

"Then you'll just have to go on being patient," Veronica countered with asperity.

"Dash it all, Ronnie. I love you. I want to marry you. All these months you led me to believe you wanted that too." His blue eyes searched her face for confirmation that he hadn't been completely wrong.

The deep furrows disappeared from her brow and her features softened as she slid back down in the bed next to him. "Of course, that's what I want, Trevor," she said as she trailed a finger along his jawline, where a muscle twitched with tension. "I love you too. Never question that. It's just—"

"Just what?" His temper flared again.

"The timing has to be right. These things must be handled with care."

"Oh, for God's sake. How much longer must I wait? A month? Two? Seven?"

"Don't be silly, darling. Soon. Very soon. I promise."

Trevor would not be mollified. "That's not good enough, Ronnie."

Trying to keep the anger from rising to her tongue, she replied, "That's the best I can do. Besides, think how it would look if I divorced your uncle one day and married you the next."

"Who cares what people think? We're the only ones who count. And Uncle Freddie. The sooner you ask him for a divorce, the sooner we can all get on with our lives. I'm rather fond of the old boy and I hate the thought of hurting him, but it's better for you to make a clean break. We can't go on living this lie forever."

"And we won't have to, darling." She pressed a kiss—calculated to make him forget any thoughts rattling around his brain—in the soft hollow beneath his Adam's apple. "I promise. It won't be much longer now. You'll see."

She was so close to getting everything she ever wanted. *So close.* She was not about to let anything stand her way. Not even Trevor. She had worked far too hard to let it all slip through her fingers now.

The telephone screamed to life on the bedside table startling both of them. "I call that bloody cheek. Who could be ringing at this hour?" Trevor muttered as he continued to kiss her neck.

Veronica struggled to disentangle herself from his arms. "Ronnie, leave it."

"I can't. It could be Freddie."

Trevor rolled over on to his back. "Why would Uncle Freddie be ringing at this hour?"

"If I don't answer the phone, we'll never know, will we? Now keep quiet?"

Trevor twisted his fingers as if he was zippering his lips closed.

"Hello?" Veronica said tentatively. As she listened, the color drained from her cheeks. "I told you *never* to call me again. How did you get this number? Are you spying on me? Leave me *alone*." Her voice was shrill.

Trevor sat up and snatched the receiver from her. "Who is this?" He heard a soft click and then the line went dead.

He stretched over Veronica and replaced the receiver in the cradle. As he settled back in the bed, he saw that she was trembling. "Darling, are you all right?" He put an arm around her shoulders. "What did the chap say to you?"

Veronica stared dumbly back at him. Her green eyes, which usually held a look of supreme self-assurance, were now filled with something Trevor had never seen before, *fear.*

CHAPTER 8

Despite having been raised by a hypercritical and overbearing father, who took great pleasure in pitting him against his elder brother, Nigel Sanborn grew up to be one of the most genial and easy-going of chaps. He always had a kind word and a smile for everyone, whether it was the cleaning lady or one of the executives sitting across from him at the negotiating table. Perhaps because of the lack of affection he and his brother, Brian, received from their father, they became extremely close and learned to rely on each other. They trusted each other implicitly. When one needed advice, his brother was the first person to whom he turned. And so it was now.

Nigel sat in a deep armchair in the lobby of the Royal Devon. *The Times* in his hands was all but forgotten as he watched Gregory and Emmeline stop briefly at the reception desk before venturing out the double doors of the hotel. Her laughter briefly drifted to his ears, and then they were gone from sight.

For several seconds, he sat there frowning. Nigel was not a suspicious man by nature, but something was not right. His instincts had never failed him before, therefore he pulled out his mobile from the inner pocket of his jacket and punched in the number he knew in his sleep.

A familiar voice came on the line after the second ring.

"Hello, old chap. How's the working holiday in Torquay?"

Nigel's face broke into a broad grin. "Is that a hint of jealousy I detect in your voice, brother mine?"

"Indeed, it is. I'll have you know that it's pouring with rain here in London, and I've caught this dreadful cold. And my wife, who is supposed to love me in sickness and in health, says that I should buck up because I'll be as right as rain in a few days. You see, I'm doomed to be drowned in the rain and I'm getting no sympathy from my nearest and dearest. Other than that, everything's simply smashing."

Nigel chuckled at his brother's gripes. "Sorry to have to pour salt in the wound, Brian, but the weather is absolutely beautiful here. Sunny and warm. Not a cloud in the azure sky."

"Sadist. How is it that you're the one who got to go out to Torquay, while I'm stuck here in dreary London?"

"Perhaps it has to do with the fact that I'm the company's lawyer while you're merely the second-in-command."

"Is that how it works? The way I see it, you get all the plum jobs, while I have to deal with Dad."

The smile vanished from Nigel's lips. Brian's tone fairly crackled with tension. Nigel was immediately alert. "Is anything the matter?"

His brother sighed. "No, nothing I can't handle. More of the usual, really."

"Are you sure?"

"Yes," Brian said reassuringly. "Don't worry, little brother. Now, tell me how are the negotiations going? When can we expect an answer to our offer?"

Although he could tell that all was not right at the other end of the line, Nigel decided not to press Brian on the point. "I'm meeting Trevor Mayhew for lunch to discuss the contract. If all goes well, we should seal the deal in a few days."

"Splendid. Then we'll have to celebrate when you get back to London. If I'm still alive, that is. But without the tender loving care of my wife, that remains to be seen.

Women are such cruel, heartless creatures. Whoever said that they are the fairer sex must have been out of his mind. Then you'll be back by early next week?"

"Yes, I should think so, the way things are going. But, Brian, there's something else I wanted to discuss with you. Or rather, someone I'd like you to have investigated."

"Oh, yes?" His brother's ears pricked up at this. "Sounds very cloak-and-dagger. Trouble?"

"I don't know yet," Nigel paused. "Possibly. His name is Gregory Longdon."

෴

Gregory was coming out of his room, when he spied Rosemary walking toward him. "Ah, you are a feast for the eyes, dear lady. The gods were indeed smiling down upon me when they placed such a vision of loveliness on my floor." He proffered her his elbow. "May I have the honor of escorting you downstairs?"

The old woman laughed in spite of herself and lightly looped her arm through his. "How can I refuse such a handsome devil?" And indeed, he was dashing in his dove-gray suit, pristine white shirt, and red silk tie.

There was an impish gleam in his cinnamon eyes as he guided them toward the lift. "Just keep reminding Emmeline."

"She's an intelligent young woman and doesn't need me whispering in her ear. You know she only has eyes for you, so stop fishing for another compliment. I've reached my quota for the night."

The corners of Gregory's eyes crinkled together and he tossed his head back in laughter. "I see you intend to keep me on my toes, Rosemary."

"I wouldn't go as far as that," she said as she looked up at him. "I simply want the people around me—the people I care about—to be happy. Emmeline is the type of person who gets under your skin without one realizing it. She deserves to get what she wants in life. And clearly that means you, young man. So I hope you won't hurt her."

Gregory's face sobered as the lift doors slid open. "I wouldn't do that for the world. You have my word on that. I can't bear to lose her. Not again."

"Good. That's the right attitude." She patted his arm and stepped out into the lobby. "It means that I won't have to beat your senses into you with a big stick, after all."

"Heaven forbid. I stand warned." Gregory raised Rosemary's blue-veined hand to his lips and gallantly kissed it.

She waved him away. "That's enough of that. Instead of dawdling here with me, you'd do well to go over to that young lady waiting patiently over there."

He followed the direction her gnarled finger was pointing. Across the lobby, sunk into one of the deep chintz armchairs, was Emmeline. She was draped in a burgundy velvet dress with a scalloped neckline, which set off the string of cream-colored pearls that her grandmother had given her for her last birthday. Although it was not discernible from this distance, Gregory knew that she was wearing—always wore, in fact—the simple gold knot bracelet that he had given to her just before their wedding two years ago. The wedding that should have taken place, but never did because—He pushed this thought from his mind. That was the past. It never did any good to look back. It only led to trouble and heartbreak, and there had been far too much of that to last them a lifetime.

Emmeline smiled and waved when she saw him. Gregory returned her smile. It always amazed him to see the depth of love that she bore for him. Why? No one had ever loved him like that, no one. He closed the space between them in a few strides. He had been a fool, but no more. With each step, all the ghosts and demons that had been haunting him faded into the past—where they belonged and where he was determined that they would remain. Emmeline was his future.

He hitched a hip on the arm of her chair and slipped his arm around her shoulders. "Waiting long, darling?"

"No, not long," she replied as she turned her face to look into his. Her soft lips held a clear invitation, so he bent down and obliged her with a tender kiss. When they parted, he was amused to see that her cheeks had flushed a becoming shade of pink.

"If that's the reaction I receive when I'm a little late, what happens when I am terribly late?" Gregory arched an eyebrow in askance.

Emmeline swatted his arm. "In that case, I would be extremely put out. I'd probably refuse to see you again. Ever."

Gregory stroked his chin in his best imitation of Chief Inspector Burnell. "I see. How disconcerting. And there would be nothing I could say or do to change your mind? Even if I was prostrate with remorse?"

She slid a sly glance in his direction. "Well—"

"Aha. I thought so. You're simply toying with my affections. I have a good mind to return to London this instant, now that I see the kind of woman I'm dealing with."

Her dark eyes danced with laughter, and she wrung her hands melodramatically. "Oh, please don't do that. I couldn't bear it."

"You leave me no choice, Miss Kirby," Gregory sniffed and turned his head away in mock anger.

They both burst out laughing.

"Come on." He pulled her to her feet. "We've wasted far too much time already." A serious look suddenly flitted across his face. "Far too much time," he repeated in a quieter tone. Then his light-hearted mood returned. "A sumptuous feast awaits you."

"Where are we going?" Emmeline asked as he gathered up her cream-colored fringed shawl and settled it around her shoulders.

"Curiosity killed the cat. But I assure you that it will be an evening you'll never forget."

⟡⟡⟡

The taxi dropped Emmeline and Gregory off at the Osbourne, the gleaming white, crescent-shaped hotel that sat atop the spectacular cliffs overlooking Meadfoot Beach. The hotel's restaurant was renowned for its gourmet cuisine.

They were shown to a quiet corner table, which afforded them a view of Torbay. Emmeline was mesmerized. Silvery embers of moonlight plummeted from the charcoal wisps of clouds drifting indolently in the cobalt sky and were swallowed up with a velvety hiss by the undulating waters. "Beautiful," she murmured under her breath.

Gregory reached across the table and took her hand. "Only the best for you, my love."

She tore her gaze from the window and simply smiled at him. She didn't have to say anything. The look in her eyes said it all.

He squeezed her hand and then relinquished it. "Shall we order?" He glanced down and started perusing the menu.

"Yes, I'm suddenly quite ravenous," she replied as she flipped open her menu.

They made their decisions quickly and soon the waiter returned with a bottle of Barolo. He uncorked it and placed it in the center of the table to allow it to breathe a little.

"Now, Miss Kirby," Gregory said after the waiter had gone. "We have some wedding plans to discuss."

"Wedding plans? What wedding plans?" Emmeline remarked coyly.

"Ours, naturally."

"That's funny. I don't remember you actually *asking* me to marry you."

"Emmy, darling, are you becoming senile in your old age?"

"Old age? I'm twelve years younger than you are, so you had better watch out who you are calling old."

"A mere technicality of birth." He dismissed this with a wave of his hand. "You're beyond your age in wisdom, but we're deviating from the topic at hand. Namely, our wedding. We must set a date."

A smiled played at the corners of her mouth as she gave him an innocent look. "I repeat. You have not asked me. Two years ago, yes, but not now."

Gregory rolled his eyes. "Women," he mumbled. "The things I do for love." He cleared his throat and reached for her hand again. "Miss Kirby," he said in a formal tone. "Will you do me the honor of becoming my wife?"

Emmeline rested her chin on her free hand and leaned toward him. She waited several long seconds before giving him her answer. "Well, I suppose so."

"Suppose? Is that yes?"

She couldn't contain her giggles any longer. "Of course, it's yes, you great oaf. Do you think I would marry anyone else?"

"Well, thank God for that. Now that we've gotten that out of the way, dates. When would you like to get married, my love?"

"There's something else we must discuss first."

Gregory groaned. "Emmy, you are making this unnecessarily difficult."

She ignored this remark. "It is the little matter of your chosen profession."

He sighed. "Not this again."

"Oh yes. I was perfectly serious yesterday. I will not become the wife of a jewel thief."

Gregory poured some of the ruby wine into her glass. "Drink some of the Barolo. You'll love it."

She accepted the glass he offered and gently swirled it around before taking a sip. The rich, bold wine tantalized her tongue before it slipped down her throat. "Delicious. But it will not distract me from what we were discussing."

"And what was that? I'd quite forgotten," he replied with an impish grin.

"We were talking about jewel thieves. One in particular. *You.*"

Gregory clucked his tongue at her. "Emmy, this is not a fit subject for such a lovely setting."

"What is it about stealing jewels that is making you so reluctant to give it up? Is it the thrill of the chase? Rubbing the police's nose in it? What is it? Tell me. I want to understand why it is more important to you than a life together with me."

She snatched her hand away. It had ceased being a playful subject for her. A niggling fear made the hairs on the back of her neck stand on end. Perhaps, he didn't want marry her. Perhaps, he *never* wanted to marry her. Perhaps, it had all been a game from the start. Perhaps—Emmeline felt a tear prick her eyelid.

Gregory could see the thoughts racing through her mind. He knew her so well. "Emmy, nothing is more important to me than a life with you. *Nothing.* So stop imagining things that aren't true."

She lifted her chin defiantly. "I'm not imagining anything. I'm just going by the evidence before my very eyes."

"Oh yes, you are. Your thoughts are churning so fast, you could become the winner of Grand Prix this year." He took her hand in his again and kissed her fingers lightly. "First, I want to make it clear that I admit nothing, but I have been considering striking out on a new career path. Does that satisfy you? Hmm."

The knot in Emmeline's stomach eased, and she impatiently wiped away the errant tear that had escaped from the corner of her eye. "Yes. Thank you," she whispered.

Gregory smiled and touched her cheek. "Silly girl. After all this time, do you still doubt my love for—" He broke off in mid-sentence and went absolutely still.

All conversation seemed to have ceased and a nervous ripple, something like an electric shock, went through the restaurant. Emmeline swiveled round in her chair and followed Gregory's gaze to see Veronica Cabot and Trevor Mayhew being shown to their table.

Lady Cabot was dressed in an off-shoulder lilac silk sheath dress that clung to her figure. Her thick, auburn hair was swept up and fixed at the back of her head with a diamond clip. Diamonds also sparkled around her swan-like throat and at her ears. Mayhew, looking quite dapper in his navy suit, pulled out a chair for her and murmured something in her ear. As she threw her head back in laughter, her cool, green gaze locked on Gregory. Her eyes widened in surprise for a fraction of a second and then flickered over at Emmeline and back again at Gregory. Her lips curled into a feline smile before she returned her attention to Mayhew.

A frisson of—*fear? envy? jealousy?*—slithered down Emmeline's spine. She watched as Gregory, like all the other men in the room, continued to stare at Veronica Cabot. However, Emmeline didn't care about the rest of the men, only Gregory.

She cleared her throat loudly and leaned forward so that she blocked his view of Lady Cabot. "Ahem. I'm over here. You know, *your fiancée.*"

Gregory blinked and for an instant seemed not to recognize her. He soon recollected his surroundings and flashed one of those smiles that is intended to melt even the stoniest of hearts. "Of course, I know who you are. How could I possibly forget, darling?"

"You seemed terribly enchanted by the beautiful Veronica Cabot."

Gregory took a hasty sip of his wine. "Veronica...*Cabot?*"

"Yes, Sir Frederick Cabot's wife. I told you about her. She's having a not-so-discreet affair with her husband's nephew. That woman over there." She jerked a thumb over her shoulder. "The one you can't take your eyes off."

Gregory patted her arm lightly. "Don't be silly, Emmy. I only have eyes for you. Other women pale in comparison, my love. So let's hear no more about Lady Cabot."

He reached across the table and cupped her cheek. Emmeline swallowed the lump that had risen in her throat as an icy tendril of fear curled itself around her heart.

Is he trying to convince me or himself?

CHAPTER 9

Gregory had been right. It had been an evening that she would never forget—for all the wrong reasons. After the grand entrance of Veronica Cabot and her "nephew," Gregory at first tried to keep up his usual lighthearted banter and teasing. But every so often, when he thought she wasn't looking, Emmeline caught his gaze straying to the delectable Lady Cabot's table. And once, she seethed with indignation to see that the brazen woman was eyeing Gregory like a ripe strawberry. Ultimately, he withdrew into himself.

His cinnamon eyes, darkened by unreadable thoughts, stared into his glass, as if hoping to find the answers in the wine's ruby depths.

For pride's sake, if for nothing else, Emmeline pretended as if she hadn't noticed a thing. In the end, Gregory made some excuse about having a splitting headache, and they decided to call it an early night.

He could hardly wait to settle their bill and leave the restaurant. It had suddenly become claustrophobic. The walls felt as if they were closing in on him. A heaviness pressed down on his chest, forcing him to draw ragged breaths. He had to get out of there. *Fast.*

"Gregory, are you all right?" Emmeline asked in the taxi on the way back to their hotel. Her dark eyes were brimming with concern as she tried to search his face, but he deliberately clung to the shadows in his corner.

They didn't speak as they rode up in the lift to her floor. At her door, Gregory pressed a distracted kiss on the top of her head and mumbled a hasty good night. Emmeline remained in the corridor until the lift doors blotted him from view. The last glimpse she had of him, his shoulders were hunched forward and his hands were thrust deep into his pockets. His handsome features were twisted into an ugly, black scowl. The expression, *If looks could kill*, flew unbidden to her mind. And suddenly, she felt very cold.

෧෨෧

Emmeline was far from refreshed when she awoke the next morning. She had had a fitful night's sleep. The few times she did manage to drift off, she dreamed that she and Gregory were climbing up the steep staircase at Meadfoot Beach and her foot slipped again. Only in her dream, Gregory suddenly turned into Veronica Cabot, who stood their laughing as Emmeline tumbled *down, down, down.* Her hands clutched desperately at the air, but there was nothing on which to grab hold. Every time, Emmeline woke with a start just before she was dashed on the rocks below and her body was swept away by the churning waters. But Veronica Cabot's silvery laughter continued to mock her. Emmeline pressed her hands to her ears to block out that horrible sound.

Her sheets were still damp with sweat and fear. All she wanted was to feel the safety and warmth of Gregory's arms around her. For him to tell her that it had all been a bad dream.

She threw the bedclothes off and staggered toward the bathroom. Her movements were slow and clumsy, as if she were gradually coming out of a drunken stupor. She turned on the faucet in the tub and water started to spill forth with a satisfying *whoosh*. Wisps of steam wafted up toward the ceiling. A nice, hot bath would wash away the disturbing thoughts rolling around in her head. At least, she hoped so.

Gregory knocked on her door at precisely eight o'clock. He was dressed in khaki trousers, an open-necked beige shirt, and brown leather loafers. Although he tried hard to hide it, Emmeline could tell he was not himself this morning. His kiss was more perfunctory than passionate and there were purple half-moon smudges beneath his eyes. But what unsettled her the most was the awkwardness between them. A wall seemed to have been erected overnight.

"Are you still feeling a bit rough, Gregory?"

"Just this damned headache. I can't seem to shake it," he replied tersely.

"Perhaps I can help." Emmeline took his face between her hands and gently massaged his temples with her fingers. That always seemed to do the trick in the past.

He turned his head away unexpectedly. "Don't fuss, Emmy. Are you ready to go downstairs to breakfast?" There was a hint of irritation in his voice as he started pacing the length of the room.

Her cheeks burned at this rebuff as surely as if he had slapped her. "Yes. Yes, of course. I'll get my handbag."

She quickly crossed to the dresser, tossed in her keys, and slung her handbag over her shoulder. "There. All ready," she said with a brightness she did not feel.

"Right, then." Gregory held the door open. "Shall we?"

"By all means," Emmeline murmured as she walked out into the corridor. "I wouldn't want to be late for breakfast."

As it turned out, the dining room was half empty. Most of the other guests preferred to lie in and eat later. Rosemary was preparing to leave as they were seated. Emmeline waved and smiled. Rosemary stopped at their table on her way out. "Good morning, you two."

"Good morning," Gregory and Emmeline replied in unison.

"And how is it that you look even more beautiful every

time I see you?" Gregory said with his signature charm and a mischievous gleam in his eye. Emmeline was relieved to see that he appeared to have recovered from whatever—or *whoever*—had been preoccupying his thoughts since last night.

She darted a surreptitious glance around the restaurant. There was no sign of Lady Cabot. Her body relaxed. They would be able to enjoy their breakfast after all.

"You're doing it a bit too brown, my dear. If you're asking if I slept well, the answer is no. I haven't had a good night's sleep in years. Not since my poor Teddy died."

A sad sigh escaped her lips and for a moment she was lost in a sea of memories.

Emmeline squeezed her hand reassuringly and Rosemary smiled down at her. "But, as I told you yesterday, I get up early every morning and take a stroll. Sometimes, when the insomnia becomes too oppressive, I take a stroll at night too. However, that's on very rare occasions. I find a stroll does wonders to clear the cobwebs from the mind. It gives you a chance to think and helps to put things into perspective."

"True," Gregory concurred. "But sometimes you merely want to get away from everything. To forget."

"You should have learned by now that you can't outrun your past, Gregory," Rosemary remarked gravely. "No matter what you do, it's always with you."

"Yes. Quite." He nodded absently. "Always. *Unfortunately.*" This was barely more than a whisper.

This conversation had cast a somber pall over the table and the trio fell silent.

Emmeline watched Gregory. His face was set in hard lines. His mind was clearly someplace else. *To forget?* Panic suddenly seized her. Emmeline gripped the edge of the table tightly to steady her nerves.

Rosemary was saying something again. "So I thought you might like to join me."

"I'm sure she'd love to. Isn't that right, Emmy? Emmy?"

"What?" Emmeline's eyes flickered between Gregory and Rosemary. "I'm sorry. I didn't catch what you said."

"Darling, Rosemary asked if you'd like to go into Cockington with her and then do a bit of shopping this afternoon."

Emmeline stared at him in confusion. "But I thought that *we* were going to drive to Dartmouth and spend the day there."

Gregory patted her hand and flashed a smile at Rosemary. "We can do that tomorrow. I'm still feeling a bit under the weather, and I wouldn't be much company for you. Rosemary's suggestion solves two problems at one stroke. Here are the keys to my car."

"But—"

"No arguments. Don't worry about me. I'll be fine on my own here at the hotel today. You two go out and enjoy yourselves."

Emmeline opened her mouth to say something and then changed her mind as she reached for his keys. She swallowed. "It seems to be all settled then."

"Marvelous," Rosemary said. "I'll let the two of you get on with breakfast. Emmeline, I'll meet you in the lobby in about an hour. Would that be all right?"

Emmeline nodded. "That's fine."

In the end, the golden and flaky croissant remained untouched on the plate before her. Emmeline had lost her appetite. She was more upset by the change in the day's plans than she was letting on. Was she being irrational about the whole thing? Of course if Gregory wasn't feeling well, she didn't want to drag him down to Dartmouth. And yet, she got the distinct and unpleasant feeling that he was lying to her. Why? She studied him closely over the rim of her cup. What was he hiding? Just as this question flitted across her mind, Veronica Cabot suddenly materialized in the restaurant. Mayhew was nowhere in sight.

Damn, Emmeline thought. How did the woman manage to look sexy in a simple cotton blouse and twill trousers?

Gregory affected not to have noticed Lady Cabot, but Emmeline could tell by the way he was attacking his bacon and eggs that he was aware of exactly every move she was making. His body seemed to stiffen as Lady Cabot's handbag accidentally bumped his shoulder as she was whisked past their table by the hostess.

"Oh, I'm terribly sorry. Do forgive me," the woman's husky voice purred as she placed a hand on his arm.

Emmeline stared at that manicured hand as it lingered there for longer than was necessary.

"Don't mention it," Gregory replied without turning around. He shot a glance at Emmeline before piercing a defenseless piece of egg.

Lady Cabot merely smiled and continued on to her table. Emmeline scalded her tongue and her throat as she took a hasty gulp of her coffee. Gregory didn't—or wouldn't—look at her.

Emmeline stood up abruptly. "Right, I'm going now."

"What? Already, Emmy? You haven't touched your breakfast."

"I'm suddenly not hungry." Her gaze drifted to Lady Cabot, whom Emmeline saw with vexation was smiling at them in amusement.

"Emmy, that's plain silly. You must eat. Think what Helen would do to me, if she learned that I allowed her only granddaughter to wither away to skin and bones."

"Gran—I—" She could feel the Cabot woman's green eyes still on her. "I'm going. I'll see you tonight for dinner?" There was a note of anxiety in this question.

"Of course, love." Gregory stood and bent down to press a kiss against her lips. "I'll be counting the minutes until your return. You leave behind a man who will be bereft without your company."

Emmeline searched his face. "Do I?"

"How can you doubt it? But off you go. I hope you enjoy your day with Rosemary."

"I hope so too," Emmeline said *sotto voce*, "because it

certainly hasn't started out on the right foot."

She shot a sideways glance at Lady Cabot, who had her elbows on the table and appeared to be having a heated conversation into her mobile. Emmeline saw her suddenly snap the phone shut and cross her arms over her chest. The arrogant look that had been on the woman's face only a minute ago had been replaced by a scowl.

Now, it was Emmeline's turn to smile. My, my, someone had upset Lady Cabot. What a shame. Was it churlish of Emmeline to take pleasure in this fact? Definitely. However, she never claimed to be perfect. She freely admitted that jealousy was *not* one of her more admirable character traits. At the moment though, jealousy was the one that had the upper hand. There were several ideas roving around Emmeline's head and they all involved grievous bodily harm against Veronica Cabot.

CHAPTER 10

Cockington was a charming village of thatched cottages tucked in a deep valley a mere mile from Torquay. It dated back to medieval times at the very least and likely had its origins in the Iron Age. The village was mentioned in the Doomsday book and had changed little over the centuries.

And so on this sun-drenched April day, Emmeline found herself trudging dutifully beside Rosemary along the winding streets of this tranquil, rural haven. They started with a tour of Cockington Court, the historic stone manor house that was the focal point of the village.

After the visit to the house, Rosemary persuaded Emmeline to take a stroll along the ornamental lakes and formal gardens of the country park. Normally, Emmeline would have enjoyed nothing more than this bucolic ramble. After all, from the time she was a little girl, Gran had instilled in her an appreciation of nature. Emmeline used to love tramping about with her grandmother all over the Kent countryside admiring the changing seasons and delighting in the woodland birds and other creatures that crossed their path.

But today, she was blind to how the red azaleas and purple rhododendrons sparkled in the sunlight at the lake's edge or how bluebells and spring flowers ran riot in the woods. The only image that danced before her eyes was Veronica Cabot and the only thought that filled her mind was that Gregory had unexpectedly decided to remain behind at the hotel. To be with Veronica Cabot? Emmeline bit her lip. She didn't know. Or was it that she was afraid of the answer?

"Shall we stop for a spot of tea?" Rosemary asked, as she tucked her arm into the crook of Emmeline's elbow.

"Of course," Emmeline replied distractedly.

"I saw a charming little tea room as we drove into the village this morning. It's just up the road over there."

Emmeline gave Rosemary a half-hearted smile and patted her hand. "Wherever you like. I'm sure it will be fine."

Rosemary frowned and stopped in front of a gift shop selling lace tablecloths. "Emmeline, I'm sorry."

Emmeline was taken aback. "Sorry for what?"

"It was unfair to drag you out with me today. Put it down to an old woman's folly. I thought we were friends and enjoyed one another's company. Clearly, you're merely being polite."

Emmeline's cheeks burned with shame. "That's not the case at all, Rosemary. Far from it. I'm afraid I've spoiled the day, but it has nothing to do with you. I assure you."

Rosemary fixed her blue gaze on Emmeline's face. "Well then, my dear, let's get that cup of tea and you can tell me what's been preoccupying your mind."

Emmeline had to laugh. She sounded just like Gran. "Tea, the English cure-all to what ails you."

"I can't think of anything better, can you?"

Once they were comfortably ensconced at a window table and had allowed the steaming cups of Darjeeling to work their soothing wonders, Rosemary folded her hands on top of one another. "I don't want to pry, so you certainly don't have to tell me anything if you don't want to. But if I can help in any way—" She left the sentence hanging.

Emmeline smiled. She reached across and covered Rosemary's hands with her own. "I don't think you're prying. I'm touched by your concern, but I don't think you—or anyone else for that matter—can help in this situation."

"Try me. I'm much stronger than I look. Life hasn't always been so kind to me, but I've managed to muddle through. Perhaps, I can pass along some of the wisdom I've gained over the years."

"You're going to think me an utter fool." Emmeline sighed and lowered her head. "Veronica Cabot is setting her cap at Gregory and I think he's falling under her spell."

Rosemary's eyes narrowed and her brow furrowed as she sat back in her chair. "Nonsense, I've never heard anything so ridiculous in my life. That young man is besotted with you."

A tear glistened on Emmeline's eyelash. "I thought so, until *she* appeared on the scene yesterday. It's as if Gregory doesn't see me anymore. How can I compete with someone like that? The answer is I can't. Oh, Rosemary, what am I going to do? After everything that we've been through, I'm going to lose him again. And this time it's going to be for good."

It broke Rosemary's heart to hear the anguish in Emmeline's voice. She leaned across the table and lifted her young friend's chin. "Listen to me. You're going to fight for him. That's what you're going to do. You can't let women like that win. Not that I agree with your assessment of the situation. Gregory is too intelligent and too wily to be taken in by a pretty face. Besides, he doesn't know anything about this Veronica Cabot." She virtually spat these words out. "But he knows and *loves* you."

The tears now coursed unchecked down Emmeline's cheeks. "Thank you for saying that," she whispered.

"You silly girl, it's the truth." Rosemary dug a handkerchief out of her handbag. "Now, wipe those tears and let's hear no more about this. Under Veronica Cabot's spell, indeed. Hmph."

⁊⊸℅⊸

Emmeline felt better after her chat with Rosemary. In the absence of Gran, it was nice to have someone to talk to. Gran would likely have told her much the same thing, but then she was biased. Gregory had long ago twisted her grandmother around his little finger and she couldn't stop singing his praises. It infuriated Emmeline when her grandmother took his side in an argument. But in the end, she knew that her grandmother loved her more than anything in this world. How lucky she had been to have Gran when her parents died.

Emmeline's mood had lightened considerably. She and Rosemary spent the rest of the afternoon doing some shopping. Emmeline found a few gifts for Gran and a turtleneck sweater for Gregory.

But she couldn't wait to dip into the two Agatha Christie novels that she bought at the tiny bookshop next to the tea room. Torquay and the surrounding towns were proud to call Agatha Christie their native daughter and so her books could be found everywhere. Gran had whet Emmeline's appetite for knowledge by introducing her to all manner of books.

As a result, Emmeline became a voracious reader at a very young age. But what she enjoyed the most was those long winter afternoons in Kent, when she and her grandmother curled up in front of the fire with hot chocolate and an Agatha Christie mystery. Emmeline had read all of Christie's books by the time she was ten years old, but to this day she still took pleasure reliving those beloved stories.

In the end, it had been a good day. Emmeline and Rosemary were still giggling and sharing stories as they entered the lobby of the Royal Devon. "Remember what I told you," Rosemary said. "Believe in yourself and don't let that woman undermine your confidence. You're better than she is in every way."

"Thanks. I'll just keep repeating that to myself."

"See that you do. Now, go find that handsome devil of

yours. I think I'll go upstairs and lie down for a bit before dinner."

Emmeline pressed a kiss to her friend's cheek and watched as Rosemary sedately made her way to the lift bank. She was still mulling over everything that Rosemary had said, when she felt a soft tap on her shoulder.

She turned around and found herself staring up into Nigel Sanborn's warm hazel eyes. "Oh, hello."

"Hello. I've been looking for you." He shot a quick glance around the lobby. "Your fiancé not with you, is he?"

"No," Emmeline said. "He was a bit under the weather today. Mrs. Dunham and I spent the day out at Cockington. We've just returned and I was about to check on Gregory. Was there something in particular that you wanted, Mr. Sanborn?"

"Nigel, please. I thought we settled that yesterday."

Emmeline smiled. "Nigel, how can I help you?"

"Actually, I think it's I who can help you."

Emmeline's dark eyes widened in askance. "Oh?"

"First of all, I must beg your forgiveness for not realizing who you were when we first met. The name rang a bell, but it didn't click until this morning. Your reputation precedes you, Emmeline. I'm a great admirer of your work, especially that article you did last month on the Sedgwick affair. Very incisive."

A pink flush rose up her cheeks. "Thank you, but I don't see how you can help me."

"I was coming to that in my roundabout way. I happen to know—well, everyone in the news business knows—that you are no longer employed by *The Times,* despite many overtures on the part of James Sloane to lure you back to your old job as senior investigative correspondent. I also know that the offers have been flooding in, but you haven't made a move yet."

This time, Emmeline turned scarlet and her fists curled tightly at her sides. "Really, Nigel, I don't see how any of that is your business."

"Please don't be angry." He put a hand up in an apologetic gesture. "I've probably put things badly," he said in his quiet way. "You see, I'm the legal counsel for Sanborn Enterprises. It's my family's firm. My father, Max, is the chairman and my brother, Brian, is the managing director. I've spoken to Brian about this and he agreed most enthusiastically."

"But—"

"Sanborn Enterprises is the parent company of Markham Media Group International, which owns a number of prestigious newspapers and magazines all over the world, including—"

"Including the *London Clarion*," Emmeline finished for him.

"Yes, that's right. Well, we—Sanborn Enterprises, that is—would like to offer you the job of editorial director of investigative features at the *Clarion*. Naturally, you would have a substantial pay rise and full editorial control without any interference from management. What do you say?"

Emmeline's jaw dropped. This was the last thing that she had been expecting. "I—I—" She swallowed hard and her eyes searched his face to determine whether this was some sort of a joke. It wasn't. Nigel was perfectly serious and stared back at her expectantly. "I can't believe it. That's what I say."

Nigel smiled down at her. "I realize that this must have taken you by surprise—"

"That's putting it mildly."

"—but I assure you that it's a genuine offer. I could draw up a contract and you could study it at your leisure. Brian authorized me to acquiesce to any demands that you may have. That shows you how eager he is to make you a part of the Sanborn family, in manner of speaking." The corners of Nigel's eyes crinkled when he smiled again. "I could draw up the contract tonight and have a draft ready for you in the morning?" he said hopefully.

Emmeline was pensive for a long moment. Then, she

took a deep breath and extended a hand. "Yes, Nigel. Please go ahead and draw up a contract. I promise to give it my full consideration."

Nigel's grin grew wider, if that were possible. "Excellent," he replied as he shook her hand. "You won't be sorry, if you decide to join the *Clarion*. How *The Times* could have allowed you to slip through its fingers, I'll never know."

Emmeline blushed again. "Yes, well—"

"Never mind. None of my business." Nigel's gaze drifted around the lobby. "I'm sure you'll want to talk this over with Mr. Longdon. I won't keep you any longer. Have a good evening."

Emmeline watched as he crossed to the reception desk, where Connie handed him two messages. "Extraordinary," she whispered to herself. "Absolutely incredible."

Never in her wildest dreams would she have predicted that the day would turn out like this, when it had started out on such a sour note. "Extraordinary," she murmured again.

"Thank you, darling. I always knew you had good taste."

"What?" Emmeline was startled to find Gregory at her side. He wrapped his arms around her waist and pulled her toward him.

"Did you have a nice day in Cockington with Rosemary?" he asked as he pressed a kiss on her lips.

Emmeline's brows knit together as her gaze tried to penetrate the cinnamon depths of his eyes. She ran a finger along the contour of his jaw. "Are you feeling better now?"

"Like a new man. Like a new man." He kissed her again. "A little sleep and some fresh air can work wonders on the human body. Don't you find?"

"Yes," she muttered. "And nothing else is bothering you?" *Or anyone?* But she bit back these words before they slipped out. Rosemary was right. She was imaging things that weren't there. So what if Veronica Cabot had an eye for Gregory? It didn't mean that *he* was attracted to *her*. Right? *Right*, Emmeline told herself. She would simply have to go on repeating that to herself until she actually believed it.

Gregory cocked his head to one side. "Emmy, are you quite all right?"

"Yes, why?"

"Because your face just now was scrunched up into the oddest expression I've ever seen."

"Was it?" She tried to shake visions of Veronica Cabot from her mind. "I suppose I'm still a bit stunned."

"Why? What's happened?" he asked curiously.

"I've just been offered a job as editorial director of investigative features at the *London Clarion*."

"How extraordinary."

"That's what I said. Especially coming out of the blue like that. Can you imagine? Editorial director at the *Clarion*."

Gregory's lips curled into that smile that always melted her heart. "Of course, I can imagine it. You're one of the shrewdest and most intelligent journalists in the business today."

"Do you really mean that?"

"Certainly, I mean it. And I'm not saying that because you are the love of my life. It's the truth."

Emmeline reached up and kissed his cheek. "Thank you."

"But tell me, darling, who was it that made this inspired offer?"

"Oh, it was Nigel Sanborn. I ran into him here in the lobby a few minutes ago. You just missed him, as a matter of fact."

A shadow eclipsed the twinkle that had been dancing in his eye. "I see," he mumbled.

"Yes. He's the legal counsel for Sanborn Enterprises, the family business. His father is the chairman and his older brother is the managing director. Apparently, Nigel broached the idea to his brother, who enthusiastically supported it. Nigel's going to draft a contract for me to review in the morning. He already said that I would have complete editorial control *without* any interference from management. Naturally, I would still want to pursue my own stories as well. It's an incredible opportunity." She was bubbling with excitement. "They're willing to give me anything I ask. That's how much they want me."

"Who wouldn't want you?" Gregory said distractedly.

At that precise moment, Veronica Cabot and Trevor Mayhew stepped out of the lift. They were clearly on their way out for the evening. Probably to one of the nightclubs in Torquay. She had poured herself into a very low-cut black satin cocktail dress that dipped slightly below her knees and swished softly with each movement. Somehow, of the dozen or so people scattered about the lobby, her green eyes zeroed in on Gregory and Emmeline. Lady Cabot inclined her head and flashed an ironic smile in their direction.

Emmeline looped her arm through Gregory's possessively. She cursed herself for feeling the need to do so. Lady Cabot seemed to sense what Emmeline was thinking, for her smile only grew more bemused.

Just because she *has an eye for Gregory, doesn't mean* he's *attracted to her*, Emmeline's brain whispered.

Emmeline stole a sideways glance at Gregory. His face was a mask of inscrutability, but his eyes never left Veronica Cabot until she disappeared through the revolving doors.

CHAPTER 11

"Oh, Miss Kirby? Miss Kirby?" Connie called out to Emmeline and Gregory as they were preparing to leave the hotel for a drive down to Dartmouth.

They both turned around and Connie hurried out from behind the reception desk. "Good morning, Miss Kirby, Mr. Longdon." She nodded her head at them. "I'm glad I caught you before you left for the day."

"Is anything wrong, Connie?" Emmeline asked.

"No, nothing at all. I wanted to give you this." She handed Emmeline a manila envelope. "Mr. Sanborn left it with me earlier. He apologizes that he couldn't deliver it himself, but he had another matter he had to attend to. He said that it's the papers he discussed with you last night. He said to take all the time you need. He'll be available at your convenience, if you have questions."

"Thanks, Connie." Emmeline smiled as she glanced down at the envelope in her hands that would open the door to a new chapter in her career. "Thanks very much."

"You're welcome. All in a day's work. Speaking of work, I see there's another guest in need of assistance. I must get back. I hope you have a pleasant outing." She gave them both a smile and then slipped back to her place behind the reception desk.

Emmeline stared down at the envelope again.

"So you've made up your mind to take it?" Gregory asked quietly at her side.

"What?" His voice had interrupted a series of thoughts racing through her mind. "Don't be silly. I haven't even read the contract."

His cinnamon gaze searched her face. "But you're tempted."

She could feel a flush spreading across her cheeks. How well he knew her. "Yes," she admitted. "I'm very tempted. In fact, I haven't been this excited in a long time."

"Then, I must try hard to hold your attention, my love," he suggested cheekily as he waggled his eyebrows up and down.

Emmeline pulled a face at him. "You always have my full attention. But seriously, it's a marvelous opportunity."

"Yes, I know." Gregory rested his hands on her shoulders and turned her to face him. "The job would fit you like a glove. And because of that, you're going to take it." He kissed her forehead. "I know you'll make a success of it."

It wasn't so much the words, as the way he said them. There was a distinct hint of resignation in his voice.

Emmeline felt a bit deflated at this realization. "Don't you want me to take this job?"

"It's not my decision, Emmy. You must do what is best for you." This trite little speech didn't make her feel any better. He had always been extremely supportive of her career in the past. Why this tepid reaction now?

She swallowed hard. "This whole conversation is a bit premature because I haven't even read the contract yet. Just let me nip this up to my room and then we can be off. All right?"

Gregory gave her a watery smile. "Fine. I'll wait for you over there."

"I shan't be a minute."

Emmeline shot a glance over her shoulder as she stood at the lift bank. Gregory was sitting in one of the deep chintz armchairs with his elbows resting on his knees and his chin in his hands. He was frowning at some invisible spot on the opposite wall. He looked like a man with the weight of the world on his shoulders.

∽∾∾

It was five o'clock when Nigel Sanborn and Trevor Mayhew emerged from the private room that the hotel had put at their disposal for their negotiations.

Nigel extended a hand to Trevor. "Mr. Mayhew, it's been a pleasure doing business with you. I'll draw up these changes tonight and have the papers ready for your signature in the morning. I don't think Cabot Corporation will regret its decision to sell its North American media division to us."

A huge grin broke out across Trevor's attractive face as he accepted the proffered hand and gave it a firm shake. "First of all, I must insist that you call me Trevor. Second, if all negotiations could be that easy, I'd have a good deal less stress in my life. Sanborn Enterprises was more than generous. They're very lucky to have you, Mr. Sanborn. I say, you couldn't be tempted to join Cabot, could you? We could use a man like you on our team."

Nigel threw his head back and laughed. "That's very kind of you, but I'm afraid the answer is no. And I'm Nigel, by the way."

The corners of Trevor's mouth drooped. "Ah, well. I understand. Family business and all that. It was worth a try." He clapped a hand on Nigel's back. "You will at least join me for a drink in the bar to seal the deal, so to speak."

Nigel glanced at his watch. "Why not? However, I wouldn't want to put you out, if you and Lady Cabot have other plans."

"No, it's quite all right. Ronnie, my aunt," he added hastily and had the grace to look abashed, "knew that we'd be at it most of the day, so she went out on her own. We arranged to meet for dinner at eight, so there's plenty of time for a couple of drinks."

"In that case, how can I refuse? Lead the way, Trevor."

გ\~გ\~გ

Emmeline and Gregory walked back into the hotel arm in arm. In all the world, no couple could have looked more in love. He bent down and whispered something in her ear. She swatted his arm and blushed. They had had a wonderful day in Dartmouth. Nothing intruded on their bliss. Everything was back to normal between them.

They were debating where they should go for dinner, when Veronica Cabot swept through the revolving doors. Emmeline saw her first and softly mouthed "Oh, no."

Veronica, her hips swaying provocatively, was loaded down by several bags. Apparently, she had spent the day doing a good deal of shopping. As if the woman needed anything else.

She cut a swath through the lobby, heedless of the guests she jostled with her bags along the way. When she reached Emmeline and Gregory, she deliberately dropped two of her packages at his feet. "Oh, dear. How clumsy of me," she said ingenuously.

Gregory snatched up the packages and thrust them at her. Lady Cabot's hand brushed against his in the exchange. He stared down as a long, elegant finger traced an invisible line across his knuckles. He slowly lifted his gaze to her face. Their eyes locked for a long moment. Hard green on cinnamon. Then, her lips curled into that feline smile that drove men wild. "Thank you." Her tone held a seductive invitation.

She briefly glanced at Emmeline and gave her a pitying look before turning her back on them and walking away.

Emmeline was seething. Her fists were balled so tightly that her nails dug into the palms of her hands. Her body trembled. It was all she could not to run after the bloody woman and claw her eyes out. Instead, Emmeline forced herself to breathe. And her eyes pounced on Gregory.

The fiery intensity of that gaze made him flinch. He smoothed down the corners of his mustache and shifted his weight slightly on his feet. "Listen, Emmy, I—"

"Emmeline, hold on there for a moment please." She turned round to find Nigel and Trevor walking toward them.

Gregory's brows knit together in annoyance. He took her elbow. "Emmy, let's go."

She shrugged off his hand. "We can't," she said through gritted teeth. She pasted a smile onto her face and waited until the two men had reached their side. "Hello, Nigel." She was surprised at how calm and steady her voice sounded.

Nigel smiled back. "Hello. I'm glad that I caught up with you. But first, allow me to introduce Trevor Mayhew. Trevor, this is Emmeline Kirby and—" There was only a fraction of a pause before he said, "Gregory Longdon."

Trevor's blue eyes twinkled and he shook their hands in turn. "A pleasure to meet you both." After the formalities were out of the way, he murmured, "Kirby. You're not *the* Emmeline Kirby, late of *The Times*, are you?"

Emmeline blushed. "Yes. I'm afraid so."

"There is nothing to fear whatsoever. It is a great honor indeed to meet you. I'm an avid admirer. Your articles are always so fair and balanced. And you bring such refreshing insight to each story. I especially enjoyed that piece you did last year on art forgers."

"Thank you, Mr. Mayhew. It's very kind of you to say so."

"Believe me, I'm not one to toss out false compliments. I wouldn't say it if I didn't mean it. So where have you landed since your precipitate departure from *The Times*? I can tell you that it sent ripples of shock reverberating all over the London media, when the news came out that you had been sacked."

"I don't know what to say, Mr. Mayhew," Emmeline replied, embarrassed and proud at the same time to see how well respected her work was.

"How about if I tell you something? As you know, Cabot Corporation owns a string of television and radio stations, as well as several newspapers and magazines. It wouldn't be hard to find you a new home with Cabot. It wouldn't take a lot to persuade my uncle to bring you into the fold. He was very impressed with the interview you did with him a couple of years back."

Emmeline laughed. "It's very kind of you, Mr. Mayhew."

"Trevor, please."

"Trevor, it's very kind of you, but—"

"But what?" he pressed on undeterred.

"I'm afraid what Emmeline is trying tactfully to say is that Cabot is a bit late. Sanborn has already made her an offer at the *Clarion*. Besides, as of half an hour ago Cabot no longer has a magazine division. Remember? I have the signed contract to prove it." Nigel tapped the side of his briefcase.

"Yes, well, Cabot has other divisions where Emmeline— if I may take the liberty—" She briefly nodded at this familiarity. "There are other divisions where she would be perfect. Tell me you haven't signed a contract with Sanborn yet?"

"No, not yet, but—"

The corners of Trevor's eyes crinkled and he clapped his hands together. "Then I'm in with a chance. I must warn you that I'm a very persuasive fellow."

Emmeline laughed again. She had been prepared to dislike him, but he really was a nice chap. It was hard to understand why he had entangled himself with that woman. "It's very flattering to see that one is in demand. However, Sanborn has made a very generous offer and I rather think—"

"You'll accept," Trevor finished her sentence for her.

"Fair enough." He sighed and gave a little shrug of his shoulders. "I can see the writing on the wall. If you ever decide to leave Sanborn, Cabot's doors will be open." He pulled out one of his business cards from an inner pocket and gave it to her. "It's been a pleasure meeting you, Emmeline and Mr.—"

"Longdon. Gregory Longdon." This was the first time he had spoken since Nigel and Trevor appeared on the scene.

"Of course, Mr. Longdon. I'm hopeless with names sometimes." Trevor shook hands with both of them. "I'm sure we'll be seeing quite a lot of one another during our stay here at the Royal Devon." He glanced at the gold Patek Philippe watch on his wrist. "But just at the moment, I'm running a bit late. I'm afraid I must dash. Perhaps all of you will join my aunt and me for dinner one evening."

Emmeline stiffened at the mention of Lady Cabot. She didn't look round, but she could feel Gregory's eyes on her.

Nigel's intelligent hazel eyes flickered from one to the other. He sensed some sort of tension between them and frowned. Feeling the need to fill the breach, he replied, "That's very kind of you, Trevor, but quite unnecessary."

"Nonsense, old chap. Closing the deal calls for a celebration. In any case, Ronnie, my aunt—" He mumbled this last word. "—loves meeting new people. I'll discuss it with her and then I'll arrange a little dinner party for the five of us. All right? We'll be staying another week." With that, he took his leave.

Not bloody likely, Emmeline thought. *Over my dead body will I sit through dinner, making polite conversation, while that witch tries to steal Gregory from right under my nose.*

CHAPTER 12

Were you serious, Emmeline?" Nigel asked eagerly.

"What?" His question had jarred her back to the present. It forced her to concentrate on his voice, rather than conjuring up different ways to murder the beautiful Veronica Cabot.

"Were you serious when you told Trevor that you were going to accept the job at the *Clarion*? Or was it merely a polite way of brushing him off?"

"Nigel, there are three things that you must know about me. I'm extremely loyal to those I care about. I always keep my promises. And, I never say anything I don't mean."

Nigel smiled down at her. "A girl after my own heart." He cleared his throat and assumed a serious expression when he caught Gregory glaring at him. "Now then, when would you like to sit down to discuss the contract? I'm sure you must have some questions or perhaps require some clarifications. Or demands? I'm free anytime tomorrow."

"How about right now?" Emmeline said as she shot a defiant look at Gregory.

"Emmy, we have dinner plans," he reminded her, a hint of displeasure creeping into his voice.

"Well, as Nigel's here, I thought I might strike while the iron was hot." She was beginning to lose her temper. How dare he take that tone with her, especially in front of a stranger?

"Fine," Gregory tossed back at her. "I hope your evening is a rousing success." He roughly pushed past Nigel and stalked off toward the revolving doors, his shoulders were rigid with anger.

"Gregory, wait. Where are you going? *Gregory?*" she called after him, but it was too late. He was already gone.

Emmeline regretted her childish behavior and silently cursed herself. *Stupid.* She could be so stupid sometimes. This is exactly what that bloody woman wanted. To drive a wedge between her and Gregory. Divide and conquer. And she fell right into the trap. Veronica Cabot's laughter was ringing in her ears. The witch was probably watching from her window ready to pounce. Emmeline groaned inwardly. *Stupid.*

She sighed. There was nothing she could do to repair the damage at the moment. So she tore her eyes away from the doors and smiled weakly at Nigel.

"Dinner in an hour," he said. "Would that give you enough time to shower and change?"

"Oodles of time." Emmeline sighed. Time wasn't the problem. Her problem walked on two legs, had thick auburn hair and could seduce a man at fifty paces with a single glance from those hypnotic emerald eyes.

໑໑໑

Emmeline and Nigel had finished dinner around nine o'clock. It turned out to be a very pleasant meal. They found that they had a lot in common and, as a result, there were no awkward lulls in the conversation. They decided to forego dessert and instead drifted to the bar to enjoy a brandy and coffee as they finalized Emmeline's contract.

She swirled the brandy balloon in one hand and watched Nigel make a note on his legal pad. Her mind was on Gregory and the way that things had been left hanging between them.

"And that's it. I'll have the contract ready for your signature in the morning," Nigel said as he put his pen down.

"Fine. There's no rush," Emmeline murmured.

He frowned when he saw her expression. It was not the face of a woman who had been offered a dream job. "Are you all right?"

"Fine," she repeated again and then seemed to recollect herself. She smiled as she extended a small hand toward him. "I'm just a bit tired that's all. I appreciate you taking the time to go over the contract with me. I look forward to working at the *Clarion*. I assure you that your faith in me won't be misplaced."

Nigel shook her hand. She had a surprisingly firm grip—poised, confident and determined. "I had no doubts about that whatsoever. Welcome aboard, Emmeline. Sanborn is lucky to be gaining someone of your caliber. I know you will only enhance the company's prestige."

Emmeline blushed and murmured her thanks as she bid him good night. She quickly made her way across the lobby and took the lift up to Gregory's floor.

She rapped her knuckles gently on his door. "Gregory?" Emmeline waited a few seconds and then knocked again when there was no response. "Gregory? It's me. Can you open the door so that we can talk?" Silence still greeted her. "I'm sorry for the way I acted earlier. I was just being silly. *Gregory?*"

"Emmeline? Is that you?" Emmeline looked up to find Rosemary emerging from the shadows down the corridor.

"Oh hello, Rosemary. Retiring for the night?"

By this time, the older woman had come level with her. "Ah, it would be heaven if I could curl up under the covers and fall into a deep, restful slumber just for one night. My misfortune is that I'm plagued by insomnia so I'm out for a turn round the gardens to tire me out a bit."

Emmeline glanced at her watch. "It's after ten. You

shouldn't be wandering about alone. I'll come with you."

"Nonsense, my dear girl. I wouldn't dream of it. I'm perfectly capable of looking after myself. Goodness knows I've had a lot of practice."

"But—"

Rosemary tut-tutted. "There, there. Now what are you doing up here? Has Gregory locked you out? If he has I'll give him a piece of my mind, see that I don't."

She was about to knock on the door, when Emmeline stayed her hand. "No. We—had words earlier and he stormed off. I'm afraid it was my fault." She then told Rosemary about the job offer made by Nigel.

"Congratulations." Rosemary beamed and gave Emmeline a soft peck on the cheek. "That's marvelous. I'm certain Gregory was pleased for you."

"Uh. I wouldn't exactly put it like that."

"What do you mean? I can't for the life of me see why Gregory would begrudge you such an opportunity."

"Not exactly," Emmeline repeated. "For some reason that I can't fathom he has something against Nigel. What it is I don't know."

"But still that doesn't explain why the two of you would argue, unless—" Rosemary's blue eyes narrowed as her thin white brows knit together. "This argument didn't have anything to do with a certain she-devil we have both come to despise, did it?"

Emmeline lowered her gaze and shifted uneasily from foot to foot. She nodded sheepishly. "I wanted to apologize, but Gregory was gone before I had the chance."

And he's not back yet. Where is he? It's after ten o'clock.

"I'm afraid that I've ruined things between us for good because I allowed my jealousy to get in the way."

"You silly girl. I thought we had resolved this earlier. This is exactly the type of opening that woman is looking for. She's trying to undermine your confidence. And from where I stand, she seems to be succeeding. Don't let her," Rosemary said harshly as she grabbed Emmeline by the arms. She had a surprisingly strong grip for such a frail woman. "Look at me."

Reluctantly, Emmeline raised her eyes to Rosemary's face. "Don't you let that woman insinuate herself between you and Gregory. Otherwise, you'll live to regret it. You must fight for him."

Yes, Emmeline thought. *Yes, I would, if I knew where he was.*

ᘓᘐᘓ

It was just after midnight and Gregory's head throbbed. He wasn't drunk, but he had had too much whiskey tonight and too little food. Not a good combination. Then he had taken himself on a forced march around—*where*? He couldn't even remember. It was all a blur. The only thing that stood out in sharp focus was the look on Emmeline's face after their encounter in the lobby with Veronica Cabot. *Bloody woman*, he cursed as he fumbled in his pocket for his key and slipped it into the lock. *Damn bloody woman.*

Even before he crossed the threshold, Gregory knew that there was someone in his room. His body tensed. All his senses were suddenly alert. It took his eyes a few seconds to adjust from the light in the corridor to the darkness in the room. He soon made out an inky silhouette in the vicinity of his bed. Then, the heavy, cloying scent of gardenias assailed his nostrils. A scent that he hadn't smelled in a very long time. He flicked on the light switch and leaned against the door pressing it closed. "Hello, Ronnie."

There, sprawled provocatively across his bed, was Veronica Cabot at her most alluring. Her auburn hair cascaded over her shoulders and she was draped in a satin dressing gown of scarlet that partially revealed the lacy edge of a matching negligée underneath. One shapely leg was uncovered and dangled over the edge of the bed.

She sat up. "It's been ages since we've seen each other, Greg, and all you can say is 'Hello, Ronnie.'"

He sighed, but he didn't move. "I'm no longer that thirty-two-year-old idiot who couldn't see straight because of his infatuation for you. Nor am I the man who woke up one morning in a Rome hotel room five years ago to find that you had scarpered with the rubies and left me holding the bag. It *was* you who called the police, wasn't it?"

Veronica chuckled and levered herself off the bed. She walked toward him. There was a soft swish as her hips and the satin swayed in unison. "Rubies always suited me. Don't look so serious. It was merely a bit of fun. I knew you would be able to think on your feet and get out of there in time." She stood directly in front of him now and looked into his eyes. She was nearly as tall as he was, not petite like Emmeline. "Besides, I'm a nomad at heart. I don't like being tied down for very long. You should know that about me. Oh, darling, you're starting to go gray at forty-two." Her fingers lightly grazed the hair at his temples and searched his face for other changes. A few lines here and there.

Gregory grabbed her wrist and pushed her hand away. His insides were churning. He pressed his back harder against the door. "I see you haven't changed."

"How very kind of you to say so, darling. You still have a discerning eye for the ladies. There aren't many forty-year-olds who look as good as I do, I must admit that," Veronica said immodestly as she ran a hand through her lush hair.

"You're nothing but trouble. Always were, always will be." His tone was clipped.

"Trouble? I don't know what you mean," she said innocently.

"You know very well what I'm talking about."

"I'm sure I don't."

"Hmph. Why are you here? Isn't Trevor going to miss you?"

Veronica flounced back to the bed and perched herself on the edge, one leg swinging back and forth. "We gave each other the night off. He's probably tucked up in his room as we speak. Why? Are you jealous?"

"I couldn't care less, but I think your *husband* might object to you having an affair with his nephew."

She laughed again. "Freddie is so besotted with me that he can't see past the end of his nose. He believes anything I tell him. And Trevor, well—He's an amusing diversion for the moment."

Gregory shook his head. Same old Ronnie. She could twist men around her little finger and they wouldn't know what was happening until it was too late and they were trapped. "Rather an extended disappearing act. I thought you were dead."

Veronica threw her head back and her silvery laughter reverberated around the room. "Sorry to spoil things for you, Greg, but as you can see I am here in the flesh and very much alive."

"Yes, I can see that," he murmured. "Where have you been all this time?"

"On the Continent. Mostly in France."

"Is that where you met your husband?"

"Yes, it was love at first sight." She clasped her hands together in a schoolgirl gesture and sighed melodramatically. "And here we are living happily ever after."

"Ha," Gregory snorted. He squeezed his eyes shut in a bid to still his racing mind. Why did she come back? *Why?*

"Now it's my turn to ask the questions. Who's the mousy little thing you're with?"

Gregory opened his eyes and his lips twitched. Mousy? *Emmeline?* He thought of Emmeline's temper, which could flare to life in an instant, and her dogged intensity when she was pursuing a story. Emmy was so far removed from mousy that it was hysterical. However, he replied, "Emmeline's not like you—"

"That's quite obvious, darling," Veronica remarked derisively as she leaned back on her elbows. "What do you see in the little princess?"

Gregory's jaw tightened at this slight. He knew she was trying to provoke a reaction. If he wasn't careful, he would lose his temper and he couldn't afford to do that. This woman could ruin him. "Emmeline's a journalist."

"A journalist?" she asked incredulously. "My, my, Greg, you *do* like living dangerously. Tell me, have you told this paragon of virtue and defender of truth about us?"

Gregory clenched his fists at his sides. His silence spoke volumes.

"I thought not," Veronica said smugly. "Otherwise, she would have scratched my eyes out by now instead of merely giving me icy glares every time she sees me. She senses something, though. Trust me, a woman instinctively knows these things. But I must say, she doesn't look like your type."

"How would you know what my type is, Ronnie?"

Her lips curled into a malicious grin. She pushed herself off the bed and came toward him. She stood so close that Gregory could feel her warm breath graze his cheek when she laughed. "*I* used to be your type," she replied, her voice low and silky. "Remember."

"Things change." His tone was deliberately devoid of emotion.

She remained silent, but her eyes roamed slowly over his face. She took a fraction of a step closer. "Things don't change that much, Greg. You can't expect me to believe you've forgotten how it was between us." Another step closer. There was only a hair's breadth of space between them now.

"Ronnie—" The word was a ragged whisper ripped from his throat. Her scent sucked the oxygen from the air as a wave of memories crashed upon the shores of his brain.

"Damn you, Ronnie," he said as he pulled her roughly into his embrace and crushed her lips with his own.

Nothing but trouble. Always were, always will be.

CHAPTER 13

Before Gregory realized it, night had been swallowed up by the gray pearlescence of the approaching dawn. He was glad to see the back of last night. It had left a bitter taste in his mouth. He had given up on sleep. For the last two hours he had been sitting on his balcony dressed only in his pajamas, watching the sea and trying to understand how he had come to this point in time.

His skin was like ice, but he was impervious to the cold breeze. It was nothing compared to the shame and guilt that chilled his heart. He glanced over his shoulder through the glass sliding door. Although the room was plunged in gloom, he could see that Ronnie was still asleep with one arm flung over her head. He turned back to the sea. How had things gotten out of hand? How could he have allowed this to happen? How could he have done this to Emmeline? *Emmy, oh God.* He rested his elbows on his knees and dug his hands into his hair.

"Ooh, darling, it's freezing out here." He started as Ronnie slipped an arm around his neck and nibbled on his ear. "Come back to bed and I'll warm you up." She nuzzled her cheek against his hair.

Gregory shrugged off her arm and stood abruptly, nearly tipping over the chair. His chest heaved. "Ronnie, I think you should get dressed and go back to your own room."

Veronica merely stood there on the balcony with a be-mused look on her face. She pulled the sheet more tightly around her body, only her bare feet poked out. "Where are your manners, Greg? That's *not* a very nice way to treat a lady."

He snorted. "You, my dear, are no lady. You never were." He brushed past her and walked back into the room.

She followed close on his heels and slammed the glass door so hard that it rattled on its track. "Don't tell me you have a guilty conscience. I never would have believed it. What has that mousy little thing done to you? It's Emmeline's own fault if she can't keep hold of her man. All's fair in love and war, after all."

Gregory stopped pacing the length of the room and, in a flash, lunged at her. He pinned her to the bed with the full weight of his body and wrapped his fingers around her swan-like throat. He loomed over her.

"Don't ever let her name cross your lips again," he snarled through gritted teeth. "You're not fit to be in the same room as Emmeline, let alone breathe the same air."

Veronica laughed. "She can't inspire that much passion, if you invited *me* back into your bed last night, now can she?"

Gregory increased the pressure of his fingers. "You should never have come back, Ronnie. You should have remained dead."

"Well, I'm not. So you had better get used to the idea. Besides, it's much more fun this way." She tried to wriggle her body out from under him, but was unsuccessful. "After this childish display of yours, I have a good mind to wake up the little princess and give her an account of exactly what happened last night. I think she would find it highly enlightening to learn all the gory details about our past, don't you?"

Her green eyes gleamed with spite. He knew she would do it. But he could cause trouble for her too.

He felt the vein in his temple throbbing. His voice was

pitched very low. "Go anywhere near Emmeline and I'll kill you."

Veronica laughed again. "Oh, darling, idle threats don't scare me."

He smoothed a stray auburn strand off her forehead and took her face in his hands. "A gentleman never makes threats. A gentleman—"

She cut him off. "Please, Greg. You forget that I know you. And you're no gentleman."

The smile on Gregory's lips didn't touch his eyes. "Then I suggest you watch your step. It would be *such* a pity if you were to have a nasty accident."

⌁⌁⌁

Five minutes later, Veronica let herself out of Gregory's room and nearly collided with Rosemary, who was on her way to the lift to take her morning constitutional. Rosemary stopped short. Her eyes widened in disbelief as they traveled from Gregory's closed door to the half-dressed woman standing before her.

"Yes? Was there something you wanted?" Veronica asked without a shred of embarrassment at her state of *deshabillé*.

Rosemary shot her a look that was brimming with venom. However, she straightened her back and with all the dignity she could muster replied, "No, there was nothing I wanted. Nothing at all."

"Good. Then, I suggest you mind your own bloody business."

Rosemary thrust her chin in the air and without another word continued on her way.

"Nosy old cow," Veronica muttered under her breath as she watched the lift doors close.

⌁⌁⌁

Emmeline checked her watch for the tenth time. Nine o'clock. And still there was no sign of Gregory. When he hadn't come to her room this morning, she headed straight to the dining room, certain that he would be waiting for her here with that cheeky grin on his face. But he wasn't. She took a sip of her coffee, which had gone cold, and pushed away her half-eaten plate of toast. She had lost her appetite. To be honest, she had only made a half-hearted attempt at eating it.

Her stomach was twisted into a big knot. She hadn't slept a wink. Their silly argument kept going round and round in her mind. If only she hadn't been so stupid. If only she had more confidence in herself and trusted in his love for her, maybe Gregory would be here right now teasing her mercilessly.

Why was it that none of these fears plagued her when it came to her work? When she was following a story, there was nothing that stood between her and finding out the truth. She knew she was one of the best journalists in the business. So why didn't some of that confidence trickle over into her private life? After all, she was the same person.

Emmeline glanced at her watch again. It was only five minutes later than the last time she checked. Right, that's it. She couldn't sit here a moment longer. She took the napkin from her lap and deposited it on the table. She signaled the waitress to ask for her bill, paid it, and quickly threaded her way toward the door.

In the lobby, she saw Rosemary speaking with Connie at reception. She waved, but they didn't see her. Rosemary was frowning. Emmeline hoped that there was nothing amiss with her friend. They were speaking too softly to distinguish everything they were saying. Rosemary shook her head a couple of times. And at one point, Emmeline heard Connie say, "The poor dear. Why does this sort of thing always happen to the nice ones? Oh, I don't know."

"Everything all right?" Both women jumped when Emmeline sidled up to them.

"What? I mean good morning, Miss Kirby," Connie stammered. "I—I hope you're enjoying your stay. Is there anything I can do for you?"

"I'm having a marvelous time," Emmeline lied and plastered a smile on her face. "Have either of you seen Gregory by chance this morning?"

Connie and Rosemary exchanged a look that Emmeline couldn't decipher. It was a little unnerving. "Well, have you?"

"No, I'm afraid I haven't, Miss Kirby. I can ring his room if you like?" Connie lifted the receiver and held it poised in the air.

"No, that's quite all right. I'll just go upstairs and roust him out of bed. It's about time he was up."

"I wouldn't do that if I were you," Connie replied quickly and then blushed. The words had come out before she realized it.

"Why ever not?"

"Why? Well, because—Because he's probably like many of our guests who enjoy a lie-in."

Emmeline laughed. "You don't know Gregory. He's never had a lie-in in his life. I'll go up and get him. Thanks anyway. I hope you both have a nice day."

Rosemary scowled, but said nothing. "Are you all right?" Emmeline asked. "Nothing wrong with your daughter or her family is there?"

The older woman shook her head. She fixed Emmeline with that intense blue stare. "They're all fine. Thank you. But if you take my advice, you'll pack your bags this instant and go home."

"What? And leave Gregory without so much as a by-your-leave?" Emmeline was incredulous.

"Yes, go now. At once. He's not worth your time. You're better off without him."

Emmeline's jaw went slack. She was confused. "But only yesterday you told me to fight for him. Has something happened?" She clutched Rosemary's sleeve. "You must tell me if something has happened to Gregory?" She felt her features crease with worry.

Rosemary opened her mouth to say something, but then she seemed to change her mind. Her voice had lost the hard edge of a moment ago. "Go home, dear. That's all. I'm must be off."

Emmeline stared after her retreating figure as she made her way to the revolving door. Just as her brain tried to fathom what had come over Rosemary, Veronica Cabot stepped out of the lift with Trevor on her arm.

"If you'll excuse me, Miss Kirby, I have some things to attend to," Connie said as she scurried toward Mr. Harcourt's office. Emmeline couldn't blame her for wanting to avoid an encounter with Lady Cabot.

Emmeline squared her shoulders and headed straight toward them. She was determined not to let the woman intimidate her anymore. She couldn't pretend that she hadn't seen them and, in any case, that was the way to the lifts. If Veronica Cabot wanted a war, by God she was going to get one.

Emmeline's eyes met Veronica's as she came level with them. However, Trevor was the one who spoke.

"Good morning, Emmeline. What a pleasant surprise. Well, not that much of a surprise, since we're all staying at the Royal Devon," he said cheerfully.

"Good morning, Trevor," Emmeline replied quietly. She wished she could slap that smirk off of Veronica's face.

Trevor, misinterpreting the look that passed between the two women, said "Where are my manners? Veronica, this is Emmeline Kirby, the famous journalist. Emmeline, this is my aunt, Veronica Cabot."

Emmeline felt sorry for him. How could the male mind be so oblivious to the fact that she and Veronica were barely restraining their primitive instincts to claw out each other's eyes. Emmeline tightened her grip on the strap of her handbag. "How very nice to meet you, Lady Cabot. I had the honor of interviewing your husband two years ago." She was astonished at how congenial she made the words sound.

Veronica smiled, but there was no warmth in it. "Did you really? Miss... *Kirby* is it? I never heard Freddie mention your name. But then, he's so busy he can't possibly remember everyone he meets. Especially journalists, who are almost as bad as private detectives, don't you find? They're always skulking about in bushes and prying into people's dustbins because their own lives are so dull and they have nothing better to do with their time."

Veronica heard the sharp intake of breath and was pleased to see that the insult had hit its mark.

Emmeline struggled to keep her temper in check. She swallowed hard and clenched her fists at her sides. "Lady Cabot, I assure you that there are a great many of us who have scruples, a sense of decency, and are only determined to find the truth."

"If you say so, I suppose you must know. But *I've* never come across anyone like that."

"Present company excepted, of course," Trevor interjected quickly.

"Of course, Trevor." Veronica slipped her arm through his and smiled sweetly at him. Then, she turned back to Emmeline. "I'm absolutely famished, Miss Crumby, so you'll excuse us."

"Kirby," Emmeline said through gritted teeth.

Veronica smiled again. "Oh, yes, Kirby. How silly of me."

Trevor inclined his head toward Emmeline and then they were gone.

⌘

"Viper, witch, parasite, gold-digger, leech, bloodsucker," Emmeline fumed as she exited the lift and stomped down the corridor to Gregory's room. What did men see in Veronica Cabot? Behind that beautiful face lurked an ugly black heart and a nasty, vindictive nature.

Why was it that only women recognized these things?

She was mulling over the latter question when she raised her hand to knock on the door. There was no response. "Gregory? Are you up? It's Emmeline."

She knocked again. "Gregory?"

He leaned against the door and squeezed his eyes shut. Perhaps, if he didn't say anything, she would go away.

"I know you're in there. I can hear you moving about. Open the door. I want to talk to you about yesterday."

Gregory froze. Had Veronica made good on her threat and told Emmeline everything? "About yesterday?"

"Yes, I wanted to apologize."

"*Apologize?*" His body relaxed. She didn't know. But what the devil was she talking about? "I don't understand."

"We can't keep talking through the door. Can't you let me in?"

"Emmy, I'm not up to this right now. I'm feeling a bit rough. Why don't you go off on your own?"

There was silence for a moment. "You have every right to be upset with me. I've been acting like a jealous schoolgirl the past few days, but I promise no more. I'm also sorry about throwing the contract with the *Clarion* in your face like that. It was simply a bit of spite. Can you forgive me?"

He heard her lean against the door and touched it with his fingertips. A lump rose in his throat. *Forgive* you? *Oh, Emmy, I don't deserve you.* Aloud he said, "Go, Emmy."

"You sound strange. Open the door. I want to make sure you're all right."

Gregory groaned. Why couldn't she just go away? Why did she always have to make things so difficult? Because she was Emmy and she thought that she could make everything right with the world, could help everyone.

He shook his head. He was no good for her. Couldn't she see that it was all wrong? He'd been a fool to think he could have a normal life.

And they certainly couldn't have a future together, not after last night.

Gregory saw that he would have to take things into his own hands. He jerked the door open suddenly and Emmeline practically tumbled into the room.

"It's about time—" She sucked in her breath when she straightened up. His eyes were bloodshot and the stubble creeping up his face gave him a haggard, careworn look. "What's the matter?"

She reached up and touched his forehead to see if he had a fever, but his skin felt cool. He sighed and roughly pushed her hand away. There was a strong smell of whiskey on his breath. In fact, the room reeked of it. What her probing gaze saw reflected in the cinnamon depths of his eyes sent a frisson up her spine.

"Please go, Emmy." It was a hoarse whisper, almost pleading. "*Now.*"

"I'm not leaving until you tell me what is going on around here. It's not like you to drink to excess."

A mirthless laugh escaped his lips. "There's a first time for everything."

"I don't believe it. What's going on?" She would not be brushed off.

"Why can't you accept things at face value? Why does everything have to have a hidden meaning?" he groused. "Why are you always sticking your nose in where it doesn't belong?"

Emmeline gasped at this outburst. "Because you're the man I love and, if you're in trouble, I want to help you. That's all. It can't be as bad as all that. Won't you trust me?" Her voice was full of tenderness. "Please."

Gregory looked down at the small hand she extended toward him and, for a moment, almost folded it into his own. Trust? Trust was something he learned long ago never to do. And as for help, nobody could help him. His life was thrown into upheaval all because of Veronica. He dropped his hand. "I don't want your help. I want you to leave me alone," he bellowed.

Emmeline took half a step backward. He saw her face crumple, and it broke his heart.

She ran out of the room without another word.

CHAPTER 14

Nigel had been working night and day on the Cabot contract for the last two months and decided to reward himself for finally closing the deal, as well as the unexpected coup of hiring Emmeline at the *Clarion*, by taking the morning and most of the afternoon off. He had always loved the outdoors, so he had slipped on some sturdy shoes and made his way toward one of the hundreds of coastal walks around Torbay. He enjoyed nothing better than being alone with his thoughts as he wandered across greens, through woods, up hills and down dales. And the views were simply spectacular.

After being rejuvenated by his bucolic rambles, it was time to turn his mind back to work. He would be checking out the day after tomorrow and he had to prepare a brief for a series of meetings that his father and Brian were going to hold early next week.

But instead of staying cooped up in his room, Nigel took his laptop and several files down to the conservatory to take afternoon tea. He was slathering a second scone with thick Devonshire cream and strawberry jam when the e-mail message from his brother flashed up on his screen. He put the scone down on his plate and brushed the crumbs from his fingers.

Nigel had anxiously been awaiting this report. He

clicked open the message and quickly perused its contents. When he was done, he dashed off a reply to tell Brian that his plans had changed and he would be spending an extra few days in Torquay to tie up a few loose ends. He promised to explain everything once he got back to London.

Nigel stretched his long legs and crossed them at the ankles, as he leaned back in his chair. He thoughtfully sipped his Darjeeling as he contemplated the implications of the report that he had just read.

While it left a lot of unanswered questions, for the first time he was certain that he was on the right track. He downed the rest of his tea in one gulp. Right, first things first. He signed his bill, gathered his things and headed straight for reception.

"You're in luck, Mr. Sanborn," Connie said. "We've had a cancellation, so it won't be a problem to extend your reservation another few days."

Nigel smiled. "Marvelous. You're an angel, Connie. Thanks."

Connie returned his smile. "All in a day's work. We're glad that you're enjoying your stay at the Royal Devon."

"Let's just say that it's far more intriguing than I had anticipated."

Connie frowned. "If you say so, Mr. Sanborn. However, I would never have associated the Royal Devon with intrigue. It's the farthest thing, in my opinion."

"Ah, but you're wrong there. Very wrong, indeed. There are secrets and lies all around us." He waved a hand to encompass the entire lobby. "Even in a lovely hotel like this. You can't escape it. But then, lies always have a way of unraveling."

Her blue eyes were fixed intently on his face. "Do they?" she asked quietly.

"Oh, yes. As a lawyer, I've seen it hundreds of times. The truth is a very powerful weapon. Lies stand no chance when confronted with the truth."

"That's all very fascinating, Mr. Sanborn, but I can't

stand here chatting with you all afternoon. Mr. Harcourt may pop out of his office at any moment."

"Yes, of course. Wouldn't want to get you into any trouble. Sorry to have chuntered away like that. Occupational hazard, I'm afraid. Thanks for fixing my reservation," he replied cheerfully and walked toward the courtesy phone on the other side of the lobby.

Nigel dialed the number and waited. It rang and rang. He pursed his lips as he replaced the receiver in the cradle and headed for the lift.

The doors opened on the fifth floor. Nigel's footfalls were lost in the thick carpeting as he made his way down the corridor. He stopped in front of room five-twenty-two and knocked. Nothing. He rapped his knuckles a second time, more insistently. Still nothing. "I know you're in there, so it's no use pretending otherwise. You can't go on avoiding me. We need to talk."

The door rattled on its hinges as it flew open. Gregory swayed slightly from side to side, but his eyes burned with a mixture of anger, hatred, and self-pity. "You can go to the devil for all I care. I have nothing to say to you." He slurred his words slightly.

Nigel pushed past him and entered the room. "Well, I have a lot to say to you, so sit down and listen." He poked away an empty whiskey bottle with his toe and watched in disgust as it rolled under the bed. "You don't seem to be in a fit state to do much else, anyway."

⁊⁊⁊

Nigel wasn't the only one who had decided to spend the day communing with land, sea and air. Emmeline had bolted from the hotel after her disturbing encounter with Gregory, her mind racing and her heart heavy. She tramped along the lonely cliff paths for hours, trying to understand what was happening. How had they come to this point in time? *I want you to leave me alone*. Those words kept ringing in her ears. She and Gregory had had arguments before, but not like that. He had *never* spoken to her that way. Emmeline had wasted months fighting her feelings for him and when she was finally ready to accept that she loved him—had never stopped loving him—it was too late. Gregory was slipping away from her. She had always prided herself for being in control, but now she was helpless. And frightened. Frightened by what she had seen in his eyes.

Emmeline was plunged in the black depths of this melancholy when she wandered into the conservatory late that afternoon and ordered a pot of strong tea. Tucked in a corner that looked out over the garden, she was grateful for the quiet. The low murmur of voices simply washed over her. What should she do? Should she swallow her pride and attempt to see Gregory again? Should she give him some space and wait until he came to her? But what if he didn't? Should she go back to London and forget Gregory Longdon ever existed? Only that morning Rosemary had told her not to fight for him, that he wasn't worth it. Was she right? Did Rosemary see something in him that Emmeline didn't—or wouldn't?

She dropped her head between hands and squeezed her temples. She tasted the salty tears as they trickled down her cheeks and rolled off her chin into her lap. She simply didn't know. And she couldn't call Gran for advice. That was out of the question. What would she say? That she thought Gregory had fallen for another woman. No, she couldn't call Gran.

Emmeline took a deep, shuddering breath and lifted her weary head. Her throat ached from crying. She fumbled in her handbag for her handkerchief and hastily wiped away her tears. Then she took a gulp of tea to steady her nerves, but only ended up spluttering the scalding liquid when she saw Veronica at the opposite end of the conservatory. She watched as Veronica calmly settled her bill and gathered up her handbag.

Emmeline slammed her cup down so hard that tea sloshed everywhere and the saucer rattled on the table. She was on her feet now. That woman was the source of all the trouble between herself and Gregory. Emmeline didn't know what she was going to say, but by God Veronica Cabot was not going to leave this room without knowing where things stood. Emmeline dropped a few pound notes on the table. She was halfway across the room when Connie came in and handed a note to Veronica.

Emmeline heard a gasp and watched as her rival's complexion became ashen. The hand that held the note trembled. "Who gave this to you?" Veronica asked. "I said who gave this to you." Her voice rose an octave as she took a menacing step toward Connie, waving the note in her face.

Connie's blue eyes were wide with bewilderment. "I—I really couldn't s—say, Lady Cabot. I just came on duty and the note was sitting there on the desk. Someone said that you were in here and so I brought it to you. I thought it might be important."

Veronica was silent for a long moment. Connie squirmed under the intensity of that cold, green gaze. "Oh, very well. You delivered the note. Now, go back to doing whatever it is that you do."

"Yes, Lady Cabot." Connie didn't need to be told twice. Relief was clearly etched on her face as she scurried out of the conservatory, trying to put as much distance between herself and Lady Cabot as possible.

Veronica was reading the note a second time, when she bumped into Rosemary who was walking into the conservatory. Veronica looked up. "Why don't you watch where you're going, you old cow?"

"I beg your pardon?" Rosemary replied quietly. "I think you'll find that you collided with me."

"You're bloody right you should beg my pardon. Now, get out of my way." Veronica pushed past the older woman.

Rosemary stared after Veronica, openmouthed, and then shook her head. The expression on her face was one of resignation as she made her way toward a sofa by the window. But Emmeline seethed at the blatant lack of respect and rudeness. Another black mark against Veronica Cabot. Another reason to give the woman a piece of her mind.

Emmeline caught up with Veronica in the lobby. "Lady Cabot?"

Veronica turned and her eyes narrowed when she saw Emmeline. "Oh, it's you, Miss Crumby. What do *you* want?" She had dropped the veneer of politeness. The gloves were off.

"It's Kirby, as you very well know."

"I could really care less. What do you want?"

"Your manners, or rather your lack of them, leave a lot to be desired. I saw the whole incident in the conservatory just now. You nearly knocked over poor Mrs. Dunham."

"What is it to you? The old cow should be more careful."

"It's *you* who should be more careful and learn how to behave like a human being instead of chasing every man that catches your fancy like a dog in heat. The world doesn't revolve around you."

"Why you interfering little—" Veronica took a step toward her, but Emmeline stood her ground, despite the difference in their heights. "How dare you? You don't know who you're dealing with. I can crush you. Just like that." She snapped her perfectly manicured fingers. "I can see to it that you never work again—"

"Your threats don't frighten me, Lady Cabot. I know exactly who and *what* you are."

"What do you mean?" All at once, there was a hint of uncertainty in Veronica's tone. She looked down at the crumpled note in her balled fist and then leveled her gaze again on Emmeline. "You're responsible for this, aren't you?"

Emmeline stared at her in confusion. "I've no idea what you're talking about."

"Of course, it all fits. Who else but a nosy reporter would be behind this *and* all the phone calls over the last several months?" She waved the note under Emmeline's nose. "Well, I'll tell you one thing. You're not going to get away with it. I'll see you burn in hell first." Her voice dripped ice.

"Not only are you the most narcissistic creature that walks the earth, but you're also unhinged," Emmeline hissed through clenched teeth. Her temper was in full throttle now.

They both looked up to see Gregory exiting the lift. Veronica's mouth twisted into a scornful smile. "I just want to know one thing. Did Greg put you up to this? I wouldn't have thought so, but perhaps this is some sort of payback for Rome."

"*Gregory*? What does he have to do with any of this?"

As if sensing that he was being discussed, Gregory suddenly stopped in his tracks. He found two pairs of eyes staring at him from across the lobby. One glacial green and the other like burning coal.

Veronica rounded on Emmeline, a malicious gleam in her eyes. "Why don't you ask your boyfriend? Better yet, why don't you go to Wickersham? It's only a stone's throw from Torquay and there you'll find the ugly truth about your precious boyfriend." She tossed the note in Emmeline's face and turned her back on her.

The heels of Veronica's designer Italian shoes clicked angrily against the marble floor as she sliced her way through the lobby. For an instant, Gregory's eyes locked with Emmeline's. He took half a step toward her. Emmeline held her breath. But then, he seemed to change his mind and hurried after Veronica instead.

Emmeline blinked away the tears that stung her eyelids. She covered her mouth with one hand and collapsed onto a nearby armchair. *He chose her.* It didn't matter what Veronica did, as long as Gregory was indifferent toward her. But clearly that was not the case. Veronica had won. *I was a fool to think that I ever stood a chance*, Emmeline reproached herself bitterly.

She watched as Gregory caught up to Veronica near the

lift. He grabbed her arm and pulled her to a corner. Veronica was nearly his height and their heads were bent very close together, their voices hushed.

Emmeline couldn't look anymore. It hurt too much. She dropped her chin to her chest and sighed. Then, her gaze alighted on the note at her feet. The note which had elicited such a violent reaction from Veronica.

Emmeline reached down and picked up the small sheet of plain paper. She smoothed out the wrinkles against her knee. There were only two lines of typed text.

The blood of Edward Prichard is on your hands.
The time has come to forfeit your life.

Emmeline slipped the note into her handbag. "Well, well, well, Lady Cabot," she said aloud as she watched Gregory and Veronica still deep in conversation. "It seems that you have secrets of your own to hide."

The tears had dried on her lashes. Emmeline stood up with renewed purpose. She had every intention of finding out who the late Edward Prichard was and what Veronica Cabot had to do with his death. Emmeline had a strong suspicion that there was a very interesting story lurking just below the surface.

വരെ

In two long strides, Gregory had caught up to Veronica and snatched her elbow. "Ronnie, wait."

She struggled to free herself. His fingers were biting into her arm through the thin sleeve of her blouse. "Let go of me, Greg, or I'll scream."

He maneuvered her away from the lift and into a corner where no one could overhear them. "I warned you to stay away from Emmeline."

Veronica laughed in his face. "When have you ever known me to shy away from a challenge? For the record, your little princess came after me. It seems she can't keep her nose out of other people's business."

"Leave her alone."

"You should try telling her that." Her anger matched his own.

Gregory took a step closer to her. His jaw was set in a tight line. "I can ruin you."

"You mean you tried, darling," she replied as she brushed an invisible piece of lint from his collar, "But I'm on to the scheme that you and the little princess cooked up. I don't know what it is that you think you've discovered, but it's not going to work."

Gregory ran a hand through his wavy hair in confusion. "What are you on about?"

Veronica sighed. "Don't, Greg. Remember it's me you're talking to. Let's not play games. We were always honest with each other."

It was his turn to laugh. "You don't have an honest bone in your body. You wouldn't know the truth if it was dangling in front of your face."

"How quickly they forget," Veronica murmured. "This entire conversation has become too tiresome." At last, she shrugged off his arm. Her usual arrogance and vindictiveness had returned. "Despite last night, my darling, I will take tremendous pleasure in seeing that you wind up the loser."

Gregory's voice was dangerously low, his head close to hers. "It seems to me that you have a great deal more to lose than I do if your husband finds out."

"Blackmail is so dirty." She made a moue of distaste. "I'm surprised that you would soil your hands with it, Greg. I thought you were better than that. Do you prize revenge against me so far above your precious Emmeline? Because I promise you, both of you *will* pay. I will see to it."

"Why you—" Gregory grabbed her arms and shook her so hard that her teeth rattled. "I'll see you dead first."

"Veronica, what's going on here?"

Veronica and Gregory looked up, startled by the inter-ruption. They had been so intent on their argument that they had quite forgotten their surroundings.

A tall, distinguished gentleman with a thick head of white hair tucked something into the inside pocket of his double-breasted suit, snatched up his bag, and started walk-ing toward them.

Veronica composed her features into an expression of surprise and stepped away from Gregory. "Why, Freddie, how marvelous. You were able to get away, after all." She met her husband halfway and looped her arm through his elbow as she kissed his cheek.

CHAPTER 15

Sir Frederick ignored Veronica's half-hearted attempt at wifely affection. He was much more interested in Gregory. The two men eyed each other warily. "Was this man bothering you, Veronica?" His question was directed at his wife, but his blue gaze never wavered from Gregory.

Veronica scowled at Gregory, but she kept her tone light. "Bothering me? No, of course not. Where would you get such an idea?"

"I don't know. Perhaps it was something about the menacing way he was looming over you and shaking you at the same time."

Veronica's silvery laughter filled the space between them. "Shaking me? Don't be silly, Freddie." She patted his arm. "I tripped and Mr..."

Gregory picked up his cue. "Longdon. Gregory Longdon, Sir Frederick." He extended a hand toward the other man, who regarded it with suspicion and refused to take it.

"Yes, Mr. Longdon," Veronica babbled on. "That's right. He happened to be on the spot and gallantly caught me before I twisted an ankle."

"Ah, I see," Sir Frederick replied noncommittally. "Well, thank you for assisting *my wife*, Mr. Longdon. Now that I'm here, I will see to her needs myself."

Gregory had been unceremoniously dismissed. "Of course. Glad to have been of service, Sir Frederick, Lady Cabot." He inclined his head toward each in turn, but the look he shot Veronica told her that their discussion was far from over.

Husband and wife had scarcely had time to recover from this uncomfortable little scene, when a voice boomed from behind them. "There you are, Ronnie. I've been looking all over for you."

Veronica's green eyes widened and Sir Frederick's back stiffened. Slipping an arm around his wife's waist, he pivoted around.

"Good God, Uncle Freddie." Trevor stopped short and quickly tried to cover up his shock. His face broke into a broad grin. "How lovely to see you."

His uncle's brows knit together. "Trevor, I must say that I didn't expect to see *you* down here. You're supposed to be in London finalizing the Sanborn deal."

Trevor squirmed under the intense scrutiny, but he held his ground. "Actually, sir, the deal's done. Nigel Sanborn and I just closed on the last details yesterday. The papers are all signed. You see, when I heard that you had to remain in London at the last moment to tie up some loose ends, I persuaded Sanborn to meet here to finalize the contract. That way Ronnie wouldn't be alone, and I could keep an eye on her until you arrived."

"Wasn't that sweet of Trevor? Naturally, he wasn't you, darling. But he's been an absolute angel while you were in London. He saw to all my needs."

Rosemary stifled a smile and took this opportunity to slip out from the shadows of a nearby column. She didn't wait to hear Sir Frederick's response. She was quite certain that they were too engrossed in their touching family reunion to notice her. She hadn't dared make a move earlier because Veronica and Gregory would have seen her. And the things she had overheard. Goodness it was enough to set one's head reeling.

c/ɔɛ/ɔ

Nigel found Emmeline on the terrace by the pool. She was leaning on the parapet, staring out at a rocky outcropping at the end of the point without really seeing it. Her mind was clearly on other matters.

The sun was just beginning to set and the sea was an undulating netting of liquid silk. Its surface tinged a misty mauve. A slight breeze stirred the air and made Emmeline shiver.

"You really should go in now. The nights can still be a bit chilly at this time of year."

Emmeline spun round. "Oh, it's you, Nigel. I thought perhaps it might be—Well, it doesn't matter what I thought." She managed a weak smile.

He felt a pang of sympathy for her. "Is it as bad as all that? Can I help at all?"

"What? I—No, it's very kind of you, but I'll have to muddle my way through as best I can."

"How about if you join me for dinner again? I promise not to ask any embarrassing questions." He crossed two fingers over his heart.

Emmeline smiled. "Thank you, but no. I wouldn't be very good company."

"Nonsense, you underestimate the powers of your charm."

This elicited a laugh. "No, really. Another night, perhaps. If Gregory…" Her voice trailed off, leaving the unfinished thought hanging in the air between them.

Nigel touched her arm. "Things may look bleak at the moment, but everything will right itself in the end. I assure you."

Emmeline's dark eyes searched his face. What was he trying to tell her? What did he know? Was she the only one around here who was stumbling about blindly? But that wasn't quite true. There was one thing she was certain about. Veronica Cabot was desperate *and* scared. This combination did not make for sound, reasoned thought. And it all had to do with Edward Prichard, a dead man.

Emmeline wished Nigel a good night and made her way back inside the hotel. There were a number of phone calls she wanted to make in the privacy of her room. However, one thing gnawed at the back of her mind. What was she going to do if Gregory was somehow involved?

ℰℬ

Emmeline yawned as she sat down in the conservatory the next day. She had tossed and turned all night, only managing to get a couple of hours of sleep toward dawn. This only left her feeling more tired. But she was making progress with her inquiries into Edward Prichard. One of the calls that she had made the previous evening was to Felicity, her friend and colleague—well, former colleague now—in the research department at the *Times*. In an hour, Felicity was able to provide a brief sketch of Prichard. Apparently, the young Edward was an Englishman who had moved to Toronto, Canada, and became the protégé of Henry Cummings, a supremely wealthy financier. Although they enjoyed a father-son relationship by all accounts, many details about how the two became acquainted remained hazy.

But Felicity had saved the best tidbit for last. Cummings was murdered in 1997 shortly after discovering that someone had systematically embezzled thirty million dollars from his company over the course of a year. The thefts had begun soon after the old man had taken Edward under his wing. Old-fashioned, painstaking detective work soon led the police to a secret bank account in Zurich into which Prichard was making a hefty deposit every month like clockwork. After that, the rest of the case fell into place rather quickly. Under intense questioning, Prichard's distraught fiancée, who was highly strung and terrified, let it slip that Edward had told her that Cummings had written a new will leaving his entire estate to him, except for a few small bequests. And finally, the gun which was used to kill Cummings was discovered in the basement of Edward's apartment building. With these pieces of solid evidence in hand, Prichard was arrested. His trial garnered major head-lines for two months because of Cummings' high profile. In the end, Edward was found guilty of murder. A Superior Court judge sentenced him to twenty years in prison. But Edward was never to serve his time because he hanged himself in his cell.

What intrigued Emmeline about this sordid story was the fact that Prichard continued to protest his innocence, even after being sentenced. No one would listen, though. And yet, with the scant information culled thus far, she was in-clined to believe that Prichard was indeed not guilty of murder. She didn't know how she knew it, but she did. Emmeline was less certain about the embezzlement aspect. But murder? No, it didn't seem to fit with the picture that she had drawn in her head about Edward.

Emmeline threw her hands up in frustration, urging her mobile to ring. If only she were back in London, she wouldn't have to rely on Felicity or her friend Patrick at the *Toronto Globe & Mail* to ring her back with information. Oh why hadn't she just stayed at home? Emmeline chided herself. Because she came to Torquay to get away from the stress of London. She gave a scornful laugh. Some holiday this was turning out to be. She hadn't seen Gregory all day. Or Veronica Cabot for that matter. However, she wasn't overly troubled about the latter. Emmeline just hoped that it was a mere coincidence and not that they were off some-where together.

"Miss Kirby, isn't it?"

The voice jarred her back to the present. Emmeline looked up to find the handsome face of Sir Frederick Cabot smiling back at her.

"Yes, it is." He extended a hand toward her. "I thought I recognized you."

Emmeline stood and shook his hand. "I feel honored that you remember me, Sir Frederick."

The gentleman chuckled. "How could I not remember such a lovely and intelligent young woman? I must confess that I have never spent such a pleasurable two hours talking since I granted you that interview a couple of years ago."

Emmeline felt her cheeks suffuse with heat. "You're very kind, Sir Frederick. I must admit that the interview was among my favorite stories."

He returned her smile. "I was about to take tea. Would you care to join me? I thought it might be nice out on the terrace as it's such a mild afternoon."

"I would like nothing better."

"Splendid. Splendid." He rubbed his hands together. Emmeline gathered up her handbag and graciously accepted the elbow he proffered.

Sir Frederick was right. It was beautiful outdoors. It could have been a June day, rather than April. They chose a table overlooking the garden and the sea below. They ordered a pot of Earl Grey accompanied by a selection of tiny sandwiches and scones with Devonshire cream and strawberry jam. They fell easily into conversation. Sir Frederick was delighted to learn that they shared a love of history, which led to a wide-ranging discussion that started in ancient Rome and wound its way to a debate about the current political landscape in Whitehall.

They had just ordered a second pot of tea and were chatting about books they had recently read, when the angry voices of a man and woman floated up to their ears. Emmeline and Sir Frederick couldn't hear what was actually being said, but it was abundantly evident from the tone that the conversation was extremely heated.

Then, quite clearly, they heard, "Well, you can think again. I will never agree to it."

"Why? What's the use of hanging on? It makes absolutely no sense, especially after all these years."

Emmeline stiffened. She stood and went to the parapet. Sir Frederick rose as well. Emmeline could feel him hovering just behind her right shoulder. They looked down into the garden and their suspicions were confirmed, not that they needed any confirmation. There below them in the shadow of a palm tree were Veronica and Gregory. They had no idea that they were being observed.

Emmeline gripped the parapet until her knuckles turned white. Sir Frederick stood there stoically, his lips pursed. A gust of wind came off the water and drowned out the rest of the argument. After another minute, Gregory stormed off as Veronica remained rooted to her spot a smile playing upon her lips.

Sir Frederick watched Emmeline closely as her dark eyes followed Gregory until he disappeared around a corner. "A friend of yours?"

She nodded dumbly, summoning all her willpower not to start crying. She swallowed hard. "Actually, he's my fiancé. At least, I still *think* he is." This last bit came out as a hoarse whisper as her gaze shifted to Veronica.

"Hmm," was all Sir Frederick managed when he saw his wife turn and wander down a path in the opposite direction.

"Our tea is getting cold," he said briskly. "We can't allow that to happen, can we, Miss Kirby? Miss Kirby?"

"Oh, sorry, Sir Frederick. No, of course not."

He held out her chair for her and then resumed his own seat. They both took a contemplative sip of tea.

Sir Frederick studied Emmeline as she stared out at the sea. "You love him very much, don't you?"

She didn't react, her eyes remained fixed on the rugged beauty of the cove. Then, he saw her nod imperceptibly and a shuddering sigh rippled through her body.

Sir Frederick stirred his tea. His spoon made a tinkling sound as he tapped it against the cup. "Whoever said that women were the weaker sex was dead wrong. It's we men who are the weak ones. We're like a moth to a flame. It's exciting, dangerous. Just like my wife."

Emmeline turned her head sharply at this remark, but said nothing.

"Men can't help being attracted to her," Sir Frederick went on. "And oh how she likes keeping us dancing to her tune. We give her anything she wants because she's so beautiful, and we want to be near her no matter how outrageous her behavior. She makes us feel—Well, never mind. What I'm trying to say is don't blame your chap for being attracted to her. I don't. Really. I quite understand."

Emmeline couldn't believe her ears. She took another sip of tea to quiet her racing mind. She felt sorry for Sir Frederick. The poor fool was so besotted by the unfaithful creature he unwisely married that he was actually *defending* her. There was absolutely no way he could persuade Emmeline to feel anything approaching sympathy for his wife. The only thing that she harbored for Veronica was pure, cold hatred. And that would never change as long as they both lived.

CHAPTER 16

There was a major hue and cry the next day. And who should be at the center of it, but Veronica. The rare pink diamond pendant that Sir Frederick had given her as a wedding present had been stolen. It had simply vanished. *Poof.* She had taken it out to wear to dinner the previous evening, but at the last moment changed her mind. Veronica told anyone who would listen that she had been too lazy to put the necklace back in the safe and instead left it out on her dressing table. She had quite forgotten about it until this morning, when she realized that it had gone missing.

She had enlisted the aid of several maids, but a search of her room had yielded nothing.

Needless to say, this unpleasant news traveled swiftly and threw the Royal Devon into a tizzy. Mr. Harcourt and the rest of the hotel staff were doing their utmost to reassure the other guests, but panic was simmering just below the surface. Already several people had checked out.

Detective Chief Inspector William Ashcroft and Detective Sergeant Paul Dandridge arrived just after ten to find Veronica ensconced in a chintz armchair in the lobby, dabbing at her red-rimmed eyes with a wrinkled handkerchief. Her husband was at her side, patting a hand soothingly.

The prurient and the merely curious, their interest piqued

by the unexpected theft, hovered nearby hoping for a scintillating scrap of gossip.

After taking statements, the detectives were shown the Cabots' room. They made a preliminary examination and then Ashcroft called the station to have a team come down and dust the room for fingerprints.

"Is that all you're going to do?" Veronica asked incredulously.

"I'm afraid, Lady Cabot, that's all we can do at the moment."

"I would think that at the very least you could search every room in the hotel?"

"We will naturally question the staff and other guests, as well as conduct a thorough search of the hotel and the grounds. But I must be honest with you, Lady Cabot, it is highly unlikely that we will find the diamond. The thief has had plenty of time in which to dispose of it."

"I find that a very cavalier attitude, Chief Inspector Ashcroft. Do you know who my husband is?"

Ashcroft stiffened. He hated snobs like the Cabots, who pulled rank at the drop of a hat. "I'm well aware of who Sir Frederick is."

"Then, you must know that he counts the prime minister among his closest friends. One call and you could be out of a job, *if* you're not careful, Chief Inspector."

"That's quite enough, Ronnie," Sir Frederick said firmly. "Please forgive my wife, Ashcroft. She is a bit overwrought."

The detective inclined his head, accepting the apology. "Of course, Sir Frederick. It's only natural that Lady Cabot should be upset." He stood. "I give you both my assurance that the Devon and Cornwall Police will do everything in its power to try to recover your diamond."

"I should hope so," Veronica replied petulantly. "It's what you're paid for, after all."

On this sanguine note, Chief Inspector Ashcroft took his leave.

৵৵৵

By one-thirty, Ashcroft had grown weary. He sighed and ran a hand through his red-gold hair. A sweep of the room had elicited nothing but the Cabots' and the maid's finger-prints. The detective had already ruled out the maid. None of the guests had seen anything suspicious. The staff inter-views were proving to be fruitless as well, until Tracy, one of the maids, slipped into the chair before Ashcroft and Ser-geant Dandridge. The hotel had put the ballroom at the de-tectives' disposal to conduct their interviews.

Tracy, a pretty thing with an oval face and thick chestnut hair piled high on her head, winked one of her gold-flecked hazel eyes at Ashcroft. "You're rather dishy, aren't you? It's hard to believe you're a policeman."

Dandridge tried to stifle a smile, while Ashcroft chose to ignore her comments. He wasn't here to chat up anyone. He was here to find a thief. Ashcroft cleared his throat, in an attempt to inject a little formality into the proceedings. He fixed her with a brown stare. "Now then, Miss Woodward, did you see Lady Cabot's diamond necklace anywhere?"

"Only when she showed it to me a day or two back. She was going on about how lucky she was to have a doting husband who showered her with expensive gifts. Her clothes are ever so lovely as well."

"Well, never mind all that. So that was the first and last time you saw the necklace?"

"Oh, no, Chief Inspector, Sergeant." She flashed a row of perfectly white teeth. "I came across it again today."

"You what?" Ashcroft was on his feet. "And you didn't say anything to Lady Cabot or the police?"

"I'm telling you now, aren't I?" Tracy went on calmly. "I just finished my shift not half an hour ago. There are ever so many rooms to get through. It's not easy."

"Yes, yes," Ashcroft sat down again and took a deep breath to quash his rising impatience before he lost his temper. "Why didn't you tell Lady Cabot that you had found the necklace after you had made her room?"

"Oh, but I haven't done the Cabots' room yet because your chaps are still mucking about in there."

"Then *where* exactly did you see the necklace?" The chief inspector asked, puzzled.

"It was in Mr. Longdon's room. It fell out of the pocket of the jacket he wanted to have pressed."

"Are you certain it was the necklace?"

"Quite certain. You don't forget something so beautiful."

"I see. This Mr. Longdon is in room—"

"Five-twenty-two."

"Do you happen to know when he checked in?"

"On Sunday. A few days before Lady Cabot."

"Was he acting suspiciously in any way?"

"A bit fickle, if you ask me."

"In what way?" Ashcroft prompted.

"Well, when Mr. Longdon first arrived, he was going about everywhere with Miss Kirby. She's in room three-oh-three. They seemed all lovey-dovey. Then, *bang*, the minute Lady Cabot appeared on the scene, he only had eyes for *her*. She *is* beautiful, I grant you that. But poor Miss Kirby."

"That's very interesting, Tracy. Anything else you can tell me about Mr. Longdon and Lady Cabot?"

She lowered her voice conspiratorially, although the three of them were the only ones in the empty ballroom. "I saw her sneak out of his room early on Wednesday morning." She raised one brow and nodded her head significantly at the detectives.

"Indeed."

"They pretend like they don't know each other, but you can tell they are old lovers. They also had two major rows. One in the lobby on Thursday and one in the garden yesterday afternoon."

"You're just a font of information, aren't you, Tracy?"

She smiled at them both in turn. "My mother always told me that it pays to keep your eyes and ears open."

"Very wise woman, your mother. Now, one last thing before I let you go. Where's the necklace?"

"I knew you'd ask me that." Tracy dug a hand into her pocket and triumphantly drew out a knotted handkerchief.

She handed it to Ashcroft who carefully untied the bundle. There suddenly splayed before their eyes was a four-carat, pear-shaped pink diamond that dangled from a choker of white diamonds. The exquisite piece caught the light and mesmerized with its fiery beauty.

♥∂♥

"It's ludicrous, Chief Inspector," Gregory said as he casually crossed one leg over the other. "I have never seen that necklace before in my life. I would have thought that the Devon and Cornwall Police CID division would recognize a frame when they saw it."

"So you deny that you stole this necklace from Lady Cabot?"

"Categorically." Indifference was reflected in Gregory's eyes, which held the chief inspector's gaze.

Ashcroft thought that Gregory was either a supremely confident actor or else utterly reckless, or perhaps both.

"What would you say if I told you that I don't believe you, Mr. Longdon?"

Gregory smiled and smoothed down the corners of his mustache. "I'd say that's your prerogative. But it doesn't change the fact that I'm being stitched up."

It was Ashcroft's turn to smile. "I've done a little checking on you, Mr. Longdon, and I've learned a good many interesting facts from our friends at Interpol and Scotland Yard."

Gregory leaned forward and put his elbows on the table, his chin resting on both hands. "Do tell. I hope they had kind things to say."

Arrogant bastard, the chief inspector thought. "It seems that they are well acquainted with you. In fact, they are very eager to have a chat with you about a string of jewel thefts that have taken place all across the Continent since the mid-1990s."

"That's fascinating, Chief Inspector. But alas, I will have to disappoint your colleagues because I am quite ignorant about any jewel thefts. I'm a respectable, law-abiding citizen. I would never partake in, nor condone, such illegal acts. Really, it goes against the grain," Gregory clucked his tongue and shook his head. "I am an Englishman, after all. It's simply not done," he remarked in an aggrieved tone.

"Hmph," was Ashcroft's response to this speech. What utter rubbish. He hated when people waved the Union Jack to excuse their actions.

Gregory stood and shot his cuff to glance at his watch. "If that's all, Chief Inspector, I do have dinner plans."

Ashcroft's gray eyes narrowed. "Sit down, Longdon." Gregory noticed that *mister* had been dropped. "This interview will conclude when I am satisfied that we have ascertained all the facts. Do you understand?"

Gregory once again resumed his seat. "Of course. I don't see what else you'd like to discuss, but by all means fire away with your questions. I can spare you oh, let's say, another half-hour at the most. Would that do?" he asked expectantly.

Sergeant Dandridge saw one of the chief inspector's fists curl into a tight ball in a bid to rein in his temper. "Now then, how long have you known Lady Cabot?"

Gregory arranged his features in what he hoped was a bland expression, but his heart pounded against his rib cage. "Lady Cabot? Sir Frederick's wife?" Ashcroft nodded. "I don't actually *know* her. I bumped into her a few times. You know how it is in a hotel. You tend to see the same people everywhere you go."

"So how do you explain that she was seen sneaking out of your room in the wee hours of the morning? In addition, the two of you were observed having a heated argument on at least two occasions." Ashcroft crossed his arms over his chest. "I'm waiting, Longdon."

"My dear Chief Inspector Ashcroft, I'm at a loss for words because I don't know why someone would concoct such a lie."

"Then, you deny it?"

"I most certainly do. As I said before, I may have happened upon Lady Cabot in passing and exchanged a desultory word with her, but that's all."

Ashcroft was not satisfied, but for the moment he couldn't do anything. All his instincts told him that Gregory was hiding something. "You may go, Longdon, but I advise you to retain a lawyer. It's quite likely that you'll be needing one in the next few days."

Gregory pushed his chair back and rose to his feet. "It's been a pleasure, Chief Inspector. I will await our next meeting with bated breath." He gave the two detectives a cheeky salute.

With masculine grace and self-assurance, Gregory glided across the ballroom, his shoes barely making a sound against the polished wood floor. *Arrogant bastard*, Ashcroft thought again. But he called out after him, "Don't forget the lawyer, Longdon."

Gregory didn't break his stride and continued on his way.

However, Emmeline, who was waiting to be interviewed next, heard what the chief inspector had said.

She put a hand on Gregory's arm as he passed her. "Lawyer? Why would you need a lawyer? The police can't possibly think you had anything to do with this."

Gregory looked down into the eyes of the woman he loved and saw the concern written all over her face. "Actually, Emmy, it seems that the necklace was found in the jacket I had sent down to be pressed."

"What?" Her dark eyes widened in surprise. "That's nonsense. Someone's trying to frame you."

Gregory smiled and patted her hand. "It seems that we

are the only two people in this entire hotel who are of that opinion."

"I'll tell them that they're mistaken." She started toward the door of the ballroom, but Gregory pulled her back.

"Don't, darling. Don't do or say anything. It will only make things worse. I'll handle this myself."

"But—"

"No, Emmy. Do not interfere. I have a fairly good idea who's behind this." She saw the muscle in his jaw twitch and followed the direction of his gaze.

Veronica Cabot had just entered the lobby.

"Oh, why won't you let me help you?" Emmeline beseeched as she tugged at his sleeve.

Gregory saw Veronica's lips curled into a smile. Until that instant, he didn't know it was possible to be consumed with such hatred for another human being. "I don't need your help, Emmy. Just stay away from me." The words came out more harshly than he intended. He simply wanted to protect her from Veronica's wrath, but all he seemed to do was to hurt her. "Please, Emmy," he said more gently, but the damage had already been done.

Emmeline tossed her head back and squared her shoulders. "Sorry to have made such a nuisance of myself." With that, she turned on her heel and left him standing there alone.

Veronica had watched the encounter between Gregory and Emmeline with amusement. She couldn't resist rubbing salt in the wound. "My, the little princess did look upset. I hope you didn't have a tiff on my account," she teased as she passed Gregory.

Gregory grabbed her arm roughly and pulled her aside. "I know this is your doing, Ronnie. Don't think you can get away with it."

"Oh, but I already have, darling. I already have," she purred. "Now, do be a good chap and let go of my arm before I add assault to the theft charge." Veronica smiled sweetly at him, but her green eyes were full of malice.

Gregory dropped his hand and cast a quick sidelong glance around the lobby. "I'll go to your husband and tell him everything. Then, where will you be? All the jewels and the money will be gone, and you'll be out on the streets."

"I wouldn't do that, Greg. Remember if I go down, so will you. I thought this little exercise just proved that to you. Think about it carefully." She patted him on the chest. "If the truth comes out, your precious Emmeline will run as far and as fast as she can away from you. You'll never see her again. Do you really want that?"

"What do *you* want?" he asked at last.

Veronica threw her head back and laughed. "The world, darling. I want the world. Now, I'm sure that we can come to some mutually beneficial arrangement if we put our heads together."

CHAPTER 17

It was ten o'clock and the news on BBC 1 was just starting, but Emmeline flicked off the television. She was not in the mood to listen to a roundup of the day's events. She unlatched the sliding door and stepped out onto her balcony. She needed some fresh air to help settle her restless mind.

Emmeline hugged herself tightly as she was assaulted by the bracing air. The wind was picking up, sending ominous charcoal clouds scudding across the cobalt sky. The night was heavy with moisture. The weather forecasters had warned that a major storm would be making its way across the southwest overnight.

Emmeline leaned on the railing and gazed out at the sea. Just before the moon was vanquished by the darkness, she caught a glimpse of Veronica hurrying away from the hotel in the direction of the garden. She stopped twice to glance over her shoulder. Emmeline slunk into the shadows when Veronica passed under her balcony. *Lady Cabot doesn't look like the outdoors type, so what is she up to at this hour when a storm is approaching,* Emmeline mused. *Nothing good, that was certain.*

Emmeline shivered. Her toes were suddenly like icicles. She was about to go in, when a movement down below caught her eye. She squinted into the darkness. Even without the benefit of the moon, she knew instinctively who this second person was. How could she fail to recognize the man she loved?

Emmeline sighed and went back inside her room. She plopped down onto her bed. What did Gregory see in that woman? She thought she knew his heart, but it was now beginning to dawn on her that she didn't know anything about him at all.

Veronica's voice reverberated in her ears. *'Why don't you go to Wickersham? It's only a stone's throw from Torquay and there you'll find the ugly truth about your precious boyfriend.'*

The ugly truth, Emmeline thought, *but am I strong enough to face it?*

She slid her legs beneath the covers. Perhaps she would go to Wickersham tomorrow. *Isn't knowing better than not knowing?* Yes, she would go.

Now, that she had made her decision she felt more at ease. Emmeline reached out on the bedside table for the copy of Agatha Christie's *Ten Little Indians*, which she had bought the other day when she went into Cockington with Rosemary.

She opened the cover and settled back against the pillows. She began to read: *In the corner of a first-class smoking carriage, Mr. Justice Wargrave, lately retired from the bench, puffed at a cigar and ran an interested eye through the political news in the Times.*

Soon though, Emmeline's eyelids began to droop and sleep pushed all thoughts of Mr. Justice Wargrave from her mind.

***

The grandfather clock in the corner of the lobby struck eleven. Sir Frederick stepped out of the lift. He was tieless and his shirt collar was unbuttoned. His hair was slightly damp and tousled. His hands were plunged into the pockets of his tan trousers. The lines on either side of his mouth seemed more pronounced and the wrinkles fanning out from the corners of his blue eyes looked deeper.

He stopped at the reception desk. "You haven't seen my wife by any chance this evening, have you?" he asked Connie.

"No, Sir Frederick, I didn't. Is anything wrong?"

He smiled weakly. "No, I don't think so. I'm afraid she doesn't sleep well and likes to take a walk at night before she retires. It's just that—well, you see, I came out of the shower not five minutes ago and realized that she hasn't returned yet. I'm getting rather worried. That's a nasty storm raging out there. And I don't know where she could have gotten to."

They both listened to wind-driven rain lashing the windows. However, Connie tried to reassure him. "The likely explanation is that your wife took refuge somewhere and at this moment is waiting until the storm dies down before she makes her way back to the hotel. That's what I'd do."

The furrows on his brow cleared. "Yes, I'm sure you're right. But if that's the case, why hasn't she called to let me know that she's all right. She knows I'd be worried." Although he had to admit to himself that it was not the first time that Veronica had been so thoughtless.

"Sir Frederick, please don't upset yourself. There's nothing to worry about. I'm sure everything is perfectly all right," Connie said.

Their eyes, which were almost the same shade of blue, locked and then Sir Frederick nodded. "Yes, of course you're right. I'm just being a silly old man. Please forgive me for troubling you."

"It was no trouble at all. However, if it would ease your mind, I could have a couple of the chaps go out and search the grounds."

"No, no, out of the question. I wouldn't be caught dead on a night like this, let alone send out two hard-working fellows. Thank you, but no. As you said, Ronnie is probably holed up somewhere. But, I think I'll hang about down here for a bit. It's less claustrophobic than waiting in our room."

"Of course. I'll ask the kitchen to make you a pot of coffee while you wait."

"That's very kind of you. Thank you."

Connie smiled and reached for the receiver. Sir Frederick cast a glance around the lobby. It was deserted at this hour, except for an older woman sitting on a sofa in the corner knitting. He chose a deep armchair nearby and picked up a week-old copy of a popular magazine. He began to flip through the pages disinterestedly. He put it down and selected another magazine.

At this point, the woman looked up and smiled. "Good evening."

"Good evening," Sir Frederick nodded and replied courteously. "Rather a terrible storm, isn't it?"

The woman put down her knitting in her lap. "Indeed it is, Sir Frederick. I attempted to take a stroll, but the storm forced me to turn back before I'd gotten very far."

"So you know who I am."

The woman laughed. "Everyone knows who you are, Sir Frederick. Your face is in the papers or on television nearly every day."

"Ah, there you have the advantage of me. I don't know who you are." He rose and gestured at the sofa. "May I?"

"Please do. And my name's Rosemary Dunham." She proffered a hand, which Sir Frederick graciously shook as he lowered himself beside her.

"A pleasure to meet you, Mrs. Dunham."

They were from the same generation, perhaps only a few years separated them. Therefore, they fell into conversation easily.

"Likewise. I must say, I very much admire your philanthropic work. Very commendable."

"Thank you. One does what one can, but it is never enough."

"One person can't cure all the world's ills single-handedly."

"I suppose not, but sometimes I wish—" He was cut off in mid-sentence when one of the kitchen staff suddenly appeared.

"Sir Frederick, your coffee," the young man said as he placed a tray with a pot of coffee and a cup and saucer on the low table in front of the sofa.

"Thank you very much." Sir Frederick scrounged around in his pocket and pulled out a couple of pound coins. "Would it be possible to get another cup for Mrs. Dunham?"

"Certainly, sir. I'll be back straightaway."

Sir Frederick turned his attention once again to Rosemary. "I never like to drink alone, you see."

They both chuckled. "Well, thank you, Sir Frederick."

"I must insist that you call me Freddie. Sir Frederick seems so stuffy and despite what you may read in the papers, I'm a very simple chap at heart."

"Then, Freddie it is. And I'm Rosemary."

He smiled. "That's better. Rosemary is such a lovely name. There's something musical about it."

"Do you think so? I've never thought about it."

"Oh, yes, indeed. Just like Veronica. That's my wife's name." A shadow darkened his face at the mention of his wife. His gaze darted toward the double doors, hoping that he would see her walking back in.

The young man reappeared with a second cup and saucer. He poured out the coffee and bid them good night.

Rosemary patted Sir Frederick's arm lightly. "I'm afraid I couldn't help overhearing your conversation with Connie. She's right. Don't fret about your wife. You'll only make yourself sick with worry. The people down here are very warm and welcoming. Someone probably saw your wife wandering about in the dark and took her in for the night. When she saw what time it was, she likely thought you were asleep and didn't want to disturb you."

"Do you think so?" he asked, eager to cling onto anything that could dispel the uneasiness in his mind.

Rosemary smiled. "Yes. After all, Torquay is not London. What could possibly happen to your wife down here?"

ℰↃℰↃ

Emmeline woke with a start. The book had slipped from her hand and crashed to the floor at precisely the same moment that a tremendous clap of thunder unleashed its vengeful wrath on an unsuspecting sky. She fumbled on the bedside table for her watch. It was a few minutes after eleven. The thin drapes at the window were flapping wildly as if possessed by spirits from the netherworld. The culprit was the sliding door, which was open a crack. She had neglected to make sure it was locked when she had been on the balcony earlier.

She quickly padded out of bed and gave the door a hard push. Then, she clicked the latch into place. Emmeline touched the cool glass with her fingertips as she lingered at the window, mesmerized. The slanting rain's angry onslaught only seemed to grow in intensity as each white flash of lightning seared the inky blackness, turning night into day.

Her breath caught in her throat and icy fear clutched at her lungs. For a brief instant, during one of those violent bursts of light, she had glimpsed Gregory hurrying back toward the hotel. His hair was plastered to his forehead and he was soaked to the skin.

CHAPTER 18

When morning at last made its appearance, the fury of last night's tempest was a distant memory. Those fortunate enough to be sound sleepers were completely ignorant of the fact that there had been a storm at all, let alone one of such ferocity. Everything sparkled with dewy freshness as the sun's first rays kissed the trees, flowers and rolling lawns where raindrops yet clung.

On the other hand, Emmeline's usually sunny disposition was absent. Instead of bursting with energy, she felt utterly drained, both mentally and physically. It was as if someone had beaten her senseless, then sluiced her with cold water and started over again and again. She couldn't sleep after she had seen Gregory. Could she have been mistaken? He was there one second and gone the next time lightning cracked its fiery whip.

She must have been wrong. *After all, he could have been*—No, she shook her head abandoning that thought. She sat up in bed excitedly, *or he could have*—No, she dismissed that idea as well. Hard as she tried—and she harnessed every hidden corner of her intellect—Emmeline couldn't come up with a plausible reason why Gregory would be prowling about the hotel's gardens at eleven o'clock on a night when the heavens had been ripped open and a watery assault was loosed upon mankind.

Emmeline reached for her watch. She groaned. It was only six-thirty. However, she couldn't remain in bed any longer. Sleep would never come now. So she threw off the covers and padded to the bathroom to take a shower. Her stomach was so tied up in knots that she would forgo breakfast and go straight to Wickersham. Until she learned all there was to know about Gregory, Emmeline was certain that she wouldn't be able to touch food. She would walk down into Torquay and catch the bus to Wickersham. Ordinarily she would have asked to borrow Gregory's Jaguar, but in view of the way things stood between them it might be a bit awkward. Who knows, if he found out where she was going he might try to stop her. And she couldn't have that. Emmeline had to find out whatever *it* was that he was hiding.

In twenty minutes, Emmeline had showered and dressed. She rode down in the lift alone, thankful that she didn't have to make cheery chitchat. She crossed the lobby quickly and slipped out of the Royal Devon. Her stride was purposeful and determined, while her mind was focused on its mission.

୧୬୧୬

Emmeline arrived in Wickersham just after nine. The bus station was in the center of the quaint little village. One side of the high street featured charming shops selling lace and other handmade goods, while across the road snuggled between a bookshop and an antiques dealer was The Witch's Brew Tea Salon. If she continued to the end of the road, it opened onto the village green and the Red Lion pub. A few steps in the opposite direction, the road curved and took one over a humpbacked bridge made of buff-colored stone. The bridge crossed a babbling brook that wended its merry way past clusters of cottages, the woods and the church.

Where to start? She needed to find a place where the locals gathered and might easily fall into conversation. The likely choice would be the pub, but it was too early. Therefore, it had to be the Witch's Brew.

Emmeline waited for a car to pass and then crossed the road. A bell tinkled overhead as she pushed open the door. The tea room was larger than it looked from the outside. Despite its name, it was warm and cozy.

Plush apple-green carpeting muted one's footfalls and cream-colored wallpaper decorated with tiny pink rosebuds pleased the eye. Each table was draped with a lace tablecloth upon which rested a glass vase that cradled a single yellow rose.

There were a handful of customers chatting quietly, while they sipped tea from Royal Doulton cups graced with forget-me-nots and munched on the freshly baked goods.

"Just one, miss?" a plump, middle-aged woman with ash-blonde hair heavily streaked with grey and large brown eyes asked cheerfully. From the way she carried herself, it was obvious that she was the proprietress.

Emmeline returned her smile. "Yes, just one. Can I have that table in the corner?"

"Of course, you can, love." The woman led her to a table where Emmeline could observe everyone in the room.

Once settled, Emmeline ran an eye down the menu with its elegant calligraphy writing. Everything looked so tempting. In the end, she ordered a pot of Earl Grey, a blueberry scone with homemade lemon curd and a small raspberry tart.

As she devoured her delicious little feast, Emmeline tried to think what would be the best way to broach the subject of Gregory. The tactics she generally used when interviewing difficult and elusive politicians back in London would not work in Wickersham. The pace of life was slower here and the people did not have devious, hidden motives for all their actions. Only when the last crumb of the raspberry tart had been washed down by tea did Emmeline decide on her plan of attack.

"I do like to see people enjoying their food," the proprietress said as she came to clear away the plates.

"Everything was absolutely delicious. If I lived in the village, I'd be in here every day and likely gain ten pounds in no time."

The woman chuckled. "Well, you could do with a bit of fattening up, no offense intended. But I'm glad that everything was to your liking. Another pot of tea, love?"

"Oh, no, I'm quite stuffed. And no offense taken. Actually, you sound exactly like my grandmother. She's always making huge meals every time I go down to Kent to see her. She thinks I don't eat in London."

"London? I thought as much."

Emmeline bent her head conspiratorially. "I hope you won't hold that against me. There are a lot of us in London who are nice, you know."

A laugh rumbled from deep within the woman's chest and erupted from her throat. "I knew I liked you the minute you walked in, miss. You have a kind face and lovely manners."

Emmeline smiled. "Why thank you. Gran would be glad to hear that her years of indoctrination have paid off."

"I don't think it took all that much, miss. You don't strike me as the type to stir up trouble."

"There are a number of politicians and businessmen back in London who would disagree with you on the point. I'm a journalist, you see."

"Ah, a journalist. How interesting. I bet you meet fascinating people all the time." The woman sat down at the table and rested her chin on her hand.

Emmeline bit back a smile. "I grant you that I've really enjoyed meeting some of the people I've interviewed. But then there are others—" She made a sour face. "—who I couldn't get away from fast enough, Mrs...I'm sorry. I'm afraid I didn't catch your name."

"It's Millie Tavistock. But my friends just call me Millie."

Emmeline proffered her hand. "I'm pleased to make your acquaintance, Millie. I'm Emmeline Kirby."

"A pretty name for a pretty young woman. Your parents must be very proud of you." Emmeline's face clouded over at the mention of her parents. "I'm sorry. Have I said the wrong thing? Arthur, my husband, is always saying as how I find a way of putting my foot in my mouth."

Emmeline managed a weak smile and touched Millie's arm lightly. "No, you didn't say anything wrong. I assure you. It's just that my parents died when I was five years old. Gran is the one who raised me."

Millie covered Emmeline's smaller her hand with her own. "Oh, you poor dear. It's even more remarkable how you've turned out. Others would have grown up bitter. Your grandmother must be a very loving woman."

"Indeed, she is. There's none better in the world. She's my best friend. Speaking of friends, another friend of mine, Gregory Longdon, told me about how lovely Wickersham was. So as I was on holiday in Torquay, I took the bus down to see your charming village. I think Gregory said that he still had relatives here. I thought I'd pop over to say hello. You wouldn't by chance know where they live, would you?" Emmeline hoped her voice didn't sound too eager, but she kept fingers crossed under the table.

"Longdon? I'm afraid I don't know any Longdons. But then, Arthur and I are new to Wickersham ourselves. We only moved down here seven months ago, after Arthur retired. He was in insurance in Manchester. We always used to come to Devon on our holidays. We fell in love with Wickersham the minute we laid eyes on the village and said that this would be place where we would live out our final years."

"Oh, I see," Emmeline said, a bit deflated.

"However, you could ask Barbara about your friends. She's lived here all her life. Barbara and her husband run the Red Lion. It's the pub on the other side of the village."

"Thanks very much. I think I will speak to Barbara. I

would hate to think I came all the way to Wickersham and didn't at least make an attempt to see Gregory's relatives."

"Of course, not. I'll just get your bill. It's been a pleasure chatting with you, Emmeline. Good luck finding the Longdons and enjoy the rest of your holiday."

"Thank you, Millie. I will tell all my friends, if they're ever down this way to make a point of stopping at the Witch's Brew."

Millie pushed herself to her feet. "I appreciate that, love. Word of mouth is always the best way."

ⅇⅉⅇⅉ

Barbara and her husband Tim were gregarious and welcoming, as were a number of the regular characters who frequented the Red Lion and were already ensconced in their favorite booths or bar stools. Emmeline delighted in soaking up the local color and listening to village lore. However, at the end of two hours, all she had learned was that Ralph and Jane Longdon had left Wickersham years ago. No one could remember exactly when or where they had moved.

Emmeline bid goodbye to all her new friends and promised to stop by, if ever she found herself in Wickersham again. She stepped out into the brilliant sunshine and hesitated on the threshold. She gazed out across the green, whose perfectly mown blades of grass sparkled in the light as a gentle breeze tiptoed by.

Her excursion to Wickersham was not a total loss because she had met some very kind people, who treated a stranger as one of their own. Nonetheless she was disappointed because her main objective was not accomplished, or rather, in unvarnished terms she had hit a dead end. But it begged the question, why had Veronica Cabot sent her on a wild goose chase? What had she been trying to tell her? As far as Emmeline could tell, there were no ugly secrets remotely connected with Gregory here in Wickersham. If only the Longdons still lived in the village. How were they related to Gregory? Were they his parents? An aunt and uncle? Cousins? Emmeline simply didn't know and now never would.

It went against her journalist's instincts to give up, but she supposed the only thing she could do was to get the bus back to Torquay. Perhaps, if Gregory were in a less prickly mood when she returned to the hotel she could ask him about last night—and Wickersham.

The church bell tolled twelve times as Emmeline started to cross the green. The sound made her halt in her tracks. Of course, she chided herself, why hadn't she thought of that before? The church had to have records of births, deaths and marriages. Maybe she could find a clue there about the Longdons. Or better yet, perhaps the vicar would be willing to speak with her for a few minutes. The church usually was the center of village life in tight-knit communities like Wickersham and the local clergy took an active interest in its residents.

Emmeline headed toward the bridge and followed the two-lane road past the woods. The happy chatter of the starlings and chaffinches frolicking amongst the leafy branches lifted her spirits. Suddenly, she was certain that in St. Margaret's church she would find the answers to all her questions. It was not far. She couldn't get lost because the church spire came into view around the next bend.

A field path at the edge of the woods led to the churchyard. It was so quiet and peaceful. The little church with its walls of old red brick and flint, and its partial covering of ivy, was set against a backdrop of ancient trees. Emmeline walked through an open gate, which was also draped in ivy. A gravel path led straight to the church's sturdy oak door. She hesitated before twisting the heavy metal ring.

Emmeline blinked to adjust her eyes from the bright sunshine to the dimness inside the church. After a few seconds, her gaze roamed from the wooden pews to the chancel and stained-glass window. Although she was Jewish, she appreciated the simplicity of this church. There were no murals or paintings, just clean white walls and brick columns. St. Margaret's somehow reverberated more strongly with her than the grand cathedrals of Europe, which were steeped in gold, silver and other treasures.

She clung to the shadows at the back of the church, careful not to disturb the handful of villagers sitting in the pews either at prayer or in quiet contemplation.

"May I help you?" a kindly voice asked.

Emmeline turned to find herself being addressed by the vicar himself. Dressed in his simple uniform of black trousers and vest, his crisp white shirtsleeves rolled to the elbows, he smiled down at her from a round, ruddy face. His clear, gray eyes were crinkled at the corners, as if amused by something. He was bald, with only a few wisps of silver hair ringing his head. And, if the way his vest was stretched tautly across his stomach was anything to judge by, the vicar was always ready for a hearty meal.

"May I help you?" he repeated. "I'm John Foster, the vicar of St. Margaret's."

"It's a pleasure to meet you, Reverend Foster. My name's Emmeline." She extended a hand, which he pressed between both of his.

"Delighted, Emmeline. Are you just visiting Wickersham or are you staying with friends down here?" Before she had a chance to reply, he waved a hand in the air and went on. "Or are you just interested in church architecture? I can tell you that parts of St. Margaret's date from Saxon times, but much of the chancel and tower are Norman. Of course, the building has been added to and developed over the years. If you look there, you'll see that the Tudor side chapel was integrated into the rest of the church by the Victorians—"

"Actually, Reverend Foster," Emmeline interjected before he really started warming to his subject, "I was hoping to locate some old family friends, the Longdons. Ralph and

Jane? I understand that they moved away some years ago. Did you know them?"

"Well, well, well." He clapped his beefy hands together. "Ralph and Jane Longdon. Indeed, I knew them very well. Now let's see, if I'm not mistaken—"

"Oh, Mr. Foster, there you are. Thank heavens." A plump, middle-aged woman in a shapeless maroon dress came bustling down the aisle all in a tizzy.

"Please excuse me, Emmeline. My housekeeper," he explained. "Calm yourself, Mrs. Dean. Whatever is it?" The vicar met her halfway.

"You must come to the vicarage at once. That Mr. Chadwick is back again and he insists on speaking to you. He's in a foul mood too."

Mr. Foster patted her arm soothingly. "All right. I'll be there in a tick." He turned back to Emmeline. "This shouldn't take more than a few minutes. If you'd care to wait, I'd be glad to tell you about the Longdons."

"Of course, Reverend Foster. Thank you very much. As it's such a glorious day, I'll be out in the churchyard."

"Splendid. I'll be back with you soon." He smiled and scurried after Mrs. Dean as quickly as his portly frame would allow.

Emmeline slipped out of the church and turned her face up toward the sky to drink in the sun's warmth. It had been chilly inside the church. She ambled down the gravel path glancing at some of the tombstones that spoke of past lives. Some stones were tilted at angles, like crooked teeth sticking up out of the ground, while others were so old that their inscriptions were virtually illegible. She stopped at one with an elegant script that read:

Mary Pierson
Beloved wife and mother who was taken away too soon
1892-1915

A sad smile touched Emmeline's lips as she came upon

similar inscriptions as she zigzagged among the neat rows in the churchyard.

Something caught her eye and made her look up. She stopped dead. Her hand flew to her mouth as she stumbled backward. "Oh, my God," she gasped.

And then she started to run.

CHAPTER 19

Emmeline was still trembling when she walked back into the Royal Devon an hour later. She had run all the way to the bus station in Wickersham. On the drive back to Torquay, she was haunted by what she had seen in the churchyard. What was she going to do?

This thought was suddenly pushed from her mind. Gregory came running up to her and pulled her into a rough embrace. "Emmy, thank God. Oh, thank God, you're all right." He held her away from him and fixed her with a hard stare, concern etched in every line of his face. He touched her cheek, smoothed back her curls and then pulled her against his chest once more. His warm lips pressed soft kisses on the crown of her head and against her temple. "I was so afraid, darling," he whispered as his arms tightened about her waist. "So afraid that I had lost you. Nobody had seen you since this morning."

For the past two days he couldn't stand the sight of her and now he was beside himself with worry. Emmeline was confused and rattled by this *volte-face*.

She looked up into his cinnamon eyes. "Gregory, what's going on here?" For the first time since she had returned to the hotel, she realized that all the guests were gathered in the lobby. They were huddled in little groups or pairs. Everyone was speaking in hushed tones. There was a nervous tension in the air. "And *what* happened to your face?" With light fingers, she stroked an ugly bruise that had formed on his right temple.

Although her touch had been gentle, he winced and grabbed her wrist. "It's nothing," he said dismissively and kissed her fingertips. "I was just a bit clumsy. That's all. Nothing to worry about."

Emmeline's brow furrowed. Gregory was too poised and in control to be clumsy and she had never known him to be accident-prone. She opened her mouth to question him further, but was prevented from doing so because Rosemary came up to them.

"Ah, there you are, Emmeline."

"Yes, and she's perfectly all right. We were all worried about her, weren't we, Rosemary?"

Rosemary lifted her chin in the air. "I really couldn't imagine what *you* were thinking, Mr. Longdon," she replied stiffly, "but I was quite certain that nothing had happened to Emmeline. She's too intelligent and sensible."

"*Mr. Longdon?*" Gregory's right eyebrow arched upward. He was taken aback by her sudden coldness toward him. What could have brought this on? "Since when have we become so formal, Rosemary?"

"It's Mrs. Dunham to you."

Even Emmeline was stunned by her attitude. She looked from one to the other. Had they quarreled about something?

"What's going on around here? Everything seems to be helter-skelter."

"Darling, hadn't you heard?"

"Heard what?"

"A woman's body was found on Meadfoot Beach this morning. Apparently, a step broke and she lost her footing and plunged to the rocks below."

Emmeline buried her head against his chest as she remembered her narrow escape only the other day on that same rickety staircase. "How horrible."

He held her close. "Now you see why I've been going

mad for the past two hours. But you're safe. That's all that counts."

Emmeline stood away from him. "I'm afraid I still don't understand. It's very tragic, but—"

"Emmy." He grabbed her by the shoulders and shook her slightly. The words came tumbling out in a rush. "The woman was a guest here at the Royal Devon. Then one of the staff said that he saw you leaving early this morning and when I couldn't find you anywhere—"

Her eyes widened with comprehension. "You mean that you thought it was *me*?"

Gregory swallowed hard. "Yes. All I could think of was how beastly I'd been to you and that I might never see you again. Can you forgive me? Can we simply forget that the past few days ever happened? *Please, Emmy.*"

Emmeline's heart soared at these words. Oh, yes. She wanted to forget everything. She searched those much-loved cinnamon eyes, trying to read whether he was sincere. She hoped so. She wanted so much for things to go back to the way they were before Veronica bloody Cabot made her grand entrance and turned their lives upside-down. The question was did he?

Emmeline ran a finger along his jaw, but remained silent. Gregory's body was tense as he awaited her answer. Then, she sighed. She loved him. Nothing would change that. "Yes, let's forget everything. We were both silly," she said quietly.

Gregory visibly relaxed and pressed his lips against hers. He didn't need words. Everything was in his kiss— tenderness, passion, desire and relief. A little breathless, they both laughed when they finally pulled apart.

Rosemary shook her head and her eyes narrowed in disapproval. "Like a lamb to the slaughter. Some people never learn, do they?" she scoffed.

Emmeline tilted her head to one side as Gregory slipped his arm around her shoulders. She couldn't fathom what had come over her friend. "Rosemary, is anything the matter?

You don't seem like yourself today. Has something happened to your daughter or her family?"

The older woman opened her mouth to say something and then seemed to change her mind. "No, Rosie and the family are perfectly fine. But thank you for your concern. You're such a thoughtful girl."

"Then what is it? Perhaps I can help."

Rosemary's blue gaze settled on Gregory as she replied, "Emmeline, let me give you a little advice. If you don't take care of things closer to home first, someone can come along and snatch it all away from you when your back is turned."

"What is that supposed to mean? If you have something to say, just say it straight out." Emmeline was beginning to get annoyed by this cryptic conversation. Clearly Rosemary was upset about something and for some reason she was taking it out on Gregory.

However, they were spared further awkwardness. The crowd suddenly parted as two constables made their way to Mr. Harcourt, who was pacing back forth at the reception desk. Emmeline watched as the three men huddled their heads together and murmured softly.

"Yes, I see. Sad business," she heard Mr. Harcourt say, a grim expression on his long, angular face.

"Chief Inspector Ashcroft is on his way. In the meantime, if we could have a private word with Sir Frederick," one of the constables replied.

Mr. Harcourt nodded. "Certainly, I will see to it that the ballroom is at the police's disposal. If the chief inspector needs anything else, please let me know and I will have my staff attend to it at once. I believe Sir Frederick and his nephew, Mr. Trevor Mayhew, are in the conservatory. I'll have one of the lads get them."

"No, it's all right, sir. Just point us in the right direction, we'll take it from there. These things are always difficult. The word will get about soon enough."

"Indeed. The conservatory is down that corridor to your right."

"Thank you for your assistance, Mr. Harcourt. Now, please have your guests remain here until Chief Inspector Ashcroft arrives. He'll want to interview everyone after he visits the scene."

"Of course." Mr. Harcourt watched the two policemen sedately cross the lobby and then he turned to Connie, who stood wide-eyed behind the desk.

"Did you hear what they said?" a woman whispered loudly to Emmeline's right. "It's Veronica Cabot. The woman who died is Veronica Cabot. I can't believe it."

Emmeline trembled and Gregory's arm tightened about her shoulders. She eyed him suspiciously. Was he upset by this unexpected news? But she couldn't gauge his reaction because his face was turned away from her. His eyes raked the guests milling about the lobby. Emmeline followed his gaze and was surprised to see that it had settled on Nigel Sanborn.

✐✐✐

Slick and dripping with sea spray, the jagged rocks glistened in the bright sunshine. Two seagulls made elegant arcs in the cerulean sky, as they swooped down to the water and then soared high up into the clouds. It was a beautiful day, except for the forensic team working on the beach. And the dead body covered by a white sheet, who was oblivious to everything.

Chief Inspector Ashcroft and Sergeant Dandridge stood at the bottom of the staircase. They shielded their eyes to look up at the cliff path. "What possessed her to come out here?" Ashcroft scratched his head, his red-gold hair set alight by the sun. "Not even the most intrepid of nature lovers would venture out in the middle of a raging storm. And Lady Cabot certainly didn't strike me as the outdoors type."

"No, sir, I would say most definitely not," Dandridge concurred. "A rendezvous? Suicide?"

The chief inspector gave him a pointed look. "Women like Lady Cabot don't have trysts on the beach. She's more of the dirty weekend in Monte Carlo type. And suicide is an even less likely possibility. It doesn't make any sense. I don't like it."

"You're going to like what I have to say even less," Dr. Clarke, the medical examiner, said as he walked up behind them and shut his black bag with a resounding snap.

Ashcroft turned around and shook hands with Clarke, who nodded his head toward the sergeant. "Hello, Peter. So what did you find?"

"She has a broken femur and her neck is cracked in two places."

"Well, that's not inconsistent with her fall, is it? I'm surprised more bones weren't broken. It's a long way down, after all." They all cast a glance at the shaky staircase.

"No, it's not inconsistent with her fall, but the stab wound that I found between her shoulder blades is."

Both Ashcroft and Dandridge shot him surprised looks. "What? Do you mean—"

"It was murder. Yes. I'm fairly certain of it, in fact. She was stabbed first and then was either pushed or fell from the cliff path. Of course, the post mortem will tell me more. Good day, chaps," Dr. Clarke said cheerily, as he left them to ponder this unexpected twist in an already unpleasant case.

CHAPTER 20

Sergeant Dandridge swung into an empty space in the car park of the Royal Devon. He cast a sidelong glance at his superior as he turned off the ignition. Ashcroft had stared out the window, lost in thought, on the short ride from Meadfoot Beach to the hotel. "Sir? We're here."

"What?" The chief inspector tore his gaze from the window and blinked twice. "Oh, yes, so we are." He sighed wearily and rubbed his stomach. "Well, I suppose we better get on with it, hadn't we, Dandridge? Damn."

"What is it, sir?"

"My ulcer is acting up. Never a good sign."

The sergeant silently agreed. The chief inspector's ulcer only made him more irritable.

Ashcroft winced and sighed again. "There's nothing for it. No good postponing the inevitable. Come on." He opened the door and stepped out of the car. Dandridge dutifully followed.

Hands thrust deep in his pockets, a lugubrious expression creasing his features, the chief inspector said, "I've been thinking."

"About possible suspects?"

"Yes and no. I was thinking about something Lady Cabot said the other day when we interviewed her about her so-called stolen necklace."

The sergeant's brow puckered together in surprise. "So-called stolen? But that maid found it in Longdon's room. And when I ran a check on him, I discovered that Interpol and Scotland Yard are well-acquainted with his escapades, although they have never been able to catch him with the goods."

"Yes, yes, I know all that," Ashcroft griped. "But as much as I dislike the fellow, in this instance I don't believe he committed the crime. I'm certain that he was set up, but we are straying from our current problem."

"Well even if your assumption is correct, sir, I can't understand what our interview with Lady Cabot and Sir Frederick has to do with her murder. I don't remember her saying anything of particular importance. She was not exactly solicitous. In fact, she was rather rude and condescending. And she went out of her way to put us in our place by reminding us of her husband's connections."

"Precisely, sergeant. It's for that reason that I think we should call in Scotland Yard and turn the case over to them. We don't want to tread on any delicate toes, now do we? The Yard is much better-equipped at dealing with such personalities. I don't know about you, but my ulcer doesn't need such excitement."

"You're right, sir. Why invite trouble? Much better all around to have the Yard step in."

"Right." The chief inspector put a hand on Dandridge's shoulder. "Let's go see Sir Frederick and his nephew."

❧❦❧

Sir Frederick had dark shadows beneath his eyes, which made the pallor of his skin seem even more pronounced. His blue eyes stared vacantly at some invisible spot on the other side of the conservatory. He wore the same shirt and trousers as he had on last night when he had come down to look for Veronica.

Slumped beside his uncle on the sofa was Trevor. If anything, he was even more ravished by shock than Sir Frederick. He hadn't moved or uttered a word in over an hour. Only the rhythmic rise and fall of his chest betrayed that he was still breathing.

Sir Frederick turned and watched his nephew. He recognized that look. It was a man in love. Trevor had loved Ronnie as much as he had. Frederick couldn't deny it anymore. He couldn't really blame his nephew. They had been bewitched by the same spell that Ronnie cast on all men. He reached out and patted Trevor's knee. "Come on, old chap. This won't do you know. She wouldn't have wanted this."

Trevor didn't reply. He simply continued to stare unseeingly into space. Sir Frederick thought he hadn't heard him. He shook his nephew's arm. "Trevor?"

After a long moment, Trevor slowly turned to face his uncle. What was etched on those handsome features were too painful for words. "She can't be dead, Uncle Freddie." This came out as a hoarse croak. "It's simply not possible. Not Ronnie. She was so beautiful—so full of life. And I—" He swallowed back what he had been about to say. That he had loved her. "And now I'll—we'll never see her again." His chest heaved as he choked back a sob.

Sir Frederick's throat constricted with his own emotions. He gave Trevor's shoulder a hard squeeze. "I know, old chap. I know," was all he could manage to say.

"Excuse me, Sir Frederick. I'm terribly sorry to intrude at such a difficult time."

Sir Frederick shifted his gaze and found himself looking up into Chief Inspector Ashcroft's gold-flecked hazel eyes. He started to rise, but the chief inspector held up a hand. "Please don't."

The two policemen settled themselves onto the sofa opposite. "I just wanted to extend my condolences, Sir Frederick."

Sir Frederick cleared his throat. "So there's no doubt, then?"

Ashcroft shook his head. "I'm afraid not. Of course, we'll need you to come down to identify the body. But it *is* Lady Cabot."

"Yes, I see. Naturally, you'll let me know when..." The rest of the sentence trailed off.

Trevor put a fist to his mouth to hold back a sob. The chief inspector cast a quick glance at him, but turned back to his uncle. He licked his lips before speaking again. "Unfortunately, there's something else I must tell you both. Something rather unpleasant."

"Unpleasant? What could be more unpleasant than discovering that my wife—my beautiful young wife died in a tragic accident."

"That's just it, sir. It's my unenviable duty to have to inform you that Lady Cabot was murdered."

Two pairs of blue eyes impaled him. "What?" they said in unison.

"I don't understand," Sir Frederick replied querulously. He suddenly looked his age. The skin of his face sagged and the lines on either side of his mouth appeared deeper. "What are you saying? You're wrong. I won't believe it." He slapped his open palm against his thigh. "I tell you I won't believe it."

"I'm afraid that your wife was murdered," the chief inspector repeated patiently. Denial was a common reaction when receiving such news. "There's no doubt. None whatsoever."

Sir Frederick stared at him for a very long moment and then slumped back. "No doubt," he mumbled. "None whatsoever. I see."

"Well, *I* don't accept it." Trevor jumped to his feet. "You're mad. Who would want to kill Ronnie?"

"Sit down, Trevor. Making a spectacle of yourself won't help matters. The police are simply trying to do their job. Now sit," his uncle commanded.

Trevor stood a moment longer and then heavily dropped back onto the sofa. He crossed his arms over his chest mutinously. "I won't believe it, I tell you. I don't mean to be rude, Chief Inspector, but have you ever handled a case like this before?"

"Really, Trevor," Sir Frederick chided. "That's quite uncalled for."

"No, it's all right, sir. Mr. Mayhew is perfectly within his rights. I was discussing the matter with Sergeant Dandridge earlier and we came to the conclusion that it might be best to call in Scotland Yard. In view of your position."

"Is that really necessary, Chief Inspector Ashcroft? I'm perfectly comfortable having you carry on with the case, despite what my nephew says."

"No, Uncle Freddie. I think it's a very sensible suggestion." Trevor inclined his head toward Ashcroft. "I apologize, Chief Inspector. No disrespect was intended. I assure you I didn't mean to offend you or to undermine your authority."

"No offense taken, Mr. Mayhew. Well, gentlemen, I'll just get on to the Yard." The chief inspector slowly rose and extended a hand to uncle and nephew. "Again I'm terribly sorry about Lady Cabot."

Sir Frederick nodded silently as he clasped first Ashcroft's and then the sergeant's hand. He was emotionally drained. So much had happened in the last twenty-four hours. And now, the chief inspector had left him with a lot to think about. His brow puckered into a frown. A lot of bitter, disagreeable things, indeed.

CHAPTER 21

The mood was subdued in the dining room the following morning. As if in tacit deference to poor, dead Lady Cabot and her distraught husband—who had taken refuge in his room since the police had broken the sad news—everyone spoke in hushed whispers and kept his or her eyes lowered.

If by chance one's eyes happened to stray, the guilty parties quickly averted their gaze.

Emmeline watched Gregory closely over the rim of her cup. To all outward appearances, he was his usual suave, confident self. But she knew him, and there was a restlessness lying just beneath the surface. This unnerved her so much that she took a large swallow of coffee and ended up burning her tongue. "Ow," she said as she patted her napkin against her lips.

"Emmy, are you all right?"

"Yes, fine. Just a bit careless."

"Everyone seems to be a bit…off-kilter this morning."

"Yes," she replied slowly, her eyes fixed on his face. "Some more than others apparently."

"What?"

"Nothing. It doesn't matter. I was merely thinking out loud."

"Oh, right." Gregory leaned back and hooked an elbow

around the chair. "It's not every day that one finds the body of a beautiful woman lying crumpled on a beach."

"Beautiful, yes," Emmeline murmured.

She clenched her fists tightly in her lap. Why couldn't she escape Veronica Cabot's presence? The bloody woman was dead, for heaven's sake. Would her ghost forever be hovering in the background? Emmeline had believed Gregory the previous afternoon when he said that he wanted them to forget the past few days and to start over. Was it only an act for her benefit? After all, he had said it before they found out that the woman on Meadfoot Beach was Veronica Cabot.

"Does her death upset you?" she asked, holding her breath for his answer.

"Darling, why would you ask me that? *I* didn't know the woman." But she noted that he didn't look her in the eye when he uttered this last remark. "You must admit, though—" He said as he traced patterns with his fork on the snowy tablecloth. "—it is disturbing in a broad sense. As any unexpected death would be."

"I see. You're sure that's all?"

"Of course, what else would there be?" Gregory replied. Although his handsome face was devoid of expression, his eyes darted about warily. "Now then, let's talk about something more pleasant." He reached out to caress her cheek as he flashed a broad smile.

Emmeline pressed his hand against her face as love and suspicion warred with each other inside her brain. In the end, she sighed. "Yes, let's. Perhaps if we—" But she broke off in mid-sentence as Nigel passed their table.

"Good morning, Emmeline, Mr. Longdon," he said with a quiet nod.

"Good morning," they replied in unison.

Gregory watched as the other man was seated at a table not far from them. Nigel snapped open a copy of the *Times* and set it before him. However, he must have felt Gregory's gaze upon him because he looked up. In that instant, Emmeline felt as if the two men had silently communicated something to one another. But what? She turned back to Gregory and realized something else as well. His hostility and defensiveness toward Nigel, if not completely evaporated, at least seemed to have abated.

Emmeline knew she should be happy that the two men appeared to be getting on. But she wasn't. One simply didn't change one's opinion overnight, especially when Gregory had taken so strongly against Nigel. No, all her instincts told her that she was missing a vital piece of information. She cast a sidelong glance at Nigel. They both looked guilty. Curiouser and curiouser. *So what are they hiding and why?*

"You and Nigel appear to be more cordial toward one another," Emmeline commented casually.

"I don't know what you mean, love. Shouldn't we be cordial toward each other? Besides, I'm charm personified toward everyone," Gregory replied with a chuckle.

Was this answer a little too forced?

"Ha," Emmeline said as she crossed her arms over her chest. "I very much doubt whether Chief Inspector Ashcroft or Chief Inspector Burnell, for that matter, would concur. For some reason, your charm, as you put it, fails to win over the police to your cause. Quite the contrary, in fact."

Gregory clucked his tongue. "Darling, I'm shocked that you could even suggest such a thing. Where did you get such an idea? It is so far from the truth that it borders on the realm of fantasy."

"Oh, yes?" She arched an eyebrow and bit back a smile. "Then, how do you explain the fact that every policeman you meet wants to put you in prison because he has some strange notion that you're a *thief.*"

"There's that nasty word again." He wagged an admonishing finger at her. "We must do something to clean up your vocabulary. English, after all, is the language of Shakespeare."

"Mmm. I can't think of a more polite word for thief."

He shook his head again. "And you call yourself a journalist. For shame."

Emmeline giggled. "In any case, you promised to find some other form of employment if I'm to accept your marriage proposal. You do remember that, don't you?"

"Wait a minute, love. Let's get our facts straight. First and foremost, you have *already* accepted my proposal."

"Have I?" She tilted her head to one side and put a finger to her temple, making a show of trying to recall something. "Oh, yes, I believe you're right. But it was with the stipulation—"

"Yes, yes." He waved his hand dismissively in the air. "We've been through all that. As you know, I'm a man of my word—"

"Ha."

"Not very elegant, Emmy. As I was trying to say when I was so *rudely* interrupted, I'm exploring several options."

Emmeline leaned her elbows on the table and rested her chin on her hands. "Yes, but thus far you have not told me what those *options* are."

He took one of her hands and kissed her fingertips one by one. "All in good time, darling. All in good time. Who knows? You may be pleasantly surprised by my choice. I might even decide to become a policeman."

Emmeline pushed him away. "Oh, get on with you. Now, you're just being silly."

"No really. Policeman is on my shortlist of careers. I was thinking of asking Chief Inspector Ashcroft for his advice on the matter when he returns this morning to conduct his interviews. He seems like such an amiable chap, don't you think?"

"Despite the fact that he believes that you tried to steal Lady Cabot's necklace?" A shadow darkened his brow for a second time at the mention of Veronica's name, but Emmeline ignored it. "Besides, hadn't you heard? Chief Inspector Ashcroft is no longer on the case."

"No? Why, what's happened?"

"I overheard him telling Mr. Harcourt yesterday afternoon that he was going to call in Scotland Yard, in view of
the Cabots' position. Apparently, some high-flyer from the
Yard—a superintendent, I think—is due to arrive by noon to
take over."

"I see," Gregory murmured, as his eyes narrowed and he
smoothed down the corners of his mustache.

Emmeline sensed the change in his mood. "Anything
wrong?"

One of the corners of his mouth quivered into a half-
smile. "What could possibly be wrong?"

∞∞∞

The two men barely elicited a second glance as they
crossed the lobby and headed straight toward the reception
desk. The older one was slightly shorter with a thickening
stomach, which peeped out every now and then as his unbuttoned suit jacket shifted with each step. At a guess, he
was in his mid- to late-fifties. He had thinning snowy hair
and a neatly trimmed matching beard that molded to the
contours of his rounded face. However, his most arresting
feature was his deep blue eyes. They danced with a fiery
intelligence.

At times, he came across as ruthless because in his job
he had to be. And yet, much to his embarrassment, there
were those who could tell you that he was generous to a
fault, sensitive and kind. His companion was about twenty
years younger. A tall, strapping chap with broad shoulders
and a slim waist. His straight reddish-brown hair fell diago-
nally across his unlined forehead. He wouldn't be considered a handsome man, but he was attractive. His warm,
brown eyes were set wide apart in a long, oval face that
quite often broke into a smile. However, it would be a mistake to underestimate the fellow because behind those plac-
id eyes lurked a sharp mind.

"Good afternoon, gentlemen. How may I help you?" Connie asked with her usual friendly smile.

The older man returned her smile as he reached into his inner pocket and pulled out his wallet. "Good afternoon. I'm Superintendent Burnell," he said as he flashed his warrant card. "And this is Sergeant Finch. May we speak with Mr. Harcourt?"

The smile faded from Connie's lips and a shiver slithered down her spine as she looked from one detective to the other. She lowered her voice to a whisper. "You're here about—about poor Lady Cabot, aren't you?"

Burnell nodded solemnly. "I'm afraid so. We've—"

Connie shook her head and cut him off. "It's all so sad—and shocking. I mean a woman like that—I can hardly believe it. I overheard Chief Inspector Ashcroft say that she was murdered. Is it true? I barely slept a wink last night. You just ask my husband. To think that here in Torquay someone would be murdered." Her hand flew to her throat. "It's shocking. Simply shocking."

Burnell and Finch exchanged looks. "Yes, well, Mrs..."

"What? Oh, my name's Connie Crawford. My husband and I and the children—I have two boys—recently moved down here. I started working here at the Royal Devon two weeks ago. We—"

"Yes, yes, Mrs. Crawford. We'll get your statement with the rest of the staff all in good time. But first, we'd like to have a word with Mr. Harcourt and we'd appreciate it if you wouldn't go around speculating about Lady Cabot's death. This is an active investigation."

Connie's back stiffened. "Yes, of course, but Chief Inspector Ashcroft said—"

"Mrs. Crawford, Chief Inspector Ashcroft is no longer on the case," Burnell remarked, his tone leaving her in no doubt about who was in charge. "Now, we'd like to see Mr. Harcourt."

"If you'll just wait a moment, I'll fetch him," she replied stiffly. Connie scurried toward a door at the other end of the desk and tapped lightly. A muffled voice told her to enter.

When she had disappeared inside, Burnell muttered out of the corner of his mouth, "I hope the rest of the staff's not like that one." He jerked his thumb in the direction of Harcourt's office. "Otherwise, we'll never have a moment's peace. Damn busybody. Have I ever told you how much I hate busybodies?"

Finch stifled a smile. "Yes, sir. Frequently."

Burnell shot him a look. "Yes, well, I'll let that remark pass for the moment. Chief Inspector Ashcroft has a lot to answer for. I knew I didn't like the man when he showed us the crime scene. Too fawning for my taste. What possessed him to open his mouth and go babbling on about the case? Especially when you have someone like that around with big ears and a wild imagination."

"She seems harmless enough. Just a bit of morbid curiosity, I'd say."

"Harmless? Busybodies are never harmless, Finch. They're the bane of a policeman's existence. They're always getting under your feet. I want a peaceful life. Is that too much to ask for? Perhaps I should retire to some nice little cottage in the country and grow marrows."

"You'd be bored out of your mind in ten minutes, sir," the sergeant replied matter-of-factly. He knew Burnell didn't mean a word of what he said. He often spoke about retiring when he was irritated. It was his way of letting off steam. "Besides, you can't retire now. Not after being promoted."

Burnell stroked his beard meditatively. "There is that."

However, further conversation was curtailed when Connie emerged from the office followed closely by a tall, thin gentleman with a dour face, whom the superintendent assumed was Mr. Harcourt.

The man extended a hand to the two detectives. "Good afternoon, I'm William Harcourt, the manager of the Royal Devon. Chief Inspector Ashcroft rang earlier to let me know that you were on your way. I'm placing a small, private conference room at your disposal. But is there anything else you need?"

"We'd like a list of all your guests and staff."

"Of course. Constance, please go print out the lists for Superintendent Burnell. *Now*, Constance," Harcourt said a bit more forcefully when she hadn't budged.

"Oh, right. Straightaway, Mr. Harcourt. I'll be back in a tick."

Harcourt cast a sidelong glance at her retreating figure. "I apologize, gentlemen. Something like this has never happened at the hotel before. We're all a bit unnerved by Lady Cabot's death."

"Quite understandable, Mr. Harcourt. However, we'd appreciate it if you could stress to your staff that they are not to discuss this case at all. There's no need to frighten your guests unnecessarily. And we will try to conduct our inquiries as discreetly as possible and with as little disruption to the hotel's operations."

Harcourt visibly relaxed. "Thank you very much, Superintendent Burnell. I will speak to the staff. Is there any other way that I can be of assistance?"

"Not at the moment. We'll let you know. Thank you."

"Fine. Ah, here's Constance. Thank you." He took the two sheets of paper from her and handed them over to the superintendent. "I'll leave you to it then, gentlemen. Constance will show you to the conference room. I'll have the kitchen send round a pot of coffee and a tray of sandwiches." He nodded to Burnell and Finch.

"Thank you again, Mr. Harcourt. You've been very helpful."

Connie came out from around the desk and led the detectives down the hall. Burnell suddenly stopped and grabbed Finch's arm. "Bloody hell," he exclaimed.

"What is it, sir?"

"Here. Look for yourself." The superintendent jabbed his finger at the guest list.

Finch took the sheet of paper. And then he understood. His eye stopped when it reached a certain name. *Gregory Longdon.* Bloody hell, indeed.

CHAPTER 22

Burnell pinched the bridge of his nose and squeezed his eyes shut. They felt dry and itchy, like sandpaper. He glanced at his watch. Three o'clock. They had been interviewing the staff for two and a half hours.

"I don't know, Finch," he said as he scratched his chin and stood up to stretch his legs. He paced the length of the small room. "We're no further than when we arrived. None of the staff seems to have seen Lady Cabot slip out of the hotel last night. Why? That's what I want to know. Why did she go out? What would make her go out on a night like that?"

"Isn't it rather a question of who was she going to meet, sir? That's the only thing that makes sense."

Burnell stopped his pacing and plumped back down into the chair opposite Finch. "Yes. You're right. A lover? But who? And why go all the way out to Meadfoot Beach? No, someone lured her there."

"Blackmail seems to be the only logical conclusion. As for a lover, her husband's nephew, Trevor Mayhew, fits the bill. I spoke to several of the staff earlier. Apparently, Mayhew accompanied Lady Cabot down to Torquay. They arrived a few days before Sir Frederick and they made no secret of their relationship. Very cozy the two of them were. 'Very tactile' was the way one of the lads on reception enviously described them. And when Room Service brought up breakfast the other morning, the maid caught a glimpse of Mayhew still tucked up in Lady Cabot's bed."

Burnell grunted and took a gulp of the now cold coffee in his mug. "The more I hear about our victim, the more this case leaves a bitter taste in my mouth. However—" He leaned forward and rested his elbows on the table. "—we're not here to like or dislike the late Lady Cabot, just to find out who wanted her dead."

"Right, sir. Shall we get on with the interviews or would you rather stop for the afternoon?"

The superintendent sighed wearily. "No, let's press on. I think we've given Sir Frederick enough time to get over the initial shock, don't you? Let's have him in here. *And* the nephew."

Finch nodded and got to his feet. "I'll fetch them, sir."

ℰↄℰↄ

"You see, Sir Frederick, we were wondering whether you could shed any light on your wife's murder," Burnell said quietly, deferentially almost, as he folded his hands in front of him on the table and fixed his gaze on the bereaved husband's face. This was a studied pose—authoritative, but not threatening—that the superintendent had cultivated over the years. It was meant to put the other person at ease, to loosen his or her tongue. "Why, for example, did she venture out at that hour of the night in middle of a filthy storm?" A faint frown tugged at the corners of Burnell's mouth, as he waited patiently until Sir Frederick was ready to speak.

Finch was at his elbow, pen poised over a notebook. He had a talent for melting into the background. Oftentimes, those being interrogated forgot that the sergeant was even there.

But that suited him very well because it meant that they

let down their guard, allowing him to observe them to determine what was the truth and what were lies.

Sir Frederick cleared his throat, but no words came out. He looked up pitifully at Burnell, whose blue eyes were a shade deeper than his own, and tried again. "Ronnie." There was a catch in his voice as he uttered his wife's name.

Trevor, looking just as miserable beside him, squeezed his shoulder silently. Sir Frederick swallowed hard and sat up straighter in his chair. "Ronnie had difficulty sleeping some nights. She often takes—took—a turn round the garden before coming to bed. It seemed to help."

"I see," Burnell murmured. "That's all very well and good, Sir Frederick. But didn't it concern you that she decided to go on one of her nocturnal jaunts when there was the very devil of a storm?"

"I didn't realize that she had gone out. I was in the shower, you see. Otherwise, I would have stopped her, naturally. When I came out of the shower and saw that she wasn't in our room, I dressed straightaway and went down to the lobby. I can't tell you why. I just had this feeling that something was terribly wrong."

"Mmm," Burnell said, as he stroked his beard.

Sir Frederick hesitated, confused by this noncommittal response. His hand trembled slightly. "I came down to the lobby," he repeated slowly. "I stopped at reception and asked that nice young woman—Connie, I think her name is—if she had seen my wife. She hadn't, but she was very kind. She told me not worry. She said that Ronnie was probably sheltering somewhere, until the storm died down sufficiently for her to return."

"But wouldn't Lady Cabot have called you to let you know? Surely she would have realized that you would be worried."

"Superintendent, our marriage is—was—not like that. I'm a good deal older than she was, and I didn't want her to feel stifled. You don't keep a beautiful, vibrant woman like Ronnie tethered."

"I bloody well would have kept the minx under lock and key with the antics she got up to," Burnell mumbled out of the corner of his mouth so that Finch was forced to look down at his notebook to hide his smile.

"What was that, Superintendent?"

"I said please go on, sir. We need to gather all the facts."

"Well, I decided to wait in the lobby. I thought that at any moment Ronnie would walk through the door. I tried flipping through a magazine, but couldn't concentrate. The words blurred before my eyes. You know how it is. I finally gave up on the magazine and tossed it back on the table. At that point, I realized that I was not alone. There was another guest nearby. She was knitting. I hadn't noticed her earlier because my mind was so preoccupied about Ronnie. I nodded at the woman and we exchanged a few words. Then, we got to talking. She has trouble sleeping too. Her name's Mrs. Dunham. Very pleasant. A widow, I believe. She helped to ease my anxiety about my wife."

"Until what time did you remain in the lobby talking with Mrs. Dunham?"

"It was a little after midnight, I think, when we said good night."

Trevor frowned and half-turned toward his uncle. But before he could say anything, the superintendent chimed in again. "You mean, although you were so worried about your wife, you went to bed?"

Sir Frederick gave a pathetic shrug of his shoulders and ran his hand distractedly through his hair. "I didn't know what else to do. The storm had worsened at that point and it was clear that Ronnie was not going to be returning. My mobile was up in the room and I thought perhaps that she might have rung and left me a message. There was no message. I contemplated going out to look for her, but I had no idea where to start. In the end, I convinced myself that everyone was right and she had found a refuge for the night. So I went to bed. I didn't get wink of sleep, though."

Burnell and Finch exchanged glances. Both detectives

were extremely dissatisfied. If Sir Frederick hadn't had witnesses to attest to the fact that he was indeed in the hotel
last night, he would have made an ideal candidate for the
prime suspect.

The superintendent remained silent for a few moments
gathering his thoughts. His blue gaze shifted from uncle to
nephew. "And you, Mr. Mayhew, where were you last
night?"

"I dined here at the hotel with Nigel Sanborn. He's another guest. We were celebrating the successful sale of
Cabot's magazine division to Sanborn Enterprises."

"Until what time were you with Mr. Sanborn?"

"We finished dinner around nine-thirty. Then, we went
to the bar for a nightcap. I'm a little fuzzy on the time, but I
think it was just after eleven when I got back to my room.
You can check with Mr. Sanborn. I'm sure there were at
least a dozen people who saw us together."

"We intend to check with Mr. Sanborn *and* the dining
room staff. Now, can you tell me when was the last time
you saw your aunt?" Burnell was amused to see Trevor's
handsome face flush slightly at the word *aunt*.

Trevor shifted in his chair. "I hadn't seen her since the
early afternoon. I'm not really sure what plans she had."

"I see." Burnell leaned back in his chair and steepled his
fingers over his ample stomach. "I know Chief Inspector
Ashcroft informed you gentlemen that Lady Cabot was
murdered."

"Yes, he did tell us, but I can't believe it. Who would
want to murder Ronnie?" Sir Frederick murmured.

"That's what I'm here to find out. Did your wife have
any enemies?"

"None whatsoever," Sir Frederick answered without hes-
itation. "Everyone loved Ronnie."

"I'm afraid the fact that she was murdered points to at
least one enemy. Had anything or anyone been worrying
your wife lately? Did she seem preoccupied or frightened?"

"No, nothing at all. Ronnie was her usual self."

"Yes," Trevor said softly.

Burnell cleared his throat and sat up in his chair. "Mr. Mayhew, if you know of anything that can help us find Lady Cabot's killer, I beg you to tell us."

"Ronnie had been receiving phone calls. I don't know for how long. It was several months at least that I know of. I—I happened to be with her on three occasions when she got one of these calls. Whoever it was really frightened her. I snatched the phone from her, but when the chap heard my voice he rang off."

"What?" Sir Frederick exploded, his blue eyes bulging from his head. "Why wasn't I told about this?"

Trevor looked sheepish as he faced his uncle. "Ronnie didn't want to worry you, Uncle Freddie. She said that she could handle the situation." He turned back to the superintendent. "I urged her to ring the police, but she wouldn't. If only I had insisted, perhaps..." His voice trailed off miserably.

"Recriminations are of no use to anyone, Mr. Mayhew," Burnell replied sympathetically. "Do you have any idea what the calls were about?"

Trevor threw his hands up in the air. "I wish I did. I would have wrung the chap's neck. Ronnie was terribly shaken. Each call seemed to frighten her even more."

"I can't believe this." Sir Frederick pounded his palm on the table. "My wife was threatened and you didn't have the decency to inform me. It's unforgivable, Trevor."

"Uncle Freddie, you have to understand—"

"The only thing I understand is that my wife was murdered and you could have prevented it."

⋆⋆⋆

"Well, that was rather interesting, wasn't it, Finch?" Burnell said after Sir Frederick had stormed out of the room, his nephew close on his heels trying to make amends.

"And I thought that this was going to be a boring case."

Finch chuckled. "Yes, sir. Do you think Sir Frederick suspects about Lady Cabot and Mr. Mayhew?"

"I very much doubt it. The poor sod put her on a pedestal. You heard him. She could do no wrong in his eyes."

"Meanwhile, she was carrying on with his nephew behind his back," Finch said significantly.

"Yes, but that still doesn't get us any closer to finding her killer. Or why she was being blackmailed." The superintendent rubbed his eyes and sighed wearily.

"And then there's the other odd piece in the puzzle, sir." Burnell raised a quizzical eyebrow in response. "Longdon. Why is he here?"

"Ah, yes. Our old friend Longdon. Funny how he always turns up like a bad penny when there's trouble brewing. Where's Ashcroft's file? I seem to remember a note he made." The superintendent pulled a buff folder toward him and flicked through a couple of pages. "Here it is." His lips curled into a smile. "Finch, listen to this. Lady Cabot's diamond necklace went missing the other day."

"Really, sir? Sir Frederick didn't mention anything about that. Was Ashcroft able to recover it?"

"Oh, it was recovered all right. But you'll never guess *where* it was found." Finch understood this to be a rhetorical question so he simply waited for the superintendent to tell him. "*In Longdon's room.* In a jacket he'd sent out to be cleaned."

"What?" The sergeant's brown eyes widened in surprise. "Much as I'd like to see Longdon behind bars, sir, that seems a bit careless, don't you think?"

"To my chagrin, I have to agree with you, Finch. According to this file," Burnell tapped the folder with his stubby forefinger, "Ashcroft believed the whole thing was a set-up. He seemed to think that Lady Cabot tried to implicate Longdon for some reason."

"That's interesting. I wonder why."

Burnell's chair creaked as he leaned back. He smiled and

stroked his beard. "Why don't we have Longdon in for a little chat?"

"Yes, sir." Finch grinned as he rose and crossed to the door.

He was startled to find an old woman hovering in the corridor as he pulled the door open. "May I help you, madam?"

"Yes. That is no," she said nervously as she half-turned to go then changed her mind and took a half-step into the room.

Finch shot a questioning look over his shoulder at Burnell.

The superintendent shrugged and stood up. "Perhaps we can be of some assistance, madam?" he asked gently.

"Well." The woman hesitated, unsure of what to do. Her blue eyes flickered from Finch to Burnell. She was tall, but slender and delicate. Her slightly stooped shoulders made her appear fragile, like a fine porcelain figurine.

"Won't you please sit down?" Finch pulled out the chair he had just vacated, before closing the door quietly behind her.

Once she was settled, Burnell tried again. "There that's better," he said with a reassuring smile. "Now, how can we help?"

For a few minutes, the woman didn't utter a word. She simply sat there twisting her fingers mercilessly in her lap, as her steady blue gaze took the measure of them. In the end, she must have decided that they were trustworthy.

She cleared her throat and straightened her back. "You're the ones who have been sent from Scotland Yard, aren't you? To investigate—" Her voice dropped to a whisper even though they were the sole occupants of the room. "—to investigate the murder of Lady Cabot."

"That's right. I'm Superintendent Burnell and this young fellow is Sergeant Finch. Was there something in particular that you wanted to tell us, Mrs...Forgive me, but I'm afraid I don't know your name."

"It's Dunham. Rosemary Dunham."

"If I'm not mistaken, you're the Mrs. Dunham who chatted with Sir Frederick Cabot last night in the lobby. Isn't that correct?"

"What?" Rosemary looked from one detective to the other in confusion. "Yes, but—"

"Around what time would you say, Sir Frederick came down to the lobby?"

"I'm afraid I don't know *precisely*. I was knitting, you see. I've suffered from insomnia for years, ever since my older son died. I usually take a walk before I retire for the evening, but unfortunately I couldn't do so last night because of the storm. I did venture out for a few minutes, but I had to return virtually immediately because it was such an awful night. I wasn't tired at all, so I decided to knit for a while down in the lobby."

"I see," Burnell replied patiently. "So you don't know when Sir Frederick came downstairs?"

"It was lateish. As best as I can guess it was somewhere around eleven, I think. There weren't many people in the lobby at that hour."

"Very well." The superintendent decided not to press the point further for the moment. "You struck up a conversation with him?"

"I believe I said good evening and then we just started talking. You know how it is. I could see the poor man was beside himself with worry, but he was trying to put a brave face on things. I had overheard him asking Connie if she had seen his wife. I tried my best to ease his mind. We sat there chatting. Connie was kind enough to have someone bring us a pot of coffee."

"I see. About how long did you spend chatting with Sir Frederick?"

"Not very long. Sir Frederick was a perfect gentleman and insisted on seeing me back to my room. I know it was eleven forty-five when I let myself back into my room because I happened to glance at the clock radio on the bedside table."

Well, that crossed Sir Frederick off their list of suspects, Finch thought.

Rosemary was speaking again. "But none of this is why I wanted to see you, Superintendent Burnell."

"It isn't, Mrs. Dunham? Do you know of something else that can shed light on Lady Cabot's murder?" Burnell asked curiously.

Rosemary started twisting her fingers in her lap again. "That's for you to judge." Her composure slipped slightly. "I would like to preface it by saying that I'm not a gossip by nature."

"Of course not, Mrs. Dunham. No one would think such a thing. But if you have information that can help with this case," Burnell prompted gently, "it is your duty to tell us."

Rosemary lapsed into silence again and the two detectives saw her wrestling with her conscience. Finally, she nodded her head. "Yes, you're right. A woman was murdered after all. It's just that Emmeline is such a lovely girl and the last thing I would want to do is hurt her. I couldn't bear that. Superintendent Burnell, before I go any further, you must promise me that you won't breathe a word to Emmeline."

Burnell and Finch exchanged looks. "Emmeline? You don't mean Emmeline Kirby, by any chance?"

Rosemary's face broke into a smile. "Yes. Do you know her? Such a dear, thoughtful girl. It's so rare nowadays that you find someone like her." The smile faded from her lips. "That's why what I'm about to tell you is so difficult." She took a deep breath. "The other morning, I was on my way to the lift when—" Rosemary stood up suddenly. "No, this was a mistake. I can't do this. It's wrong."

"Please, Mrs. Dunham." Burnell and Finch got to their feet. "I assure you that what you say to us will be kept in the strictest confidence. You have my word on that. Now, won't you please sit down again?" Burnell gestured toward her chair.

Rosemary bit her lip and then slowly lowered herself back down. Her blue-veined hands gripped the armrests. "You won't tell Emmeline?" Both detectives shook their heads solemnly. "All right, then. The other morning, I was on the way to the lift when I ran into Lady Cabot coming out—coming out of Mr. Longdon's room. It was very early and all she was wearing was a negligée. A very revealing negligée. Clearly, she had been there all night. It didn't take much imagination to realize what they had been doing. Bold as brass, she was. She had no shame whatsoever."

"I see," Burnell mumbled.

"Poor Emmeline. Anyone can see that she's madly in love with Mr. Longdon and he—he's a good-for-nothing scoundrel."

Yes, well, there was no adequate reply. Spot on, he'd have to say. Burnell never would have thought Longdon capable of betraying Miss Kirby but, once again, human nature had proven him wrong.

"I've been trying to avoid Emmeline," Rosemary went on in a rush. "I felt so embarrassed. And as for him—" A deep line appeared between her eyebrows as she frowned. "—well, I can tell you I had a good mind to confront him, but I thought it would only make an already distasteful situation worse. So I've been giving him the cold shoulder."

Burnell and Finch both suppressed a smile. "Of course, Mrs. Dunham. I would have done the same in your shoes," the superintendent said.

"It's all so sordid. But I've been keeping my distance from Mr. Longdon ever since Lady Cabot's body was discovered because I've been afraid."

Burnell's ears pricked up at this. "Afraid? Why afraid?"

Although they were the only ones in the conference room, Rosemary cast a quick sidelong glance to her right and left. She leaned her elbows on the table and licked her lips. "Because I—I think he—That is—I think he killed poor Lady Cabot," she said, her voice barely above a whisper. Her hand flew to her mouth, as if wishing to recall her words.

Burnell stared at her dumbfounded for several seconds and Finch's hand was suspended in mid-air above his notebook.

Burnell swallowed his surprise. "That is a serious accusation, Mrs. Dunham. What would make you say such a thing?"

"Oh, I know, Superintendent Burnell." Her voice cracked and tears welled up in her blue eyes. "It's extremely serious indeed."

The detectives waited for her to regain her composure. "You see, I overheard him threatening Lady Cabot the other afternoon. I wasn't spying and I certainly never meant to eavesdrop. In fact, I very much wish I hadn't."

"Yes, yes, Mrs. Dunham, no one is accusing you of anything," Burnell replied a little hastily. His patience was beginning to wear thin. "Simply tell us what you overheard, as accurately as you can remember."

"Right. They were arguing about something. Mr. Longdon had grabbed her by the arm. I couldn't hear what was being said at first, but it was very heated. From what I could gather, Mr. Longdon threatened to tell Sir Frederick something. I didn't catch what it was. Lady Cabot replied, 'Blackmail is so dirty.' and 'I'll make you pay.' Their voices dropped for a bit at that point. And then—then I heard Mr. Longdon distinctly say, 'I'll see you dead first.' If you had seen his face, there would have been no doubt in your mind that he meant every word."

Rosemary's hand was trembling when she had finished. Her chest was rising and falling. It had taken all her courage to come forward. "I hope I did the right thing by telling you all of this, Superintendent Burnell."

A heavy silence hung upon the air as he stared back at her, stunned. "Yes, Mrs. Dunham. You were quite right."

CHAPTER 23

Finch dispatched Rosemary from the room as politely as he could, all the while trying to reassure her. The second that the door closed behind her, he exhaled loudly.

"Do you think that she was telling the truth, sir?"

The superintendent sighed wearily and shrugged. "What reason is there for her to lie?"

"Yes, what reason," Finch echoed glumly as he plunked down heavily in the chair Rosemary had just vacated. "I never would have pegged Longdon as a murderer. He seems to be above it."

"Yes, well, the law says that every man is innocent until proven guilty. Even Longdon. And we are guardians of the law, so let's not jump to any hasty conclusions, shall we? Get him in here, *now*, Finch. Longdon has a lot of explaining to do."

The sergeant rose slowly to his feet and shuffled toward the door. With his hand on the knob, he stopped and looked back at his superior. "What about Miss Kirby, sir? This is going to come as quite a shock. Isn't there some way we can spare her?"

"We'll deal with that, if and when it comes to it. If we handle this carefully, there's no need for her to know. On the other hand, we can't sweep it under the rug."

"But, sir, doesn't she have a right to know? I mean if he's—"

Burnell slammed his palm on the table. "Finch, we're police officers. Our duty is to uphold the law. Right now, our job is to find out who murdered Lady Cabot. We are not in the business of giving advice to the lovelorn. Do I make myself clear?"

"Yes, sir. Perfectly clear. But Miss Kirby is not just anybody, is she?" Finch said huffily and then flung out of the room before Burnell had a chance to respond.

"No, Finch," the superintendent said to the empty room. "No, Miss Kirby is not just anybody, but we can't play favorites. Unfortunately." He ran a hand wearily over his face. "Some days I hate this bloody job."

☙☙☙

Finch was still seething from his confrontation with Burnell. He admired the superintendent tremendously, felt it was a privilege to work with him, but he couldn't understand why Burnell would keep the truth from Miss Kirby. She had a right to know what a despicable scoundrel Longdon was, before she got too deeply involved with him— *again*. Because that's the direction things were going. The writing was on the wall. Everyone could see it. So why would Burnell want to protect Longdon? The superintendent didn't even like the bloody man. How could he? Longdon was a thief.

Finch shook his head and sighed. One of the porters had said that he had seen Gregory headed in the direction of the conservatory. Right. Time to make the bastard squirm. "Bloody hell," Finch muttered as he pushed open the door.

There across the room he saw Emmeline huddled close to Gregory on a sofa as they enjoyed afternoon tea. She threw her head back and laughed at something Gregory had just whispered in her ear. Finch's face fell. "Why? Why did she have to be here *now*?" This was going to make things much harder. As if they weren't complicated enough to begin with.

Finch threw his hands up in the air in a resigned gesture. There was nothing for it. He had a job to do, as Burnell had said. He squared his shoulders and crossed the room.

"Excuse me, Miss Kirby, Mr. Longdon," Finch said quietly.

Emmeline was the first to look up. Her dark eyes widened for a second and then her face broke out into a smile. "Sergeant Finch? What a pleasant surprise. What are you doing here?"

Pleasant? No, things are far from pleasant, Finch thought.

"Freed yourself from old Oliver's clutches for a holiday break, did you?" Gregory asked in his usual flippant manner.

Finch clenched his fists at his sides and gave Gregory a withering look. "Superintendent Burnell and I are here on a case, Mr. Longdon."

"*Superintendent* Burnell. Well, well, well. When did all of this happen?"

The sergeant tried to keep his temper in check. "The promotion was fairly recent, not that it's any of *your* business."

"Feeling a bit touchy today, are we, Finch?" Gregory said, taking pleasure in goading the sergeant.

Emmeline reached out a patted his sleeve with one of her small hands. "Gregory, that's enough. Sergeant Finch, you said that you were here on a case. You don't mean the Cabot murder, do you?"

Finch's brown eyes widened. "Who said anything about murder?"

"Word quickly spread throughout the hotel that Lady Cabot's death was not the result of an accident."

"I see," Finch murmured.

The mischievous gleam had disappeared from Gregory's

eyes and his mouth was set in a hard line. "I thought that Chief Inspector Ashcroft was handling the case."

"I don't have to give you any explanation. But if you must know, the chief inspector felt that he was bit out of his depth and called in Scotland Yard. So here we are."

"Yes, here you are indeed," Gregory mumbled under his breath.

"Now, if I've satisfied your curiosity, Longdon, Superintendent Burnell would like to have a chat with you—"

"Would he really? Oliver misses me that much does he?"

"—about Lady Cabot's murder."

Emmeline swiveled round. "Why would Superintendent Burnell want to ask Gregory about Lady Cabot's murder? He doesn't know anything about it." There was an edge to her voice.

Gregory slipped an arm around her shoulders and pressed a quick kiss against her curls. "There's nothing to worry about, darling. Oliver just misses me, I told you."

"If you'll follow me, Longdon."

Gregory got to his feet and casually flicked a piece of lint from his sleeve. "Certainly, Sergeant. I'll see you later, Emmy." He bent to kiss her cheek. "Remember, the dinner reservations are for eight."

The two men started to walk away. "Wait. I'm coming too," Emmeline called as she caught up with them. "After all, Gregory is my fiancé. I have a right to be there. We have no secrets from each other."

Finch stopped dead. He shot a look at Gregory. "Fiancé? That's rather sudden, isn't it?"

Gregory flashed a smile at him as Emmeline replied, "Not really. Actually we would have been married two years ago, if certain things hadn't intervened." A shadow flitted across her features and then was gone. "But that's all water under the bridge now. The important thing is that we're back together. Where we belong. Isn't that right, Gregory?"

"Where we belong. No secrets. Of course, darling," he

mumbled distractedly. But she missed the frown that had etched itself across his brow.

❧❧❧

Burnell was pacing the length of the room, his head down, his hands behind his back. He turned at the sound of the door. "You took your sweet time, Finch..." His words trailed off and he swallowed hard. "Miss Kirby, always a pleasure." He extended a hand toward her.

He looked over the top of her head at Finch who shrugged helplessly as he closed the door.

Emmeline shook Burnell's hand warmly. "I hear congratulations are in order, *Superintendent* Burnell."

"Yes, well," the superintendent hedged uncomfortably. "The boys upstairs, in all their wisdom, made Fenton assistant commissioner. I still have to report to the bloody man, so I suppose they gave me the promotion as a consolation prize."

"Rubbish," Emmeline said with a wave of her hand. "It's very well deserved and should have come long ago."

"Thank you, Miss Kirby. Very kind, I'm sure," Burnell replied with an embarrassed smile.

"Do I get to offer my congratulations as well, Oliver?"

The smile vanished from the superintendent's lips when his glance slid to Gregory.

"It's *Superintendent* Burnell. And I see you're as impudent as ever, Longdon."

"What can I say, *Oliver*? You wouldn't like me half as much if I didn't keep you chaps on your toes."

"I never liked you in the first place, Longdon."

"Now, now, Oliver, you know that's not true. Don't get prickly. It's not good for your heart."

There was an impish glint in Gregory's eyes. How he must enjoy these little verbal tussles. Burnell, on the other hand, was far from amused. He could feel a flush rising to his cheeks and he curled his fists into tight balls at his sides. "There's *nothing* wrong with my heart. My health is none of your concern," he said sententiously. "Now then, you've been summoned here because we have a few questions we'd like to ask you in connection with Lady Cabot's murder."

Finch had slipped into the chair by his side and flipped open his notebook.

"I'm afraid you're wasting your time. I can't help you. I didn't know the woman." Although his face still held a slightly bemused expression, the air of flippancy had evaporated.

Since she was attuned to every nuance of Gregory's character, Emmeline was the only who heard the tension in his voice. And this sent a frisson of fear up her spine. "Yes, Superintendent Burnell, I really can't understand why you've called us here," she said. "We ran into Lady Cabot a handful of times, exchanged a few pleasantries." Emmeline bit her tongue on those words. "And that's all."

"Actually, Miss Kirby," Burnell replied patiently, "we only wanted to speak with Longdon at the moment. There's really no need for you to be here—"

"I did try to explain that to Miss Kirby, sir," Finch piped in, "but she insisted on coming. It seems that she and Mr. Longdon are engaged. Again."

"What?" Burnell's deep blue eyes widened in surprise as he slowly turned toward his sergeant, who nodded glumly.

"I see," the superintendent murmured as he tried to recover from this news. He forced a smile on his lips. "May I offer my congratulations, Miss Kirby, Longdon." This last was uttered grudgingly.

"Thank you, Superintendent Burnell." Emmeline had missed the exchange between the two detectives.

"But, sir, don't you think we should—"

Burnell cut him off. "No, I don't, Finch," he countered, his tone edged with irritation. "This is not the appropriate time to bring *that* up."

"Yes, sir," Finch retorted truculently, as he settled back in his chair.

"Miss Kirby, won't you please sit down?" Burnell gestured toward the chair where only half an hour ago Rosemary had been sitting, telling them about Gregory's tryst with Veronica Cabot. "We'll try to make this as painless as possible. All right?" He shot a warning glance at Finch.

"What about me, Oliver? Aren't you going to offer me a chair as well?"

"You can go to the devil, for all I care," the superintendent muttered under his breath, but aloud he remarked, "Do as you wish, Longdon."

"Then I think I'll stand." Gregory pulled out the chair for Emmeline and flashed a cheeky grin at the superintendent.

"Always have to be difficult," Burnell mumbled as he dropped his heavy frame into the chair across the table.

Emmeline stared at the two detectives expectantly. Burnell cleared his throat and smiled weakly at her. "Now, then—Um, yes." He shuffled the file in front of him. "Miss Kirby, are you sure you want to be here? We can get your statement later."

"Quite sure." She nodded emphatically, but the superintendent saw that she held her body rigidly. As if waiting for the other shoe to drop at any moment. Lord, he was going to do everything in his power not to hurt this woman. At least not *too* much. But sooner or later the truth had a way of coming out.

"Right." Burnell became officious. "Longdon, Miss Kirby, how well did you know Lady Cabot?"

Gregory remained silent, but Emmeline answered. "As I said before, we didn't know Lady Cabot at all. We ran into her a couple of times. I gather she is—was something of a recluse. She never liked to have her picture in the papers, which is rather surprising for a woman like that."

"Like that? What exactly do you mean, Miss Kirby?"

Emmeline felt her cheeks suffuse with heat as images of Veronica's laughing face flashed into her mind and her spiteful words reverberated in her ears. "Don't you find it highly unusual for a beautiful woman—" Bile rose in her throat at these words. "—married to an influential man like Sir Frederick to shun the limelight?"

"I see. Longdon, was your relationship with Lady Cabot different than that of Miss Kirby's?"

Gregory's eyes narrowed as he met Burnell's icy blue gaze. What was the man driving at? "I didn't have any relationship with Lady Cabot. It's as Emmeline said. Lady Cabot was a fellow guest. We saw her in the company of her nephew, Trevor Mayhew, a few times. That was all."

"Are you quite sure about that?"

"Positive," Gregory replied stiffly.

The superintendent stroked his beard and contemplated him for several seconds. He opened his mouth to say something and then appeared to change his mind. "Right. You know, it's a funny thing."

"What is, *Oliver*? Tell me. I always love a good joke."

"I want none of your lip, Longdon. This is a murder inquiry. You claim never to have set eyes on Lady Cabot and yet, on two occasions you were overheard arguing, quite violently, with her. I've been given to understand you even threatened to kill her. That doesn't sound to me like you were merely on nodding terms with the woman."

One corner of Gregory's mouth twitched into a half-smile, but the color drained from Emmeline's cheeks. Her mouth felt very dry.

"What do you have to say to that, Longdon?" Burnell pressed.

"Nothing. You've got your facts wrong."

"I don't think so, Longdon. We have reliable witnesses. What were you arguing about?"

"Nothing," Gregory retorted dispassionately.

"It couldn't be that Lady Cabot accused you of blackmailing her over the past few months, could it?"

Gregory threw his head back and laughed. "I'm surprised at you, Oliver. Now, we really are delving into the realm of fantasy. Blackmail? *Me*?" He clucked his tongue and shook his head at the detective.

"So you claim not to know anything about it?"

"I wouldn't even know where to begin, my dear Oliver."

"But I do," Emmeline said. She felt three pairs of eyes suddenly focused on her.

"I beg your pardon, Miss Kirby," Burnell said, taken aback.

"I don't mean that I know about blackmail. However, Lady Cabot and I had a—few words in the lobby. She had been extremely rude to my friend Mrs. Dunham and I called her out on it. I can't abide rudeness. Well, Lady Cabot characteristically laughed off the incident and suggested none too subtly that I should mind my own business. If not, she warned that if I was not careful she, as Sir Frederick's wife, would make certain that I never worked again. Lady Cabot became more irrational and agitated as our argument went on. She started waving her hands about and suddenly seemed to remember a crumpled piece of paper she had balled in one fist. She looked down at it and then at me."

She paused for a moment and closed her eyes as she tried to recall Veronica's exact words. She nodded once and looked at the superintendent again. "She said, 'You're responsible for this, aren't you?' I told her I had no idea what she was talking about. But she wouldn't listen. 'Who else but a nosy reporter would be behind this *and* all the phone calls over the last several months?' Frankly, I thought she had lost her mind. She wasn't making any sense. Then she said, 'You're not going to get away with it. I'll see you burn in hell first.' I must admit, I was beginning to lose my temper at this stage. When Lady Cabot noticed Gregory across the lobby, she became even more inflamed. She asked, 'Did Greg put you up to this? I wouldn't have thought so, but perhaps this is some sort of payback for Rome.' She was quite rattled by the note."

"*Payback for Rome*? Those were her words?"

Emmeline nodded. "Yes, Superintendent. As you can imagine, I remember the conversation quite vividly."

Burnell's lips curled into a smile. "That's very interesting, Miss Kirby."

Gregory bent down and whispered in her ear, "Emmy, why didn't you tell me any of this?"

Without turning to face him, she said out of the side of her mouth, "It was rather difficult. You told me to leave you alone at the time."

"Tell me, Miss Kirby," Burnell went on, "do you have any idea what was in this note that so disturbed Lady Cabot?"

"I can do better than that, Superintendent Burnell. I can *give* it to you. She threw it my face as she stormed off." Emmeline rooted around in her handbag. "Ah, here it is."

The superintendent eagerly reached out to take the piece of paper. He smoothed it out on the table in front of him. "'The blood of Edward Prichard is on your hands. The time has come to forfeit your life,'" he murmured. "Very ominous. Finch, find out who this Prichard fellow was and how he was connected to Lady Cabot."

"I can help you there too," Emmeline said abashedly.

"Can you? You're full of surprises today, Miss Kirby. You wouldn't want to take over the case, would you?"

Emmeline blushed. "No. But the note intrigued me so I rang my friend Felicity in the *Times* research department. Apparently, Prichard was an Englishman who had emigrated to Toronto and somehow wound up as the protégé of a wealthy financier named Henry Cummings. From all accounts, they had a father-son relationship until it was discovered that Prichard was embezzling. Shortly afterward, Cummings was murdered and Prichard was arrested for the crime. There was a sensational trial, at the end of which he was found guilty and sentenced to twenty years in prison. However, he never served his sentence because he committed suicide the very night that the verdict was handed down. I'm afraid that's all that I was able to find out at the mo-

ment. I'm waiting to hear back from a friend of mine at the
Toronto Globe & Mail."

"I'd say that was quite enough to be getting on with,
Miss Kirby. Thank you. You've been very industrious while
on holiday. Now, I'd like to go back to this blackmail business. Longdon, why do you think Lady Cabot was so convinced that *you* were behind it?"

"I'm not clairvoyant. I can't tell you what was in the
woman's mind. Besides, blackmail is such a vile and dirty
game. I wouldn't be caught dead dabbling in it."

"I see." Burnell leaned back in his chair and stroked his
beard. "Speaking of dead, where were you last night between ten and eleven?"

The image of Gregory, trapped for a second in that
damning flash of lightning, as he hurried past her balcony
floated before Emmeline's eyes. Then her mind went back
to yesterday afternoon when he had turned away from her
and followed Veronica across the lobby. They had looked as
if they were having a serious conversation, an angry conversation. And finally, how could she forget the other day on
the terrace when her tea with Sir Frederick was interrupted
by the sound of a heated argument between Gregory and
Veronica?

"Well, Longdon? I'm waiting for an answer. And there's
another thing I've been meaning to ask. That's a rather nasty bruise you've got there on your temple. It makes you
look uglier than usual. How did you happen to come by it?"

Emmeline cleared her throat before Gregory had a
chance to open his mouth. "Oh, Gregory, it's all right. You
can tell Superintendent Burnell. After all, it is the twenty-
first century and we are all adults here." He was standing
behind her chair. She didn't dare turn around to look up at
him because she was certain she would lose her nerve. Instead, Emmeline fixed her eyes on Burnell. "Superintendent, what Gregory is trying very gallantly to do is to protect my reputation, but really it's quite unnecessary. We are
engaged."

She could feel Gregory's eyes boring into the back of her head as Burnell stared at her in confusion. "Miss Kirby, forgive me, but I don't quite understand."

She felt her cheeks warming, probably to a delicate pink hue.. "Y—You s—see," she stammered, "The fact is—that Gregory was with me last night. All n—night. In my room."

Gregory's eyebrow shot up in surprise, but he quickly recovered his equilibrium. He gently rested a hand on Emmeline's shoulder and gave it a quick squeeze. She, in turn, reached up and touched his hand lightly for a brief second. Gregory beamed down at the superintendent, who had clearly not anticipated this answer.

Burnell licked his lips and tried to regain control of this interview. "Miss Kirby, think carefully about what you're saying."

"T—there's nothing to t—think about," Emmeline stuttered nervously. "Gregory was with me all night. Obviously he's too embarrassed to tell you, so I see that I'll have to do it. Like all men, when he got up in the middle of the night, he refused to put the light on and he ended up walking into the bathroom door. Result, nasty bruise. I told you. It's all very simple. Nothing mysterious whatsoever."

Burnell leaned his elbows on the table and rubbed the back of his neck. After a long pause, he finally said, "Miss Kirby, I respect you very much—"

"Thank you, Superintendent Burnell. The feeling is mutual."

Burnell half-smiled. "As I was saying, I respect you very much. Since I know you are a woman of the highest integrity—and would never think of lying to the police—which as you are well aware is a criminal offense—" His hard blue stare made Emmeline squirm slightly in her seat. "Then I must accept your word that Longdon was with you last night."

"I'm happy to hear it. I'm glad that I was able to clear that up for you. So we can go now?" She half-stood.

"You are free to leave, if you wish, Miss Kirby. But I'm not quite finished with Longdon."

"But why?" There was a hint of desperation in her tone. The sudden desire to flee the room overwhelmed Emmeline. "We've told you everything. What else could you possibly want to know?"

The superintendent's gaze shifted to Gregory, whose features were devoid of emotion. "Although I believe *you*, Miss Kirby, I'm afraid I do not have the same confidence in Longdon. I would like to know why he has been lying to us."

"But he hasn't. I told you—" It was a plaintive plea.

Burnell ignored her. "Tell me again, Longdon, how you had never met Lady Cabot until a few days ago. From what Miss Kirby just said, Lady Cabot was convinced you were blackmailing her for—what were her exact words again, Finch?"

The sergeant flicked back through his notes, but they all knew that this was merely for show. "'Payback for Rome.'"

"Ah, yes, *Payback for Rome*. That's a rather interesting turn of phrase. It smacks of familiarity. Revenge tends to be a very personal matter. You have to know a person to seek vengeance. So I'm going to ask you once more, Longdon, did you know Veronica Cabot before you were fellow guests here at the Royal Devon?"

A heavy, uncomfortable silence filled the room. Looming, waiting. Emmeline held her breath.

Gregory looked down at her. From this angle, he could only see her profile. That face he loved so well. "Did I know Veronica Cabot?" A bitter laugh escaped his lips.

Answer him, for God's sake. Answer the bloody question, Emmeline's brain screamed.

Gregory sighed wearily. "The last time I saw her was four years ago. She had a different surname then." He felt Emmeline's body stiffen beneath his hand.

"It was Longdon. She's my *wife*."

CHAPTER 24

Y ou mean *ex*-wife, don't you, Longdon?" Burnell asked, all gruff officiousness. After all the things he had seen over the years, he didn't think anything could shock him anymore. He was wrong. Gregory's revelation had completely knocked him off balance. At his side, the superintendent heard a sharp intake of breath from Finch.

"Well, now, yes, ex-wife, Oliver" Gregory replied impassively. "But at the time she married Sir Frederick, she was still my wife. Never mind how—it's a rather long, complicated story—but I thought she was dead. I filed a swear-death-and-dissolution-of-marriage certificate four years ago, but it was only just issued in January. So as I said, Ronnie was still technically my wife—"

Emmeline leaned forward so that Gregory's hand slipped off her shoulder. Her heart was in her mouth and blood was thundering in her ears. Or was that the sound of her whole world crashing down around her?

My wife, my wife. The words kept going round and round Emmeline's head, making her dizzy.

Burnell glared at Gregory with icy disdain. He slapped his fist against his thigh, hard, in lieu of throttling Gregory, which would have been much more satisfying.

The superintendent turned his attention back to Emmeline, who sat across from him, stunned. It was unnerving how still she was. Not a muscle quivered. Their eyes met and held for a long moment. Behind the sheen of unshed tears, her dark eyes stared back at him, dull and empty. Her fiery zest had been snuffed out and only a shattered, broken shell had been left in its place. It was painful to watch the range of emotions flickering across her ashen face. Burnell reached out to touch her hand, to give her some support, to let her know she was not alone. But at the last second, he recalled their positions. He quickly curled his fingers into a ball and let his hand drop back into his lap.

They were all startled when Emmeline suddenly pushed herself to her feet.

She was surprised that she was able to stand at all. Her legs felt like water. The skin over her knuckles was stretched taut and white as she gripped the edge of the table to steady herself. The room had become stiflingly hot and claustrophobic. She had to get out. To get away. *Far away.* The look of pity in Burnell's eyes was too much to bear. How dare he pity her? She didn't need his pity. She didn't need anybody.

She swallowed the lump in her throat. "Superintendent Burnell, if you haven't any further questions for me, I'd like to go. If that's all right?" It took a tremendous effort to keep her tone even. She rubbed her temples, which were throbbing with a merciless headache.

"Of course, Miss Kirby. There's no need for you to stay," he said quietly as he watched her closely. "Finch," he jerked his head at the sergeant, "why don't you take Miss Kirby to her room?"

"Right, sir." Finch jumped up immediately, ready to be of any assistance.

"No, please, Sergeant Finch." Emmeline held up a hand to stop him. "It's quite all right. You're very kind, but I'd rather be alone—" A tremor in her voice betrayed her then.

She dropped her chin to her chest and quickly tried to skirt around Gregory, who stood between her and the door.

He grabbed her arm. "Emmy, please. Let me explain," he implored.

She shrugged off his hand without looking up and brushed past him as a sob caught in her throat. The door rattled on its hinges as she slammed it behind her.

Gregory lunged for the door and wrenched it open. "Emmy, wait," he bellowed into the corridor.

In an instant, Burnell was at his shoulder and banging the door closed with the flat of his palm. "Let her go, Longdon. You've done quite enough damage for one day."

"Get out of the way, Oliver," Gregory said through gritted teeth. "This is none of your concern."

Burnell laughed but there was no mirth in it. "Do you hear that, Finch? None of my concern, he says."

"Yes, sir." Finch had quietly moved to flank Gregory on the other side, all his senses alert. "Mr. Longdon appears to be under some misapprehension about how the law works."

The superintendent leaned his elbow on the door. His blue gaze was as hard as steel. "I'm conducting a murder inquiry, Longdon. *Everything* is my concern. And at this moment, *you* make a very convincing prime suspect." He took a step closer and poked Gregory in the chest. "Therefore I would advise you, *in the strongest possible terms*, to tread carefully. Otherwise, you might find yourself enjoying the hospitality of one of Her Majesty's prisons."

Gregory snatched Burnell's wrist in a vice-like grip and removed it from his chest. "Hate to disappoint you, Oliver old chap, but I didn't kill Veronica Cabot—"

"You mean *your wife*."

"If you insist," Gregory hissed. "Yes, my bloody wife."

"I don't insist. According to you, that's who she was."

"Arrest me, if you like. That's your prerogative, Oliver. Frankly, I hope you do. It would be rather amusing to watch you make an utter fool of yourself. But just now, my only concern is Emmeline. So get out of my way."

Gregory reached for the knob and had opened the door a crack, but Burnell slammed it closed once more.

"You should have thought about Miss Kirby *before* you set out to seduce her and ruin her life with your lies. I always thought you were a scoundrel, Longdon. However, despite your criminal tendencies, I believed you were a gentleman and truly loved Miss Kirby. Obviously, I was wrong. I never would have dreamed you would sink so low."

Gregory's back stiffened. He blinked twice. His mind was churning behind his cinnamon eyes. "This is becoming tiresome, Oliver. Are you going to arrest me?"

The two men eyed each other warily for several long seconds like rival lions circling one another in the jungle.

Burnell broke the silence. "Not at the moment. But I'd watch my step, if I were you, Longdon."

Gregory yanked the door open. His mouth was set in a tight smile as he clapped the superintendent on the shoulder. "I look forward to the chase, Oliver. I just hope in the end you get over your obsession with me and find Ronnie's killer. Otherwise, we'll all be stuck in purgatory for a very long time."

He turned his back on the two detectives and went in search of Emmeline, hoping against hope that it wasn't too late. Hoping that he could set things right. *Bloody Ronnie*, he cursed. How had he allowed himself to get tangled up with her all those years ago? She was always trouble. Gregory thought that once she was dead, it would all go away. That he would be able to get past the nightmare. That he and Emmy would be able to have a life together. Finally. He was wrong. Even dead, Ronnie was wreaking havoc.

ပာၵာ

The tears were streaming unchecked down her cheeks as Emmeline ran down the corridor. *My wife, my wife, my wife.* She couldn't get away from those two ugly words. They chased her, mocked her. It was a cruel joke someone had played on her. Only there was nothing funny about it.

Her chest heaved as she tried to fill her lungs with air. She stopped and leaned against the wall. Her entire body was trembling. "Why?" It was a pitiless cry.

"*Emmeline?*"

Although the voice was gentle, it made Emmeline jump. She swung round to find herself looking up at Rosemary's lined face, which was creased with concern. "My dear, you're as white as a sheet. What on earth has happened?" Her hand reached out and lightly touched Emmeline's arm.

This kind gesture only served to loosen the floodgates once more. Emmeline's throat ached with tears. She shook her head from side to side. In between choked sobs, she managed to say, "Oh, Rosemary, I don't know what I'm going to do. My whole world has been turned upside down."

"There, there, my dear." The older woman slipped an arm around her shoulders, which were still shuddering. "Look there's a quiet corner over there." She pointed an arthritic finger at a sofa across the lobby. "Why don't we go sit down and you can tell me all about it? All right?"

Emmeline nodded mutely and allowed herself to be led by the elbow. She tucked her head into her chest so that no one else could see that she was crying.

"Now, then," Rosemary said once they were settled on the sofa. "Out with it. I'm sure it can't be that bad."

"Oh, it's worse. Much, much worse." Emmeline took a huge gulping breath. "I discovered something horrible—about Gregory and—and Veronica Cabot."

"Oh, dear." Rosemary's cheeks had gone pale. Her fingers twisted nervously in her lap. "Please believe me, I never wanted you to find out. Superintendent Burnell promised me he wouldn't say anything to you."

Emmeline cocked her head to one side, a confused expression upon her tear-ravaged face. "I don't understand."

"I don't know what this world is coming to," Rosemary muttered angrily. "In my day, when someone promised to keep a confidence, he or she did. I thought Superintendent

Burnell was a man of his word. He promised he wouldn't tell you that I saw Lady Cabot coming out of Mr. Longdon's room the other morning dressed only in a negligée—"

"What?" Emmeline's eyes widened in disbelief as she shakily rose to her feet. "Rosemary, what are saying?"

Rosemary stared back at her in horror at the realization of what she had just done. She stood quickly. "Oh, Emmeline, I thought you knew. I thought that was why you were upset," she spluttered. "Can you forgive me? Please."

Emmeline was silent. She simply stood there, trying to absorb the shock of this latest blow. Then she started laughing hysterically. "You mean it was all a lie. Gregory never loved me at all." The laughter soon devolved into bitter tears. She clenched her fists at her sides. "It was all a bloody game. From the start. They planned to meet here. How could I have been so stupid? They were probably laughing at me the whole time—"

"Emmy, thank God I've found you." It was Gregory. He was hurrying toward them.

Emmeline's head turned slowly. Her eyes became narrow slits. The withering look that she gave him dripped icy venom. "Leave me alone," she snarled as she started backing away. "Don't come near me. Rosemary, you'll have to excuse me."

"Of course, my dear. I'm terribly sor—"

Emmeline brusquely cut her off in mid-sentence. "Never mind. None of it matters anymore." She swiftly pivoted on her heel.

"Emmy, we have to talk," Gregory called after her as she darted across the lobby in the direction of conservatory.

"Hmph," Rosemary sneered contemptuously as he drew level with her. "It seems you've finally got your comeuppance. And not before time. Your sort never learn. Pity you had to tangle Emmeline up in your lies. It's always the innocent who get hurt."

Gregory halted, his cinnamon gaze hard and unrelenting. "I don't know what you said to her, but you'll be sorry you stuck your meddlesome nose where it didn't belong." His voice was low and menacing.

Rosemary blinked twice. She gathered up her handbag from the sofa. "If I were you, Mr. Longdon, I wouldn't hurl threats around like that. It might give people like Superintendent Burnell the wrong idea. After all, murderers cover up their secrets with lies."

CHAPTER 25

Nigel was sitting in the conservatory with a cup and saucer balanced precariously on his armrest as he concentrated on the *Times* crossword in his lap. He tapped his pen against his lips thoughtfully. Number Twenty-Tree Down had stumped him. As he took a sip of coffee to stimulate his brain cells, he felt the air move. Someone had rushed past him in the direction of the French doors.

Nigel craned his neck round and saw that it was Emmeline. Her shoulders were tense and she looked distraught. He put the paper aside and rose quickly. "Emmeline," he called. But either she didn't hear him or she chose to ignore him. That was not like her at all. She was not normally rude. "I wonder what's happened to upset her," he said aloud.

As these words slipped out of his mouth, Gregory burst into conservatory. His eyes darted everywhere as he sliced his way across the room. Grim determination mingled with weariness and, yes, fear, were etched in every line of his face. His jaw was set in a tight line.

Inevitably, his eye fell on Nigel. Without preamble, he asked, "Have you seen Emmeline?"

"Yes, she came through here not two minutes ago and headed straight out onto the terrace."

"Thanks," Gregory said hastily and made to go.

Nigel reached out and grabbed his arm. "Hang on. What's happened? Emmeline looked very upset."

"What's happened? *What's happened?*" Gregory snapped. "Veronica bloody Cabot is what happened. The modern-day she-devil. The plague on mankind. And now, Emmeline knows everything."

Nigel's eyebrow quirked upward in surprise. "Everything. I see," he murmured as his gaze drifted toward the terrace. "But how did she find out?"

A bitter laugh escaped Gregory's lips. "That's the ironic thing. *I* told her. I told the woman I love that the whole time we've been together I was still married. It doesn't matter that I thought my wife had been dead for four years."

"Did you explain that to Emmeline?"

Gregory ran a hand distractedly through his wavy hair. "I didn't have a chance to explain *anything*. She ran out of the room and straight into Rosemary Dunham, who apparently took great pleasure in regaling Emmeline with the fact that my ex-wife and I spent the night together in my room. So you see, just at the moment my life is a bloody shambles."

"Indeed." Nigel nodded his head gloomily. "Shall I go after her and have a quiet word?"

"No," Gregory growled as he shook off Nigel's hand. "No, too many people have been sticking their noses in our business. This is between us. No one else." He started to walk away.

"If there's anything I can do to help..." Nigel's sentence trailed off.

Gregory stopped and glanced over his shoulder. "Be careful what you wish for. I may be needing a lawyer in the very near future."

"Why's that?" Nigel asked, perplexed.

"Hadn't you heard? Apparently, I'm to be cast in the starring role as Veronica Cabot's murderer."

⨯⨯⨯

The honeyed rays of the late afternoon sun dangled tantalizingly from the clouds as the wind's warm breath caressed Emmeline's cheek. She watched, mesmerized, from the top of the cliff as the incoming tide caressed the tawny sand, leaving a frothy trail in its wake as it rolled out again. The next wave thundered forth, chasing the seagulls and two little boys higher up the beach.

Her eyes roamed from jagged rocks slick with foam to the thick woods behind her. She sighed, marveling at what Mother Nature had toiled so hard to create on this earth. It was truly a labor of love. Tears pricked her eyelids. Emmeline swallowed the lump in her throat. There was that word again. *Love*. She couldn't escape it. Why did it have to hurt so much?

Emmeline took a half-step closer and peered over the edge of the cliff. Meadfoot Beach. That was where Veronica Cabot's body had been discovered. Broken. Twisted. *Murdered*. How could a place so lovely have been the scene of something so horrible? And yet, she was glad that the woman was dead.

Some would call her cold and unfeeling. Well, they could sod off. Emmeline felt no remorse, no twinge of guilt. With every fiber of her body, she hated Veronica Cabot. The vile and vindictive witch had it coming. But her death only made matters worse. The bloody woman—*Gregory's wife*—was still haunting her. Emmeline's chest heaved with a miserable sob. *Gregory's wife*. She couldn't fight that.

Her mind was in turmoil. She didn't want to feel this pain anymore. This longing ache in her heart for what should have been. Emmeline impatiently wiped away a stray tear from her cheek and closed her eyes. She listened as the soothing, seductive waves beckoned to her from below. Wouldn't it be wonderful to stay in this lovely place forever? To be carried in and out on the tide. Not to think. Not to feel. *Not to love*. Peace. That was all she wanted. She could have that here. Yes, she was sure of it. Her foot shuffled forward.

"Emmy, watch out."

Her eyes popped open as Gregory's strong arms clamped around her waist and pulled her from the cliff's edge.

"What were you doing?" he asked angrily. "You could have killed yourself."

She stared mutely up at him. For a minute, the past merged with the present and she leaned against his body. And then, Veronica Cabot's laughing face danced before her eyes and she struggled to break free of his embrace.

"Let go of me. I never want to see you again." She pummeled his chest with her fists. But the harder she fought, the more vice-like his hold on her became.

Gregory pulled her toward his chest and kissed the top of her head. He could feel her body shuddering as she cried. "Shh. I love you, Emmy. I never wanted to hurt you. I never wanted any of this ugliness to touch you."

That was the wrong thing to say. "Love me? *Love me?*" It was a primitive growl that came from deep within in her throat. She placed both hands on his chest and gave him a violent shove that sent him staggering backward a few feet.

"Everything that comes out of your mouth is a lie."

"It is *not* a lie. I love you. I've never lied about that. *Never.*"

She tossed her head back and laughed, but it wasn't a pleasant sound. "It's funny you claim to love me so much, and yet it slipped your mind to mention that you have a wife."

Gregory took a step toward her. "Had a wife. Please let me explain."

Emmeline put a hand up. "Stay right there. I'm not interested in your explanations."

"Well, you're going to listen whether you like it or not," he persevered. "I hadn't seen Ronnie in four years."

She snorted. "That didn't stop you from having an intimate family reunion the minute you clapped eyes on one another again. If it's true that you haven't seen her in all that time."

"I deserved that. There's no excuse for it," he said, chastened. "You don't know how sorry I am about that night. I can't forgive myself. So there is no reason why you should. I was a fool, overcome by lust and memories." He rubbed the back of his neck and a harsh laugh escaped his lips. "And the irony of it is, they weren't even good memories." Gregory fixed her with a steady gaze. Emmeline's eyes stared back at him, lost and betrayed. But she was listening. Maybe there was a glimmer of hope for them, after all. He'd have to tread carefully from here on out.

"Perhaps if I wrack my brain," he went on, "I might remember a time when we were happy. It was dangerous and exciting at the start. We were both young and reckless. The days sped by in a rush. Ronnie was so damned unpredictable. I never knew what she would be doing from one moment to the next. She would disappear for months at a time and then return as if she hadn't been gone at all. Years passed by like that. It couldn't last, of course. A relationship like that is bound to burn out sooner rather than later. As it did one gray morning, when I awoke to find myself alone in a Rome hotel room. Ronnie and the—" He swallowed the word rubies at the last second. "She was gone, but the police were banging down my door. I was lucky to make it out of there by the skin of my teeth.

"I searched for her across the Continent for six months. I couldn't find a trace of her. Ronnie had simply vanished off the face of the earth. Then after I had given up on ever seeing her again, I ran across a mutual acquaintance in London. The first thing he did was to clap me on the shoulder and offer his condolences. He asked me how I had been coping since Ronnie's death.

"You can imagine how shocked I was. However, I didn't let on that I had no idea what he was on about. I just let him talk. He said that he had heard the news only two months before that Ronnie's car had been abandoned on a lonely road somewhere in the Scottish Highlands and there had been evidence that she drowned herself in one of those godforsaken lochs that were so deep a body would never be seen again.

"It was all so difficult to digest. Wild, beautiful Ronnie, *dead*. I couldn't believe it. I had to find out for myself what had happened. The next day, I took the train up to the town...Ben something...I forget the name, exactly. I went straight to the police station to enquire about Ronnie. The constable behind the desk remembered the case quite vividly. It was the first suicide in the town's history. He confirmed that they never recovered a body. The only things they found were her handbag and her sweater neatly folded by the water's edge. I thanked the constable and asked for a copy of the file. In the absence of a body to bury, I had to have something to start the long process of having her declared dead."

"How horrible," Emmeline whispered, as she squeezed her eyes shut.

"Yes, well. After I pulled myself together, I realized that my search was over. I vowed that day I would never allow anyone to get that close to me ever again. And it worked. I relied only on myself. It was easier that way, cleaner. Until that rainy day in 2007 when I met you, Emmy. That's when a new world opened up before me. A world of endless possibilities."

Gregory held his breath as he watched her face. She didn't say anything for a long time.

"Did you love her?" Her voice cracked and she chided herself for asking the question. She told herself that the answer didn't matter. And yet, *it did*.

Gregory didn't dare come nearer. He didn't want to chase her away at this stage. "No," he said quietly as he shook his head. "At the beginning, I was deluded enough to think so, but no."

Emmeline swallowed the lump in her throat. "Then why? Why did you ever get involved with her?"

He sighed wearily. "I don't know. Loneliness, I suppose. Emmy, you're the only woman I've ever truly loved. That's the reason I left you the day before our wedding. I loved you too much."

"What?" Emmeline's eyes widened in disbelief. "You loved me, so you *left* me?" she asked incredulously.

"Yes, I know it sounds rather—"

"Insane, mad, daft, crackers. Choose whichever adjective you like," she retorted facetiously. Her body was taut with tension, her fists clenched at her sides. Not a good sign.

"Emmy, please. That day, the day before our wedding, I had been told that the swear-death-and-dissolution-of-marriage certificate wasn't finalized because of some red tape. That was bad enough. Then the other shoe dropped. I happened to be on Piccadilly, already annoyed by this complication, when I thought I glimpsed Ronnie getting out of a cab and darting into the Ritz. I told myself it was impossible. Ronnie was dead. And yet, I could have sworn that it was her. If you live with someone—albeit on and off—for close on ten years, you can't make a mistake like that. You know the tilt of her head, the way she moves. You can single her out in a crowd. I had to find out. My life...*our life* depended on it. If she *was* alive, then how could I declare her dead? Our marriage would still be valid."

"And then you would have to tell me, or were you just going to keep it an ugly secret?" Emmeline asked with disgust.

Gregory sighed. "Just hear me out," he implored. "There's more involved here. I went to the Ritz. There was no sign of the woman in the lobby. I asked at reception if a Veronica Longdon was staying at the hotel. I explained that she was an old friend and she mentioned that she would be in London for a few days. I was politely told that it was against the Ritz's policy to give out such information. Their guests insist upon a certain level of privacy. 'So she *is* a guest?' I persisted. But I was asked to leave. I took up a spot across the road and watched the hotel's entrance for hours. She finally came out again, dressed in an evening gown. The doorman hailed a taxi for her. She disappeared into the sea of cars on Piccadilly. My heart stopped because by that point I was certain it was Ronnie. This realization hit me like a ton of bricks. I couldn't marry you. How could I explain? It was all much too sordid a mess. I thought it would be kinder in the end, if I simply disappeared. Until I found Ronnie and sorted it all out, we couldn't be together. Again, my search was fruitless. I told myself I must have been wrong all along, but by that time it was too late. The search had taken months and I couldn't come back to you. I resigned myself to the fact that I would never lay eyes on you again. And then what happens? Two months ago, you literally fell into my arms down a dark alley in Venice. Well, you know the rest. End of story."

Emmeline's spine stiffened and she gave him a hard look. "*End of story*? You must be joking. Are you forgetting that your dear, departed *wife* was murdered two nights ago right here?" She swept her arm in a wide arc to encompass the cliffs and the beach below. "Not only that, but, in the intervening years, she seems to have picked up a second husband. Now it all makes sense. That's why she never allowed her photo to be taken. She was terrified that by some chance you would see it and come after her. She was living in a house of cards. It was only a matter of time before you found her. And when you did, you invited her to your room for a cozy chat that lasted all night. How the two of you must have laughed at poor, stupid Emmeline's expense."

"It wasn't like that at all, Emmy. You must believe me. Ronnie was already in my room and—"

Emmeline shook her head and waggled her finger at him. "Spare me the sordid details. I'd rather not be sick to my stomach."

In one stride, Gregory had closed the distance between them and snatched her by both arms. He shook her. "I told Ronnie that I wasn't interested in making trouble for her and Sir Frederick, although she was still my wife at the time they married. He was welcome to her. I wanted—want a life with you. As far the law is concerned, Veronica Longdon is dead and our marriage has been dissolved. No one would have to be the wiser. We could both go on our merry way."

Emmeline twisted in his arms. "How perfectly charming. I take it *your wife*—" Gregory winced at this, but she ignored it. "—readily agreed to this proposal?"

"Actually, she didn't. Ronnie said that she couldn't bear to be parted from me ever again. She wanted to go on seeing me, but first I would have to dump you. I refused. I pointed out that she had much more to lose if I went to Sir Frederick. But Ronnie was dangerous. That's when she threatened—"

"Threatened? Threatened what?"

Gregory was silent for a long moment. His eyes raked her features, trying to gauge how she would react when he told her.

"Well? You can't leave me hanging now? It's time to air out all your dirty laundry."

Gregory cleared his throat. "Part of the reason I stayed with Ronnie all those years was because she knew—she knew I had killed a man."

The blood drained from Emmeline's cheeks. "What?" It was barely a whisper.

"I killed a man in Spain in 2005, the year before Ronnie disappeared. I assure you, Emmy, it was in self-defense. He was a drunken lout who came after me with a knife in an alley of the Gothic quarter in Barcelona. The only problem was, he was the scion of one of the country's most prominent families. No one would believe me. Ronnie was there that night. She knew what happened, but she kept the knife with my fingerprints. It amused her to know that she held my life in her hands. You can't imagine what it's been like having this threat hanging over my head for the last five years. But that was Ronnie."

"Is that what the two of you were arguing about in the garden the other day?"

"Yes, and in the lobby after your little contretemps with her."

Emmeline nodded. "When she accused us of colluding together? So you *were* blackmailing her. What does this chap Edward Prichard have to do with any of this?"

"I have no idea who this Prichard fellow is or how Ronnie was connected to him. And I would *never* stoop to blackmail."

"Oh, yes, I forgot. You prefer clean and tidy endings. Blackmail could go on indefinitely. But murder on the other hand, well that could silence a problem just like that." She snapped her fingers in his face. "Although you must admit, that, too, could get messy."

Gregory released her and stepped back, stunned. "Emmy, what are you saying?"

"I *saw* you that night," she hissed. "First, *your wife*—forgive me, ex-wife, I lose track of your notorious marital status—passed below my balcony and then not five minutes later I saw you skulking in the shadows. About an hour later, you came back in the middle of that wild storm but there was no sign of the late, lamented Lady Cabot, née Longdon. Now, tell me again how you got that nasty bruise on your head?"

He blinked twice. "I was going to try one last time to persuade her to agree to turn over the knife. We had arranged to meet that night, but someone coshed me on the head. I never saw the blow coming. When I woke up, Ronnie was nowhere to be found. I assumed she got tired of waiting and went back to the hotel. After all, it was coming down in buckets by then." An uncomfortable silence fell between them. Gregory was the first one to break it. "You can't possibly think—Darling, you *know* me."

"I thought I did. Now, I realize that everything I believed was a lie."

"Is that why you told Burnell we spent the night together? Because you think I killed Ronnie. I may be a lot of things, but a murderer is not one of them. You *know* it."

His shoulders sagged forward, and he suddenly looked older. His eyes held a wounded expression and the lines on either side of his nose appeared deeper. Emmeline's gaze scoured his handsome face, stripping him bare. What she saw before her was a stranger.

"Perhaps, once, I could have said so with certainty, but not now. You just admitted that you killed a man. You *say* it was in self-defense. But how do I know that? I only have your word for it." There was a slight tremor in her voice. "After all, it's not that big of a leap from liar to murderer. Both are steeped in deception and *betrayal*."

She squared her shoulders and thrust her chin in the air, leaving Gregory standing on that lonely cliff top watching, open-mouthed, as the silhouette of her small figure slowly disappeared into the setting sun. Not once did Emmeline look back.

CHAPTER 26

For ten minutes, Trevor had been hunched over the bar, his head hung low as he rolled his whiskey glass between his hands. He wasn't drunk—perhaps that was the trouble. He merely moistened his lips with his drink and then sat staring into its amber depths searching for answers to questions that didn't make any sense. Questions that gnawed at his brain and left him uneasy. No matter which way he twisted it around, it was too much of a coincidence. But if he was right, what did it mean?

He let out a low, pitiful sigh. He *had* loved Ronnie. She was vain and beautiful, a liar and a schemer, but he loved her nonetheless. He would have done anything for her. They understood one another. They were cut from the same cloth. They had to fight for everything, but that made the victory all the sweeter. Trevor frowned in consternation. However, things seemed to change when Longdon appeared on the scene. Trevor vividly remembered that night in the dining room, when he looked up and caught the wicked gleam in Ronnie's green eyes. Like the cat that just ate the cream.

She thought he hadn't noticed that throughout their meal her gaze kept straying to Longdon and Emmeline's table. Trevor had taken an instant dislike to Gregory that night and he vowed to keep Ronnie as far away from the chap as possible. But now, in retrospect, Trevor had the uncomfortable feeling that his efforts had failed. He pushed himself to his feet.

By God, he wanted to wring the fellow's neck. But first things first. He fumbled around in his pocket and tossed some money down on the bar. Then, he strode purposefully out into the lobby. He was on his way to reception. He would get an answer, one way or the other. If a little money had to exchange hands, so be it. There was a girl at the desk. She was just picking up something from the printer and had her back toward him. Something about her was familiar.

"Excuse me, miss. I was wondering if you could help me." But he would never get a chance to ask his question.

"Ah, there you are, Trevor. It's about time you surfaced." Sir Frederick Cabot, his distinguished features marred by sadness and a lack of sleep, was headed straight toward his nephew.

"Damn," Trevor muttered under his breath. Aloud he said, "Yes, Uncle Freddie?"

When Sir Frederick drew level, his eyes roamed over his nephew. "Where the devil have you been all afternoon? I had Parker on the phone three times about the Sanborn acquisition. I told him you were handling the matter, but he said he couldn't get in touch with you."

"Sorry, Uncle Freddie," Trevor replied noncommittally.

"It's no good being sorry about it," Sir Frederick grunted. "I expect you to take care of it. If you can't handle the job, I'll give it to someone else. I can't be bothered with all that right now. Not with Veronica barely cold." These last words caught in his throat and it took him a moment to get his emotions under control.

Trevor knew just how the old boy felt. He put a hand on his uncle's shoulder and gave it a reassuring squeeze. "We—everyone loved her, Uncle Freddie. She touched everyone she met."

Sir Frederick violently shrugged off Trevor's hand. "But she was *my wife*. Don't forget that."

His nephew was stunned by this reaction. "No, of course not. No one is forgetting that fact."

"Your behavior says otherwise," Sir Frederick remarked frostily.

"If this is about that blackmail business—"

"If? Why wasn't I told about it?"

"Ronnie didn't want to worry you unnecessarily. She swore me to secrecy. She thought the whole thing would blow over."

"How dare the two of you decide what I should and shouldn't be told? I was her husband." Sir Frederick's voice was low and shook with anger. "I had a right to know if my wife was being threatened by some deranged lunatic, who ended up killing her. If I had known, I could have protected her. She would never have ventured out that night. But the two of you robbed me of my right. What else were the two of you hiding?"

Trevor squirmed under the icy blue intensity of Sir Frederick's gaze, which was so similar to his own. His uncle couldn't possibly have known about his affair with Ronnie, could he? They had been so careful. At least he'd tried to be discreet, for the old boy's sake. However, he had to admit that Ronnie was reckless and loved to dance with fire. Trevor swallowed hard. He'd have to broach the matter delicately because his uncle was rather prickly at the moment. He cleared his throat. "Uncle Freddie, there's something I've been meaning to ask you about what you told Superintendent Burnell. It rather confused me."

"What are you driveling on about? Don't think you can change the subject."

"I'm not trying to change the subject, Uncle Freddie. I'm simply trying to get things clear in my mind about the night that Ronnie was—was murdered."

"Well, what is it?" Sir Frederick countered irritably.

"You said that you became anxious and came down to the lobby in search of Ronnie." His uncle nodded. "And then you decided to hang about and wait for her. In the interim, you struck up a conversation with another guest, a Mrs. Dunham."

"Yes, that's right. A very nice woman. But I really don't see what you're driving at."

Trevor rubbed the back of his neck. "The devil of it is— What I mean is, I was wondering whether—"

"Sir Frederick, I'm terribly sorry to interrupt." It was Mr. Harcourt, the hotel manager. He was barreling down on them. He inclined his head toward Trevor. "Mr. Mayhew, good evening. I'm afraid I must have a word with your uncle."

"It's quite all right, Mr. Harcourt," Sir Frederick replied affably. "We were quite finished with our conversation, weren't we, Trevor? See to it that you call Parker and straighten out the Sanborn acquisition."

Trevor sighed. "Yes, Uncle Freddie. I'll get onto it straightaway."

"Good. Now, Mr. Harcourt, my attention is all yours. How can I help you?"

"Well, you see sir—" The rest of their conversation died away as Harcourt led Sir Frederick toward his office.

Trevor pursed his lips and shrugged. Oh, well, he would have to try again later. At the moment though, he had better go to his room and ring London to see what Parker wanted. He crossed the lobby and punched the button for the lift.

He slipped his hands into his pockets and contemplated his feet as his mind mulled over his conversation with his uncle. There was a lot of damage to mend. He hoped it wasn't irreparable.

Ding. Trevor looked up when the doors slid open. His eyes widened in disbelief. "Good God, it's *you*."

౭౧౭౧

Superintendent Burnell impaled a defenseless sausage with his fork, studied it for a moment, and put it back down on his plate. Then, he pushed the plate away. His scrambled eggs had already gone cold. When he had woken up this morning, he had been ravenous. It was not surprising considering that he hadn't eaten anything since the tuna mayonnaise sandwich he had hastily wolfed down yesterday afternoon before that disconcerting interview with Gregory and Emmeline. If this case went on much longer, he might end up losing some weight. At least, his doctor would be pleased about that.

Damn, this case, Burnell thought. The thing that kept running through his mind was the image of Emmeline's face when Gregory said that Veronica Cabot was in reality the ex-Mrs. Longdon.

"I've never hated a case more in my life, Finch. I hate everything about it. Everything," he spat in disgust as his sergeant watched him take a sip of coffee.

"Yes, sir. It's been very...enlightening." Finch was just as disturbed as his boss. His full English breakfast remained untouched.

"Too bloody enlightening in some respects, but it hasn't brought us any closer to finding Lady Cabot's killer."

"So you don't believe it's Longdon?"

Burnell's exhaled wearily. "God knows I *want* it to be Longdon. To see that scoundrel behind bars, where he should have been long ago, would be a triumph."

"He had motive," Finch pointed out. "He wanted to keep his marriage a secret from Miss Kirby."

"Can you really picture Longdon resorting to blackmail *and* murder? It's simply not his style. Very messy. And the chap's far too smooth and cunning."

"On the other hand, time and time again, we've come across those precise qualities in a murderer."

"Yes, but for Miss Kirby's sake, I hope it's not him."

"Miss Kirby," Finch murmured as his brow wrinkled. "You don't think she would take him back, do you? Not after everything we've discovered. I mean she's finally had her eyes opened to the kind of man Longdon really is."

"I've learned never to second guess women. They have an uncanny ability to surprise you. And Miss Kirby, well, we both know that she is—different." He had been about to say *special*, but caught himself at the last moment. He didn't want Finch thinking he'd gone soft. Burnell had a certain image to maintain. However, he suspected that he and the sergeant both had a tender spot for Emmeline, although neither one would ever admit it. There was just something about her that got under one's skin.

They both fell into a troubled silence. Burnell swirled the dregs of his coffee round and round in his cup, while Finch stared off into space. The superintendent suddenly groaned.

"What is it, sir?"

"I'm not looking forward to telling Sir Frederick that his marriage was a sham."

"Oh, yes. I'd been so focused on Miss Kirby and Longdon that I'd quite forgotten about Sir Frederick. How do you think he's going to take the news?"

Burnell threw his hands in the air and shrugged his shoulders. "Your guess is as good as mine, Finch. Well, no use putting it off." He signaled to the waitress who brought their bill. The superintendent signed it and they slowly got to their feet, girding themselves for the day ahead.

They had reached the lobby when Burnell's mobile started to squeal in his jacket pocket. "Burnell," he barked down the line. He listened for a few seconds and then an eyebrow shot up. "I see. That's very interesting. Thanks, Ashcroft. I'll have Finch drop by the station to fetch the file."

He snapped the phone shut and turned to his sergeant. "As you've gathered, that was Chief Inspector Ashcroft. Apparently, Sir Frederick changed his will shortly after his marriage, leaving his entire fortune to Lady Cabot upon his death."

"Surely, that's not unusual. She was his wife. Well, he *believes* she was his wife."

"No, it's not unusual." The corners of Burnell's mouth curled into a smile. "But what's interesting is that before Sir

Frederick met Lady Cabot/Longdon, his nephew Trevor Mayhew was his heir, lock stock and barrel. Under the new will, Mayhew only inherits if Lady Cabot predeceases him."

"Ah," Finch said. "Do you think he could have killed her? Ashcroft told us that Mayhew and Lady Cabot were having a not-so-discreet affair. Could it have been a ruse on Mayhew's part to get Lady Cabot out of the way and his hands on the money?"

"There's only one problem with your theory, Finch. Sir Frederick is still alive."

"Yes, but perhaps Mayhew killed Lady Cabot first to throw off suspicion and, in a few months' time when the dust settles, the old boy will meet with an accident or die in his sleep one night and no one would be any the wiser."

Burnell nodded. "It's possible. And yet, I don't think it's that simple." His brow puckered into a frown. "There's something else going on here. Something larger."

"But what, sir?"

"I can't quite place my finger on it, but I can feel it right here." The superintendent patted his balled fist against his ample stomach. "I just know it."

"If you ask me, I'd say either Longdon or Mayhew could have killed Lady Cabot. Neither one has an alibi."

"You're forgetting that Longdon has an alibi. Miss Kirby insists that he was with her *all night*," Burnell said pointedly.

"Oh, come on, sir. We both know that's a lie. It's obvious she was covering for him. Even Longdon looked surprised. But perhaps now that Miss Kirby knows about Longdon and Lady Cabot, she'll change her story."

"I doubt it. She's already hurt and humiliated."

"All the more reason to throw Longdon to the wolves and have done with him once and for all."

Burnell clapped the sergeant on the shoulder and gave him a piteous look. "Finch, sometimes I despair of you and your powers of observation. Miss Kirby will never be done with Longdon. She loves him. Always has. She will never stop loving him. Ah, ah—" He put a hand up to stop the protest percolating in the sergeant's throat. "It's no good arguing the point. What such an intelligent woman sees in that rake I'll never understand, but there it is. We can't change it, much as we'd like to."

"No, I suppose you're right, sir."

"However, you realize that knowing this only makes our job that much harder. Because if Longdon *is* the murderer, Miss Kirby is never going to accept it and she's going to fight us tooth and nail. And we know first-hand how she can get when she's pursuing a story."

Finch's lips twisted into a half smile. "Yes, sir. Like a bull dog. With a temper. She never lets go."

"Indeed. I'm not looking forward to that prospect. So I suggest that you pop along to the station and get that file from Ashcroft. Then have a little chat with Mayhew and try to sound him out about the will. Tactfully, of course. In the meantime, I'll go and inform Sir Frederick that he was not legally married to his wife. Lucky me." Burnell pasted a smile onto his face. "Now, why is it that people are always chuntering on about the perks of the job and rubbing shoulders with those in high places? I certainly do not consider this a perk. In my opinion, this whole case is like being pitched into the center of a volcano that's about to erupt."

Finch stifled a smile. "Good luck, sir."

CHAPTER 27

Superintendent Burnell found Sir Frederick out on the terrace, elbows resting lightly on the arms of his chair as he tapped his steepled fingers to his pursed lips. His blue eyes roamed over the cliffs and the cove without really taking in their beauty. A copy of the *Times* lay unopened in his lap.

As the superintendent approached, Sir Frederick's shoulders trembled slightly as a sigh shuddered through his body. His head drooped forward, shaking from side to side as if he was answering some internal voice. It struck Burnell that Sir Frederick suddenly looked all of his seventy-two years. He no longer cut the dashing figure of *a man of a certain age*. Just an old man who was grieving for his wife.

"Excuse me, Sir Frederick," Burnell said quietly. "I'm terribly sorry to intrude, but I was wondering whether I could have a word with you."

Although he had kept his tone deliberately gentle, Sir Frederick still jumped. "Oh. Oh, it's you, Superintendent Burnell. I'm sorry. My mind was a million miles away." He waved a hand toward the empty chair next to him. "Please sit down."

"That's quite understandable," Burnell replied as he eased his bulk into the seat. "You have a lot on your plate at the moment. And I'm afraid I'm not going to help matters.

You see, we've discovered something..." How should he put this delicately? His mind struggled over the right words.

Sir Frederick sat up straighter. "Something about Veronica's murder? You've found her killer?"

His eyes eagerly searched the superintendent's face, hoping to divine the answer. There was something else in that gaze. What was it? Fear? Trepidation?

"No, not yet, sir. We're still working on that aspect of the case."

"Oh." Sir Frederick's shoulders sagged and his attention strayed back toward the water. "Then, I'm at a loss to understand."

Burnell cleared his throat and plunged right in. "In the course of our investigation, we've discovered that—that you and Lady Cabot—were not legally married."

Whatever Sir Frederick had expected, it certainly was not this. His head snapped back so hard that the superintendent wondered whether he had done himself an injury.

"What the devil are you playing at, Burnell? What do you mean that Veronica and I weren't legally married?"

"I'm afraid," Burnell continued calmly, "that Lady Cabot was already married. Had in fact been married for nearly ten years—to Gregory Longdon. Their marriage hadn't been dissolved at the time of your—nuptials. It was only finalized two months ago."

"What?" Sir Frederick's blue eyes burned with anger. The hand that gripped his knee was white, the skin stretched taut across the back of his knuckles. "You're mad. That's the only explanation there can be for this...this..."

"I know it must come as something of a shock—"

Sir Frederick cut him off. "*Shock*? It's a bloody lie. Why would you say such a thing?" His voice was starting to rise, attracting the attention of some of the other guests sitting nearby.

Burnell cast a quick glance over his shoulder. "Perhaps, we should continue this discussion at another time, Sir Frederick, when you've had a chance to digest the information. I assure you it's the truth. We've checked."

Sir Frederick slumped back in his chair, suddenly deflated. "I don't understand," he murmured. "Veronica—I don't understand. Did she care for me at all? Or was she only after my money? I wasn't egotistical enough to believe that she could love an old man. That's why I tolerated her—her liaison with Trevor." Burnell's eyebrows arched up in surprise at this. "However, I thought at the very least she cared about me and enjoyed my companionship. Goodness knows I gave her everything she wanted. Everything. But Ronnie and—and *Longdon*. It's simply too much to bear." He shook his head in confusion.

An uncomfortable silence fell in the space between them. The superintendent was the first to break it. "Since you mentioned your nephew, I have a few questions about—"

Sir Frederick stood up abruptly. "You'll have to excuse me, Superintendent. As you can imagine, what you have just told me has come as a tremendous shock. I need some time alone."

Burnell got to his feet as well. "Of course. Perhaps I could meet with you and Mr. Mayhew this afternoon?"

Sir Frederick waved a hand dismissively. "Yes, yes. But for God's sake, *not now*." He was already walking away.

Burnell watched him hurry across the terrace, his stride clipped, his shoes clicking hollowly against the flagstones. As he stood there silently stroking his beard, the superintendent wondered what the man was hiding. *Or who he was protecting?*

∽∾∽

Emmeline heard the knock on her door. Again. This was the fourth time. But she didn't stir from the chair on her balcony. She knew who it was even before the muffled voice called, "Emmy, please open the door. We need to talk."

She stared out at the water, which shimmered as the late morning sun tiptoed across the surface.

"You can't barricade yourself in there forever. You have to come out sometime."

Do I? Emmeline asked silently. *What possible reason could there be?*

"Emmy, I love you. Please open the door," he replied as if he had read her mind.

A single tear slipped out from the corner of her eye. She impatiently swiped at it with the back of her hand. In doing so, her gaze fell on the gold knot bracelet dangling from her wrist. The bracelet Gregory had given her so long ago. The bracelet she always wore. The salty ambush of more tears assailed her.

Love? What about your dead wife? Did you give her *a bracelet as a token of your affections too?*

"I have nothing to say to you. Go away," Emmeline said at last, her throat swollen with emotion. "Just leave me *alone.*"

☙❧

Sergeant Finch thanked the clerk politely and turned away from the reception desk. A perplexed expression creased his features as he tapped his notebook against his open palm. He had only walked a few steps, when Burnell cornered him. "Finch? *Finch?* I'm sure your daydreams are quite enticing, but can you spare your attention for a few moments on the case?"

"What?" The sergeant looked up, startled. "Oh, sorry, sir. I was distracted."

Burnell fixed his gaze on Finch. "That was obvious. Now, did you get the file on Sir Frederick's will from Ashcroft?"

"Yes, yes. Here it is." Finch pulled it out from under his arm. "It's just as Ashcroft told us earlier. Until Sir Frederick married Lady Cabot, Mayhew was his sole beneficiary."

The superintendent took the file and flicked through its contents quickly. "What did Mayhew have to say when you questioned him?"

"Nothing."

"What do you mean nothing?" Burnell asked irritably.

"I never had a chance to speak with him. Apparently, Mayhew's checked out. He left in a hurry early this morning. He had been booked in until the end of the week."

"Checked out? In the middle of a murder inquiry? Well, well. Human nature is a fascinating thing. Now, why do you suppose he would leave in such a rush when his dead lover is barely cold in her grave? What could be more important than finding her killer? If he loved her, that is."

"Perhaps, it became too much for him. After all, we didn't explicitly say that he *had* to remain in Torquay. Mayhew must have told Sir Frederick where he can be reached."

"Speaking of Sir Frederick, one or two interesting points came up during our conversation." Out of the corner of his eye, Burnell caught a glimpse of Connie hovering nearby ostensibly checking the computer. But her head was tilted just that little bit to one side that it made it clear that she was straining to hear what they were saying. He slipped his arm around Finch's shoulder. "Here, come with me, and I'll fill you in," he said as he maneuvered the sergeant to the other side of the lobby and out of earshot.

∽∾∽

The lift doors slid open with a *ding* and a swish, disgorging Sir Frederick into the lobby. It barely registered that he had bumped into one of the other guests, who gave him a dirty look. On the other side of the lobby, he saw Burnell and Finch deep in conversation, their heads bent close together. Jarring thoughts roiled his brain. And they all had to do with Gregory. *Bloody Longdon*, Sir Frederick cursed inwardly. He ran a hand through his crisp white hair. For a man who prided himself on always being calm and in control, he suddenly felt all at sea.

"Excuse me, Sir Frederick. Are you all right?" Connie had materialized at his elbow, her blue eyes full of concern.

He blinked at her in silence and then gave a slow, weary shake of his head. "I—No, I haven't been all right since my wife died. My whole world is in utter chaos and—" He broke off in mid-sentence, his attention arrested the minute Gregory stepped out of the lift. Sir Frederick's jaw clenched into a hard line, the muscle convulsed beneath his skin. "And it all has to do with *that* man."

"Mr. Longdon? Whatever does he have to do with any of this?" Connie asked.

Sir Frederick turned back to face her. He met her gaze frankly and was silent for a long moment. Then he gave her forearm a gentle squeeze, as if he were patting a dog on the head in dismissal. "Forgive me, dear. You'll have to excuse me." And he started to walk away.

"But, Sir Frederick," Connie called after him. "I really don't think it's wise to quarrel with Mr. Longdon, whatever it may be about." But her entreaties bounced off his stiff shoulder blades and were swallowed up into the ether.

She frowned and pinched the bridge of her nose. There was nothing for it. With a shrug of resignation, she returned to the reception desk.

The minute Gregory set foot in the lobby, the hairs on the back of his neck prickled. First, he caught a glimpse of Burnell and Finch huddled together in a corner. Then Sir Frederick came into his line of vision. Damn. The man had seen him too and was stalking toward him.

Gregory steeled himself for the inevitable confrontation. "Canons to the right of me. Canons to the left of me. Into the Valley of Death rode Gregory Longdon," he muttered under his breath.

"Longdon, I'd like a word with you," Sir Frederick said in clipped tones as he drew level.

"Certainly, Sir Frederick," Gregory replied as pleasantly as possible under the circumstances. "How can I help you?" He attempted to defuse the situation by forcing his lips to curl into a smile.

"Let's drop the pretense, shall we, Longdon?"

Gregory's eyebrow quirked upward. "And exactly what pretense would that be?"

"You know very well what I'm talking about," Sir Frederick growled as his hands flexed and unflexed at his sides. "It's about my wife and *you.*"

Gregory straightened his spine. The smile vanished. He felt rather than saw Burnell and Finch watching him. He would have to tread carefully. "In the interest of accuracy, I believe you mean *my* wife, don't you? Your marriage wasn't legal. At the time, she was still technically my wife."

Sir Frederick's eyes narrowed and his blue gaze shot daggers at Gregory. "So you admit it."

"At this stage, there is no reason to lie. It's a matter of public record," Gregory said dispassionately. "If it's any consolation, I hadn't seen Ronnie in four years. In fact, I thought she had died."

Sir Frederick took a step closer to Gregory. They were virtually the same height. "I don't give a bloody damn what you thought." His voice dripped ice. "Whatever you were scheming, you had better forget it. I'm wise to you now and I'm going make sure you get everything that's coming to you."

One corner of Gregory's mouth twisted into a smile, but he held his ground. "I'd be careful if I were you, Sir Frederick. That sounds very much like a threat and I don't take kindly to threats. So you had better—"

"Longdon, what's going here?" Burnell said.

Gregory flashed a cheeky grin at his old nemesis. "Oliver, old chap. Finch." He inclined his head at the sergeant. "It's always nice to see you both. Been enjoying your little sojourn here in Torquay? Oh, no, I forgot." He snapped his fingers. "This is more of a working holiday for you, isn't it? Pity that."

The superintendent's cheeks flushed and he replied through clenched teeth, "I hope you weren't harassing Sir Frederick."

"Me?" Gregory put a hand to his chest in mock surprise. "I wouldn't dream of it, Oliver. We were simply exchanging our views on current events and had a minor difference of opinion, isn't that right, Sir Frederick?"

The older man held his body rigidly and for several seconds couldn't bring himself to utter a word. One hand trembled at his side. "*You.*" It was a guttural snarl ripped from his throat. Then, he seemed to remember himself and his surroundings. He squared his shoulders and swallowed hard. "This isn't over, Longdon."

He shoved Gregory aside before the last vestiges of his self-control deserted him.

The two detectives watched Sir Frederick's retreating back as he stalked off toward the conservatory. Once he had disappeared round the corner, Gregory found two pairs eyes, one blue and one brown, studying him intently.

To be the subject of such fervent scrutiny would have unnerved anyone else, but not Gregory. He relaxed and smiled. "Well, chaps." He rubbed his elegant hands together. "I don't know about you, but it'll be lunchtime in a couple of hours and I'm famished. I discovered a great little pub in town the other day. Why don't you join me and we can have a good old chinwag to catch up? What do you say?"

"You must be joking," Burnell replied, watching the mischief dance in Longdon's eyes as they flitted between him and the sergeant. "I'd rather join Socrates for a heaping bowl of hemlock."

"I assure you that the pub meals are a far sight tastier and the company will be a good deal more stimulating."

"Stimulation is the last thing that I need at the moment,

Longdon. Especially from you. I have a murder inquiry to conduct."

Gregory clucked his tongue and shook his head. "I'm disappointed, Oliver—"

"*Superintendent* Burnell. Will you *never* learn?"

Gregory shrugged nonchalantly and turned his attention to the sergeant. "Finch, you'll join me, won't you?"

Finch sneered. "Not bloody likely."

Gregory affected a crestfallen expression. "If I didn't know better, I'd say you didn't like me. But we all know that's far from the truth."

The corners of Burnell's eyes crinkled as he laughed. "Truth? You wouldn't know the truth if it was dangling in front of your face. Now, go off and find someone else to annoy. But mind you—" He lowered his voice. "—don't wander off too far. We'd like to have another chat with you. Finch and I have a whole list of questions to ask about you and Lady Cabot—uh, Longdon—and the night she was killed."

"I wouldn't miss it for the world, *Oliver*." Gregory reached out and straightened the superintendent's collar and plucked a piece of lint from his sleeve. "I'll be counting the minutes until our next *tête-à-tête*."

Burnell snorted. "Hmph. Come on, Finch. I need some air."

"Cheery bye, then." Gregory gave them a cheeky little salute, which they ignored.

As soon as the two detectives were gone, his irreverent mood evaporated. He stood there in the middle of the lobby, arms folded over his chest, the wheels of his brain clearly spinning, and his attractive features twisted into a black scowl. It sent a shiver down Connie's spine as she watched him from the reception desk. Until that moment, she hadn't realized Gregory was a dangerous man. A very dangerous man.

CHAPTER 28

Sir Frederick, I'm afraid you can't keep avoiding us," Burnell said as he and Finch loomed over the older man's table.

"What now, superintendent? Can't a man even enjoy a late breakfast in peace? Is nothing sacrosanct to you chaps? Do your superiors know how you hound innocent people?"

"Naturally, we apologize for any intrusion, sir, but we are investigating your wife's murder. I would think that you, of all people, would want us to carry on. You *do* want your wife's killer brought to justice, don't you?"

"Wife. Ha," Sir Frederick replied bitterly. "It seems that my life for the last eight months has been a charade. What I thought to be the truth was..." He allowed this thought to trail off, shrugged pathetically, and shook his head. "Well, it doesn't really matter now. It's not going to change anything. Forgive me." He waved a manicured hand toward the empty chairs opposite him. "Please sit down. Ask me whatever you like."

"Thank you, Sir Frederick, for understanding that we are simply doing our jobs," Burnell said deferentially as he and Finch slipped into the seats indicated.

The waitress appeared and Sir Frederick turned to the two detectives. "Would you like some coffee or breakfast?"

"Coffee would be lovely, Sir Frederick. Thank you," the superintendent responded. Sir Frederick nodded.

Burnell waited for the waitress to leave. "Now then, sir," he started as Finch casually flipped open his notebook. "There are one or two points we'd like to clarify. According to your statement, while you were taking a shower, Lady Cabot left your room."

"That's right. I didn't find it odd at all because, as I told you, Veronica had trouble sleeping and often took a walk before coming to bed. But when the storm started intensifying and she still hadn't come back, I began to become concerned. That's when I went down to the lobby."

"Yes," Burnell said quickly. "Mrs. Crawford, the girl at the reception desk that night, and Mrs. Dunham have corroborated your statement."

"Then I fail to see how going over it all again helps."

"Forgive me if this sounds indelicate, but we were wondering whether at some point before you went downstairs you stopped by your nephew's room."

"Trevor's room? No. Why would I pop over to Trevor's room? I was looking for my wife—Oh, I see." Sir Frederick stiffened and his face darkened. "If you're asking me whether I was spying on my wife, the answer is no. I knew my wife and Trevor were having an affair, yes. But I had no desire to confront the two of them like some outraged husband in a Victorian melodrama."

"So, that night, it didn't even occur to you that she might be with Mr. Mayhew?"

"No, it did not. Ronnie was discreet. She would never rub my nose in it like that."

Burnell and Finch exchanged glances.

"I see," Burnell murmured. "What was Lady Cabot's relationship with Mr. Mayhew like?"

"I beg your pardon, Superintendent." Sir Frederick had trouble keeping his voice even. "What the devil do you mean by asking me something like that? Isn't it obvious what kind of a relationship they shared?" His breathing was very rapid and ragged.

"You mistake my meaning, sir," the superintendent replied soothingly. "How did Lady Cabot and Mr. Mayhew get on?"

Cabot scratched his head in confusion. "They—they got on fine. I don't understand what you're getting at."

"Please bear with me, Sir Frederick. To your knowledge, did their affair begin before or after you changed your will and made Lady Cabot your sole beneficiary?"

"My *what*? How dare you? You people have no right to go digging into private matters." Sir Frederick stood up abruptly.

"Please sit down, sir," the superintendent said firmly. "In a murder investigation, we have a right to pursue *any* line of inquiry that might lead us to the killer."

"Yes, but—but," Sir Frederick stammered.

"The most common motives for murder," Burnell went on calmly as Sir Frederick lowered himself once more onto his chair, "are money, jealousy, and revenge, or a combination thereof. Now, before you married Lady Cabot, your nephew inherited everything upon your death."

"Yes," Sir Frederick replied, his tone hushed. His cup shook as he attempted to take a sip of coffee and then set it down again, sloshing some of the liquid onto the saucer. "But I don't see—"

Burnell didn't allow him to finish this thought. "Would you say that Mr. Mayhew was upset when you changed your will?"

"I wouldn't say upset exactly."

"Then how *would* you characterize his reaction when you informed him of the fact?" Burnell pressed.

"Surprised. I'd say he was surprised. But he took the news in stride," Cabot said quickly. "Surely he couldn't have believed I would leave matters as they stood when I had a new wife?"

"Perhaps Mr. Mayhew saw no reason to change things.

After all, he is your second-in-command at Cabot Corporation. Perhaps he has his own ideas on how the company should be run and didn't like the fact that you made Lady Cabot a member of the board. So I'm going to ask you again. When did you become aware of your wife's affair with Mr. Mayhew? Before or after you changed the will in her favor?"

"I—I—" Sir Frederick shot a desperate look at the two detectives. He clasped his hands tightly on the table in front him to stop them from trembling. "It was after," he whispered hoarsely. "Their affair started after I changed my will."

Burnell leaned back in his chair and stroked his beard meditatively. "Mmm, I thought as much."

"But you can't possibly think that Trevor had anything to do with Ronnie's murder. *For money?* That's absolutely ludicrous. Why are you going after my family like this when that rogue Longdon is wandering around out there? If there was ever a more perfect candidate for the role of killer, it's that man," Sir Frederick lashed out savagely. "Why aren't you going after him?"

"Because Mr. Longdon is still here at the Royal Devon, while your nephew is gone."

"What do you mean *gone*?"

"Just that, Sir Frederick. Mr. Mayhew checked out in a hurry early this morning. Now why do you think he would do that?"

Sir Frederick's complexion turned a very unbecoming shade of gray. "I—I don't know." His blue eyes were wide with bewilderment. "*I don't know.* But I'm afraid you gentlemen will have to excuse me. I'm suddenly not feeling very well."

"Of course, Sir Frederick." Burnell and Finch stood as the old man somehow managed to stumble his way out of the restaurant.

"Poor chap," Finch said sympathetically.

"I'm not surprised he's feeling ill," the superintendent murmured as they sat down again to mull over the interview over their coffee. "It must come as a bit of a shock to realize that someone you trust is not who you think he is."

⋆⋆⋆

Emmeline took a deep breath and squared her shoulders as she stepped off the lift. Everything felt strange. It all looked the same and, yet, it was different. Or perhaps *she* was the only one who had changed? She swallowed down the lump that formed in her throat. Her heart still felt raw, like it had been raked over hot coals in the nethermost regions of hell and then pummeled into insensibility. However, she couldn't hide in her room forever. She would have to confront Gregory at some point. Unconsciously, she fingered the gold bracelet he had given her. Despite everything that had happened, she couldn't bring herself to take it off. But what would she say to him if she saw him? How could one put the pieces back together after something like that? More importantly, did she *want* to? She simply didn't have any of those answers.

One thing that Emmeline *did* know was that she had to find out who killed Veronica Cabot. She wouldn't be able to put that particular ghost to rest until she did. Instinct told her it held the key to everything.

Where to start, though?

Come on, Emmeline, think, she told herself. *Listen to your instincts*, her brain pressed. *They have never failed you before. Well, almost never.*

Emmeline crossed one arm over her chest and cocked her head to one side, resting her cheek against the curled fist of her other hand. She made a mental list of the facts: Veronica Cabot was killed approximately between ten-thirty and eleven. From what Emmeline had been able to piece together—from snippets of conversation she had overheard between Chief Inspector Ashcroft and his sergeant before Superintendent Burnell took over the case—Lady Cabot had been lured out to Meadfoot Beach. She had been stabbed and then either pushed or fell from the cliff path. But what could have compelled the woman to go out in a violent storm? What or *who*?

Unbidden, the image of Gregory clinging to the shadows in Veronica's wake and then hurrying back to the hotel *alone*, soaked to the skin and with a nasty bruise on his temple flared before her eyes.

'*The last time I saw her was three years ago. She had a different surname then. It was Longdon. She's my wife.*'

My wife...My wife...My wife...

The words continued to rattle around her brain in the same sickening, staccato fashion. Over and over and over again. Emmeline squeezed her eyes shut and clamped her hands over her ears. A shudder rippled through her body. No, she would not allow it to beat her. To steal her sanity as well as her heart. She was better than that. Much better.

She took a deep breath and nearly jumped out of her skin when she felt a hand upon her shoulder.

"Forgive me, Miss Kirby, I didn't mean to startle you. Are you quite all right? You look a little peaked."

Emmeline opened her eyes to find Burnell and Finch frowning at her in concern. "What? Yes. I'm fine. Fine." She sounded as if she were trying to convince herself rather than the two detectives. Burnell and Finch exchanged skeptical looks. She sighed. "Really. I'm fine. Just a momentary wave of light-headedness. That's all."

The superintendent shrugged and decided to let it go. "Then may I ask you a question?"

"Only if I'm allowed to ask a few of my own, Superintendent Burnell."

Burnell sighed and shot Finch a glance that said, *Here we go.* "If it's possible to answer your questions without compromising the case, then I will endeavor to do so."

Emmeline smiled for the first time since this mess descended upon her. "Fair enough."

She extended a small hand and Burnell shook it. They understood and respected one another. Neither would do anything to break that trust.

"We're still attempting to determine everyone's movements the night that Lady Cabot was murdered. And we were wondering whether you wanted to change your statement. About Mr. Longdon's alibi."

The smile faded from Emmeline's lips and her mouth suddenly felt very dry. "I—" Her gaze flickered from Burnell to Finch and then Gregory came into her line of vision across the lobby. Their eyes locked for a second. Emmeline quickly looked away. She swallowed hard. "There's nothing I want to change. I stand by my statement."

She turned to go, but the superintendent put out a restraining hand on her arm. "Miss Kirby, it won't help him—or you—to lie," he said gently. "I should hate it very much to have to arrest you for perjury. In the end, the truth always comes out."

Emmeline's back stiffened and she tossed her head back. "You needn't remind me. I assure you I'm very, *very* well acquainted with that fact."

Burnell released her. "Yes. I'm sorry," he replied, suitably chastened.

Out of the corner of her eye, Emmeline saw Gregory making his way toward them. "May I go, Superintendent?"

Burnell glanced over his shoulder and then turned back to her. "Of course. Just think about what I said. Lying will only make things worse."

A bitter laugh escaped Emmeline's lips. "I've never been called a liar before. I should resent it, but somehow I can't muster the energy to do so. Besides, how much worse can it get?"

Burnell's gaze swept over her face and saw the pain—still raw and fresh—reflected in her troubled dark eyes. "I didn't mean to offend you, Miss Kirby. I'm simply doing my job. In this instance, it's not so much a case of lying as a misplaced sense of loyalty."

Finch, who had kept his tongue during this exchange, chimed in now in a low voice, "Is he worth it, Miss Kirby? He hasn't done anything to merit such loyalty. He's certainly abused your trust."

Burnell shot him a warning look, but Emmeline wasn't angry. She was too numb for anger now. "Perhaps you're right, Sergeant Finch. I know you both mean well, but things aren't as easy as all that. Emotions are messy and complicated things. You can't switch them off just like that." She snapped her fingers. "You can't help *feeling*. At least, you can't if you're human. And it can take a long time to get over—" A sob suddenly caught in her throat. "Forgive me. I have to go." She hurried off, her dark head tucked down, before the two men could utter another word.

"Emmy, wait," Gregory called as he brushed past, ignoring the detectives.

Burnell clapped a strong hand on his shoulder. "Let her go, Longdon."

Gregory rounded on the superintendent. Although outwardly calm and in control, his cinnamon eyes burned with a mixture of resentment and irritation. "Oh, leave off, Oliver. This is none of your concern."

"On the contrary, Longdon, anything or *anyone* who is connected with this murder inquiry is my business."

"I—didn't—murder—Ronnie." Gregory enunciated each word slowly through clenched teeth.

"That remains to be seen. What I *do* know is that you're hiding something, and I promise you that I'm going to find out what it is."

Gregory finally shrugged off the superintendent's grasp. "Believe what you like. I have more important things to attend to at the moment." He started to walk away.

"Haven't you hurt her enough?" Finch couldn't resist this parting shot.

Gregory stopped in mid-stride and turned on his heel. He

came back and stood in front of the sergeant. Their noses were practically touching. Finch could feel Gregory's warm breath brush his cheek. "Stay out of it."

"If I were you, Longdon, I'd be careful. Threatening a police officer is a serious matter."

Gregory took half a step backward and smiled. But there was no mirth in his eyes, only cold, hard anger. "And I'd say you and dear, old Oliver here—" He inclined his head toward the superintendent. "—are overstepping the bounds of your duties. Highly improper, to say the least. I think your superiors would frown upon you allowing personal prejudices to cloud your professional judgment."

Burnell quickly snatched Finch's arm before he did anything rash. "Off you go, Longdon."

"Your wish is my command, Oliver." Gregory gave them a little salute and was gone.

"Sorry, sir," Finch said when they were alone again.

Burnell sighed. "Lad, you played right into his hands. You have to be smarter than that. He lives to set us off-balance. The trick is not to let him. Now, collect your wits about you. We have a devil of a case to solve."

"Yes, sir. It won't happen again," the sergeant replied contritely.

"Right. Then we'll say no more about it. I think we need to—" Burnell's mobile rang at that moment. He flipped it open. "Burnell." He listened intently for a few seconds. "Is he indeed? No, no. Just watch him. We'll take care of the rest. Thanks for following up." He severed the connection.

Finch was looking at him in askance.

"It appears Mayhew has surfaced in London," Burnell said. "I want you on the next train back to Paddington. Go and have a nice little chat with our friend about why he was in such a rush to leave Torquay. Press him about Sir Frederick's will and his relationship with Lady Cabot."

The sergeant tucked his notebook into his jacket pocket. "Right. I'm on my way."

"Ring me when you've seen him and then come back as

quick as you can. Something tells me that I'm going to need you."

Finch grinned. "You won't even have a chance to miss me, sir."

"Miss you? Hmph. As if I would." He jerked his head toward the lifts. "Now, go on."

Burnell lingered in the lobby after the sergeant had gone, his lips pursed as he stroked his beard. He could feel his thin white brows knit together as his mind turned over the facts that they had gathered thus far. There was something he was missing. It was right there in front of him, but he couldn't place his finger on it. And it bothered him. It bothered him very much because the killer was watching and waiting as he and Finch stumbled around blindly.

CHAPTER 29

E mmy, you can't run forever," Gregory said as he cornered her in the hotel's garden. At this time of the morning, the sun filtered through the trees alternately plunging them into shadow and light. Hovering and uncertain. Never one or the other. The tulips and daffodils stood tense and alert, silent witnesses, as a gentle breeze dandled the air around them. "Turn around and look at me. Please."

Emmeline stood rooted to the spot. She gripped her elbows, hugging herself hard in a bid to remain in control.

Gregory saw her shoulders tremble slightly. He ached to pull her into his arms and hold her until he could fix everything between them. If that were possible.

"I can't do this right now. I think it would be best if you go." Her voice was low and remote, with only the merest trace of a tremor.

"I'm sorry, Emmy. I'm sorry for everything, darling. I have no right to ask you, but please give me a chance. That's all I want. A chance."

Emmeline shook her head. She turned around slowly. Her dark eyes were bright with unshed tears. "You've had too many chances already. Nothing you say or do can make up for all the lies you've spun."

"I love you. That's not a lie. You can't tell me that you don't love me anymore." He closed the space between them and put his hands on her shoulders. She didn't resist, but she stared straight ahead. "I can see it in your eyes that you still do."

She finally looked up into his face and sighed. "It's not enough. Not anymore. It hurts too much. I don't know which is worse, losing the baby or finding out about you and—" She broke off, her voice stolen by the tears swelling in her throat.

Emmeline leaned her head against Gregory's chest and wept. He folded her into his embrace and let her cry. He rested his chin on her head, murmuring softly as he smoothed her dark curls.

They stood like that for a long time. She was the first to pull away.

He pressed a kiss to her forehead. "I promise you I will make this right again."

"How can you? We can't—much as I would like to— pretend that your—your *wife*—never existed. Her murder only complicates matters. Burnell knows that we weren't together that night. He knows I lied. You needn't worry. I won't change my story, but you have to tell me what happened that night. I saw you pass beneath my balcony." Gregory's eyes widened in surprise. "First *her*, then you," she went on in a rush. "An hour later you came back alone. And now you have that bruise on your temple. So tell me what really happened. I'll stand by you, as long as you tell me *everything*. I want there to be no more secrets between us. That's the only way we can get past this nightmare."

He looked down at her expectant face. "I—I can't tell you any more than I already have."

"What do you mean you can't?" Emmeline snapped, a quiver of anger in her voice.

"I can't," he repeated softly.

"Then you can go to the devil. We have nothing left to say to one another." She turned on her heel and stalked off in the direction of the terrace.

Ten minutes later, Nigel quietly ambled into the garden and plunked himself down next to Gregory on a stone bench. He stretched his long legs out in front of him, crossed them at the ankles, and cast a quick sidelong glance at Gregory, who hadn't said a word.

Nigel frowned. "I just came across Emmeline. Actually, it would be more accurate to say that she nearly ran me down in her haste. I don't even think she realized it was me. She had a face like thunder and was muttering something unintelligible under her breath."

Still Gregory said nothing. He continued to stare at some spot on the other side of the garden.

Nigel exhaled heavily. "After that, I simply followed the trail of blood until it led me to you. It doesn't take Sherlock Holmes's powers of deduction to see that the two of you have had a row. I can only assume it was about one topic."

Without turning, Gregory said, "Emmy thinks I killed Ronnie."

Nigel saw the muscle pulsing in his jaw. "What do you expect her to think? Did you tell her?"

Gregory jumped to his feet. "No, of course I didn't tell her," he lashed out. "How could I?"

"So you'd rather she believed that you're a murderer than tell her the truth. I don't understand it." Nigel threw his hands up in the air in exasperation. "You're a bigger fool than I thought."

"I don't need a lecture from you," Gregory retorted with icy disdain. His eyes were hard and unyielding. "I didn't ask for your advice. In a matter of days, you've insinuated yourself into my business. Why? Why are you here?"

Nigel fixed a steady gaze on Gregory. "Because you were always reckless and someone has to save you from yourself."

Sergeant Finch waylaid Trevor as he was hurrying up the steps into his club. "Mr. Mayhew, I'd like a few moments of your time."

Trevor halted in mid-stride. The hand that clutched the mahogany handle of his umbrella tightened. Finch could see the man's knuckles turning white. "I'm afraid I can't right now, Sergeant. I'm late for a luncheon appointment. Besides, I already gave you chaps my statement. I have nothing else to add. So if you'll excuse me."

He took one step up, but Finch reached out and checked him. "I can wait until you've finished your lunch or you can come down to the Yard. It's entirely up to you, sir." The sergeant gave him a pleasant smile and waited for his answer.

Trevor ran a hand distractedly through his blond hair and licked his lips, all the while weighing his options. He glanced at his watch and shrugged his shoulders in resignation. "I can give you ten minutes, no more," he said curtly. "Come with me."

"Thank you for being so accommodating, Mr. Mayhew."

"You've left me very little choice," Trevor mumbled to himself as the doorman ushered them inside and took his umbrella.

As they shook themselves free of rain and surrendered their coats to the doorman, Finch's eyes darted round the lobby. It was tasteful and elegant, and rather imposing, all at the same time. A handful of landscape oil paintings graced the walls, which were made of solid oak paneling. To their right was the cloakroom, while to their left a short corridor led to some unknown area of the club. Directly in front of them was a doorway that opened onto a large room, also done in oak paneling, where Finch could see several Chesterfield sofas and wing chairs upholstered in claret leather that were scattered about in little groupings. There was also a bar.

"Mr. Mayhew," the doorman said. "About a quarter of an hour ago, Mr. Galbraith rang up to say that he was unavoidably detained and would be late for your lunch appointment."

Trevor's forehead creased into an annoyed frown. "Thanks for the message, Whitcombe." He saw the doorman shoot a questioning glance at Finch. "This is Mr. Finch. He's a friend of mine. I'll vouch for him. He'll only be here a few minutes. He's on his way out of town and just dropped in to say a quick hello. It's lucky he caught me. Isn't that right, Finch?" There was an undercurrent of bitterness in his tone.

The sergeant smiled broadly and played along. After all, it wouldn't do to have it known that one was consorting with Scotland Yard. "Yes, that's right. It's been ages since we've seen each other."

The doorman sniffed, but accepted this explanation. "Very good, Mr. Mayhew."

"We'll be in the reading room. Send Galbraith straight in when he gets here, will you?"

"Of course, sir," the doorman replied with a solemn nod.

There were only a few men in the reading room. They were either carrying on hushed conversations or had their noses buried in the *Financial Times*. Trevor led Finch to a couple of empty chairs by the Adam fireplace, where they wouldn't be overheard.

"Now then, Sergeant Finch, *what* is it that you want to ask?"

Finch removed his notebook from his inside pocket and flipped it open. "First off—"

"Good afternoon, Mr. Mayhew," a waiter interrupted. "May I get you and your guest something to drink?"

"Two coffees," Trevor said quickly without asking Finch.

"Right away, sir."

Once he was gone, Finch started again. "First, Mr. Mayhew, can you tell me why you felt the need to leave the Royal Devon in such a hurry without letting anyone know?"

"Not that it's any of your business, but I had business

here in London. A big deal that I had to finalize." He leaned back in his chair and propped his elbows on the armrests as he crossed one leg over the other. "As for not telling anyone, I don't know what the devil you mean. Uncle Freddie knew I was coming back to London. In fact, he insisted that I go."

One reddish brown eyebrow arched upward. "Did he, indeed?" Finch remarked as he tapped his pen against his notebook. "That's very interesting, sir. Because when we spoke to your uncle this morning, he had no idea that you had checked out."

"What?" Trevor asked, his face a study in perplexity. "I don't understand."

At this point, the waiter arrived with their coffees and their conversation ceased until they were alone once more.

"I don't understand, Sergeant. Ronnie's murder must be taking a greater toll on Uncle Freddie than I realized, if he forgot that I had gone back to London."

"Ye—es," Finch replied circumspectly as he jotted a quick note. "Now then, about the night your aunt—Lady Cabot—was killed. You said..." He flipped back a few pages. "...yes, here it is. You said that you hadn't seen her that night."

"Yes, that's correct. I had dinner with Nigel Sanborn that evening."

"And Lady Cabot didn't come to your room later on?" Finch pressed.

A flush rose from Trevor's jaw all the way up to his ears. "No, Ronnie didn't come to my room that night, Sergeant. Regardless of what you might think, we didn't rub Uncle Freddie's nose it. We were both fond of the old boy and would never have...seen...each other while he was at the hotel."

"I see. So you retired to your room that evening alone?"

"Yes. I had some paperwork to do, and then I went to bed."

"How do you explain the fact that you were seen by one

of the other guests in the corridor outside your uncle's room?"

"I—I—who saw me?"

"That's not really important, Mr. Mayhew. Please answer my question."

"It *is* damn well important. I have a right to know."

Finch remained silent, waiting.

Trevor put his coffee down on the table between them. "All right. Yes, I went to their room. I had to ask my uncle a question about this deal. I knocked, but there was no answer."

"Why didn't you simply call your uncle's room?"

"It was—" Trevor sat back in his chair and tapped his fingers nervously on the armrests. "I don't know. It was easier to go down and see him. But as I said, I knocked and no one answered. Uncle Freddie must have been in the shower, at the point, and couldn't hear."

"About what time was that?"

"I don't know…ten, ten-thirty…something like that, I think. I didn't check my watch."

"Pity that. So you have no alibi for when Lady Cabot was murdered? By your own admission, you were not in your room as you had originally claimed."

"What are you saying?" Trevor sat bolt upright. Several heads turned in their direction, when they heard his raised voice. He leaned forward and whispered, "What are you implying, Sergeant?"

Finch eased himself to the edge of his chair and rested his elbows on his knees. "Tell me, Mr. Mayhew, did you know that Sir Frederick had changed his will in favor of Lady Cabot upon their marriage?"

Trevor's blue eyes widened in bewilderment. "Well, yes, he told me that he was going to do so. It was only right."

"Very noble attitude, I'm sure. Therefore, you weren't upset that you were no longer going to be the heir to your uncle's vast fortune?"

"Look here, I don't like the turn that this conversation is

taking. What are you accusing me of?"

Finch ignored this question and posed his own. "How soon after your uncle changed his will did your affair with Lady Cabot begin?"

Trevor sucked in his breath, bristling with indignation. "I see your little game now. You think I romanced Ronnie and then killed her for...for what?—to get Uncle Freddie's money?"

"Is it so farfetched, Mr. Mayhew? After all, with Lady Cabot out of the way, it was highly likely that you would once more inherit everything. You didn't happen to lure her out to the cliff that night with some story or other, did you?"

"I'd tread carefully if I were you, Finch," Trevor snarled, his voice full of menace. His clenched fists trembled and his cheeks were suffused an angry shade of crimson.

The sergeant sighed and shook his head as if he were speaking to a naughty child. "Mr. Mayhew, threatening a police officer could be misconstrued. You wouldn't want people to think that you have something to hide, do you?"

"How dare you? I have nothing to hide. I didn't kill Ronnie, and I don't know anything about what happened. Now, get out of my sight before—"

Finch stood and casually tucked his notebook into his pocket. "Before what, Mr. Mayhew? If you were going to issue another threat, I'd reconsider. In a court of law, it would most certainly go against you."

Trevor jerked his head toward the door. "Get out. If you have any other questions, contact my solicitor."

"Ah, there you are, Mayhew," a gruff voice said from behind Finch.

They both turned to find a rather stout gentleman with a balding head and ruddy complexion smiling at them without guile. "Sorry, have I interrupted something? The chap outside said I'd find you in here."

"No, no, Galbraith. We've finished here. Mr. Finch was just leaving." Trevor gave the sergeant a pointed look.

Finch favored him with a broad smile. "Good afternoon,

Mr. Mayhew. It's been very enlightening. I'm certain we'll be in touch again." He inclined his head toward Galbraith and left before Trevor could reply.

Trevor stared after him, troubled thoughts darkening his mind.

"Everything all right?" Galbraith asked.

"What? Oh, yes." Trevor forced his mouth into the semblance of a smile. "Nothing to worry about. Won't you sit down? I know it's late already, but I thought we'd have a quick drink in here before we go into lunch. All right?"

"Fine by me," his companion agreed readily and took the chair Finch had just vacated.

They ordered two gins and chatted about desultory matters as they waited. But only half of Trevor's mind was focused on what Galbraith was saying. The other half went back over every word of his conversation with Finch. He slapped his hand against his thigh. "Damn, I forgot to tell him that I saw—Oh, never mind," he mumbled under his breath. "Let the insufferable chap find out on his own. It can't have anything to do with Ronnie's murder anyway."

And yet...Trevor frowned as he recalled the night Lady Cabot was murdered.

CHAPTER 30

As soon as Finch had concluded his interview with Trevor, he rang Superintendent Burnell and gave him a succinct resume of what he had discovered. Burnell found it extremely interesting that Sir Frederick had been well aware that his nephew had checked out and was back in London. So why lie? And why try to incriminate Mayhew? The other day, the superintendent had had the strong impression that Sir Frederick was protecting someone. At the time, Burnell had believed that it was his nephew. But, after this little episode, he wasn't so sure.

Finch's train wouldn't arrive back in Torquay until around seven that evening. That was not for another four hours. In the interim, Burnell decided to go tackle Sir Frederick about his faulty memory and anything else he might be hiding.

The superintendent went to the reception desk. "Ah, Mrs. Crawford, you haven't seen Sir Frederick by chance this afternoon, have you?"

Connie smiled pleasantly. "As a matter of fact, I saw him going toward the conservatory not more than a quarter of an hour ago. I believe he's having tea. Has anything else happened?" she asked, suddenly anxious.

"No, no," Burnell reassured her. "I merely wanted to clear up a few points. That's all."

"Oh, I see," Connie replied unconvinced but, as there was nothing left to say, she gave him a wan smile and bid him good afternoon.

The superintendent found Sir Frederick in the conservatory, engrossed in the *Times* crossword. He tapped his pen to his lips and stared up at the ceiling, as if hoping to find the answer there.

"Excuse me, Sir Frederick."

"Oh, it's you, Superintendent Burnell. I'm afraid you've caught me."

"I beg your pardon, sir?"

"The crossword." The older gentleman waved his paper in the air. "I'm normally able to breeze through this in fifteen minutes at breakfast. However, since Veronica…well since she died…I find my mind wandering. I can't seem to concentrate on anything for very long."

"That's understandable." Burnell cleared his throat. "I'm afraid I have a few more questions for you."

Sir Frederick sighed wearily and tossed his paper on the table in front of him. He waved a hand at the chair opposite. "I suppose we'd better get it over with. Sit down."

Burnell had barely lowered his bulk into the rather uncomfortable chair, when Sir Frederick shook his head. "I must say that I'm not very impressed with the job Scotland Yard is doing. You chaps keep mucking about, but you're no closer to finding my wife's killer."

The superintendent didn't allow this dig to nettle him. "I assure you that we *are* making progress."

"Indeed? I'm jolly glad to hear that. So what is it that you want now?"

"It's really a matter of clearing up a little discrepancy that seems to have arisen."

"Discrepancy? Well, spit it out, man," Sir Frederick prompted irritably.

"It seems—" Burnell smiled weakly. "—I sent my sergeant up to London today. In fact, he's on his way back now."

"Is he? How interesting. Is there a point, Superintendent?"

Burnell curled his right hand into a fist but carried on. "I sent Finch up to London because we learned that Mr. Mayhew was back in town. He made no attempt to hide his movements from the officers the Yard sent to follow him."

"*Follow him*? Are you telling me you have my nephew under surveillance? That's outrageous, Superintendent." Sir Frederick was incensed. "Why is the Scotland Yard wasting taxpayers' money following an innocent man?"

"Forgive me, Sir Frederick, but Mr. Mayhew did leave Torquay rather unexpectedly and did not inform us of his intentions."

"And why should he? He's not a member of the criminal classes like that Longdon fellow. Now there's a real criminal, if ever I saw one. *He* should be locked up."

Burnell ignored this outburst. "You must admit that Mr. Mayhew's actions were rather suspicious."

Sir Frederick slapped his open palm on the table rattling his cup and saucer, and attracting the attention of two elderly ladies sitting near the window. "Why do you chaps insist on harassing my family instead of doing your job to find the real killer? I could have you sacked for this, if it continues."

The superintendent smiled, but he was certain that his eyes were like steely blue daggers. All the better to make witnesses squirm. "I strongly advise you to rethink your stance, Sir Frederick. In a murder inquiry, I am duty-bound to follow all leads that are presented to me. Now, can you explain to me why you told us this morning that you were utterly unaware that your nephew had left the hotel? Mr. Mayhew told Sergeant Finch that you *knew* that he was planning to return to London. In fact, he said that you insisted that he go back to close a particular deal or other."

The color drained from Sir Frederick's cheeks. All the bluster was gone, snuffed out in an instant. He slumped back against the sofa. A trembling hand raked through his snowy hair. "I—I—"

Burnell stared at him, waiting patiently. When no answer was forthcoming, he said, "It strikes me as rather incongruous, you know. I don't like inconsistencies in a case." His knees creaked and he slowly pushed himself to his feet. "It tends to set me thinking about all sorts of things. However, I'll leave you now. Perhaps some time alone will help to refresh your memory. I suggest you think long and hard about your statement. And anything else that you'd like to tell us."

Sir Frederick looked up at the superintendent in mute appeal. He opened his mouth to say something and then changed his mind, clamping it shut once more. No, far too much had been said already.

҂҂҂

"All alone? May I join you, then?" Nigel asked the next morning as he approached Emmeline's table at breakfast.

"What?" Emmeline started. Then she smiled and waved to the empty chair opposite her. "Oh. Of course."

"Thanks. Coffee and eggs and bacon," he told the waitress who had appeared to top off Emmeline's cup.

Emmeline stared at him uncertainly over the rim as she took a sip. Nigel smiled in return. There was something about the gleam in his warm hazel eyes that was familiar, but for the life of her she couldn't put her finger on it.

"Bloody cheek, I know," he said. "Pushing myself on you like this."

"Oh, no. Not at all. You're always pleasant company."

"The feeling is mutual."

She inclined her head to accept the compliment. "But I was wondering whether you had a particular reason for wanting to see me."

Nigel tapped the side of his nose. "Smart girl. I knew I was right to insist that you come and work at the *Clarion*. As you have correctly surmised, I do indeed have something, or rather someone, I'd like to discuss with you."

"I thought as much." Emmeline leaned her elbow on the table and rested her chin on her hand. "Out with it."

"It has to do with—with Gregory."

The smile faded from her eyes. She sat back in her chair, crossed her arms over her chest, and thrust her chin in the air defiantly. "There is *nothing* I'd like to discuss on that particular subject."

"I have to disagree with you. An awful lot has been left unsaid—"

"Why are you getting involved in this?" Irritation was creeping into her voice. "None of this has anything to do with you."

"It seems to me I've heard that before," he murmured under his breath, but louder he said, "Let's just say that I'm protecting a Sanborn Enterprises investment. Turmoil in one's private life is not good for business."

"I assure you, I *never* allow my private life to interfere with my job."

"Forgive me. I didn't mean to offend you. I know you're a consummate professional. Otherwise, I wouldn't have pushed my brother and father to hire you. But from my vantage point as an outside observer, you can be rather mulish, like our friend Gregory." He held up a hand to prevent angry words tumbling from her lips. "Now, listen. He has his faults, I grant you, but you can't really believe that he murdered Veronica Cabot, can you?"

"I—I—If I'm honest, no," Emmeline admitted at last with a sigh. "No, I don't think he did it."

"Well, at least one of you has some sense."

"What do you mean?" She gave him a quizzical look and then her dark gaze narrowed. "You know, Nigel, it strikes me—and not for the first time, mind you—that you know a lot more about what's going on than you're letting on. Why is that?"

"I have no idea what you are implying." He arranged his face into a picture of innocence. "I think it must be an occupational hazard. You journalists tend to see conspiracies everywhere."

"That won't wash. Tell me what you know about all this. About Gregory."

"My dear, I'm afraid it's not my place. I'm a lawyer. I can only advise. If you want answers, go to the horse himself."

She slumped back again. "I can't."

"You mean you *won't*."

Emmeline closed her eyes and pinched the bridge of her nose. "Too much has happened. Too many lies. Too many secrets. I can't forget." She opened her eyes again. "He's hurt me once too often."

"Rubbish. You're not a porcelain doll. You're made of sterner stuff than that. You have to be, to be such a great journalist."

"Who says I'm a great journalist?" she asked innocently.

Nigel gave her a pointed look. "Stop fishing for compliments. You know you're good. Damn good. Not only that, you've got integrity, class, and intelligence. That's a hell of a combination. So don't tell me you can't get over what's happened. I don't condone what Gregory's done. In fact, I'd like to give him a good thrashing." Emmeline giggled at this. Nigel grinned. "But when it comes down to it, you love him."

There was an interminable pause and, for a second, Nigel thought he had been mistaken.

"Yes, God help me, I love that insufferable, incorrigible, irritating man. Why? I don't know, but there it is," she whispered at last.

Nigel inwardly breathed a sigh of relief. "Naturally, you're under each other's skin. You can't help it. No matter how stupid the fool has been, he loves you. Go and talk to him. Make him tell you everything. That's the only way." He reached out to give her hand a reassuring squeeze and smiled. "Well, that's me done. This giving advice business really gives one an appetite," he said as he proceeded to tuck into his steaming plate of bacon and eggs.

Emmeline laughed.

"Oh, look, you're in luck," Nigel said. "The devil himself just walked through the door. His ears must have been burning."

"What?" She swiveled round in her chair and saw Gregory. Then she turned back to Nigel. "You didn't plan this by any chance, did you?"

"Me?" He put a hand to his chest in mock innocence and sniffed. "As if I would."

"Uh huh. I pity any opponent that comes up against you in court, Mr. Sanborn. He or she has absolutely no idea how utterly devious and underhanded you can be."

"I hope that was meant as a compliment. I choose to take it as such."

"Take it however you like. You always have a card up your sleeve, don't you, Nigel? No, don't worry," she said as she pushed herself to her feet. "It was a rhetorical question. But you stand warned. I'm going to find out why you've taken *such* a great interest in Gregory and me. I find it very strange that, for two men who could barely tolerate one another a few days ago, you seem awfully cozy all of a sudden."

"Gregory's over there." Nigel pointed to his left, making his expression as bland as possible.

Their *tête-à-tête* was over. Emmeline was not going to get anything else out of him. *For the moment*, she told herself.

∽∾∽

"Your new best friend Nigel thinks we need to talk," Emmeline plunged in without preamble as she pulled herself to her full height, which was still a head shorter than Gregory. "He said that there are things you haven't told me that I need to know."

Gregory glanced over the top of her head at Nigel, who returned his stare without blinking. Gregory smiled down at Emmeline—one of those dazzling, engaging smiles that made her heart flutter and her knees go weak. He took her elbow and bent down to give her a kiss. "It's heartwarming to see that you've forgiven me, darling."

Emmeline turned her cheek away before his lips could brush against hers. "I didn't say I had forgiven you," she said quietly. "I don't know if I *can* forgive you. All I'm prepared to do at the moment is to listen. I'm making no other promises."

Gregory straightened up and smoothed the corners of his mustache. "Fair enough. At least, you're still speaking to me."

"It remains to be seen for how long." She removed his hand from her arm. "So start talking. And it had better be the truth. *All of it.*"

"I promise to tell you everything, Emmy." He pulled her aside and waved his hand to encompass the restaurant. "But we can't talk here. Too many people. Let's go to your room, where we can be alone."

"No. I want people about." She crossed her arms over her chest and locked her gaze on his face.

There was a bemused gleam in his cinnamon eyes. "Why, love, you don't think I would take advantage of the situation and ravish you, do you?"

"I wouldn't put anything past you. I warn you that my tolerance threshold is very low. I'm *not* in the mood for any more of your games." She held her body rigidly and tossed her head back. A sure sign that her temper was smoldering at present, but could flare into life any second.

"Right, let's go into the lobby. We can find a quiet corner, while at the same time you won't have to worry about my nefarious intentions. After you, Emmy." He stood aside and gave her a little bow of his head.

"You better not have any nefarious intentions," she murmured under her breath as she swept past him. To her chagrin, she heard him chuckling softly behind her.

There weren't too many people milling about the lobby as they made their way to two chintz armchairs that were set a little apart. Emmeline perched herself on the edge of one chair and sat stiffly with her hands clasped tightly in her lap.

Gregory frowned. This was not going to be easy. He wasn't going to be able to charm his way out of this one. But where to begin? And more importantly, when he had told her, would she stick by him or would she run as far and as fast as she could?

He reached out to take one of her hands and then thought better of it. Curling his fingers into his palm, he let his hand drop. "Emmy, I didn't kill Ronnie. Whatever else I've done, you must believe that."

Emmeline looked at him from beneath her lashes. "I never really believed you were capable of murder. I was hurt that day on the clifftop. I was lashing out because I had just found out about you and—and *her*. Oh, *why*, Gregory?"

Even though she had promised herself she would be strong, she dropped her head into her hands and started to cry. She felt him caress her hair.

"I'm sorry," he whispered in the space between them. "I will be sorry for the rest of my life that I hurt you like this."

Her head snapped up. "Again. That you hurt me again, you mean. This was a mistake." Emmeline jumped to her feet. "Why should I listen to you? Everything that comes out of your mouth is a lie."

She began to walk away, but Gregory grabbed her wrist. "Please, darling. Please. I promise no more lies." He turned her hand over and tenderly kissed her palm.

Emmeline hesitated. He looked so earnest. She wanted to trust him, but could she?

"Please," he whispered again.

She sighed and sank back down into the chair.

"I didn't kill Ronnie, however she—" But Gregory never got a chance to tell Emmeline.

There was a sudden commotion at the reception desk.

They both turned to see one of the maids gesticulating and talking excitedly to Connie.

The only thing that floated to their ears was Connie exclaiming in disbelief, "You stupid girl. What do you mean Sir Frederick is dead?"

CHAPTER 31

"Sir Frederick can't be dead. He *can't* be." There was a tremor of fear in Connie's voice. "He was probably taken ill. Peter," she called to her colleague, who was punching some information into a computer. "Ring Dr. Bradford. Tell him one of the guests has been taken ill. Then inform Mr. Harcourt about Sir Frederick."

Peter gave a curt nod, his hand already reaching out for the phone. Connie turned back to the maid, who began trembling and sniveling. She took her by the shoulders and gave her a good shake. "Pull yourself together. Becoming hysterical will not help anyone. Not to mention it will upset the other guests."

Connie cast a surreptitious glance around the lobby. At once, her gaze fell upon Emmeline and Gregory, who stared back at her. Her spine stiffened, but she quickly turned her attention back to the maid. "Now, come with me," Connie said as she grabbed the pass key. "We'll go up to Sir Frederick's room together." She gave the maid a gentle push forward. "Come on."

Emmeline and Gregory watched the two women disappear into the lift. They were both silent for a long moment.

"Do you think it's true?" Emmeline whispered, at last.

"I don't know," Gregory replied tersely.

It was more the tone of his voice than what he said that

caused her to shiver involuntarily. The planes and angles of his face stood out starkly. The two lines on either side of his nose seemed deeper. And his cinnamon eyes were clouded by something dark and unreadable.

He seemed to sense that Emmeline was staring at him. He did his best to shake off his black mood, patted her arm reassuringly, and gave her a half-smile. "Don't worry, Emmy. If Sir Frederick *is* ill, his money will ensure that he receives the finest medical care."

"I'm sure he will. What are you worried about?"

"Me? Why should I be worried about anything, darling?"

"I know you and something's bothering you. I thought there weren't going to be any more secrets between us. What was it that you were going to tell me?"

Gregory took one of her small hands in his. "Oh, it's nothing that can't wait," he said nonchalantly.

He saw disappointment flicker into her dark eyes. However, now was definitely not the appropriate time to tell her of Ronnie's devious plan.

"I see," Emmeline mumbled as she slipped her hand from his grasp. "If you can't trust me, then there's very little else we have left to say to one another."

"It's not a question of trust."

"Isn't it?" she scoffed. "That's what it looks like from my vantage point."

He grabbed her arm roughly. "Then you're wrong. You're the only person in this world who I trust with my life."

"If that's case, what could be so horrible that you can't tell me? I already know about your wife and the man you killed in Barcelona."

"Damn it, woman. You don't make things easy. If I tell you, you'll run and never look back."

Emmeline leaned toward him. "I assure you that's exactly what will happen if you *don't* tell me." Her features had hardened into that bull dog expression that struck fear into the hearts of unsuspecting men and women when she was pursuing a story—the look that said that she would never give up. *Never*. Until she had her answer.

"Darling, I—"

Across the lobby, the lift doors slid open and Connie stumbled out with the maid close on her heels. Even from this distance, Emmeline and Gregory could see that things were very wrong indeed. Both women appeared stunned. Their movements were slow and awkward. Their complexions had taken on a grayish hue.

Connie went to the reception desk and spoke in hushed tones to Peter, who once again picked up the receiver. He spoke succinctly for a minute and then returned it to its cradle. Within a few minutes, Superintendent Burnell and Sergeant Finch came bustling into the lobby.

"Dear God, then it's true. Sir Frederick *is* dead," Emmeline said.

"Yes," Gregory mumbled. "How...unexpected."

⊘⊘⊘

Mr. Harcourt accompanied Superintendent Burnell and Sergeant Finch to Sir Frederick's room and let them in with the pass key.

"Nothing's been touched?" Burnell asked as his practiced eye swept over the room in an initial survey.

"Not as far as I know," Harcourt replied gravely. "From what Constance told me, the maid—her name's Nancy, by the way—tapped on the door to ascertain whether it would be all right to make up the room. When there was no answer, she opened the door and found Sir Frederick." He waved his hand vaguely toward the bed where the older man lay, head slumped to one side. Harcourt kept his gaze firmly directed at his feet. "Nancy apologized for disturbing him and said that she could come back later. When there was no reaction, she went closer to the bed and realized that he was dead. She immediately went downstairs and told Constance. The rest you know."

"Yes," murmured the superintendent as he approached the bed. He kept his hands in his pockets and bent down to scrutinize the body. "Thank you, Mr. Harcourt. I've called Chief Inspector Ashcroft and he's dispatched the forensics team. The medical examiner is on his way as well. I'd appreciate it if they could be shown up here as soon as they arrive. And another thing." Burnell straightened up. "We'd like to keep the news of Sir Frederick's death quiet for as long as we possibly can."

"Naturally, that goes without saying. You can rely on me, Superintendent. I will speak to the staff. The Royal Devon has had far too much publicity already."

Burnell smiled briefly. "Good man. Now, if you could let Sergeant Finch and me to get on with this grim business, we'd appreciate it."

"Of course. Just ring the desk, if you need anything at all."

"We will. Thank you." The superintendent nodded politely. As soon as the door had closed behind Harcourt, he said, "I thought he'd never leave. Anything over there?"

"Nothing obvious from a cursory glance, but then I don't want to disturb anything until forensics has had a go at it."

"Right, come here. Take a look at this."

Finch walked over to the bedside table, where Burnell was standing. On the table was half a glass of water, a bottle of prescription medication, and a single sheet of paper. "Read it," the superintendent directed.

The sergeant cocked his head to one side, his lips moving silently as he read the handwritten note. His brown eyes widened in disbelief. "Suicide? I never would have pegged Sir Frederick as the type to take his own life."

He read the note again. This time aloud.

"'I killed my wife. God forgive me. I loved Veronica, but I found I could no longer turn a blind eye to her infidelity. Playing the part of the old cuckold had become too much for me to bear. I don't want anyone else to suffer for what I alone have done.'"

"Sir, what do you make of this development?"

Burnell had one arm folded over his chest and the other hand was stroking his beard. "What do I think? I don't like it. Who was he trying to protect with this grand gesture?"

"Well, it certainly wasn't Mayhew. He wanted us to believe that his nephew had scarpered, when *he* was the one who had sent Mayhew back to London on business."

"Yes, but don't forget that with Lady Cabot dead Mayhew now inherits the lot."

Finch's brow furrowed and he shook his head. "Despite his recalcitrance when I spoke to him yesterday, I really don't believe that Mayhew murdered Lady Cabot."

Burnell was silent for a long moment, his gaze fixed on the late Sir Frederick Cabot. "I think you're right, lad," he said, at last. "His uncle likely wanted a bit of revenge for the affair. He wanted to make things a little uncomfortable for Mayhew, to teach him a lesson. However, when Sir Frederick saw that we were taking a serious interest in his nephew, he vowed to do anything necessary to protect the family name and so sought to divert our attention to Longdon."

"But suicide, sir? That's a bit drastic, isn't it?"

"A man who sees nowhere else to turn does desperate things. What if Sir Frederick knew who murdered Lady Cabot? What if this was the only way to protect that person? Someone we don't know about or who has slipped under the radar unnoticed until now."

"But who? And why?"

Burnell put an arm around the sergeant's shoulders. "Finch, as highly trained policemen, that's exactly what we're going to find out. And we had better uncover something soon before our killer becomes impatient and strikes again."

∽∾∽

"I can't be sure until the toxicology tests come back, but

I'd have to say that he took his own life. There are no other signs of violence," Dr. Clarke, the local medical examiner, said as he peeled off his latex gloves.

"Thanks, Dr. Clarke. I'd appreciate it, if you could expedite those tests," the superintendent pressed.

"Anything for Scotland Yard. I should have them back in a day or two."

"The sooner, the better." Burnell extended his hand to the doctor. "Thanks again for coming out so quickly."

"All in a day's work. I must say that with all these mysterious deaths, the Royal Devon is beginning to garner a rather notorious reputation. Pity that. It's such a lovely place. Ah, well, I must be off. Happy hunting, chaps."

"Happy, indeed. This sordid affair has been wrapped in gloom and doom from the outset," the superintendent told Finch once the doctor had left. They were waiting for the forensics team to finish up dusting for fingerprints and cataloguing evidence so that Sir Frederick's body could be removed. The photographer had already gone.

"Superintendent Burnell, I think you ought to see this," called a young constable, dressed in the white jumpsuit that the team had donned to protect against contaminating the crime scene.

Burnell shuffled over to the desk. "I found this note under the credenza. I don't know whether it has any bearing on the case."

The sheet of paper had been sealed in a clear, plastic bag. It was typed.

Ronnie,
Tonight at ten-thirty. Don't be late, darling. You might live to regret it.
Greg

"What is it, sir?" Finch was at his side, craning his neck to get a glimpse. Burnell passed the note to him.

"This rather puts paid to Longdon's alibi."

Burnell gave him a pointed look. "Only a gullible fool would have accepted Miss Kirby's story at face value. It was patently obvious that she was lying to protect him. At the time, though, there was no way to disprove it. Now, we can press him for answers. And yet—" He frowned at the piece of paper.

"What is it, sir?" Finch asked, perplexed.

"I find it rather curious that this has shown up all of a sudden. Tucked under the credenza of all places. Why wouldn't Lady Cabot have destroyed it? And why is it *typed?*"

"To make it more difficult to identify the source. If you remember," Finch pointed out, "the blackmail note that Lady Cabot crumpled and accused Miss Kirby of sending was also typed."

"Hmm. It appears our killer has a penchant for neatness. The only thing is blackmail and murder are far from neat and tidy."

Burnell and Finch stood aside as Sir Frederick was zipped into black body bag and wheeled out on a stretcher. The old gentleman left a lot of unanswered questions behind him.

"Finch, let's have another chat with Longdon and Miss Kirby."

❦❦❦

With his copy of the *Times* tucked under his arm, Nigel whistled tunelessly as he left the dining room. For once, he had lingered over his eggs and bacon as he attacked the crossword.

He sighed. It was his last day in Torquay and he intended to make the most of it. Tomorrow, he had to return to London and the madness that awaited him at the office.

Ah, well, all good things must come to an end sometime.

He started whistling again as he planned out a long walk

along the cliffs, before having a spot of lunch down by the harbor.

As he crossed the lobby, he caught a glimpse of Emmeline and Gregory—heads bent together and talking in hushed tones. He smiled to himself. Well, at least that little problem had worked itself out.

He walked over to them. "I'm glad that the two of you have resolved your differences." At the sound of his voice, Emmeline and Gregory's heads shot up in the same instant. However, the thunderous looks on their faces told him that all was far from well.

"Ah," Nigel murmured.

Emmeline jumped to her feet and waved her hand in Gregory's general direction. "Thanks to the reticence of your lying, secretive, treacherous, devious friend here, nothing can ever be resolved." She was so angry that her balled fists were shaking at her sides.

Nigel reached out and put a restraining hand on her arm to prevent her from walking away. "Emmeline, I'm sure if you just listen to what Gregory has to say—"

She violently shrugged off his hand. "Listen? *Listen*? I was willing to listen. Despite everything he has done, I came to hear him out. But he won't *tell* me anything." Her voice was rising with each word that came out of her mouth. "He says that he *can't* tell me. If he doesn't trust me, you can't expect me to moon about after him. I'm washing my hands of the whole situation. You're welcome to him."

Gregory reluctantly rose to his feet, ignoring the dark look Nigel shot at him. "Emmy. *Darling*. Please calm down and be reasonable. There are some things that it is better for you not to know. Believe me. It's for the best."

"Ooh," she groaned. She hated—*absolutely hated*—when people told her to calm down. She was perfectly calm until the very moment they said that to her. "What do you do with a man like that?" The question was directed at Nigel, but both men knew it was purely rhetorical and would be dangerous to venture a response. "And another thing—"

Emmeline was in full verve now, waggling a finger at them, but she would never be able to finish her train of thought.

"Longdon, Miss Kirby," Burnell called as he and Finch approached the trio. "We'd like to have a few words with you."

Nigel didn't miss the exchange of glances between Emmeline and Gregory. "Superintendent Burnell, what's all this about?"

"Respectfully, Mr. Sanborn, this is none of your concern."

Nigel smiled pleasantly. "As Miss Kirby is now an employee of Sanborn Enterprises and I'm the company's corporate counsel, I have every right to inquire what this is about."

Burnell sighed. "Mr. Sanborn, there's no need to go all official. In light of the new situation, we would like to clarify some discrepancies regarding Miss Kirby's and Longdon's statements."

"I see," Nigel replied noncommittally without looking at either Emmeline or Gregory. "What new situation would that be?"

"Oh, Nigel, hadn't you heard?" Emmeline said. "Sir Frederick Cabot is dead."

CHAPTER 32

"What?" Nigel's gaze darted from Emmeline to Superintendent Burnell and Sergeant Finch. "When did this happen?"

Burnell glanced over his shoulder and lowered his voice. "Miss Kirby, we'd appreciate your discretion in the matter. We are trying to keep the news quiet for as long as possible."

A flush rose upon Emmeline's cheeks. "Of course. You have my word that I won't report anything until you've made a statement. However, may I ask, was Sir Frederick murdered as well?"

"We are not at liberty to say at the present time."

"Oh, come on, Oliver," Gregory chimed in, flashing a grin at Burnell. "You're among friends. If you can't tell us, who can you tell?"

The superintendent's icy blue stare was full of venom. "I'd watch my step if I were you, Longdon. You have a lot of explaining to do about the night Lady Cabot was murdered."

"And why is that?" Gregory asked.

"Because," Burnell said through clenched teeth, "we've come across a piece of evidence that makes it clear that you have *no* alibi for that night." He concluded this pronouncement with a pointed look at Emmeline.

The color drained from Emmeline's cheeks. She tried to say something, but the words simply would not come out. She cleared her throat and tried again. "Evidence? That's ridiculous, Superintendent Burnell. What evidence could you have? I already told you that Gregory was with me that night. All night," she insisted.

Burnell turned to Emmeline and his face softened. But his tone was stern. "I know what you told me, Miss Kirby, but I'm afraid you lied to me."

She blushed and lowered her gaze. She truly felt remorseful at having deceived him, but she had no other choice at the time. She couldn't allow him to find out that Gregory had followed Veronica Cabot that night. And returned alone.

"Now, if the two of you would be so kind as to come with us."

"I will be joining you for this interview," Nigel said.

"Mr. Sanborn," Burnell retorted irritably, "I assure you that Sanborn Enterprises has nothing to worry about. We do not intend to charge Miss Kirby with perjury or perverting the course of justice. Longdon is our primary concern."

"Then I'm still coming."

"For Heaven's sake, why?" Burnell protested.

Without flinching, Nigel replied, "Because Mr. Longdon is my client as well."

"*What*? Since when?"

"Since five minutes ago."

Burnell and Finch exchanged an annoyed look.

"So shall we proceed with these questions that you have? I take it that you are not going to conduct this interview in the middle of the lobby."

Burnell pursed his lips and shrugged. "Very well, Mr. Sanborn. Have it your way. The hotel has put the private conference room at our disposal. If you would all follow us."

"Of course, Superintendent Burnell," Nigel said. "Anything to help the police in this matter."

"Hmph," Burnell grunted.

Nigel, Emmeline, and Gregory silently followed a few paces behind the two detectives. Nigel's gaze met Gregory's over Emmeline's head. Gregory's cinnamon eyes narrowed slightly and he gave an imperceptible shake of his head. Otherwise, his features were arranged in a neutral expression.

Emmeline lightly touched Nigel's arm. He looked down at her and she mouthed, "Thank you."

He gave her a reassuring smile and patted her small hand. "Don't worry," he whispered. "Everything will be all right."

Emmeline cast a sidelong glance from under her lashes at Gregory. "I hope so."

That was all that they had time for. They had arrived at the conference room, where Burnell was standing in the doorway waving his hand at them impatiently. "All right. Let's get a move on."

Finch was already settled at the table with his notebook open. Burnell closed the door as they took seats opposite Finch. Emmeline sat in the middle, flanked by Nigel on her left and Gregory on her right. Her hands were folded on the table to prevent them from trembling. Gregory reached over and put one of his hands protectively over hers. Without looking at him, she slipped them from his grasp and into her lap. This was not lost on Finch, who looked from one to the other.

"Now then, Longdon," Burnell said as he came round the table and wearily lowered himself into the chair across from Gregory. "We know that you were *not* with Miss Kirby the night Lady Cabot was killed. So where were you?"

Gregory smiled and didn't answer at first. He leaned back in his chair and crossed one leg over the other. "You know it's not very nice to contradict a lady. How do you know that I wasn't with Emmy?"

Burnell smiled, but his eyes were hard as steel. "Show him, Finch."

The sergeant produced the note they had found in Sir Frederick's room and slowly pushed it across to Gregory, who glanced at it with a bemused grin. "Oliver, I must say that I'm extremely disappointed." He clucked his tongue at the superintendent. "This is *not* worthy of you."

"Let me see that," Nigel said.

Gregory casually slid it over to him without taking his eyes off Burnell.

Emmeline craned her neck to see the note over Nigel's shoulder. Nigel shook his head. "I'm afraid my client is right, Superintendent. Anyone with access to a computer or a typewriter could have written this. Clearly, it was the real killer's intention to divert suspicion from himself by incriminating Mr. Longdon." He pushed the note back to Finch, unconcerned.

"Nevertheless, the fact is that Longdon does *not* have an alibi and he has failed to explain how he got that bruise on his temple." Although Burnell was speaking to Nigel, he fixed his gaze on Emmeline.

Unconsciously, she fingered the gold bracelet Gregory had given her. A tense, uncomfortable silence closed in around them, intimidating with its stealthy approach.

At last, Gregory cleared his throat. "I didn't kill Ronnie," he said quietly. "I'll tell you everything that happened that night as long as Emmy leaves this room *now*. She has nothing to do with any of this. We all know she was simply trying to protect me. But really, darling—" He turned to her, "—it's not necessary." He lifted her hand to his lips and grazed her knuckles with a kiss. Then he looked back at Burnell. "Don't prolong this, Oliver. It's me you want, not her."

Burnell stroked his beard thoughtfully and then jerked his head toward the door. "Go on, Miss Kirby. Longdon's right."

"Thanks, Oliver," Gregory mumbled.

"That's *Superintendent Burnell* to you for the millionth time."

Emmeline snatched her hand away and glared at Gregory. "I see. All boys together, is it? You can bloody well think again. I'm staying, whether you like it or not." She tapped a finger impatiently on the table. "I'm fed up with being kept in the dark. I'm not some mindless female who needs to be coddled and sheltered. Whatever you have to say, you can say it front of me."

She thrust her chin in the air, daring any of them to contradict her. The only one not stunned by this outburst was Nigel, whose lips convulsed into a smile.

Burnell shrugged. "You heard the lady, Longdon. Start talking."

Emmeline crossed her arms over her chest. Her back was ramrod straight, the expression on her face was intractable.

Gregory sighed. "All right. As you've already surmised, I went to meet Ronnie that night. However, *she* was the one who arranged the meeting not me. I did not write that note, and I didn't murder her."

"That remains to be seen, Longdon. On several occasions you were overheard threatening Lady Cabot. Why did you go to meet her that night?" the superintendent pressed, stone-faced.

Gregory hesitated. His gaze snaked over to Nigel, who nodded. "Because she threatened to destroy Emmeline's career, if I didn't kill her husband."

CHAPTER 33

Whatever Emmeline had been expecting, it was certainly not this. She stared at Gregory open-mouthed. "What do you mean? How was she going to ruin my car—"

"Pardon me, Miss Kirby," Burnell interrupted. "But the more important question is how did she intend to kill her husband? I find it fascinating because Sir Frederick just happens to be dead. You didn't by any chance have a hand in it, did you, Longdon?"

The room fell silent once again and all eyes were focused on Gregory.

"I told you, Oliver. I didn't kill *anyone*. But I can't deny that I wanted Ronnie dead. I didn't care about myself. She could do anything she wanted to me, but when she threatened Emmy—" His hand clenched into a tight fist on the table. "Well, that was quite another story. I couldn't have that. I told her that I wouldn't contest her marriage to Sir Frederick, even though our swear-death-and-dissolution-of-marriage certificate had not been issued at the time they wed. We wouldn't have to see each other ever again and could go on with our lives without anyone being the wiser. After all, we hadn't been husband and wife in years. I wasn't interested in coming between her and Sir Frederick. He was welcome to her.

"But our Ronnie—" Gregory's lips curled into a bitter smile. "—bless her mercenary little black heart had a vindictive streak *and* was greedy. She always wanted what she couldn't have." He gave Emmeline a significant look to emphasize this last point. "She saw the way things were with Emmy and decided to come between us out of spite. She said that seeing me again rekindled all the 'old feelings' and she couldn't imagine another day without me. Then Ronnie came up with this far-fetched plan to kill Sir Frederick so that she could inherit his entire fortune. She said that we could take the money and start over again anywhere in the world we wanted."

Burnell's right eyebrow arched upward in surprise. Gregory sighed. "When I told her that getting back together was simply not on, she began to lash out. Ronnie didn't take rejection well. She said that if I didn't kill her husband then she would drop a word in some well-placed ears and make it known that the reason Emmy always managed to get such spectacular scoops was because she wasn't above dabbling in blackmail. Ronnie said that she'd make sure that Emmy would never be able to show her face in journalism circles—anywhere—ever again. I have no doubt whatsoever that Ronnie meant every word. Sir Frederick knew a great many people in the industry."

Gregory heard a sharp intake of breath from Emmeline. He automatically reached out and took her trembling hand in his own, his thumb caressing along the edge out of long habit. "I tried several times to make her see the sheer folly of what she suggested," he continued. "But there was no reasoning with Ronnie. She was fixated on the idea. In the end, I lost my patience with her. Those were likely the occasions when I was 'overheard' threatening her. However, I would never have touched her."

"A bit late for that, wasn't it? I mean after your torrid night together," Emmeline said bitterly as if they were the only ones in the room. She tried to pull her hand away, but Gregory held it firmly.

"Emmy, I told you that was a horribly stupid mistake that I will regret for the rest of my life. Call it a momentary lack of sanity. Lust. Whatever you like. But I assure you, it meant *nothing*. Ronnie could never hold a candle to you, darling. I hope, in time, you will be able to forgive me," he replied quietly.

Burnell cleared his throat and Finch fingered his tie in embarrassment at this little speech. Nigel remained impassive.

The superintendent tapped the table with his forefinger to get the interview back under control. "Let's not get distracted from our purpose here today, Longdon."

"Right, Oliver. Well, the night Ronnie was killed, she rang me and said that she had a change of heart and wanted to meet to discuss things. I was wary of this *volte-face*, but I agreed to a meeting to try to find out what she had up her sleeve. Because I was certain that her devious mind was plotting something.

"We arranged to meet on the cliff path above Meadfoot Beach at a quarter past ten. But it was an utter waste of time. She started spouting more of the same rubbish about killing Sir Frederick so that the two of us could get back together. We argued and then I got fed up. I turned my back on her and left. I can still hear her calling after me that I would be sorry when Emmeline found herself blacklisted.

"Ronnie was very much alive when I left her. However, as I made my way back through the woods, before I realized what was happening, someone gave me a whopping great crack on the head. I don't know how long I was out, but it was pouring with rain when I regained consciousness. I hurried back to the hotel and that was that. End of story."

The room fell silent as each of them mulled over Gregory's tale. Burnell stroked his beard, fixing his hard blue stare on Gregory, who sat so still beside Emmeline that it was unnerving.

"Well, Superintendent Burnell, have you nothing to say?" Nigel was the first one to break the spell. "My client has told you the whole story now. If you have nothing further—" He put his palms on the table and pushed himself to his feet.

"I wouldn't be so hasty, Mr. Sanborn. It's a very pretty tale, but you can hardly expect us to believe it."

Nigel exhaled wearily and plunked back down into his chair. "And why not? It happens to be the truth."

Burnell snorted as he exchanged a brief look with Finch. "Truth? Unfortunately—or perhaps you have been fortunate—you haven't known Longdon as long as Finch and I have. The truth and Longdon are at opposite ends of the spectrum. Lies are second nature to him. And he tells them with just the right degree of pathos to elicit sympathy from unsuspecting persons with kind hearts." Although his last words were directed at Nigel, the intended target was Emmeline.

She cleared her throat. "Superintendent Burnell, surely after everything that's happened, I'm the last one to defend Gregory. But in this instance, he *is* telling the truth. I can corroborate his story."

Burnell and Finch groaned simultaneously. "Not again, Miss Kirby, I beg you. This case is already complicated enough."

"I'm not lying. Honestly." She rested her elbows on the table and leaned forward. Her dark eyes were earnest and imploring. "I apologize for my earlier statement. You've proved that I was lying. I had no intention to mislead. I just wanted—I just—" The words caught in her throat.

Burnell didn't want to prolong her discomfiture. "It's all right, Miss Kirby. We know." His gaze strayed to Longdon. He shook his head, wondering once again what the devil she saw in him. Even now. Then, to Emmeline, he said, "There's no need to trouble yourself. We understand."

Emmeline had regained control of herself once more. "But that's just it, you don't. I saw Lady Cabot *and* Gregory that night."

Out of the corner of her eye, she saw Gregory turn his

head toward her. But she kept her gaze fixed on Burnell and continued, the words tumbling out in a rush. "They passed below my balcony. It was precisely ten o'clock. The reason I know is that the news was starting on BBC1, when I turned off the television and went out on the balcony to get some air. The wind was beginning to pick up, sending clouds across the moon. Some movement caught my eye and that's when I saw Lady Cabot pass under my balcony. I huddled in the shadows so that she wouldn't see me, but it wasn't necessary. She had her head down and appeared intent on hurrying off toward the garden and the woods beyond. I was about to go back into my room, when not five minutes later I saw Gregory skulking after her."

The corners of Gregory's mouth quivered into a bemused smile. He smoothed down his mustache. "Skulking, darling? I'll have you know that I *never* skulk. It's rather common."

"Oh, do be quiet, Longdon. No one's interested in your comments at the moment," Burnell said impatiently.

Gregory sniffed. "I must say that's a rather high-handed attitude to take, Oliver."

The superintendent grunted and turned back to Emmeline. "Do go on, Miss Kirby."

"The storm was coming and it was getting cold. There wasn't much point hanging about on the balcony. I went back into my room and tried to read for a bit to get my mind off—off things. I must have fallen asleep because I woke with a start, when the book slipped to the floor at the same instant that a great clap of thunder let loose its fury. The curtains were flapping wildly in wind. That's when I realized that I hadn't latched the sliding door earlier. I quickly got out of bed to do so. I wanted to shut the storm out. It was getting rather violent outside. I'm not normally skittish, but that night I was for some inexplicable reason. As I was locking the door and about to pull the curtain, a white flash of lightning seared the sky and I caught a glimpse of Gregory. Coming back to the hotel. Alone."

"Interesting," Burnell murmured. "Is that all, Miss Kirby?"

"Yes, that's it." She didn't like the superintendent's tone and the way he fixed on Gregory. "So you see, Gregory *was* telling the truth."

"Actually, I'm afraid, Miss Kirby, your statement rather raises more questions than it answers."

"But you can't seriously believe that he could—" Her dark eyes found Nigel's warm hazel ones and silently pleaded with him.

Nigel patted her arm reassuringly. "Look, Superintendent Burnell—"

Burnell cut him off. "Mr. Sanborn, what Miss Kirby has just told us puts an entirely different complexion on the case. It places Longdon at the scene of the crime. No one else, as far as we've determined thus far, knew that he and Lady Cabot had an assignation." Emmeline winced at this. "We only have *his* word for it that someone hit him in the dark. Lady Cabot could have lunged at him with a rock. Longdon himself said that they had argued."

"It's not true," Emmeline said hotly, tears shimmering on her eyelashes. "Can't you see? It must have been the real murderer who hit Gregory so that he wouldn't have an alibi. To make you—" She waved a hand wildly about, encompassing the two detectives. "—think exactly what you're thinking. But you're wrong." She suddenly jumped to her feet, nearly overturning her chair in her haste. "*You're wrong.*"

"Emmy, please. It's all right." Gregory stood up and tried to take her in his arms to still the anger rippling through her body, but she shrugged him off.

The other three men rose as well. "Miss Kirby, we are merely trying to ascertain the facts," Burnell said. "We have to follow the evidence wherever it may lead us."

"*Evidence?*" she wheeled on him, her voice shrill. "Superintendent Burnell, we both know that evidence can be fabricated. As it has been done here, only you refuse to see it because you and Sergeant Finch—" Her eyes slid for a second toward the sergeant. "—are prejudiced against Gregory."

Her chest heaved and her breath was coming raggedly. Both Burnell's and Finch's jaws went slack. They stared at Emmeline in disbelief, taken aback by her vehemence.

"Oliver, this isn't necessary, nor is it helping. Please let Nigel take Emmy away. She's tired. It's all the strain of the past few days. You can put me under hot lights, subject me to sleep deprivation—or anything else that crosses your plodding police mind—but Emmy does *not* need to be here anymore."

Gregory touched her cheek lightly and smoothed away an errant tear with his thumb. She lifted her eyes to his face and pressed his hand to her cheek. But suddenly, the image of Veronica Cabot's arrogant face reared before her eyes and the tender moment was gone. She pulled away from Gregory.

"Darling?" he probed, baffled at her coldness after her impassioned defense of him. He took a step toward her, but she shook her head and backed away. His brow furrowed and, for a second, she glimpsed the hurt in his eyes before his features arranged themselves into an inscrutable mask.

"Nigel, please take her away from here. *Now,*" Gregory mumbled hoarsely.

"Longdon, you're in no position to give the orders around here."

Gregory shot Burnell a warning look.

The superintendent was not of a susceptible nature and therefore unimpressed by such emotional displays— especially by the criminals within his custody. However, he, too, agreed that Emmeline had been through quite enough for one afternoon. And probably one lifetime. "Go on, Miss Kirby," he said kindly.

Their eyes met and held. He could see the wheels of her mind racing behind those troubled dark eyes. Burnell jerked his head toward the door. "Mr. Sanborn, I think a good cup of tea is what's needed."

Nigel nodded and gently took Emmeline by the elbow. She resisted.

"Don't worry, Miss Kirby," Burnell continued. "I'm not going to arrest Longdon the minute your back is turned. We simply want to talk with him. To sort things out." He saw her body relax slightly. "Go get that cup of tea. It will do you a world of good."

As door closed behind them, Gregory heard Nigel's words drift to his ears *sotto voce*, "I rather think a stiffner is what's called for."

This made his lips curl into a smile. "If I were you, I'd wipe that smile off my face, Longdon. For Miss Kirby's sake, I said that I wouldn't arrest you *for the moment*. But things could change."

Gregory crossed one leg casually over the other and there was a mischievous gleam in his cinnamon eyes. "Oliver, I realize that I'm the only thing that provides any excitement in your otherwise dull and sheltered life, so by all means do carry on." He waved an elegant hand at the superintendent. "I wouldn't want to deprive you of your fun."

Burnell's eyes sliced Gregory to pieces. The superintendent wondered—and not for the first time—what he ever did that was so bad that he deserved to be plagued by such an unabashedly unrepentant rogue. "I want none of your lip now."

"Yes, Oliver, whatever you say," Gregory replied, as he bit back a smile.

Damn, Burnell thought, *why does the man always have to have the last word*?

CHAPTER 34

Emmeline sat huddled in a corner of the sofa in the conservatory, staring into the steaming depths of her teacup.

"Drink it. It's Darjeeling, not poison," Nigel said, in an attempt to lighten the mood, but she wasn't listening to him.

She fixed him with a confused gaze. "What? Poison? Lady Cabot wasn't poisoned."

Nigel sighed and slumped back in the chair opposite Emmeline. "Oh, never mind. It wasn't important."

"Then why say it in the first place?" she mumbled. Her brow was knit in concentration, but he was happy to see her take a sip of tea.

"Look, Emmeline." He hesitated. "Do you think you'll be all right on your own here for a bit?"

"Hmm," she replied distractedly as she looked up at him.

"The thing is I have to go up to my room to make a few calls. Would you mind terribly?"

His eyes searched her face in concern. She smiled and reached out to give his hand a grateful squeeze. "Of course not, you go on and do whatever you need to do. I'm a big girl. I don't need a babysitter. I'll be fine. Thanks for everything you've done, Nigel. You've been a brick."

Her words put him at his ease and he didn't feel so guilty leaving her. "I haven't really done anything."

"Don't be so modest."

"Well," he said awkwardly as he rose. "Don't worry. Gregory can take care of himself. Everything will come right in the end. You'll see."

"I know it will," she replied with conviction. "Because I'm going to find the murderer and prove Superintendent Burnell and Sergeant Finch wrong."

Nigel didn't like the determined look in her eyes. There was something vaguely reckless about it. "On second thought, the calls can wait till later."

Emmeline threw her head back and laughed. "Don't be silly. Go do your work. You've wasted far too much of your day already. Besides, I need some time alone. To think."

"I wouldn't say wasted," Nigel murmured.

It took a few more minutes, but Emmeline was finally able to shoo him away.

※※※

Think, that's what I told Nigel. She needed to clear her brain. She asked for another pot of tea and pulled out her ever-present notebook. There had been too many distractions in the case up until now. What she had to do was separate the wheat from the chaff. As any good journalist would do, Emmeline began dutifully jotting down the facts that had come to light. Some niggling voice at the back of her brain kept whispering that it was all right there under her nose. She simply had to put the puzzle pieces together. However, thus far she had been too blinded by her jealousy of the beautiful Veronica Cabot—and hatred, if she were honest with herself—but no more. Cooler heads had to prevail. She couldn't allow her temper to supplant her reason.

Emmeline took a fortifying sip of tea. What did they know? Someone followed Lady Cabot out to Meadfoot Beach and overheard her argument with Gregory. That gave the killer the idea of framing him. The killer had to have worked quickly, though, to have knocked Gregory out in the woods and then retraced his steps to murder Lady Cabot. But that was taking a very big risk. Veronica could easily have gone back to the hotel by the time the killer returned, or Gregory could have regained consciousness. Emmeline groaned in frustration. It didn't make sense. None of it made sense.

Perhaps, if she concentrated on a motive she would have better luck. Love? Jealousy? Revenge? All three? The killer had to be someone who hated Veronica *and* Gregory. Why? Because the killer found out about their night together? The only people who would have been upset by that revelation—aside from herself, that was, and Emmeline knew that she didn't murder Veronica, much as she would have liked to—were Sir Frederick Cabot and Trevor Mayhew. She wouldn't have said that either man was a very likely suspect. And yet, Sir Frederick committed suicide and left a note confessing to the crime. This bothered Emmeline. It apparently bothered Burnell and Finch too. Yes, Sir Frederick grew up in an era when protecting the family honor was all-important. But murder? No matter how embarrassed he was about his wife's infidelity and the subsequent discovery that they were not really married, Emmeline couldn't fathom Sir Frederick taking his own life. After all, he *had* turned a blind eye for months to Veronica's affair with his nephew. Something, Emmeline judged, would have been a much more serious transgression.

She stared down at her notes. What was she missing? Then she remembered the threatening note Veronica had received. How did the elusive—and long dead—Edward Prichard fit into the equation?

Emmeline took another sip of tea and munched on a biscuit without really tasting it. At least it was quiet here in the conservatory. For the first time in a week, her mind had a chance to find a little peace. Peace? *This* was peace? she snorted silently. Superintendent Burnell was preparing to arrest Gregory and she was sitting here calmly drinking tea.

She really must have lost her mind. Or was it only her heart that she had lost?

Emmeline tasted the salty tears as they began to trickle one by one out of the corner of her eyes and down her cheeks. "Damn." This was followed by the jarring chink of china upon china being set down none too gently on the table at her elbow. "Damn," she said again as she rooted in her handbag for her handkerchief.

She dabbed her eyes with the delicate dainty white square. "Oh, Gregory. Why? Why did you have to lie to me? I loved you so much. I would have forgiven you *anything*, if you only would have told me the truth from the start. But now?" The question was left hanging in the air.

And Emmeline didn't have answer.

If only Gran were here, she thought. No, much as she loved her, she couldn't tell Gran about this nightmare. But she *could* tell Maggie. Her best friend, well she was really more like the sister Emmeline never had. Yes, she'd give Maggie a ring. Maggie would listen without judging. Emmeline would be able to get everything off her chest and then Maggie would give her some much needed advice. Dear old, Mags. A weak smile played around Emmeline's lips as this old nickname flew to mind. Magpie, her older brothers used to call her when they were children because she used to hide their toys. On the other hand, she was always Margaret to her father and Peggy to her mother. Maggie or darling to her husband, Philip. Mummy to her twin boys. But in the end, all the names described the same woman. One in a million. And Emmeline loved them all. Yes, Maggie would set her straight.

Emmeline flipped open her mobile and checked her watch. Maggie would still be at the office. She started to punch in the number she knew by heart, however, her attention was arrested by the appearance of Connie.

Emmeline was struck by how tense and drawn the woman looked. Connie's usual cheerful demeanor and bright smile were nowhere to be seen. She twisted a handkerchief between restless fingers as her blue eyes scanned the conservatory. She made a tour of the room before asking one of the waiters a question. Emmeline saw him shake his head. Then she heard Connie say, "Thanks anyway, Colin. I'll check the lobby again."

Head bent, Connie made her way toward the door. But in her haste, the handkerchief slipped from hands. Emmeline saw it flutter to the floor.

"Hey, Connie," Emmeline called out, but Connie didn't hear her. So she got up and scooped up the handkerchief. "Connie, wait. You dropped this," she said when she finally caught up with her.

"What?" Connie swung around at the sound of her name. "Oh, it's you, Miss Kirby," she replied, her voice tinged with impatience. "How can I help you?"

Emmeline smiled. "Actually, I can help you. You dropped this."

Connie looked down at the handkerchief with its embroidered monogram in the corner. The calligraphy letters *RCD* were delicately entwined together with tiny pink rosebuds. Her blue eyes opened wide and she shoved it back at Emmeline as if it was a venomous snake. "Why are you giving this to me? That's not mine."

Emmeline frowned. "But I just saw you drop it." She offered it to the other woman again and was repulsed a second time.

"I tell you it's *not* mine. I don't know why you insist—"

"Ah, Connie, you are a clever girl. You found my handkerchief. I thought it was lost for good."

Emmeline and Connie were startled to find Rosemary suddenly at their side. They hadn't heard her approach. Rosemary snatched the handkerchief from Emmeline's hand and hugged it to her stomach possessively. "It has tremendous sentimental value to me. My son Teddy gave it to me as a birthday present when he was ten years old. It's come to mean more to me since…well, since his death. I always carry it with me. To keep him close." She sighed wistfully.

"I was so afraid I had lost it. Thank you, Connie." She stretched out a blue-veined hand and gave Connie's arm a light squeeze.

The two women's eyes met and held for a long moment. Blue gaze upon blue. Almost mirror images of one another in shade and intensity. Connie straightened her shoulders, but seemed to visibly relax. She cleared her throat. "I was trying to find you, Mrs. Dunham. You must have dropped it in the corridor. One of the maids found it and brought it to me. The minute I saw it, I knew it must be yours."

"Well, thank you." Then, to Emmeline, "Oh, my dear, forgive me. I was so relieved to get my handkerchief back that I didn't say hello. How rude you must think me. "

"No, no. It's understandable," Emmeline murmured.

Connie nodded. "I must apologize too, Miss Kirby, for being brusque with you just now. As you can well imagine, the whole situation around here is rather distressing, and it's getting on everyone's nerves. First, Lady Cabot was murdered, and now poor Sir Frederick. Such a kind and distinguished gentleman." She shook her head, her eyes bright with unshed tears. "Suicide? Bah," she spat in disgust. "If you ask me, that Mr. Longdon killed Sir Frederick—" She broke off abruptly, shamefaced. "I'm sorry, Miss Kirby. I know that you and he—that you are well..." Her words trailed off, when she heard the sharp intake of breath from Emmeline.

An uncomfortable silence fell as the three women looked awkwardly at one another. Emmeline swallowed down the anger rising in her throat. "Gregory did not—" she said through clenched teeth, "—I repeat *did not* kill anyone. Do I make myself clear?" Neither Rosemary or Connie uttered a word. "And what's more, I'm going to prove it to you and to the police."

"If you ask me, you're on a fool's errand," Connie sniffed coldly. Emmeline's hands balled into fists at her sides as she glared at Connie. She opened her mouth to reply, but Connie swept on, heedless to the animosity she had instilled. "I overheard Superintendent Burnell talking with his sergeant. They are preparing to prefer charges against Mr. Longdon for the murder of Lady Cabot at least."

"What?" Emmeline's eyes widened in disbelief. "But that's ridiculous. Superintendent Burnell must have lost his mind. There's no concrete evidence that ties Gregory to the murder. It's all circumstantial."

Connie shrugged her shoulders. "I really wouldn't know about that, Miss Kirby. But the police must have *something*, if they're going to arrest Mr. Longdon." She tried very hard to keep the smug tone of satisfaction out of her voice.

Emmeline wanted to throttle her. She was desperately holding onto the last threads of her temper, but this woman was determined to push her to her limits. Connie didn't know what a terrible mistake she was making.

"You must admit that, Emmeline," Rosemary said, catching her off guard.

"What? I'm sorry. My mind drifted for a moment."

"I said that Connie is right. Scotland Yard is not in the habit of arresting innocent people. Therefore, Superintendent Burnell and Sergeant Finch must have *something* incriminating against Mr. Longdon."

Emmeline shot a thunderous look at both Connie and Rosemary and realized that it was useless to argue further. They had already made up their minds. But they were wrong and she would show them. She would show them all.

Emmeline took a deep, cleansing breath. She plastered a smile on her face and squared her shoulders. "Well, if the two of you will excuse me, I have a thousand things I must attend to."

"Of course, Emmeline," Rosemary replied with a tight smile. "Perhaps we'll see each other later at dinner."

"Perhaps," Emmeline said aloud. But her mind screamed, *Not bloody likely.*

"Yes, I must get back to reception," Connie mumbled. "Mr. Harcourt told me that Mr. Mayhew is on his way back to the Royal Devon."

Rosemary turned her elegantly coiffed head toward Connie. "Is he?" she asked casually. "Well, yes of course. The heir apparent. I suppose that was to be expected after Sir Frederick's untimely death. When is he scheduled to return?"

"I believe sometime tomorrow afternoon."

"I see." A shadow passed over Rosemary's wrinkled features for an instant and then it was gone. Or did Emmeline simply imagine it in the first place?

"Good afternoon, Emmeline. I would wish you happy hunting, but I'm afraid I can't honestly say that I support you."

Emmeline smiled stiffly. "Everyone is entitled to his or her own opinion." Although she knew she was being rude, she turned her back on Rosemary and Connie.

Emmeline made her way back to the sofa where she had been having tea earlier. She plopped down heavily, every nerve end in her body was seething. The whole exchange with Rosemary and Connie had left a bitter taste in her mouth. They had already tried and convicted Gregory based solely on hearsay without any corroborating facts whatsoever. As a journalist, this went against the grain and grated on Emmeline's sense of fairness and objectivity.

She ordered another pot of tea and leafed through her notes again. The words started to blur on the page. It struck her forcefully, all at once, that she had missed something. Something important. It was hovering at the outer edges of her consciousness, just waiting for her to pluck it from the air. But *what* was it? She flipped through pages impatiently.

The waiter arrived and set the tea tray down on the table. She nodded politely as he melted away to see to another guest. Frustrated and disgusted with herself, Emmeline poured herself a cup and allowed the curative powers of the Earl Grey to soothe her nerves and focus her disjointed thoughts. As she leaned back against the sofa, taking tiny sips, her gaze settled on Connie and Rosemary, who were still huddled together. She watched them curiously. How could they be so judgmental? She went over their entire exchange again in her head. What was it that bothered her? Aside, that is, from their undisguised prejudice against Gregory.

Connie and Rosemary seemed to sense her intense scrutiny and hastily concluded their conversation. Rosemary waved her handkerchief in the air and appeared to thank Connie again for finding it. Then they both disappeared in opposite directions. Connie went out into the lobby and Rosemary headed toward the terrace.

Emmeline frowned, feeling two vertical lines etch themselves between her eyebrows. This whole case had set everyone on tenterhooks and was a mass of convoluted strands. And yet. She had the strong feeling that she had found the thread that would untangle the whole mess. She just needed to talk it through with someone. Emmeline set the teacup and saucer down on the tray and pulled out her mobile to ring Maggie as she had originally intended to do before she was distracted by Connie and Rosemary.

Emmeline punched in the number and waited. One ring. Two rings. Three rings. "Come on, Mags, pick up," she mumbled under breath.

Four rings. "Hello, you've reached Maggie..." Emmeline severed the connection. She didn't want to leave a message. She needed to talk to Maggie *now*.

"Oh, Maggie, Mags, Margaret, Peggy, where are you when I need you?" Emmeline asked as she shoved her handkerchief aside and dropped her mobile back into her handbag. Maggie, the lady of a thousand names, could be in any number of places. Emmeline would simply have to try again later.

Wait a minute! Names. Something to do with names. The words that would haunt her for the rest of her life came flooding back once more. Only this time, they took on a new meaning.

'The last time I saw her was four years ago. She had a different surname then. It was Longdon. She's my wife.'

Emmeline sat bolt upright on the edge of the sofa. Yes, of course. The same woman, just a different surname. *Her married name.*

An idea was beginning to crystallize at the back of her mind. But how would she prove what she suspected?

CHAPTER 35

Emmeline burst into the lobby just in time to see Superintendent Burnell and Sergeant Finch leading Gregory toward the car park. Each detective had a hand on Gregory's upper arm. Nigel was following close on their heels. All four men looked grim.

"Superintendent Burnell," she called. "Wait a minute."

As she drew near, she realized that Gregory's wrists were handcuffed. Her eyes traveled from the steel bracelets to Burnell's face. "Then it's true. You're arresting Gregory."

"Now, Miss Kirby," the superintendent said as he raised his hands to forestall the angry cascade that was about to be unleashed from her lips. He well remembered her reaction the last time they attempted to arrest Gregory for murder.

But she was having none of it. "Why are you doing this?" It was more of an accusation than a question.

Burnell cast a quick glance around the lobby and saw Connie watching them from reception. He lowered his voice, hoping Emmeline would do the same. "By his own account, Longdon was at the scene of the crime *and* he had a strong motive for murdering Lady Cabot and possibly Sir Frederick as well. Now, please stand aside and allow us to do our job."

"I most certainly will not." Emmeline took a step forward to stand in front of Gregory, as if to shield him with her body. To the outside observer, the scene smacked of the ridiculous, in view of the fact that the four men all dwarfed Emmeline by a foot.

"You're making a terrible mistake," she snarled.

Gregory awkwardly took her by the elbows and gently moved her aside. "Emmy, everything will be all right. Don't get upset. Let Oliver and Finch do their job."

She rounded on him. "How can you be so calm about the whole thing? This is taking stiff upper lip a bit far. Don't you realize that you're being arrested for *murder*? This isn't a game to pass the time."

Gregory's gaze slid sideways to Nigel, who chimed in. "Emmeline, please let me handle the situation. You'll only make matters worse at this stage. If—"

"*Worse?*" A bitter laugh escaped her lips. "How could matters possibly be any worse?" Her eyes swept over in each man in turn. No one chose to respond. "Would it make a difference if I told you I *know* who killed Lady Cabot?"

Burnell and Finch exchanged surprised glances. "Know, Miss Kirby, or suspect?" the superintendent asked.

Emmeline wavered, but only for a fraction of a second. "Well, I have a strong suspicion. But—"

The two detectives seemed to visibly relax. Burnell smiled at her. "I see, Miss Kirby. The problem is that we need proof, not suspicions." He took hold of Gregory's arm again and tugged him half a step toward the door. "Come on, Longdon. We've wasted enough time."

"If you would only hear me out," Emmeline implored, her voice rising in frustration at the stupidity and stubbornness of the male species. Sometimes they could just be thick.

"The time for talking is over, Miss Kirby. I was under no obligation to give you any explanation, especially in view of the fact that you are a member of the press. I only did so out of courtesy. You're only getting in our way by playing at detective." This came out more harshly than he had intended and, for that, he was truly sorry. He heard her sharp intake of breath and felt the volley of icy daggers flying in his direction from those unblinking dark eyes.

Emmeline's back stiffened at the rebuff. "At least I know where we stand, Superintendent Burnell. I won't keep you and Sergeant Finch from your duty, but stand warned—" She took a step closer to him and drew herself up to her full height, which at this moment was on par with a giant. "—if you thought I was a nuisance before 'as a member of the press,' I'm going to become your shadow now. You see, I'm editorial director of the *Clarion* as of two days ago. That means I have full control over content and which stories I choose to pursue *personally*. I'm *not* dropping this one. Not until I bring you the real murderer's head on a platter. You should know that about me by now. I *never* give up."

Burnell was silent for a long moment. Then, he cleared his throat. "A very pretty speech, Miss Kirby. It's too bad you're wasting your time."

Before she could articulate her riposte, he had hustled Gregory out into the car park. Nigel and Sergeant Finch lingered awkwardly by her side for a moment, clearly not knowing what to say. In the end, succumbing to the typical male instinct to avoid controversy and further argument, they decided it was better to leave her to cool off.

Finch managed a weak smile and Nigel gave her arm a quick, reassuring squeeze. Then they were gone.

ᗉᕯᗉᕯ

Emmeline grew more angry and determined to find the irrefutable proof to support her theory, which she was becoming more and more convinced was the truth. She had spent the past two hours on the phone with her friend David Jacobs, an investigative journalist at the *Toronto & Globe Mail*. She had pressed him for all the details of that long ago murder of financier Henry Cummings by his infamous young protégé, Edward Prichard.

Her dinner remained untouched as she scribbled furiously in her notebook. David patiently recounted what he knew of the police investigation, Prichard's subsequent arrest on embezzlement, then later murder charges, and ultimately, the evidence that came out at the trial.

"That's about everything, Emmeline," David concluded. "I hope it's helped. Now, are you going to give your old friend a tiny hint as to what this is all about or am I condemned to ignorance until your story comes out?"

Emmeline downed her third cup of coffee. "David, I can't begin to thank you for all of this information. You're a giant among men."

"But you can't tell me what you're working on," he replied matter-of-factly.

She felt herself smile for the first time that day. "But I can't tell you what I'm working on. Sorry."

"Fair enough. I won't pry. Anything else I can do?"

Emmeline flipped back through her notes to something she had underlined and next to which she placed two question marks. "There's just one point I'd like to clarify."

"Shoot. It's your phone bill."

"When Felicity pulled background for me on the case initially, she said that Prichard had a fiancée. But you made no mention of Prichard's fiancée. Whatever happened to her?"

"She dumped him the minute her greedy little eyes fell on Henry Cummings. By all accounts, she was extremely beautiful. Therefore, it wasn't surprising that when she set her cap for him, he fell hard. In two months, she became *his* fiancée. She had insinuated herself into every aspect of his life, his home, his business. In short, everything. Cummings even made her his sole beneficiary *before* he put the ring on her finger. Why is it that men can be brilliant in business and such fools in their personal lives?"

Unbidden, Emmeline's thoughts flew to Gregory. "I

wouldn't know, David. The workings of the male mind have always been a complete mystery to me. You men have quite a lot to answer for."

His hearty laughter boomed down the line and echoed in her ear. "I detected a hint of asperity in that statement. You know, women are not the coquettes and innocents they purport to be. Some can be utterly ruthless and cunning, when they want something badly enough."

"Don't I know it," Emmeline mumbled under breath.

"What was that?"

"Nothing, David. It wasn't important."

"I wasn't speaking about you, of course. You're one of the most honest and loyal women I know. Besides, with your temper I don't think you'd make a very good gold-digger."

She giggled. "Thanks. I'll take that as a compliment...I think."

"By all means, that was the spirit in which it was intended. Now, you know that I could go talking with you for hours, but duty calls."

Emmeline glanced at her watch. "I didn't realize the time. Thanks, David. You've been a tremendous help. The next time you're in London, I'll take you to dinner wherever your heart desires. No expenses spared."

"I'll look forward to it. It's been ages since I've seen you. It will be nice to catch up. Congratulations on your new job at the *Clarion*. Best of luck. Talk to you soon." There was a soft click as he rang off.

Her conversation with David had given Emmeline a lot of food for thought. He had confirmed so many of her suspicions. The adrenaline was throbbing through veins. There were several leads she needed to follow up, but she knew she was on the right track now.

Emmeline settled her bill and, in her haste to get up from the table, she collided straight into the solid golden form of Trevor Mayhew.

"Oof," she exclaimed, slightly winded.

"Emmeline, I'm terribly sorry. Are you all right?" he asked, as he grabbed her arm to steady her.

"Yes, I think so. Trevor?" She was surprised to see him. "I'm afraid it was my fault. I suppose you're back because of your uncle. My condolences. It must have come as a shock."

A shadow darkened his countenance. "Yes. Thank you," he murmured. "It's been a difficult week. First Ronnie—my aunt. And now Uncle Freddie. Suicide." He shook his head. "I can't believe it. And why would he confess to Ronnie's murder? None of it makes any sense."

They fell silent, each chasing disturbing trains of thought.

"Well, I mustn't keep you," Trevor said at last. "You appeared to be in quite a hurry."

"Yes, I was. I'm working on a story. Again, I'm sorry for your loss. If there's anything that I can do to help..." She left the sentence hanging.

Trevor managed a weak smile and gave her arm a squeeze. "Thanks, Emmeline. That's very kind of you, especially since the police have arrested Longdon for Ronnie's murder."

Emmeline squared her shoulders and thrust her chin in the air. "The police have made a mistake. Gregory didn't murder Lady Cabot."

"Forgive me, Emmeline. But I think you're allowing your personal involvement with Longdon to—"

"This has *nothing* to do with my relationship with Gregory," she said through clenched teeth. "I'm a journalist and therefore well acquainted with the basic tenets of objectivity. And I'm telling you, Superintendent Burnell has arrested the wrong man. I know who the murderer is."

"Do you? Then why arrest Longdon?"

She threw her hands up in the air in exasperation. "Because they're imbeciles. Whatever they claim to have is circumstantial. There's no possible way Gregory could have done it. Absolutely none."

She met his skeptical blue stare without blinking. "I'm sorry, Emmeline. I appreciate your loyalty to the man, but you're deluding yourself. After all, there's no smoke without fire."

Emmeline balled her fists at her sides. She was determined not to lose her temper. "On that note, I think it would be best if I said good night, Trevor."

"Perhaps, that would be wise. I'll be going down to the station in the morning to speak with Superintendent Burnell. Good night, Emmeline." He inclined his head slightly as he stepped aside for her to pass.

"Good night, Trevor," she replied woodenly.

Their once easy rapport had evaporated in the space of a few minutes. For that, she was sorry but there was no room for sentiment now. Not with a murder charge looming over Gregory's head.

"Emmeline," he called after her.

Perhaps, he wants to apologize, she thought. Well, maybe he's not that bad after all. "Yes, Trevor."

"You dropped your notebook." He bent down to scoop it up. As he was flipping it closed, his eye happened to fall on two words. "What this?"

Emmeline snatched it from him, before he could read anymore. "Just some leads that I'm following. That's all. Thank you, Trevor. Good night."

Emmeline felt his gaze boring into her shoulder blades as she threaded her way across the restaurant, but she didn't turn around.

Trevor frowned, and an uneasy feeling clouded his mind. All he could see was those two words written in Emmeline's elegant, curving hand at the bottom of the page.

Edward Prichard.

How the devil did she find out? Why was she stirring up that particular hornet's nest again? he wondered.

It only confirmed his worst fears. Emmeline had to be stopped before the distasteful truth came tumbling out.

CHAPTER 36

Edward Prichard. He was the key to everything. All of Emmeline's nerves tingled with excitement because she knew she was on the right track. Veronica Cabot had to be the mysterious fiancée who broke it off with Prichard the minute a bigger prize was dangled before her eyes. That was why she was always careful not to get her photo in the papers—that, and the fact that she was still married to Gregory.

Someone must have found out Veronica's involvement with Prichard. Someone who despised her and chose blackmail as the weapon of punishment. Judging by her reaction when she had accused Emmeline of being behind the scheme, Veronica was terrified of losing all that money if Sir Frederick found out. That last note with its vow to make her pay for her crime had escalated matters to a different level.

Was murder always part of the plan? Emmeline wondered. *The final judgment? The price Veronica had to pay for leading Prichard on and ultimately causing his death? Or did circumstances get out of hand and murder was the only option left open?*

Emmeline groaned. She simply didn't know. Her thoughts were racing in all different directions. She squeezed her eyes shut and pinched the bridge of her nose between her thumb and forefinger. Blood throbbed a relentless tattoo against her temples. She had to get out of the hotel. She needed some air.

Taking a shortcut through the conservatory and out onto the terrace, she breathed in a lungful of clean air and stretched her arms over her head to loosen the knots between her shoulder blades. Her soft-soled shoes made barely a sound as she crossed over to the parapet to watch the waves rise and fall as they rolled toward shore only to disappear into gloaming's smoky mauve embrace. Night would soon snuff out the last vestiges of day.

But, for now, the soothing hiss of the water below beckoned. Emmeline decided to take a walk before she sought refuge in her room. Without consciously planning it, she found herself following the path that led past the hotel's garden and through the woods toward the cliff path, where Veronica Cabot had waited for Gregory. And where she had been stabbed and then pushed to her death.

The shadows were thicker here and a light wind set the leaves chattering restlessly. Emmeline hugged herself as she tried to rub the goose pimples from her arms. The hairs on the back of her neck prickled and a shiver slithered down her spine. She quickened her pace, but it had nothing to do with the cool night air. Someone was following her. She hadn't been certain at first, but now she was.

A twig cracked. She stopped, her ears straining to listen, all her senses suddenly, acutely alert. The footsteps were getting closer. Emmeline started to run, her breath coming in ragged rasps. She risked a glance over shoulder. But it was too late.

The gunshot shattered the vespertine quietude. Birds nestling amongst the highest branches took terrified flight as Emmeline crumpled to a heap on the earthy floor. A thousand needles of pain radiated from the base of her neck to the top of her skull.

As the murky gloom bore down on her, Emmeline had the vague impression of a familiar silhouette standing before her. Watching, waiting. She tried to lift her head, but the pain exploding behind her eyes made focusing impossible. Then her eyelids fluttered closed. And she succumbed to the blackness.

ᥱᕲᥱᕲ

Sergeant Finch guided the car down the narrow country lane. He cast a quick sidelong glance at Superintendent Burnell, who hadn't uttered a word since they left the station. Burnell simply stared out the window without really taking in the bucolic landscape. The only thing that betrayed his deep concern was the rhythmic tapping of his stout fingers on his knee.

Finch turned the last bend in the road and rolled to a stop on the gravel drive. There, nestled amid lush grounds, a cream-colored Georgian manor house rose above the wooded hills to gaze down lovingly at the River Dart as it bid adieu to the day and surrendered to the evening's soft embrace.

"We're here, sir," he said.

Burnell stirred and blinked twice. "Here? Here where?"

Finch sighed. "Whitehurst Manor. Sir Frederick's estate."

The superintendent slowly turned his head to allow his gaze to sweep over the house and stroked his beard thoughtfully. "Right. Let's have a look round," he said as he got out of the car.

Finch watched his boss as he came round the car to join him. "Don't worry, sir. Everything will be all right. We have a man watching, Miss Kirby."

"I don't like it, Finch. I was persuaded against my better judgment—" He broke off suddenly. A dark shadow fell across his face and then after a moment, "No use worrying over spilt milk. Did you put out the word that Longdon had escaped?"

"Yes, I rang up Mr. Harcourt at the Royal Devon to alert him and his staff. You don't seriously believe he'll do anything foolish, do you?"

"Lord knows, Finch. That man is as unpredictable as they come. I wouldn't put anything past him."

The sergeant nodded. "Hmm."

"Well, we won't find any answers dawdling out here." Burnell started to walk toward the front door.

"What are we looking for, sir?" Finch asked as he rang the bell.

"Damned if I know. Hopefully something to explain why Sir Frederick took his own life and confessed to his wife's murder."

Finch opened his mouth to ask another question, but immediately bit back what he had been going to say when a tall, thin woman with chestnut hair piled atop her head opened the door.

"Superintendent Burnell and Sergeant Finch," Burnell said as they showed her their warrant cards. "We rang earlier."

"Yes, of course. I'm Martha Beresford, the house manager. Please come in." She stepped aside and ushered them into the hall. "What a terrible tragedy," she said, shaking her head sadly as she closed the door behind them.

"Yes," Burnell replied. "Can you tell us why Sir Frederick and Lady Cabot chose to stay at the Royal Devon and not here? We understood that it was Sir Frederick's habit to spend April through June at Whitehurst Manor."

"That was his custom, but this year he had undertaken some renovations on the house. Sir Frederick had been hoping that the work would be finished by now. Unfortunately, there have been some unforeseen delays. Sir Frederick had planned to come over to inspect where things stood, but Lady Cabot died and then he—" She choked back a sob. "I'm sorry, Superintendent," she said as she fumbled in her pocket for a handkerchief and blew her nose. "It's all been such a shock. A kinder gentleman and employer never walked the earth. Sir Frederick will be truly missed."

"Of course, Mrs. Beresford," Burnell murmured soothingly. "Had you worked for Sir Frederick for many years?"

A bitter smile creased her lips. "Nearly twenty years. Sir Frederick hired me shortly after my husband died."

"I see. Then you knew him quite well. And Lady Cabot? What was your impression of her?"

Mrs. Beresford stiffened. "I really couldn't say," she sniffed. "I never met the woman. The whole point of this trip was to check on the renovations and to show her the house."

"Forgive me, Mrs. Beresford. But you seem to have formed a negative opinion of Lady Cabot, and yet you contend that you never met the woman."

Mrs. Beresford was quiet for a long moment as she sized up the two detectives. "We are in touch with the staffs of the houses in Cap Ferrat and London. Naturally, one hears things or at least is able to read between the lines. Apparently, Lady Cabot was not quite...not quite in Sir Frederick's class. She was beautiful and well-spoken, yes, but breeding always outs, doesn't it? And she lacked it. A parvenu, from what I understand. Madame Gauthier, the caretaker in Cap Ferrat, said that Lady Cabot was only after Sir Frederick's money. Why, only a month after they were married, she shamelessly set her cap at Mr. Trevor. Can you imagine? Quite revolting."

"I see." The superintendent nodded sympathetically. "So Mr. Mayhew was a regular visitor at Whitehurst Manor?"

"Oh, goodness, yes. Members of the family were always popping in and out of the house." Mrs. Beresford sighed and a smile lit up her face as the memories of summers past came flooding back. "However in the last couple of years, Mr. Trevor was the only one who came down. A pity. They were always such a close-knit, devoted family. Cousins, uncles, aunts, nieces, and nephews. Ah, well." She shrugged her shoulders and another sigh escaped her lips. "I suppose things can't remain the same forever."

"I suppose not," Burnell murmured.

"Well, I'm certain you did not come here to hear me chunter on about the past." Mrs. Beresford became what he assumed was usual her brisk and efficient self once more. All nostalgia was firmly locked away. "Now, when you rang earlier you said that you wanted to go through Sir Frederick's papers. His desk and all his files are in the library. It's down the corridor to your right. I'll just pop into the kitchen and have Mrs. Pilchester prepare a tea tray for you gentlemen."

"That's very kind of you, Mrs. Beresford, but quite unnecessary."

She would brook no arguments. "Nonsense. After a long day, there's nothing better than a fortifying cup of tea."

"Thank you," Burnell and Finch replied in unison.

"Right. I'll leave you to it, then. Remember, down the corridor to your right. If there's anything else you need, simply press the red button on the telephone. It rings through to my office."

Mrs. Beresford was as good as her word. Twenty minutes later, there was a light tapping on the library door and a plump woman with snowy white hair—presumably Mrs. Pilchester, the cook—appeared with the tray laden with a teapot, cups and saucers, and plate of warm scones with homemade strawberry jam. She bestowed a shy smile upon the two detectives and then bowed herself out of the room.

Burnell and Finch had hardly had a chance to start on Sir Frederick's papers, but they had to admit that the tea was a welcome respite. The superintendent lowered his weary body down onto the well-worn, overstuffed blue-gray sofa, while Finch chose the matching armchair near the window overlooking a corner of the garden.

They sipped their tea and munched on scones in silence. Each lost in his own thoughts. The sergeant's brown eyes

roamed around the rectangular-shaped library. It was cozy
and highly conducive to allowing the mind to get lost in the
pages of a good book. The soft beige, wall-to-wall carpeting
muted one's footfalls, while the cream-colored walls pro-
vided the perfect backdrop for the delicate watercolors and
landscape paintings on one side of the room. The wall behind the sofa was covered floor to ceiling with creamy
bookshelves crammed with hardcovers and paperbacks, interspersed with a few vases and *objets d'art*.

"I could certainly get use to this, couldn't you, sir?"
Finch said.

"Hmm?" Burnell looked up from the file in his lap and
cast a quick glance about him. "Very nice. But don't get any
ideas in your head, Finch."

"No, sir." The sergeant took a sip of his tea to hide his
smile. "Anything in that file?"

Burnell set his cup and saucer down on the coffee table.
"No, nothing. I've gone through it a dozen times or so already. They all deal with Cabot Corporation."

"It would help if we knew what we were looking for."

The superintendent's knees cracked as he rose to his feet.
"Ah, well, no rest for the wicked. Time to get back to work.
I'll go through the rest of the desk. You get stuck in with
whatever is in that bureau over there."

"Right." The sergeant popped the last morsel of scone
into his mouth and washed it down with a hasty gulp of tea.

When Finch opened the bureau, he found that it was
stuffed with photo albums. The bindings on some were
frayed, as if they had been thumbed through often. He
pulled the first stack out and brought them over to the chair
he had been occupying by the window. He placed them on
the floor then settled himself into the chair. Finch picked up
the top one and rested it on his knees. He sighed as he started flipping through the pages with a distinct lack of enthusiasm. The album was filled with black-and-white photos,
probably Sir Frederick's parents and grandparents. Finch
wondered if the little boy in some of the photos was Sir

Frederick. The rest of the albums in this stack were pretty much the same, so the sergeant was able to go through them fairly quickly.

Finch cast a glance over at his boss as he returned the albums to the bureau and took out the second group. The sergeant hid a smile. Burnell was hunched over the desk, his glasses on the bridge of nose, his lips moving silently as he concentrated on a sheaf of papers. Finch resumed his seat once more. These albums were more recent photos, probably taken in the last fifteen or twenty years, of family gatherings at Whitehurst Manor and outings to nearby villages. A younger, carefree Trevor Mayhew, mugging for the camera, was clearly recognizable, as was Sir Frederick. Finch assumed the rest of the people in the photos were assorted other relatives and friends, who came down to Devon to get away from it all. He went through the first album and had only leafed through two pages in the second book, when one of the photos made him stop. He squinted at it. "It can't be," he said.

This caught Burnell's attention. "Found something, Finch?" He took off his glasses and watched as his sergeant took the album over to the lamp on the end table by the sofa.

"Sir, I think you need to see this."

Burnell put his palms on the desk and pushed himself to his feet. "Bring it over here." He took the book from Finch. "What am I meant to be looking at?"

"Family photos. Recognize anyone, sir?"

The superintendent's eyes carefully scrutinized each face in the photos and read the neat captions penned in below. His gaze halted when it fell upon one particular photo. He read the caption and then looked at the photo a second time.

Burnell nodded his head sagely. "Yes, now it's starting to make sense. I've been a bloody fool. It's been staring us in the face the whole time."

"Sir, I wouldn't say it was *that* obvious."

"No? Well, perhaps not. But it explains a lot of little things that didn't add up before."

Burnell snapped the album shut and his brow furrowed in consternation. "Come on, Finch."

"Where are we going, sir?"

"The Royal Devon. Miss Kirby is in grave danger and it's all my fault. I should have paid more attention to what she was trying to tell us." He pounded one fist against the open palm of his other hand. "Let's hope that she hasn't done anything rash to upset our killer. If anything happens to her because of our negligence—" He broke off, leaving the rest of the sentence hanging uncomfortably in the air between them.

Finch took the album from his boss and tucked it under his arm. They let themselves out of the house without taking their leave of Mrs. Beresford.

"Drive like the wind, Finch," Burnell said as he clicked his seat belt in place. "Miss Kirby's life may depend on it."

CHAPTER 37

Drip. Splash. Drip. Drip. Splash. The soft rain tiptoed through the shadows, leaving its moist kiss upon leaves and branches and the woodland floor.

"Emmeline," the voice called to her from far away. *"Emmeline."*

She tried to lift her head and open her eyes. That was a mistake because some giant had placed her head in a vice and was taking sinister pleasure in twisting it tighter and tighter. Surely, her head would explode at any moment.

She heard the voice again, only more insistent this time. "Emmeline, come on. Wake up. Wake up."

This was accompanied by some vigorous shaking of her shoulder, which only sent the pain shooting to every corner of her body.

She wished whoever it was would simply go away and leave her alone. She wanted to die in peace. Was that too much to ask?

"Emmeline, come on, old girl. Snap out of it."

She groaned and tried to roll over onto her side. Another mistake for which her head rebuked her harshly. Her mouth was parched, but she managed to whisper, "Go—away."

The shaking started again. Why couldn't this unreasonable chap understand? She had a good mind to give him a punch on the nose. The only thing stopping her was the fact that she couldn't seem to make her eyes open to see whoever this bloody prat was.

"Open your eyes. That's it, old girl. Come on. Emmeline, you have to wake up. Do you hear me?"

I hear you, all too loudly, she thought. *Maybe if I open my eyes, he'll leave me in peace?* Emmeline made a supreme effort to concentrate and managed to crack her left eye open. She felt beads of perspiration on her forehead.

"Good girl. Well done. That wasn't so hard, now was it?"

That's easy for you to say, Emmeline grumbled inwardly. *You're not the one with a ten ton brick on your head.*

"Now, open the other one."

Really, didn't anyone ever tell this chap he was too demanding?

"If you got one eye open, you can open the other as well."

She licked her lips with the tip of her tongue and filled her lungs with air. Her third mistake of the evening. The brick was now being dropped from a great height and was bouncing on her head. "Oh, please stop," she moaned.

"I'm not going to leave until you open your eyes."

Oh, it's you again. Why are you still here?

"What happened? Is she all right? Emmy?"

This was another voice, one tinged with concern and a trace of fear. She knew that voice. *Gregory?*

"I lost track of her and then I found her like this. Sorry, old chap. I let you down."

"Never mind all that now. Let's get her back to the hotel. What was that?"

They both froze and held their breath. Something was snuffling around in the undergrowth. Whatever it was, it was getting closer. They held their breath for a long moment and listened.

"Someone's coming. You can't be seen. Make yourself scarce. Go on and wait for me in my room. I'll come as soon as I take care of Emmeline."

"Promise?" Gregory said as he started moving away, his gaze darting into the shadows, trying to discern who the unexpected newcomer was.

Nigel jerked his head impatiently. "Yes. Now go."

It *was* Gregory. Emmeline's eyes flew open wide and she turned her head slightly. "Gregory, it is you. I'm so happy that you came to see me one last time before I die."

Then Emmeline's head slumped to one side and everything went dark once more.

ᘓᘓᘓ

"I say, Nigel. Am I glad to see you."

Nigel tore his eyes away from Emmeline's still face and found himself squinting up into Trevor's blue eyes. "Are you, Trevor? I must say that I'm surprised to find *you* here."

Trevor bent down on his haunches beside Nigel and smoothed back Emmeline's dark curls from her forehead. "How is she? I was taking a walk after dinner and I found her. I went back for help, but I'm afraid I lost my way. Then I thought I heard voices. And here I am. What happened to her? Do you know?"

Their eyes met in the half gloom, but neither uttered a word. Trevor was the first one to look away and Nigel wondered why the man was lying. "I have absolutely no idea what happened. Perhaps you can tell me?"

"Me? How should I know? I told you. I was walking and—"

"I know," Nigel cut him off. "And then you got lost in the dark."

"That's right." Trevor replied defensively as he put his hands on his thighs and pushed himself to a standing position. "Shouldn't we get Emmeline back to the hotel for some help?"

"Yes," Nigel mumbled. "That would seem to be in order."

"Here, I'll get her."

"No," Nigel retorted sharply as he gently eased one arm under Emmeline's shoulders and the other under her knees to lift her up. "I'll handle it."

"As you wish. No need to be so tetchy. I'm sure she only took a tumble in the dark."

"I'm glad one of us is sure. Because I'm certainly not," Nigel countered ominously. "Why don't you lead the way, Trevor? You can tell me if there are any roots I should avoid. I'll watch out for other hazards."

Trevor shrugged his shoulders and held a branch back to allow Nigel to pass unmolested with his burden.

⌒⌒⌒

The sight of Nigel carrying Emmeline—unconscious, head lolling back—in his arms sent a ripple of gasps through the guests who happened to be in the lobby. With the deaths of Lady Cabot and Sir Frederick still fresh in their minds, this scene was more than a little disconcerting, to say the least.

"You there," Nigel yelled to the young fellow at the reception desk. "Call a doctor immediately. This woman's been injured. Come on. Don't stand there gawping at me, you fool. Get a move on."

"Yes, sir." He picked up the receiver and started punching in a number.

"Trevor, make yourself useful and hurry that chap along."

"Right." Trevor made his way to desk and spoke in low tones to the young man, who was suddenly joined by his colleague, Connie.

"Thank God, you're here, Connie," the young man said, relief patently obvious on his face.

Connie ignored him and directed her attention to Trevor, her blue eyes locked on his. "What seems to be the problem, Mr. Mayhew?"

Trevor was momentarily tongue-tied. Finally, he found

his voice. "As you can see—" He waved his hand vaguely behind him. "—Miss Kirby appears to have had some sort of an accident. She needs a doctor."

Connie flicked her gaze over his shoulder and then back again. "Yes, I see. I'll take care of it," she replied as she took charge of the situation. She reached out for the receiver and tapped her forefinger impatiently on the desk, all the while watching Trevor closely.

Superintendent Burnell and Sergeant Finch walked into the lobby as Nigel was turning around trying to find a place to set Emmeline down.

"Sanborn, what the devil's happened?" Burnell asked as he and Finch rushed over to help ease Emmeline onto a sofa.

"Gregory, Gregory," she murmured over and over.

"Longdon?" The superintendent raised an eyebrow. "He's *here*?" he whispered.

Nigel slid a sidelong glance to his left, before he gave an imperceptible nod.

"That's just bloody marvelous. He's going to ruin everything."

"You really can't blame him. He was worried about Emmeline. And obviously he was right to." Nigel looked down. Her head and shoulders were resting against his chest.

"We're all bloody worried about her," Burnell grumbled though clenched teeth. "That's why we went through that whole charade this afternoon. Longdon can't—"

"*Gregory*," Emmeline mumbled at the sound of his name. "He hurt me. *Gregory*."

"Sir, we've got to keep Miss Kirby quiet. She's starting to attract attention."

Burnell shot a hard blue stare at Finch. "Really, Finch? Thank you for imparting that little bit of wisdom."

The sergeant persevered, inclining his head slightly over his right shoulder. "The wrong kind of attention, sir. The kind of attention that likely got her in this predicament in the first place."

Burnell looked about and then nodded. "Right." Then he lowered his voice as he turned back to Nigel. "Let's get her up to her room. We found something this afternoon."

"Indeed?" Nigel's eyes silently questioned the superintendent.

"Not here. Too many ears."

Nigel nodded.

"Do you think she can walk if we help her?"

"I don't think so. She keeps going in and out. From what I can tell, someone gave her a good coshing on the back of the head. I can't tell if there are any other injuries, although there's some blood on her shoulder."

Burnell looked down at Emmeline, who was moving her lips noiselessly. "Right. Finch, you take over for Mr. Sanborn."

"Yes, sir." They brought Emmeline to a sitting position. Her head slipped onto the sergeant's shoulder with her cheek resting against his neck. "Come on, Miss Kirby. We're going up to your room so that you can take a little rest. You'll like that, won't you?" Finch murmured soothingly.

Emmeline nodded. "Tired. Very tired. Hurts. It hurts."

"Don't worry, Emmeline. You'll be fine. You just need some rest," Nigel said.

"Can't. Gregory." She started to squirm in Finch's arms.

"Easy now. Don't worry about anything. Longdon's fine. He can take care of himself."

"Can't. He hurt me. I know who murdered—"

"Shh," Nigel whispered in her ear as Trevor suddenly appeared at his elbow.

"Ah, Superintendent Burnell and Sergeant Finch, how fortuitous that you happened to come on the scene at this crucial moment. They've rung for the doctor. He should be here in about twenty minutes. How is she?" Trevor asked anxiously, his brow puckered in concern.

"You can see for yourself, Mr. Mayhew," Burnell said curtly. "Now, if you would please stand aside, we're going to take Miss Kirby up to her room."

"Yes, of course. Good idea. I'll wait down here and send the doctor up as soon as he arrives."

"Very good of you, sir."

Trevor watched until the two detectives and Nigel had disappeared into the lift. Then he reached into his jacket pocket and pulled out his mobile. His eyes swept the lobby before he punched in the number.

He listened for a few seconds. On the third ring, there was a soft click. He spoke in a low, urgent tone. "We need to talk. Don't argue with me," he hissed. "You were very careless tonight. The only thing that your little stunt did was to further arouse Emmeline's suspicions. But what's even more disturbing is the fact that Longdon is nosing about. Yes, that's right, Longdon. I overheard Burnell and Sanborn talking about him. Longdon is an even bigger threat than Emmeline. Meet me in an hour by the cliff path. We can discuss what is the best way to deal with him."

☙❧

Emmeline had quieted down by the time the lift doors slid open on her floor and the odd little group made its way down the corridor to her room. Nigel slipped the key into the lock and turned the knob. They took half a step into the room and stopped dead in their tracks.

"Well, don't look at me, chaps. I didn't do it," Gregory said.

He was standing in the middle of the room, which looked as if it had been ravaged by the storm that had ripped through the other night. Everything had been rifled— Emmeline's suitcase, her handbag, the drawers, everything. The sheets were a rumpled, tangled mess on the bed. *The*

Sonnets of the Portuguese and her Agatha Christie novel were both on the floor face-down.

Nigel smoothed out the sheets and Finch gently set Emmeline down on the bed.

"Bloody hell," Burnell swore as he eased some of the detritus out of the way with the toe of his shoe.

"Oliver, you're perspicacity always amazes me, but I think you succinctly summed up the situation."

"Shut up, Longdon." The superintendent stood with his hands on his hips surveying the wreckage.

Gregory clucked his tongue and waggled a finger at Burnell. "Language, Oliver. Might I draw your attention to this artistic display, which I believe all of you missed in the initial excitement?"

They all turned in the direction he was pointing. There, scrawled in red lipstick in big block letters on the mirror above the dresser, were the words: *NEXT TIME, I WON'T MISS.*

CHAPTER 38

Emmeline sat up in bed, her head propped against several pillows. She was completely awake now, but her head throbbed mercilessly. The local doctor had been and gone. After some probing, followed by "Hmm" and "Aha" interspersed at various intervals, he determined that she would live. A diagnosis that Emmeline was very gratified to hear. However, he told her that she was lucky that someone had decided to thump her over the head. Otherwise, the bullet that had grazed her shoulder would most likely have entered through her ear and lodged itself in her brain. This tidbit was something that she was not so happy to hear.

She crossed her arms over her chest and closed her eyes. Why did people insist on using her head as a means to take out their frustrations? Why didn't they simply bang their own heads against a wall?

Emmeline opened her eyes again and found herself staring at the mirror. *NEXT TIME, I WON'T MISS* leered back, mocking her. Why couldn't they have given her a different room?

Oh yes, she remembered now. The hotel was fully booked and they wanted to get her away from the lobby, where she had become the star attraction.

"Coward," she spat in the direction of the mirror. "If you

think that you're going to scare me, you're dead wrong. Now, I know I'm right." She was going to leave the words there to prove she was not afraid. No, she wasn't afraid. She bloody furious.

She gingerly swung her legs over the edge of the bed and started to get up, when the door opened and four male voices converged into one to reprimand her.

"Miss Kirby, what *do* you think you're doing?"

"Emmeline, the doctor said that you need to rest."

"Miss Kirby, I must insist that you follow the doctor's instructions. You'll do yourself an injury if you're not careful."

And finally, "Emmy darling, there's no need to prove to us how strong and courageous you are. We all know it. Now do be a good girl and lie back down."

Emmeline's eyes locked on Gregory's face. He managed a crooked smile. "Come on, love. Lie down. You'll feel better." He bent down and lifted her legs onto the bed again.

She started to reach up to touch his cheek and then changed her mind, letting her hand drop into her lap. A low sigh escaped her lips. Absently, Emmeline went to finger the bracelet he had given her, only to realize that it was *not* there. She began to fumble frantically among the sheets and threw the pillows on the floor. The four men exchanged worried glances.

"Where is it? It has to be here?" she muttered.

Gregory kneeled down beside her and gently grabbed her upper arms to still her. "Darling, what's the matter? What are you looking for?"

She turned to him, her eyes brimming with hot tears and her face a picture of misery. "My bracelet." She lifted her naked wrist in the air. "I've lost my bracelet. The bracelet you gave me. It's not here."

Gregory smiled and straightened up. He pulled her into his embrace. "Don't worry, love. I'll buy you another one. An even nicer one."

Emmeline pushed him away. Tears streaked her olive cheeks. "You don't understand. I don't want another one. I want *that* one."

Superintendent Burnell, Sergeant Finch, and Nigel stared at one another, at a loss about what to do. Gregory, however, remained unfazed. "Don't worry, Emmy. I promise to make a thorough search for it in the morning. And I won't leave any stone unturned until I find it."

"It could be anywhere, though. I might have lost in the woods. How will you find it?"

"You leave that to me. I have my ways. And if not, I'm certain our dear representatives from Scotland Yard will be only too happy to assist me in this matter. Isn't that right, Oliver?"

He flashed a cheeky grin at Burnell, who emitted a grumpy "Hmph" at this remark.

Gregory turned back to Emmeline. "There, you see. What did I tell you? Always willing to serve the public. But it's getting late now, and you need some rest. Oliver has spoken to Chief Inspector Ashcroft, who has posted two sturdy constables on your door. They'll be there all night. They have strict instructions not to let anyone in, aside from the four of us. So you don't have to worry about our resident artist returning to create another mural in the middle of the night. And just to make doubly sure, I'll be taking up residence in that chair over there." He pointed to a straight-backed armchair that had been positioned at the end of her bed.

"Thanks. But it's really not necessary for you to babysit me. I'll be fine," she managed at last. Although she was loath to admit it aloud, her nerves were a bit shaky after everything that had occurred this evening, and she was glad that the police would be outside her door. Then another thought struck her. "Hey, what are *you* doing here? I thought Superintendent Burnell had arrested you for Lady Cabot's murder."

The room fell silent. Her eyes narrowed as she searched

all four men's faces in turn. Only Gregory's features sported a bemused expression. "There's something all of you are not telling me, isn't there?"

Not a one of them would meet her eyes.

⌘

Emmeline had slept fitfully. Aside from the fact that her mind was racing, she couldn't seem to get comfortable. At one point, she woke up with a start. She was shivering, but her body was drenched in sweat. Memories assailed her of that horrible moment in the woods when she heard the gunshot and then saw that face looming over her prone body just before she passed out.

She reached out for her watch on the bedside table. Tenthirty? This was ridiculous. She couldn't stay cooped up in her room. Half the morning was gone. She never lingered in bed this late. She was used to getting up early because she always had a story to work on. Today was no different. A little bump on the head was not going to stop her from getting *this* story. She was perfectly fine. Slightly sore, but fine overall.

Emmeline threw off the bedclothes with purpose and padded on bare feet to the bathroom. She turned on the shower and waited until smoky wisps of steam seeped out from behind the curtain. First, a hot shower to ease her stiffness. Then a turn round the hotel garden before she hunted down a killer. No need to tell Gregory and the others about her plan, seeing as they had chosen to keep her in the dark about what *they* had discovered. *Two*—or rather five, in this case, since they outnumbered her—*can play at this game*, she mused.

The shower had refreshed her and she was ready to do battle. After ten minutes of coaxing, although it went against their better judgment, Emmeline finally managed to persuade the two constables guarding her door to allow her to go down to the garden for a bit of air and exercise. Alone. However, they elicited the promise from her to return within a half-hour. Emmeline readily agreed with a smile on her lips and her fingers crossed behind her back. She squeezed past the two officers and hurried down the corridor before they could change their minds.

A light breeze dandled the tree branches as watery sunshine seeped from the ragged tear in the clouds. The garden was deserted, but the chatter of the chaffinches hidden amongst the leaves kept Emmeline company as she strolled down the gravel path. She could hear the low murmur of the sea in the distance beyond the woods. She loved the sea and normally it had a soothingly hypnotic effect upon her. But not this morning. She shivered involuntarily as cold tendrils of fear curled themselves around her heart. Her pulse quickened.

The gravel crunched behind her. Someone else was in the garden. The footfalls were soft and unhurried. But getting closer with each step. One foot in front of the other. Closer. Emmeline turned slowly, the blood roaring in her ears.

"Ah, Miss Kirby, I'm glad I've found you."

Emmeline found herself staring into Connie's smiling blue eyes. "Oh, were you looking for me for any particular reason, Connie?"

"I thought you might be missing this." The other woman stopped a few feet from Emmeline and extended a hand. There in the middle of her palm lay Emmeline's bracelet.

"My bracelet," Emmeline exclaimed with a mixture of relief and happiness. "I never thought I'd see it again." She scooped it up and slipped it onto her wrist at once.

"I recognized it the minute I saw it. I knew you would be missing it. I remember you mentioned that it had some sentimental value."

Emmeline smiled at the other woman. "Yes, it does. I'm very grateful. But where did you find it?"

"Why, in the woods where you dropped it, of course."

Connie's smile had vanished and her pleasant demeanor with it. Her frosty blue glare sliced Emmeline to the bone. Her voice was laced with acid. "Well, no matter. Your days of meddling into things that are none of your concern are over, Miss Kirby."

She pulled a gun from her pocket and pointed it at Emmeline's chest.

CHAPTER 39

Emmeline blinked twice as she stared at the barrel of the gun. Then her gaze traveled up Connie's arm, until it came to rest on the other woman's face, whose features were contorted in anger. Emmeline's heart was thundering so loudly in her chest she felt certain that Connie must be able to hear it.

Emmeline's mouth felt dry, but she swallowed hard. She couldn't allow the fear to take over. She had to keep her wits about her. Otherwise, she would never get out of here alive.

"Tell me, Rosie." Emmeline saw other woman's eyebrows lift in surprise. "It *is* Rosie, isn't it?"

The muscle in Connie's jaw quivered and the hand holding the gun trembled slightly. "You're mistaken. You know very well that my name's Connie. Connie Crawford."

"We both know that's only partly correct. Crawford is your married name, but you were born Rosemary Constance Dunham," Emmeline replied with more confidence than she felt.

When Connie remained silent, Emmeline pressed on. "It was there for all the world to see. *RCD.* The initials on the handkerchief. It was *your* handkerchief that I picked up yesterday in the conservatory. Not your mother's, although she tried to cover up for you."

Connie's blue eyes grew wider, but still she held her tongue.

Emmeline shrugged. "I'm interested to know who came up with the idea to kill Veronica Cabot, you or your mother?"

"You—you—" Connie stammered. "You're mad."

"Am I? I don't think so. Your reaction rather belies that statement. Now, let's see if I've got it all straight in my mind."

Emmeline took a big chance at this point and turned her back on Connie as she started to pace back and forth along the path. If she could throw the woman off guard, perhaps she could make a run for it. "I haven't quite worked out all the pieces, but you or your mother managed to discover that Veronica Cabot and your oldest brother's fiancée were one in the same woman. Edward Prichard was your brother, wasn't he?"

Emmeline turned on her heel to face Connie again. "Still no answer? It doesn't really matter. The question was rhetorical, in any case. Veronica dumped Edward in a heartbeat when she caught Henry Cummings's eye, didn't she?"

"Yes. And poor Teddy took his own life, all on account of that self-centered viper."

Both Connie and Emmeline whirled around when they heard Rosemary's voice behind them.

The sudden appearance of her mother had the effect of snapping Connie out of her stupor. She hurried to Rosemary's side.

Emmeline was outnumbered, but she stood her ground. Her eyes flickered from mother to daughter. Now that they were side by side, and she knew the truth, it was quite obvious that the two women were related. They had the same eyes, the same tilt of the head, the same mannerisms. That's why Rosemary had seemed so familiar when she met her along the promenade her first day in Torquay. It wasn't that she reminded Emmeline of her grandmother, it was that Rosemary reminded her of Connie, whom she had met at the hotel only an hour earlier when she had checked in.

"Emmeline, you had no business interfering in any of this," Rosemary said sternly, her brows knit together in vexation. "It was a family matter, and the family always takes care of its own."

"But murder, Rosemary?" Emmeline asked incredulously.

"No, not murder, my dear. Justice. That woman killed my son as surely as if she were in his cell, pulling those sheets tighter and tighter around his neck until his life was squeezed from his body. She had Teddy so wrapped around her finger that he was willing to do anything for her. And how did she repay my sweet and generous boy? By dumping him and making it look as if he embezzled from the company."

"There must have been another way—"

"Another way? The only way to stop a woman like that is if she's dead. That way, she can't hurt anyone else. She was wicked. The devil incarnate. She took good men and twisted them inside out, simply to do her bidding. It had to stop. She had hurt the family too much. Emmeline, you, of all people, should be thanking us for getting rid of that woman, although I don't understand why you would want Mr. Longdon after discovering that he betrayed you with *her.*"

Emmeline sucked in her breath. This stung as surely as if she had been slapped. "How dare you throw that in my face? This is not about me and Gregory."

"Isn't it, Emmeline? You claim to prize the truth above all else. Be honest with yourself, if with no one else. That man is so deeply embedded under your skin that you can't see straight. He keeps betraying you and yet you keep coming back for more."

"Why, you witch. How could I ever have believed that you were a lonely widow with a kind heart? You're nothing of the sort. Only someone as cold and calculating as you could have hatched up this ruthless scheme. And your daughter there—" Emmeline jerked her head toward Connie. "—is no better."

An ugly crimson flush rose upon Connie's cheeks. She raised the gun and waved it in the air. "I should kill you right now. You have no right to judge us." Then she turned to Rosemary. "Mum, Trev was wrong. She's more of a threat than Longdon ever was or could be."

"Trev?" Emmeline asked, perplexed. "You don't mean Trevor Mayhew, do you?"

A sinister smiled played about Connie's lips. "Yes, that's right."

"What does Trevor have to do with any of this?"

"Oh, so Miss Nosey Parker doesn't know everything, after all? I thought you would have realized by now, Trev is my cousin. Well, third cousin, if you want to be technically correct. Uncle Freddie—we all called him uncle—but he was really our second cousin. He and Mum were first cousins. Such a darling man."

Emmeline opened her mouth, but no words came out.

"You remember, Emmeline, I told you that first day we met," Rosemary picked up the thread in the tale, "My parents sent me down to Torquay during the Blitz to stay with my aunt and uncle, and their three children. Two daughters and a son."

"And the son was Sir Frederick?" This came out as a hoarse croak. Emmeline felt the bile rising in her throat. She squeezed her eyes shut and shook her head, as if to deny this startling revelation.

"Got it in one. After years of hiring private detectives to find that woman with precious little to show for their efforts," Rosemary said bitterly, "out of the blue, Freddie announced one day last spring that he had come across an English beauty in Cannes, who gave him the eye. Freddie was quite certain that she was the same Veronica who had killed my poor son. You see, Teddy and his uncle were very close, like father and son. Freddie took it extremely hard, when Teddy died. In some ways, I think Freddie took the news harder than I did. That's how close the two of them were. The minute Freddie rang me about the woman in Cannes. I knew it had to be *her*. It was divine justice.

"Freddie lived in the South of France most of the year. However, I urged him to come back to London immediately for a family conference on how we should proceed. Freddie was the one who came up with the idea of marrying her. I wouldn't allow it at first, but he persuaded me that it was the only way. They'd play newlyweds for a few months, then when the time was right we'd arrange for young Lady Cabot to have an accident. Freddie would be the grieving widower for an appropriate period and then gradually things would return to normal." Rosemary looked into the distance for a moment and let out a deep sigh. "And the world would be a better place without *her* roaming about in it. It was the perfect plan. Perfect."

"If you're related to Jack the Ripper," Emmeline mumbled.

"Don't take that superior tone with me, my dear," Rosemary sniffed. "That woman got what she deserved. Now, where was I? Oh, yes. Unfortunately, Freddie, like all the men, soon fell under that woman's spell. He said that we must be wrong about *his* Veronica. She couldn't possibly have had anything to do with poor Teddy's death. Freddie actually called me a liar. Me. Can you imagine? It was too much. In the end, Rosie and I made him see that it was a matter of family duty."

"I can't believe what I'm hearing. Sir Frederick Cabot, businessman, philanthropist, patron of the arts, willingly married a woman for the sole purpose of murdering her."

"I told you, my dear. It was a family matter. We take care of our own. When someone hurts one of us, he—or she, in this case—hurts all of us. We had planned to wait a year, before dealing with Veronica. But our plans had to be hastened when she got her clutches into Trevor. We couldn't allow him to become another Teddy. First, we started with the anonymous notes and phone calls to make her look over her shoulder. It was such fun watching her unravel bit by bit. Then the trip to Torquay was arranged. Rosie and I were in place, ready to play our respective roles. Veronica didn't suspect a thing."

Something finally clicked into place in Emmeline's head. "Of course, it's all so clear now. All those times in the lobby—when you pretended to feel faint, Rosemary, and, Connie, when you cut our conversation short the minute Veronica and Trevor exited the lift. You weren't trying to avoid Veronica at all, which I thought at the time. The two of you were afraid Trevor might see you and the game would be up. I'm right, aren't I?"

"You think you're very clever, don't you?" Connie took a step closer to her. "You think you're better than we are. You prance about all high and mighty. Well, let me tell you something." Another step closer. "You're nothing. Do you hear? *Nothing*," she spat this word like a bullet.

Emmeline swallowed hard, but managed to look Connie directly in the eye. "It was there right in front of my face the whole time, but I allowed myself to be distracted. I saw what you wanted me to see. Perhaps, if I had been paying closer attention..." Her voice trailed off and she bit her lip.

Perhaps if I hadn't allowed my jealousy to get in the way I would have seen, she thought silently. *Oh, well, too late for recriminations. In for a penny, in for a pound.* She had to know the truth, every odious detail. "So now that you've regaled me with the background on your 'perfect plan,' tell me about the *coup de grace*. The night you murdered Veronica Cabot."

Connie laughed in her face. The sound sent a frisson of fear down Emmeline's spine.

"Wouldn't you like to know, Miss Nosey Parker? Well, seeing as you're dying to know—dying, get it?" Connie elbowed her in the ribs.

Emmeline kept her eyes fixed on the gun in the other woman's now trembling hand.

"I'll have to oblige. I wouldn't want you going to your

grave ignorant. Veronica made it rather easy. All we had to do was follow her to her assignation with Longdon. We really have to thank your boyfriend. He was our unwitting ally. We watched them argue, and then he stalked off. I trailed after him, caught up to him in the woods, and gave him good thump on the head. After all, he was no saint. Clearly, he was in league with her and he would have to pay for his sins sooner or later. I opted for sooner. As murderers go, he fit the bill. Better him than us, eh?" Another jab in the ribs. "Then I double-backed and met Mum and Uncle Freddie."

"Sir Frederick was there? You don't mean to say that he actually helped you?"

"No," Rosemary replied quietly, as she picked up the story. "No, in the end, the old fool lost his nerve and couldn't go through with it. Men. And they call us the weaker sex." She sniffed with disgust. "Connie and I had to finish the job, while he scurried back to the hotel and pretended he had been in their room all evening. You should have seen the surprise on Veronica's face when we confronted her. Nothing gave me greater pleasure than plunging that knife between her shoulder blades. I thought it would be difficult, but it was easy. Oh, so very easy. You know, she had the gall to laugh and turn her back on me. She called me an old cow. Well, I had the last laugh, didn't I?"

CHAPTER 40

Emmeline's jaw dropped. She was stunned at how nonchalant Rosemary had been in describing the whole thing, as if it was an everyday occurrence. They murdered a woman in cold blood. *Murder.* Her mind simply couldn't comprehend it. No matter how much she hated Veronica Cabot—and there was no doubt about it, she hated her with every fiber of her being—she would never have contemplated murder. It went against everything that had been instilled in her by her grandmother and what she had been told about her parents' views of right and wrong. Life was too precious.

Emmeline's gaze hovered between mother and daughter. They stood there preening. It was sickening. She cleared her throat. "Instead of taking things into your own hands, you should have gone to the police. That's what they're there for. To hunt down killers and bring them to justice."

"Ha. Don't be naïve, Emmeline. You know as well as I do that the police wouldn't have given us the time of day. Don't think that your Superintendent Burnell and Sergeant Finch wouldn't have willingly looked the other way, if the price had been right."

Emmeline straightened her spine and her chin jutted forward. "You do Superintendent Burnell and Sergeant Finch a grave injustice." She blistered with indignation.

"They are two of the most respected, hardest-working, honest, and thorough police officers on the Metropolitan Police force. If you had gone to them with your suspicions and evidence, they would certainly have listened to you."

Rosemary's lips curved into an amused smile. "Really? I rather doubt it. But we'll never know, will we? Unfortunately, Emmeline, you're the only one who has miscalculated in this sad business. You should never, *never,* have gotten involved with Gregory Longdon. If you hadn't, you would have been much happier, less insecure. As it is, you must understand that Rosie and I cannot allow you to share what you've discovered today. It's going to have to be our little secret. A secret I'm afraid that you will have to take to your grave."

Emmeline took a half-step backward. "You're mad. You're going to kill me *here* in the garden within a stone's throw of the hotel?" She was stalling, her mind working furiously to think of a way to escape from this nightmare alive. "I would have thought that was rather messy. How would you explain it? Besides, someone could come along at any moment to take a stroll round the garden."

"Oh, Emmeline, stop putting off the inevitable. You know everyone has to die. Your time happens to have come a bit sooner than anticipated." Connie sounded almost reasonable, almost. However, the malevolent gleam in her blue eyes belied her calm tone. "The three of us have been here for a good half-hour and no one has come along to disturb us. But you're right, of course. We can't stay here. Too many questions would be asked. We had another place in mind. Distinctly more suitable. Now, come on."

She grabbed Emmeline roughly by the arm and pressed the muzzle of the gun deep against her rib.

"I hope it's as nice as you say. I wouldn't want to be disappointed." Emmeline tried to be flippant, but she couldn't keep the tremor from her voice.

The gravel crunched noisily beneath her feet as Connie dragged her down the path that led toward the woods.

"I shouldn't worry, Emmeline," Rosemary said as she followed in their wake. "It will be over so quickly, you won't have time to feel disappointed."

Emmeline swallowed hard. She couldn't think of how to reply.

"I rather resent being left out of all the fun. Not very sporting." A male voice floated to their ears.

Emmeline stiffened. Her self-possession suddenly abandoned her and panic started to rise within her breast. They turned around to find Trevor hurrying toward them.

ᗒᗒᗒ

Superintendent Burnell and Sergeant Finch stepped out of the lift and they immediately knew something was wrong. Down the corridor, Nigel was talking heatedly with the two constables standing guard on Emmeline's door.

"And you just let her go?" Nigel asked, the exasperation palpable in his tone.

"Mr. Sanborn, sir, our orders were to see that no one enters Miss Kirby's room. Neither Chief Inspector Ashcroft nor Superintendent Burnell said anything about preventing her from leaving."

"You bloody great oafs. Don't you realize that someone tried to kill her last night and may very well do so again?"

"What's going on here?" Burnell demanded gruffly as they came level with the trio.

"Superintendent Burnell, thank God you've come," Nigel said. "These two constables have allowed Emmeline to go out *on her own* to take a stroll in the garden."

The superintendent's eyes narrowed, dissecting the two constables.

"S—sir, we had our orders to guard the room. H—how were we to know?" one of them stammered.

"Did you think it was more important to guard an empty room than to protect the woman who resided inside it?"

"No, sir. Of course not, sir. But no one explained the situation."

"Explained. *Explained*," Burnell exploded. "Obviously what little bit of brain the two of you possess failed you completely. Ring Chief Inspector Ashcroft *now*. Explain the situation and tell him to send some men to the hotel. Then, get out to that bloody garden. And you had better pray that you find Miss Kirby lolling on a stone bench, or I'll have your badges for this. Do I make myself clear?"

"Yes, sir," the constables said in unison. They were already scurrying toward the lift.

Burnell slammed his fist against Emmeline's door. "It's a bloody shambles."

"Sir, I'll go downstairs and speak to the hotel staff. Perhaps someone saw Miss Kirby. Perhaps she changed her mind and decided to have a late breakfast in the dining room," Finch offered optimistically.

Burnell balled a fist and pressed it against his ample stomach. "Something in here tells me that's wishful thinking, Finch."

"I'll go check with Longdon. Let's hope for once that Miss Kirby's with him."

"I'm afraid Gregory's not in his room," Nigel said. "I thought he might be with Emmeline. That's why I came down. The rest you know."

"You see, Finch. My stomach never lies. Longdon picked a fine time to make himself scarce. I would have thought he would be glued to Miss Kirby's side. More to the point, where's Mayhew? Has anyone seen *him* this morning?"

Both Finch and Nigel shook their heads glumly.

"I hope to bloody hell that Miss Kirby hasn't walked into a trap because we overplayed our hand."

৩৩৩

"I'll take that, Rosie," Trevor said as he eased the gun

from Connie's hand and firmly gripped Emmeline by the upper arm. His cousin had no choice but to yield to him.

Trevor favored Emmeline with a smile which made her blood run cold.

"I—I thought—that is—I thought you weren't part of this ghastly scheme," she stammered.

Connie threw her blonde head back and laughed. "Oh, poor Emmeline, you're not as astute as I gave you credit for. We didn't involve Trev. The whole point was to protect him from that witch. He just sort of stumbled upon our little plan by chance. Who do you think coshed you over the head last night?"

Emmeline's eyes widened in disbelief. "*You?*"

Trevor inclined his head slightly. Then to Rosemary and Connie he said, "And it's a good thing, too, that I came along when I did, otherwise, Rosie would have made a right hash of it. Killing her in the woods, really?" He shook his golden head at his relatives. "Much better this way. Make it look like she took her own life, eh?"

"You're right, Trevor dear," Rosemary replied. "Now, let's not linger around here any longer."

"Right. Shall we?" Trevor tightened his hold and shoved Emmeline forward. She winced as she lost her footing for a moment. His fingers bit into the soft under part of her arm.

"I don't know how you think you're going to get away with this." She tried to keep calm, but it was becoming distinctly more difficult, as the seconds ticked by, to display the trademark British stiff upper lip.

"No more talking. Just move."

They followed the walkway out of the garden and onto the footpath that led through the woods and which became the coastal trail high above the jagged outcropping of rocks.

Trevor and Emmeline were a few feet in front of the others. The sound of the incoming tide mingled with the screeching of two seagulls wheeling gracefully through the thickening clouds. They were near the edge of the path. She felt light-headed and didn't dare look down, but out of the corner of her eye she caught the movement of the angry rollers rumbling toward the rocks. Coming closer. *Ever closer.* One wrong step and she would slip. There would be nothing to break her fall. Except the rocks. The hard, sea-slicked rocks, glistening with salty foam.

The wind was picking up and rain started to seep from the charcoal sky, gently at first and then more insistently. Tiny droplets clung to Emmeline's cheeks and moistened her hair. She cast a nervous sidelong glance at Trevor. He held himself erect, his blond hair plastered to his scalp. All she could see was his profile. He stared straight ahead, so she couldn't read the expression in his eyes. But his jaw was clenched in a tight line.

Suddenly, Trevor stopped and pulled Emmeline to one side so that she was forced to look out at the sea. Her knees felt like water. Her legs couldn't support her weight any-more. Surely, she would tumble over the edge. Trevor must have sensed this because he roughly pulled on her arm, at once propping her up. In the process, he stepped slightly in front of her. "I think this is far enough," Trevor called out to Rosemary and Connie, who were still a little ways back.

Connie shrugged. "It's as good a place as any." She turned to Rosemary. "What do you say, Mum?"

The older woman glanced down at green-gray waters slapping against the rocks. "It's fine. Let's just get this over with."

Emmeline struggled to break free of Trevor's grasp, but he was too strong. "You'll never get away with this. No one will ever believe that I committed suicide."

"They will when they find the note you left," Connie said with a malicious grin.

"What note?"

"Don't you remember? The note you left with me with strict instructions to give it to Superintendent Burnell in one hour. Plenty of time for you to take a little leap into the chil-ly water. Poor Emmeline, so overwhelmed by Longdon's betrayal, she took her own life." Connie shook her head and clucked her tongue. "Such a tragedy that she had to die so young."

"You're mad. Utterly mad."

"Oh, Emmeline." Rosemary sighed, and, for a second, a pained expression flitted across her features. "Don't think that I enjoy this. Far from it. I regret that things have come to such an end. But you must see that we have no other choice. We cannot possibly let you live, now that you know the truth. At least you understand why that creature had to die."

Emmeline opened her mouth to reply, but she was forestalled by Trevor. "The thing is, Aunt Rosemary, I don't understand it. Not one bit. So why don't you explain it to me. And 'that creature's' name was Veronica, by the way."

In one swift motion, Trevor had pushed Emmeline behind him, so that he blocked her with his body, and turned the gun on his aunt and cousin. Emmeline couldn't see their faces, but she was certain that they mirrored her own stunned expression.

"Trevor, what is the meaning of this? Have you taken leave of your senses?"

A bitter laugh escaped Trevor's lips. "You have the nerve to ask me *that*? You ruthlessly plotted to kill the woman I love—loved—in cold blood and you ask me that? Emmeline's right. You're sick."

"Pull yourself together," Rosemary commanded, a sharp edge to her tone. "It was a family matter. You must see that. That woman drove my Teddy to his death and she had to pay. The family had to make her pay. The family always takes care of its own."

"Really? How did the family take care of Uncle Freddie, eh? The family—the two of you—" He pointed an accusatory finger at them. "—badgered him until he didn't know which way was up and the only way to get some peace was to take his own life. Doesn't that bother you?" Trevor's voice was hoarse and thick with emotion.

"Oh, come off it, Trev," Connie countered. "Veronica was a gold-digger to the core. The only person she cared about was herself. She would have thrown you over in a heartbeat, if a bigger prize was dangled in front of her greedy eyes."

"That's it. I've heard enough. Did you really think I would sit by and let you get away with it?"

Emmeline heard the soft click as Trevor eased the safety catch off the gun.

"No," she mumbled, but it came out as a garbled croak. "No, you can't." She clutched at his moistened sweater, but he ignored her.

"Trev, you can't be serious. You can't do this. We're family." Connie's voice shook. Her confidence had abandoned her. She was no longer so bold and condescending.

"Listen to her, Trevor," Rosemary murmured soothingly. "When you've thought about it for a moment, you'll see that we were right. We had to kill Veronica. It was the only way. Now, you don't really mean to harm us, do you, my dear?"

Trevor raised his arm. Emmeline squeezed her eyes shut. This was *not* happening. She couldn't stand here and be an eyewitness to a murder. "Trevor, please don't do this," she managed at last. "You're better than they are."

He suddenly dropped his arm to his side and tilted his head slightly toward his shoulder. "You're right, Emmeline," he said out of the side of his mouth. "I *am* better. Heard enough, Longdon?"

Gregory emerged from the woods. "Every word, loud and clear. Modern technology never ceases to amaze me." He waved a small recorder in the air as Trevor removed the wire from inside his jacket.

Emmeline peeped out from behind Trevor. "What? I don't believe this. *You?*"

Gregory winked at Trevor and flashed a cheeky grin at her. There was a mischievous gleam in his cinnamon eyes. "Emmy, you didn't really think that I was going let you out of my sight after last night, much as you tried to be the avenging angel."

"So the two of you—the whole time—" Her eyes narrowed. "You could have let me in on your plan. Instead you allowed m—me t—to—" she spluttered indignantly.

"To do what you do best, my darling, seek out the truth and vanquish evil. Only you *must* admit that you needed a tiny bit of help this time." He and Trevor exchanged a laugh at her expense.

"Beast," she muttered. "I always said that you were a heartless beast."

This only made the two men laugh harder.

Unfortunately, they let their guard down just long enough for Connie to lunge for the gun. The sound of the shot was snatched up by the wind and carried out over the cliff before it drowned in the churning waters below.

CHAPTER 41

Emmeline was knocked to the ground and lay there on her back, momentarily dazed as she tried to catch her breath. She rolled her head slowly to one side, her cheek resting against the rough path. Someone quite close by was screaming. And then Emmeline realized that *she* was the one screaming.

Trevor was huddled next to her, unconscious, his mouth slightly open, and an ugly red stain quickly seeping through his pearl-gray sweater. "Trevor," she whispered as she rolled onto her side and propped herself up on one elbow. She reached out and softly touched his cheek. His skin was warm, but fast turning the same shade as his sweater. He was losing a lot of blood. "Trevor," she tried again. "I know you *must* try to wake up."

However, her efforts to rouse Trevor were interrupted by the sight of Gregory tussling with Connie for the gun. An icy, naked fear clutched at Emmeline's heart as she watched with horror. They were getting closer and closer to the edge of the cliff.

The animal grunts emitted by Connie rent the air. There was a wild, glazed look in those cold blue eyes, which darted right and left as she searched for a way to escape.

Emmeline slowly got to her knees, and waited. She held herself perfectly still. *Now.* Another part of her brain took over. Adrenaline coursed through her body, propelling Emmeline to her feet. She held her head down and her shoulder low.

"Watch out," Rosemary cried out to her daughter.

But it was too late. Emmeline had used all the weight of her body to take Connie unawares, ramming her shoulder into the other woman's rib cage.

The gun made a small arc as it flew through the air to land several feet away. Connie tumbled to the ground with a hard *thud*. Emmeline winced as she heard bone crunching against bone, followed by a low moan. She took her eyes off Connie for a fleeting moment to ascertain where the gun was. That's when she made her mistake.

Connie had just enough strength to reach out and grab Gregory's ankle. He lost his footing, wobbled back and forth for a paralyzing instant as he tried to desperately regain his balance. Then, gravity won.

"*No.*" It was a single, anguished word, ripped from Emmeline's throat. The sound was inhuman.

She scrambled to her feet, stumbled, and then slithered on her stomach. "Gregory." Only the wind echoed in her ears. He had to be all right.

Please God, he has to be all right, she implored the heavens. Hot tears blurred her vision as she pulled herself toward the edge. "*Gregory.*"

Relief flooded her body, but only fleetingly. Gregory was alive, just. But he wouldn't be for long if she didn't think fast. He was slightly below her and conscious. That was the good news. The bad news was that he had only managed to get hold of a ledge with one hand and Emmeline could see the veins bulging through the taut skin of his hand as that arm was taking the entire weight of his body.

She braced herself by grabbing onto a large rock by her side and leaned out further over the edge. "Gregory, take my hand."

He looked up into her anxious eyes and his mouth

quirked into a crooked smile. "Oh, hello, love. Came to admire the view with me? It's absolutely marvelous." The words were light-hearted, but his handsome features were strained by tension.

"Shut up and give me your hand, you bloody man."

"Really, Emmy. There's no need to be dictatorial," Gregory chided.

Emmeline grunted as she leaned her torso closer to him and stretched her arm out as far as it would extend. "I always said that you were incorrigible. The minute you get back up here, I'm going to kill you—"

"Darling, I hate to point out the obvious but that would rather defeat the purpose of this diverting little exercise."

"Ahh. Take my hand. *Now*," she commanded through clenched teeth.

"A simple please would have sufficed," he murmured, still trying to alleviate some of the stress of the situation.

Emmeline ignored him. "On the count of three, grab my hand. Ready. One…two…"

"Three," Gregory finished for her as he clutched at her hand.

Tears streamed from the corner of her eyes and they exchanged a brief smile. But now she had to pull him up. She hoped all her hours at the gym lifting weights and taking long runs in the park on the weekends had paid off. This was the moment when she needed all her strength. Otherwise, Gregory would—

No, she wasn't going to follow that particular thought to its unhappy conclusion.

Emmeline groaned as every muscle in her body strained to pull Gregory up with one arm. He was heavier than she had expected. "Come on," she mumbled under breath. Her other arm tightened its grip around the rock.

Out of the corner of her eye, she became aware of some movement. Emmeline tilted her head back and wished she hadn't. Her mouth went suddenly dry. Rosemary was standing over her with the gun held in one very steady hand.

"Emmeline, you really should have taken my advice when I told you to leave the Royal Devon. It would have saved you all this unpleasantness."

"Unpleasantness? You murdered a woman. But it's not too late, Rosemary. Put the gun down and help me. I promise to put in a good word for you with Superintendent Burnell. Please, Rosemary." She felt Gregory's fingers starting to slip from her grasp. "*Help me.*"

Rosemary remained silent for an agonizing moment and Emmeline thought she had gotten through to her. Then, the older woman released the safety catch and replied, "I rather think not."

Emmeline swallowed hard and turned her attention back to Gregory. If it was the last thing she did, at least she was going to make sure he was safe. "Do what you want. I have more important things to attend to."

Rosemary's blue eyes widened in surprise and she hesitated for a fraction of a second. Then she squared her shoulders and pressed the trigger.

EPILOGUE

Being in such close proximity, the shot was amplified and made Emmeline's body shudder. She steeled herself for the pain, but instead felt two pairs of strong, very male arms reach over her to get at Gregory. Another pair of arms wrapped itself around her waist and dragged her away from the edge.

Emmeline found herself looking into Superintendent Burnell's worried face. "Are you all right, Miss Kirby? Are you hurt anywhere?"

"Superintendent Burnell, what—how?" she stammered in confusion. "Gregory?" She glanced round anxiously and started to crawl away from him, but he put a restraining hand on her shoulder.

"He's all right, Miss Kirby. See for yourself," he said gently.

She looked in the direction his finger was pointing. Gregory was sitting on the path, slightly winded, but, apart from a few bruises and scratches, he seemed to be in one piece. She saw him extend a hand to Nigel and Sergeant Finch as he murmured his thanks.

"Gregory." She shrugged off Burnell's hand and flung herself at Gregory.

She took his face between both her hands and started to kiss his eyes, his nose, his forehead, his cheeks, his ears.

Gregory's arm slipped around her waist and he chuckled. "Steady on, old girl. What will the others say?"

Emmeline laughed through the tears that were flowing with unrestrained joy. "I don't care. I love you and I was so afraid that—"

"Shh, Emmy. Everything's fine." He pulled her into his embrace. "Don't you know by now that you can't get rid of me that easily?"

"More's the pity," Burnell mumbled.

Emmeline pressed her cheek against Gregory's neck and held him close. Never wanting to let him go again.

Chief Inspector Ashcroft and his men appeared. There was a lot of commotion for a while. Someone very kindly wrapped a blanket around her and Gregory after ascertaining that they had not suffered any serious injuries. Then, Emmeline saw two constables lift a black body bag into the back of a waiting van.

"Trevor?" She became very agitated. "Dear God, *not* Trevor."

Gregory tightened his arm around her shoulder. "No, Emmy. Trevor will be all right. He's been taken to hospital. That—" He jerked his chin in the direction of the departing van. "—was Rosemary. Sergeant Finch shot her."

Emmeline's gaze locked with his for a long moment. "Oh. Oh, I see. And Connie—I suppose I should say Rosie?"

"She has two cracked ribs and a concussion, but, it appears, no permanent damage."

"I see," Emmeline murmured again. "It's all very sad."

"Yes," Gregory replied as he pressed a kiss against her curls and looked out at the sea. "Revenge eats away at you, until only an empty shell of your former self is left. Very sad, indeed."

❧❧❧

Two days later, it was time to go back to London. Home.

It's funny, Emmeline thought, as she crossed the terrace of the Royal Devon to get a last glimpse of the beautiful view. She had come to Torquay to get away from it all, only discover that life and its rivalries, its pain and complications, were the same to a greater or lesser degree everywhere. She sighed. *A pity.*

Emmeline was about turn and go back inside the hotel, when she caught sight of Gregory and Nigel down below in the garden. Their conversation appeared intense. Gregory was pacing back and forth, his hands thrust deep into his pockets. She saw him stop at one point and shake his head at something Nigel had just said. "No, Nigel." The words floated up to her ears. "For the last time, I'm not going to tell Emmeline. And neither are you."

"Not my place, old chap." Nigel sighed. "I suppose there's nothing left to say. Will I see you again back in London now that Emmeline works for *The Clarion*?"

"I don't think that's such a good idea, considering everything, do you?"

"No, I suppose you're probably right. Take care of yourself at least and don't give Emmeline too much grief. You're very lucky to have her. Not many women would put up with you."

Nigel extended a hand to Gregory, who stared at it for a moment and then shook it. One corner of his mouth curved into a half-smile. "I know. Emmy's one in a million. Take care, Nigel."

Emmeline stepped away from the parapet so that the two men wouldn't realize that she had witnessed their little exchange. She hurried back into the hotel and was waiting for Gregory out front when he emerged.

"Ready to go, darling?" he asked.

"Yes, I think it's about time we went home."

"There's just one small detour I want to make first," Gregory said as they walked toward his blue-gray Jaguar and held the passenger-door open for her.

"Oh? Where?" Emmeline asked, her curiosity piqued.

He closed the door and slipped into the driver's seat. "I'll tell you when we get there."

৩৩৩

Emmeline awoke an hour and a half later when the car rumbled to a stop. She yawned and blinked the sleep from her drowsy eyes. Her face froze when she gazed out the window. "Why are we here?"

"Darling, you look as if you've seen a ghost. What's the matter?" One of his eyebrows arched upward.

"Nothing," she said quickly. "Why did we come here? I thought we were going home?"

"Emmy, I told you I wanted to make a stop before we returned to London. This is it. We're in the village of Wickersham and this is St. Margaret's."

"Yes, I know. But *why* are we here?" She was getting agitated.

"You know? How do you know?"

"Never mind. It doesn't matter. Are we going to sit in the car all day?"

Gregory fixed her with a hard cinnamon stare, but she didn't flinch. "No, let's go inside," he said. "I want to show you something. Then there won't be any more secrets between us."

She recalled his words to Nigel back at the hotel. '*For the last time, I'm not going to tell Emmeline.*'

Perhaps Gregory had changed his mind. Perhaps they could truly start fresh.

He led her inside the quiet church she had visited only a week before. Dust motes danced upon the strands of sunlight streaming in through the windows. The church was empty, save for the vicar, who was walking down the aisle toward them.

His round face broke into a smile when he saw her and he took her hand in both of his and shook it vigorously. "Oh, hello again. It's Emmeline, isn't it?"

"Yes," she mumbled. She could feel Gregory's eyes on her. "I'm sorry I ran out like that the last time. I remembered a very pressing appointment."

"Perfectly understandable," the vicar replied good-naturedly.

"You've been here before, Emmy?" Gregory asked. "Why?"

Emmeline sighed and faced him. "If you must know, Veronica suggested I come here. She said that I would find out something that you were hiding. But as I told Reverend Foster, I had to leave unexpectedly."

Gregory's eyes widened in surprise. "Ronnie. I see. I think I know what she wanted you to discover." Then he turned to the vicar. "Do you still keep all your marriage registers here in St. Margaret's?"

"Yes, of course. Thanks to my niece, all the records are scanned and computerized these days. She's marvelous, my niece. With the click of a mouse, I can retrieve any record going back to 1930. Can you imagine? It's quite wonderful. Follow me into the office and I can find the information you're looking for."

Emmeline hesitated for a second.

"Come on, Emmy. You wanted the truth."

"I still do."

"Then let's not keep Reverend Foster waiting. I'm sure he's a very busy man."

"Oh, dear me, yes," the voluble little vicar replied. "I'm afraid you caught me in the middle of things, but no matter. I'm here to serve."

Emmeline and Gregory were silent as they followed Reverend Foster through a door at the back of the church, down a corridor and into a tiny office. He put his glasses on the bridge of his nose and flicked the switch on the computer. Instantly, the screen lit up.

"Now then, young man, what was it you were looking for?"

Gregory cleared his throat. "June 22, 2000."

"All right. Let me see." With two fingers, Reverend Foster pecked the date into the keyboard. "Ah, here it is. Only one marriage that day. A Gregory Longdon and a Veronica Hammond. Wait a minute, Longdon." He turned to Emmeline. "Wasn't that the name you asked about last time?"

"Yes," Emmeline whispered. "It was. So this is what she wanted me to see."

"Well, I'm glad that you found your answer," Reverend Foster replied cheerfully.

Gregory shot a quizzical look at Emmeline, but thanked the vicar, and gave him something for the church fund.

"Oh, thank you. Very kind, I'm sure. Now, I must get back to the church hall."

"Of course, sir. Don't let us keep you from your duties a moment longer. We can see ourselves out."

"Well, if you're sure. A pleasure meeting you both." He shook their hands and bustled out the door.

Emmeline remained silent all the way back to the car.

"Darling, are you all right?" Gregory asked, as he slipped the key into the ignition and turned on the engine.

"Yes." But it didn't sound convincing, even to her own ears.

"I know it will take time for you to get over my...my indiscretion with Ronnie. But now there are no more secrets between us. The past is behind us. We can start with a clean slate."

"Can we?" Emmeline's eyes searched his handsome face. She knew every line, every curve, of that much-loved face.

"Of course, we can. There's nothing to stop us."

"No, nothing," she murmured as the car rolled past the churchyard.

Her mind flew back to that day she was wandering among the tombstones. That day she had run all the way to the bus station with her heart racing. What she had seen had shaken her to her very core. It was one lonely tombstone.

Gregory James Anthony Longdon
December 21, 1967-March 3, 1970
In loving memory of a beloved son taken too soon

Emmeline looked at Gregory's profile. *How*, she wondered, *can I love a man, if I don't even know who he is?*

About the Author

Daniella Bernett is a member of the Mystery Writers of America New York Chapter. She graduated summa cum laude with a B.S. in Journalism from St. John's University. *Lead Me Into Danger* and *Deadly Legacy* are the first two books in the Emmeline Kirby-Gregory Longdon mystery series. She also is the author of two poetry collections, *Timeless Allure* and *Silken Reflections*. In her professional life, she is the research manager for a nationally prominent engineering, architectural and construction management firm. Daniella is currently working on Emmeline and Gregory's next adventure. Visit www.daniellabernett.com or follow her on Facebook and on Goodreads.

CPSIA information can be obtained
at www.ICGtesting.com
Printed in the USA
LVOW07s0345171017
552622LV00024B/1329/P